LOVE IS THE GOAL

BOOK 1

THE SOUL LOVE SERIES

SIMON NORTHOUSE

FLABBERGASTED
PUBLISHING

For information about special discounts available for bulk purchases, sales promotions, fund-raising and educational needs contact admin@snorthouse.com or visit the Author's website at www.snorthouse.com or Facebook page https://www.facebook.com/simonnorthouse

Disclaimer: This is a work of fiction. Names, characters, businesses, places, events, locales, and incidents are either the products of the author's imagination or used in a fictitious manner. Any resemblance to actual persons, living or dead, or actual events is purely coincidental.

Published by Flabbergasted Publishing

First Edition

e-book ISBN-13: 978-0-6485330-9-2

Paperback ISBN-13: 978-0-6487619-0-7

TABLE OF CONTENTS

LOVE IS...   1

1: HOPE   3

2: FAITH   15

3: LOVE   27

VICTORIA'S DIARY   37

4: LUST   42

5: ACCEPTANCE   54

6: UPWARDS   69

7: DEEDS   77

8: MADNESS   93

9: SOUL LOVE   104

10: HAPPINESS   118

VICTORIA'S DIARY   128

11: LEARNING   133

12: BEAUTY   139

13: ONLY YOU   147

14: ART   159

15: POWER   172

16: VIOLENCE   186

17: COWARDICE   194

18: TRUST   202

19: DESPAIR   210

20: ABSTINENCE   221

21: LECTURE   237

22: IDYLL   247

23: DEPARTING   258

VICTORIA'S DIARY   266

24: SACRIFICE   269

25: CONFRONTATION   274

VICTORIA'S DIARY   284

26: HOPE   288

LOVE IS...

The sleet is driven hard into our faces by a humourless wind. I have my hands tucked deep into my pockets and my head pointed towards the ground. My coat is zipped up as far as it will go. Gerry is explaining how he and his wife, Sarah, first met. Despite the conditions he has a smile on his face whenever I glance at him. He recalls his tale with obvious glee. Marky, Macca and Jonesy are trailing behind. We're making our way to the curry house to finish the night off.

Water drips from my chin. I raise my head and look ahead. A group of five lads are rapidly approaching. I can tell they are looking for trouble. It's the way they walk. There's an aggressive swagger to their gait. Their arms are further away from their sides than they need to be. Some sway from too much drink. There's something wrong with this town, with this country. Violence and hatred circle above it like vultures over carrion. I hope for the best. Hope is all I have left.

They clatter into us deliberately. They reek of cheap cider and even cheaper ignorance. One of them shouts an abusive, racist comment towards Gerry and spits in his face. Time hits the brakes and I feel like I'm in a film. The group carry on for a few more steps before they turn and yell at us. I glance at Gerry who is pulling his sleeve across his face to remove the spittle. Adrenalin surges through my body. Fight and flight stand before me—the choice is mine. I want to choose flight with all my heart. I want to run. I want to run faster than I've ever run before. I want to run and leave this dirty old town and this broken old country

1

behind me forever. I want to fly, to soar, but my wings have been clipped. There wasn't really a choice… between fight or flight. There was an impostor in the duo.

One of the lads is now pointing at me. His face is screwed up in anger and hate. Marky and the others are now on the scene. Marky yells something. The gang of thugs turn around. The mouthy one throws a haymaker of a punch at Marky. I've gone deaf and everything happens in slow motion. Marky weaves back and the punch sails harmlessly by. I gaze at a corrugated security shutter that protects a shop window. In red graffiti are spray-painted the words, "Love Is The Answer". Not on a Friday night in Leeds after the pubs have closed, it isn't. My eyes lazily swivel back towards Marky. His left hook is poetry in motion. It's as though it's on a primed spring. The hook is always hard to avoid. It must be something to do with the arc of its trajectory. Love is the answer… don't you just love irony?

1: HOPE

I'm sitting at a table in Flip Of The Coin wine bar. It's not really a wine bar, it's just a good old fashioned pub in a salubrious part of Leeds City Centre. For some reason, a lot of pubs have changed their names recently and started calling themselves wine bars. Okay, I accept it is 1984 and the age of the yuppie, but trying to make yourself appear sophisticated by doing nothing more than changing your name... is... well... a bit pretentious —in my book at least.

We, that is me and my mates, don't call it Flip Of The Coin. No, we refer to it as Tossers. Not very original or amusing, I bet you're thinking, but you'd be missing the point. You see, between twelve o'clock and two o'clock every weekday, the pub, (sorry, wine bar) fills to the brim with all the tossers from the financial district. Lawyers, bankers, solicitors and other ne'er-do-wells swagger around getting pissed, ramming pizza into their fat bloated faces whilst touching women's arses and ogling their tits. They are a disgrace! Entitled and privileged, they treat women as chattels and I abhor them for that.

However, this is our bar, the boys and mine. We've been coming here for the last two years and we aren't going to stop just because a bunch of bean-counting, lecherous suits frequent it for a few hours each week.

Leeds used to be a grim northern city, a provincial backwater full of dour Yorkshire folk, and to be honest with you, most of it still is. However, the city centre itself has undergone somewhat of a transformation of late. Many

3

multinationals have moved from that God forsaken hell hole known as London to the capital of the north—Leeds. Some guy once said to me, when I told him I came from Leeds, that, "Leeds is the gateway to the west". That poor bugger lived in Hull, so I guess anywhere was the gateway to the west for him.

It's twelve-fifteen and I'm waiting for Marky to arrive. I've known Marky since I was five years old, we started school together and have been best mates ever since. Marky is a class warrior, a highly charged political protagonist. He stands slightly to the left of Trotsky and Stalin. Even though he lives every moment of the day to overthrow the Conservative Government, I actually think he would be sad to see them go. He'd lose his raison d'etre. It's the Iron Lady and her cronies that fill his veins with molten fire. It's what makes him wake at six every day to begin the crusade for justice, reparation and a fair living wage for all. Me? I don't do politics. Put the Labour party in power and they'd just be as bad. They're all in it for themselves, feathering their own nest while spouting how wonderful they are.

Talking of Marky, here he comes now, down the steps. He's short and skinny but don't let that fool you—no, he's as hard as nails. I've seen him knock-out guys twice his size. He has a vicious left hook and he fights dirty. Marky has saved my bacon on many occasions, but he's not a violent type. I've never witnessed him start a fight, but he does manage to get himself into a lot of scrapes. Then again, if you are a communist motor-mouth I guess that's going to happen.

'Hey comrade, how's it hanging?' He holds out a clenched fist and I bump it with mine. He calls everyone comrade, you'll get used to it.

'It's all hanging fine, Marky. How's it hanging your end?'

'I tell you what mate, everything will be just dandy once we get rid of these Tory bastards and their far-right political agenda.' See what I mean?

'Yeah well, you might be waiting some time for that day to arrive. What are you having to drink? Pint of bitter?'

'Don't tell me you've got a job since I last saw you two days ago?'

'No. But, I did get my dole cheque this morning, so this shout's on me.' He reaches into his pocket and pulls out a wad of rolled-up notes.

4

'Don't be daft, I'll get them. What are you having? A pint of lager?' I nod, resigned to the fact that Marky will never let me pay for anything.

'Okay, but at least let me order—let me have some dignity.' He laughs at me as he hands over a ten-pound note. I walk to the bar where the voluptuous Jenny is busy polishing pint glasses and stacking them on a shelf behind her. Jenny is the landlady of this fine establishment. She's a widow and a bloody attractive one at that. Her daughter, Amy, is at the far end of the bar serving a guy who already looks half pissed. He wears smoked glasses and is sporting a light purple suit. He is fat and he's always jolly. Forever smiling or laughing. I frequent this wine bar quite often and he's always here before me and he's always here when I leave. He's obviously a banker of some sort. I bet he starts work at nine, makes a few phone calls for a couple of hours then heads here at opening time. Probably makes more money in two hours than I get for a year on the dole. Ah well, such is life.

Amy and I had a thing going about four months ago. The sex was great but it was purely lust. After a while we both realised there was no real spark and we ended it. We are still good friends and occasionally, very occasionally, we help each other out—if you know what I mean. Amy pulls a great pint of bitter and she is great in the sack, but being a gentleman I'm not going to elaborate.

'Hi Jenny, one pint of lager and one pint of bitter, please,' I say.

'Righto.' She picks up a glass and sticks it under the spout and pulls slow and strong on the beer pump. She has a tight grip. I'll be honest, I've got the hots for Jenny. I'm going through a bit of a strange phase at the moment. Lately, I've been looking at older women—and I've been enjoying what I've seen. Amy is twenty, so Jenny would have to be in her late thirties at least. Her husband died ten years ago and from what Amy tells me her mother hasn't had any male acquaintances since. Imagine the built-up sexual tension in her body. I keep trying to chat her up but I get short shrift.

'So Jenny, fancy going out tonight? A nice Chinese meal, then on to a nightclub to dance the night away, then back here for a few quiet drinks. Once you've got rid of the last punter we could make love on the pool table. Whaddya say?' She gives me a pouty, half-smile.

5

'Number one; I'm old enough to be your mother. Number two; you've had sex with my daughter and number three; do you know how much it costs to replace the green baize on a pool table?'

'Jenny, you've got to get over the age thing. How old are you? Thirty-four? Thirty-five?'

'Nice try Jimmy. Flattery will get you nowhere.'

'Okay, I'm nineteen and a half—let's call it twenty—and let's say you're forty. That's only a twenty-year age gap. Now imagine if you can, that you were one hundred years old and I was eighty and we got married—no one would blink an eye. Don't you see? Age depreciates with time.'

'So you're proposing marriage now?' she replies, as she puts the second pint onto a beer mat in front of me.

'Hey, let's not run before we can walk. We both need to test drive the vehicles first before we go bandying about the big "M" word.'

'That's one-pound-fifty please,' she says, ignoring my last statement. I hand over the tenner and she does her thing at the till. She's wearing a tight pencil skirt which highlights her firm womanly shape. You're probably thinking that I'm as bad as the men I just criticised—thought so. Well I'm not. You see, I am in love with the female form. It really is a work of art. When I look at a woman, it's not in a sexual way. I don't see them as a sex object. No, I marvel at their curves and shape, their beauty—inner and outer. To me every woman is a masterpiece painted by one of the old masters. I love their take on life, I admire their intelligence. They are way smarter than men—okay, that's a sweeping generalisation. What I mean is, they seem to understand what's important in life. Most of the men that I know are still boys and always will be. They play with their tanks and guns. They idolise other men who can kick a ball around or master an electric guitar. They are slaves to alcohol and tobacco and they become truculent when given sage advice. And yes, I include myself in that assertion. I think the world would easily survive without men, but without women, well, it would soon return to mother nature. Jenny hands me my change.

'You know Jenny, one day you are going to fall for my boyish good looks, rapier-like wit, sartorial elegance and silver tongue—but by then it may be too late—seize the day and be here now.' She looks at me as though I'm speaking in a foreign tongue.

'Yeah well, maybe I will—and maybe I won't.' I guess that's the end of that then.

I'm back at the table with Marky. I unzip my Harrington jacket and pull the camera from around my neck and place it on the table. Marky takes a slug of beer and smacks his lips together.

'So how has your week been, Marky?'

'Dull as dog shit. I've been stuck in court all week.' I know what you're thinking, you think Marky's a bad lad—he's not. No, Marky is a junior reporter for the Yorkshire Evening Standard, the biggest newspaper around these parts. They also do a morning edition, with the completely original name of Yorkshire Morning Standard. It sells about one hundred thousand copies a day but the evening edition hits just short of one million copies. Okay, it's not up there with the tabloids, but it's a major player for a regional newspaper.

'So any juicy bits?' I ask.

'Nah, two cases of domestic violence, one case of attempted armed robbery, one purse snatcher and a butcher who exposed himself to an elderly lady. They always give me the crap. What I want is to go undercover and do some investigative journalism. You know, the millionaire crooked businessman who has been ripping off his customers, or the well respected MP, probably Conservative, who has an appetite for young rent boys' arses. Something I can really get my teeth into.' I laugh.

'You want to get your teeth into a young rent boy's arse? I always knew you were strange.' He ignores me and takes another slug of beer.

'So Jimmy, any news on the job front?'

'Nah, not a sausage.'

7

'The problem with you, my son, is that you have a love of the dole.' I bristle at this.

'I do not have a love of the dole! Have you any idea what it's like to be on welfare? Queuing up once a fortnight with hundreds of other people to sign my name on a form at the dole office. The snotty bastards behind the counter looking down their noses at me as though I'm some sort of disease; being pulled into the office for an interrogation; "Have you been looking for work?" "Have you done any work? "You do realise that if you have been paid for any work in cash or kind then that will jeopardise your payments?" It's fucking humiliating and degrading. Even when I cash my cheque at the post office they huff and puff and treat me like a third-class citizen. You'd think it was their money they were handing over.'

'Whoa! Calm down, Jimmy,' he says leaning away from me.

'Do you know how many jobs I've applied for in the last three and a half years?'

'No, how many?'

'Well… I couldn't tell you the exact number off the top of my head, but it's a lot. Only last week I went for a job at that independent record store in the shopping centre. They had over five hundred applicants for one position and interviewed thirty—for a fucking job selling records! It's tough out there Marky—damn tough. You better than anyone should know that. So don't say I have a love of the dole!' I take a gulp of beer then bang my glass down hard on the table. Marky pats me on the back.

'Okay, okay, calm down big boy, I was only teasing. I know how tough it is. It's government policy to have mass unemployment, break the unions, then they can have their Eldorado—a free market economy. Low wages, no-contracts, no worker's rights. They are trying to break the spirit of the working man… and woman.'

'Yeah well, they're doing a fucking good job of it.'

'Never give in comrade. It won't always be like this. These times they are a-changing, the cause is gaining momentum, our day of glory will come.'

'And in the meantime I haven't got a pot to piss in.'

'All that is about to change. You've been my pet project for a while now, Jimmy, and it struck me late last night as I lay in bed.'

'I'm not comfortable with you thinking about me as you lie in bed—it's a bit odd.' He smiles and shakes his head.

'Always with the one-liners. No, listen, I'm serious.' He lights a cigarette and blows smoke out into the air. 'It's been staring us right in the face forever and a day and I can't believe it's taken me this long to suddenly notice it.' Marky has a knack of dragging things out.

'For Christ's sake Marky just get to the bloody point.' He picks my camera up.

'What's this?' he asks without a hint of sarcasm. I want to punch him.

'It's a fucking leg of lamb! What do you think it is? It's a camera!'

'No it's not just a camera. This, comrade, is your livelihood. This is your bread and butter, your passport to financial freedom. This little bit of metal, plastic and glass is your saviour and you should prostrate yourself before it.' I'm intrigued. I stare intently at him as he takes another slurp on his beer.

'Go on,' I encourage.

'All in good time, James, all in good time, but first some good news.' He wipes a line of foam from his top lip.

'Oh, yeah? I could do with some good news. What is it?'

'I've been pestering Joe Carmichael to get you some freelance photography work.'

'Who's Joe Carmichael?' Marky shakes his head in annoyance.

'Jesus, Jimmy! Don't you ever listen to anything I say? Joe Carmichael is the editor-in-chief at the Standard. He's the head honcho. I must have mentioned him a hundred times to you.'

'Sorry,' I reply as I become distracted by the fine figure of Jenny and her firm grip on the beer pump.

'Anyway, as I said, I've been pushing your name forward to get you some freelance work.'

'And?'

'He won't have a bar of it. Says the paper is going through some sort of gap analysis and they are reviewing all assets and costs.'

'Fuck, what does that even mean?'

'Yeah I know, it's management wank words. It means cutting costs, i.e. jobs, so the fat, lazy shareholders can make an even bigger profit at the end of the year. He says they can't take anyone else on and that John Arnold is adequate for their needs at present. There's a takeover brewing I can feel it.'

'Who's John Arnold?' Marky rolls his eyes heavenward and lets out a huff.

'He's the Standard's in-house photographer. Must be mid-fifties if he's a day. He's got the nickname foggy and for good reason… I reckon his eyes are shot.'

'I've got to admit that some of those photos in the paper are often quite blurry. It hurts my eyes to look at them. I thought he was exploring some new form of photojournalistic expressionism. So I may be missing the point here, but how is this good news?'

'It's Thursday right, tomorrow is the big edition of the morning paper. They all work late tonight until about 8 pm then retire to The Soldiers Arms for a piss up.'

'So?'

'You meet me there tonight and I'll introduce you to Joe Carmichael.' As good news goes—this is shit.

'Is that it? Is that the good news? What's the point of that?'

'Because comrade, he'll then be able to put a face to the name. You can chat him up with some of your sparkling banter and offer to do some work for free to prove that you can actually take good photos. Once you meet someone in person they get an impression of what you're like. If they like what they see they take a positive attitude towards you.'

I finish the dregs of my beer and stand up. 'Is that your great idea for me? My saviour, my passport to financial freedom is to meet up with a half-pissed editor and offer to work for free for him?'

'No... well yes... it's part of it. There's something else.' He glances at his watch. 'Get the drinks in and I'll go over it quickly with you but I'm running out of time. I'm due back in court in fifteen.' I head to the bar where Jenny is now replenishing boxes of crisps. She is squatting as she pushes new packets of salt and vinegar into the cardboard receptacles. Her white blouse is loose and I can see her large milky bosom slowly rise and fall.

'Ahem!' It makes her start and she jumps up.

'Oh! You daft bugger! You gave me a fright. What do you want? Same again?'

'Yes please Jenny. Has anyone ever told you that you're the most beautiful landlady in the country?' She grips that bloody beer pump tight and pulls on it slow and hard—fuck—I need to get a girlfriend.

'Yes all the time, unfortunately it's you.' She places the drinks on the bar. 'One pound fifty please,'

'Oh, give me two packets of cheese and onion as well, thanks.' She bends over and I cop another eyeful of cleavage. She takes my money and hands me some change. 'So, are we still on for tonight then?' I'm persistent, give me that much.

'In your dreams, Jimmy boy, in your sweet dreams,' she laughs.

'Oh you are always in my dreams Jenny and you get up to some wicked stuff.'

'Right bugger off, I've got work to do.' I grip the packets of crisps between my teeth, pick up the drinks and head back to Marky.

'You still trying to get off with Jenny?'

'Yep. I think she's beginning to crack. It won't be long before she's got a firm grip on me.' Marky chuckles and takes a huge sup of his beer, necking down at least half a pint in one go.

'You've no chance sunshine. She's old enough to be your mother and you've bagged her daughter. She won't touch you with a ten-foot barge pole.'

'Watch this space.'

'I don't know why you ever split up with Amy. She's a little beauty. You must be mad.'

'She's a great girl but there was no pizzazz.'

'Pizzazz eh? So that's what you're after. Do you and Amy, still… you know…'

'Yes. Occasionally, when one or the other of us is desperate.' Marky looks at his watch again as he stuffs a handful of crisps into his mouth.

'Right, back to business, where was I? Ah that's right, so meet me at the Soldiers tonight at 8 pm and we'll get the introductions out of the way and that will kick-start things.'

'Kick-start what things?'

'Next, you'll need to get some business cards printed. When you leave here go and see Jonesy and tell him to knock up a design for you.' Steve Jones is another one of my best mates. He's a student at Leeds University studying graphic design. He's also the drummer in The Hipnotikz, the finest band in Leeds. 'Then bring the design with you tonight and give it to me. I'll take it down to the print room tomorrow and get one of the guys to run you off a batch of a thousand cards. I'm also quite chummy with one of the girls in the classified ads department. I'll get her to run a small ad for you free of charge. You need to think of a name for your business, something short and catchy. Oh and don't forget to put your bloody name and telephone number on the card. Not your last name obviously, we don't want the dole snoopers following you around.' Marky has left me well behind.

'Business name? What are you talking about? And another thing, I don't have any money for all this stuff. I'm on fifty-six pounds per fortnight and sixteen pounds of that goes towards my rent. I can barely afford to feed myself.' Marky stares at me with an air of frustrated pity. He lets out a deep sigh then sculls his pint.

'You can be bloody hard work sometimes, Jimmy. You are the business. As from today you are a freelance photographer. Just think up a name like, "Jimmy's Photography" or "Photos 'r Us". Use your imagination.'

'And what exactly am I taking photographs of?'

'Anything and everything. Weddings, family portraits, business premises, baby photos. Bands! Yes, bands. Stick a business card up in all the music and record shops in town. "Get professional photos of your gigs." The world is your oyster, mate. If you can't get a job—invent your own. You're a bloody great photographer and you need to use your talent. Times are tough Jim and you've got to hustle. Make it happen. Right, I've got to go. Remember it's not going to cost you anything, initially. Jonesy will do the design for free and the business cards and ads will cost you nothing. You could do with investing in an answering machine because your phone is going to be ringing off the hook.' He stands, stuffs another handful of crisps into his face and pulls out his wad of notes. He peels off forty pounds and hands it to me.

'No Marky. I'm not taking that. It's okay you buying me a couple of pints every now and then but I'm not taking money from you.' He fixes me with a steely glare.

'Take it,' he orders. 'You'll need to stock up on film'. I reluctantly take the notes and stick them in my back pocket.

'How come you've always got so much money? A cadet reporter doesn't earn that sort of dough.' He smiles.

'No they don't. Let's just say I have a few schemes running. Most of this money goes to the cause.'

'What is this cause you keep banging on about?' I fear I shouldn't have asked that question. Marky looks bewildered.

'THE cause! The struggle. The working class revolution that will be soon hitting these shores. It's coming Jimmy, and when it does you are going to be part of that cause.'

'I am?' He clenches his fist and punches it into mine.

'Yes you are, comrade. You'll be up there on the barricades with thousands of others and you're going to capture the glorious revolution on film. You'll be a national hero. Right, I'm out of here. Tonight at eight and don't forget the bloody design!' he yells back at me as he marches out of the pub with energy and swagger. Well, I guess that told me. I love Marky like a brother but I'm not sure I want to be a national hero or part of his forthcoming revolution, it all sounds rather violent.

2: FAITH

I'm sitting in the university common room with Jonesy. We're mulling over ideas for the business card.

'Nah, "Jimmy's Photography" is a shit name and so is "Photos 'R Us". We need to come up with something sparky,' says Jonesy as he slurps on a pot noodle. He stands up, grabs a sheet of paper, a pencil and sits down at a table. I follow him and sit alongside.

'Okay, well have you any better ideas?'

'We need to brainstorm. Right, list some parts of the camera and associated words to describe the act of taking a photo. I'll jot them down as you call them out.'

'Well there's the lens, the aperture, the shutter, the shutter release, viewfinder. You can have photographs, photos, film, snaps, pictures, clicks. Hey what about "Watch The Birdy Photography" that's quite sparky,' I suggest. Jonesy looks at me with utter disdain and contempt.

'You're really crap at this aren't you? I hope your photography is more innovative than your business acumen.' He studies the words on his list. 'Hmm, I quite like snaps. It's short, sharp and sparky.' There he goes again with that word "sparky". I'm not sure what it even means.

'Hey I've got another one,' I blurt out as a sudden brain-wave hits me.

15

'Go on then, dazzle me,' he replies without much enthusiasm.

'Okay, what about, "Capture The Moment", that's quite sparky.' Jonesy stares at me, expressionless. 'Maybe with Jimmy on the end, you know, "Capture The Moment With Jimmy". Then again maybe…' I tail off quietly. He goes back to his words.

'Hmm, shutter, shutter-up…'

'Yeah, I like that. It's got a bit of humour to it. You know shutter-up and shut up.'

'Nah. You don't want humour.'

'I don't?'

'No. You want to sound young, vibrant, energetic—sparky. You're the new kid on the block, the boy about town. You're about the future and hope. You need to light that spark in people.' I don't like that metaphor one little bit and let him know.

'You can't light a spark. You can cause a spark but you can't light one.' He ignores me.

'It comes down to two then. Snap or Clicks,' he states defiantly.

'I don't like clicks.'

'Why not?'

'Because it sounds a bit like "clits". The wrong overtones.' Jonesy laughs.

'Yeah, you're right. I should have spotted that but then again, my mind isn't perpetually in the gutter. Okay, "Snap Photography" it is then. Right, we just need a byline. Any ideas?'

'What's a byline?'

'A byline, you know a tagline, a slogan. A short punchy sentence to stick in the minds of potential customers.'

'So this has to be punchy, right? Not sparky?'

16

'Yeah, that's right. We've got spark with Snap. Now we need the punch.' I rack my brain to try and think of something. Then, the light-bulb moment.

'Oh yes, Jonesy. You are going to love this!' I am very excited about this one.

'I doubt it very much, but try me anyway.'

'All right, what about, "We focus on your image", whaddya think?' I hold my arms out in greatness and Jonesy beams for the first time.

'Fuck me, Jimmy! Where did you pull that one from? It's bloody perfect. It not only appeals to people who want a family portrait taken but it will appeal to business owners—you're going to improve the image of their product. Okay, done and dusted. On the front we have Snap photography – we focus on your image – call James on blah, blah, blah for all your photography needs. On the back we have weddings, family portraits, business branding – whatever your requirements are, we can meet them – call today. How does that sound?'

'Sounds bloody great—apart from the James bit.'

'James sounds professional. Jimmy makes you sound like a second-hand car dealer.'

'I think Jimmy has punch and spark, whereas James sounds like some stuck-up git.'

'Jimmy does not have punch or spark. Jimmy makes me think of a fifty-year-old slob with a beer gut and bad breath. James makes me think young, sharp, upwardly mobile—in essence—professional. James, it is. Right, is this to be in black and white or colour?'

'Fuck, I don't know. Marky never said. I can't even ring him as he's in court.'

'Don't worry. I will do one of each. I've got a free period now so I'll get to work on it right away.'

'Cheers Jonesy. You are a star my friend. Any chance of getting the design by tonight? Marky wants to get them printed tomorrow?'

'Yeah, no problem. I'm rehearsing with the band so you'll have to call into the studios to collect. We're there from six till nine, tonight.'

##

I'm making my way on foot to the rehearsal studios. It's located in a rundown area not too far from the city centre. Old car yards and decrepit looking warehouses line the streets. It's just gone 7 pm and I'm going to have to get a spurt on if I'm to get to the Soldiers Arms for 8 pm. I begin to jog. I pass a scrap metal yard and a vicious looking Alsatian jumps up at the locked gate and begins barking madly at me.

'Jesus H! You daft bastard!' I yell at the dog, which is now going berserk. I pull the camera from my neck and go down on one knee and take a few snaps. This seems to infuriate the dog even more and I get some good shots of his snarling teeth, salivating jowls and wide scary eyes. I jog on and soon reach my destination. The studio is a converted Methodist chapel situated behind a railway viaduct—it's all very Victorian. A cacophony of music blares out into the cold night air. There are at least three different songs I can detect being played. I ring the bell and Jumbo, the owner, lets me in.

'Hey Jimmy, long time no see.' Jumbo used to be a roadie for several successful bands but he got tired of being away from home for so long. He then set up this studio, a place for local bands to rehearse and record. We high-five each other.

'Jumbo, how's it going man? Keeping busy?' He's called Jumbo because he's the size of a bus, but he's a gentle giant.

'Oh, there's always something going on Jimmy. Keeps me out of mischief. You here to see the Hipnotikz?'

'Yeah. What room are they in?'

'Number four, down the end.' I walk down the corridor to the deafening sound of electric guitars, drums and vocals. I open the door, go inside and sit down on the floor. The Hipnotikz are mid-song and they all smile at me. It's a new tune that I haven't heard before and they tread their way carefully through it until it ends. I stand up and clap.

'More! More!' I bellow. Macca laughs.

'What do you reckon, Jimmy?' he asks.

'Sounds awesome—that's a new one—right?'

'Yeah, wrote it last night. Came totally out of the blue, fully formed like a newborn baby. It needs a bit of work on it but it should be ready by our next gig.'

'What's it called?'

'Backstreet Riot.'

'Another love song?' Jonesy emerges from behind his drum kit and picks up an envelope laying on the floor. I walk over to him.

'Here Jimmy, take a look at these,' he says with a certain amount of pride. 'I've done a couple of variations on the theme.' He hands me about ten business cards. The whole card is a photo of the front of a camera. SNAP! Is emblazoned across the lens with the slogan underneath and in big bold letters, my name and phone number.

'Bloody hell Jonesy, this looks magnificent. Wow!' I turn the card over and it is now the back view of the camera. It looks classy and professional. Gerry wanders over.

'Let's have a gander then,' he says with a big toothy smile. He grabs one of the cards as I look through the others. They're all pretty similar just with different fonts and text sizes. Some are black and white and others are in colour. 'So you're a freelance photographer now?' chirps Gerry as he hands the card back.

'Yep, this is the start of the rest of my life. Don't know why I didn't think of it earlier.'

'You didn't, it was Marky's idea,' corrects Jonesy. I laugh.

'Yeah, you're right. Marky can take the credit for this one.' I look at my watch and it's already past 7:30 pm. It's a good twenty minutes brisk walk to the

Soldiers Arms. 'Listen boys, I can't hang around for long, I have a rendezvous with Marky in thirty minutes.'

'It's not a clandestine meeting of The Cause is it?' laughs Macca.

'No. He's introducing me to the editor of the Standard.'

'Well, put in a good word for us, will you. Tell him we're the next big thing and he should get an interview with us before we hit the big time,' replies Macca.

'Haha! Yes, I will. Thanks again Jonesy. I owe you one.'

'No you don't. That's what friends are for, isn't it?' I sit down on the floor and listen to a couple more songs, then head out of the door.

'I'll see you tomorrow night in Tossers,' I shout back. They all give the thumbs up before ripping into another song. I knock on the reception door and let myself in. Thankfully it is heavily soundproofed and the noise diminishes as I close the door behind me.

'Hey Jumbo, can I stick one of these on your notice board?' I hand him a card. He scans and nods.

'Yeah, sure man. Good idea by the way. I'm always getting bands asking if I know of any good photographers. Mind you, they're all bloody skint so you won't make much money out of them but it will get your name out and about.'

I am out on the street jogging my way back to the city. I must have short-term memory loss as I forget about the dog and he scares the bejeezus out of me again.

'Be nice!' I yell at him. 'You have anger issues my friend and it's not passive-aggressive it's active-aggressive.' The dog goes crazy and spins around and leaps up at the gate. If he got hold of me he'd rip me apart.

I'm panting hard as I near the Soldiers Arms and I spot Marky's Vespa parked up outside. I slow down to catch my breath. As I open the pub door I can hear raucous laughter, music and I inhale the smell of ale and cigarette smoke. I go through another door into the main bar. Marky is sitting in a corner with a couple of guys.

'Hey Jimmy!' He yells and jumps to his feet. 'Did you get the design done?' I hand him the envelope and he looks at the cards. 'Oh yes, very swish, very smart. How come you've got so many?'

'Jonesy did a few mock-ups. They're essentially the same. Which one do you think looks best?

'This black and white one with the red logo. What's this James shit, at the bottom?' he laughs.

'Jonesy said it sounds more professional than Jimmy.' Marky nods, sticks one card in his back pocket and hands me the envelope.

'Right, come on. I'll introduce you to Carmichael. At the very least you'll get a free drink out of him. He sticks one hundred quid behind the bar. That's why it's so packed in here. Oh, and remember—sell yourself.' We push our way through a throng of people until we are standing behind an extremely large man sitting at the bar holding court. He's talking loudly and puffing on a smoke. Now and then someone laughs at what he's just said. Marky taps him on the shoulder.

'Mr Carmichael, Mr Carmichael, Mr Carmichael!' he shouts above the noise, but he is ignored. 'Mr Carmichael, Mr Carmichael...' The big man eventually glances over his shoulder at Marky.

'Fucking hell Marky, what is it now? You're always busting my balls.'

'Mr Carmichael, I'd like you to meet a good friend of mine.' Marky grabs my arm and pulls me forward. Carmichael slips off his bar stool, stands up and turns around. He must be well over six foot tall and at least twenty-odd stone. He has a gargantuan sized head to match his oversized body. He has the appearance of a bulldog. He towers over me—he towers over everyone. A cigarette dangles limply from the side of his mouth and he looks a tad annoyed.

'What do you want Marky?' he grumbles.

'Mr Carmichael, may I introduce you to my good friend, Jimmy Hooper. Jimmy, this is Mr Carmichael.' I hold out my hand and see it disappear into his fleshy, giant mitt as he shakes it loosely.

21

'How do you put up with this one?' he says, flicking a thumb in Marky's direction.

'It's a dirty job but someone's got to do it.' He half laughs and begins to turn away.

'You're right about that. Get yourself a drink lad, pleased to meet you.' Marky jabs me in the ribs.

'No, Mr Carmichael, you don't understand. This is Jimmy, I've been telling you about him.' The big man turns back clearly exasperated at his lost drinking time. 'Jimmy's a freelance photographer. He wants to do some unpaid work for the paper.' Mr Carmichael looks at me suspiciously.

'How long have you been freelance?' he barks. I'm about to say, "about five minutes" but luckily Marky and his gift of the gab jump in first. Marky looks at me and I look at Marky.

'Oh, it would be about eighteen months or so now, wouldn't it, Jimmy?'

'Yeah, yeah,' I say. 'Just a tad over.' Carmichael eyes us both warily.

'Have you done work for any other papers?'

'No, not yet. I'm just trying to break into the market now. I've mainly been doing business branding, weddings, family portraits… that sort of thing. I'm also putting together a portfolio of work in the hope that I can get my own exhibition.'

'Hmm, well, as I've explained to Marky we have our own photographer and a number of other freelancers on call so I can't really help you out at the moment. If you leave me your card I'll keep you in mind. You seem an industrious sort of lad which is always a good thing and if you're a friend of Marky's, then you must have street smarts.' I hand him a business card and he briefly looks at it. 'Snap Photography—punchy name,' he says, nodding his approval.

'The thing is Mr Carmichael, Jimmy goes to a lot of gigs, local bands and big name acts. He could get us fresh live photos instead of the stock images they send out. You should see his work, it's brilliant. He has a way of capturing faces.' I can tell that Carmichael is losing interest fast.

'Yeah, yeah. Well, go see Dave Dee, he's in charge of the entertainment copy.' Marky beams.

'Cheers Mr Carmichael. You won't regret it. Oh, one last thing, he'll need a press pass—to help him to get into the gigs for free.' Carmichael shakes his huge melon.

'Fucking hell Marky, you're like a dog with a bone, that's why one day you'll make a damn good reporter. Jimmy, call at the offices tomorrow afternoon and I'll authorise one. Now Marky, can you please fuck off and let me enjoy the rest of the night.' He turns and slumps back onto his barstool and shouts at a guy behind the bar. 'Bill, another whisky in here when you get a chance.' Marky pulls me away with a massive grin on his face.

'Yes! You're in!' he exclaims. I don't feel like I'm in. We collect a couple of pints at the bar and take a sip.

'He's an intimidating guy,' I muse.

'Nah! He's a big softy really.'

'He's got a head like a fucking bulldog.' Marky laughs out his beer.

'Haha, that's his nickname, "Bulldog". If you're in his inner circle you can call him that. Listen you'll hear it in a minute.' We listen intently for a few seconds and it's not long before someone calls out.

'Hey Bulldog, throw me a smoke will yer? I'm all out.'

'There's a fucking cigarette machine in the corner, you tight arse,' Bulldog shouts back but throws the guy a cigarette anyway. Marky takes me by the arm and leads me away from the bar.

'Right, you see that guy over there, the one with the glasses on?' I stare into a smoke filled corner and spot a man sitting alone busily scribbling notes.

'The one who's writing?'

'Yeah, well that's Dave Dee, the guy I keep telling you about, you remember?'

'Oh, yeah,' I reply. To be honest, I don't remember at all. Marky drops that many names in a conversation, and talks so fast, that sometimes I zone out. 'He's the one who runs the show really. Dave does the full page spread on Saturdays about the forthcoming week's entertainment. He's a good bloke but the poor bugger is always snowed under. Look at him now, still working away while everyone else gets pissed. I reckon you pitch it to him that you provide him with two or three concert reviews a week along with accompanying photos. He'll snap your hand off.' We make our way over and Marky does the introductions again. We shake hands and all sit down.

'So Dave, Jimmy here is going to be doing a bit of work for us,' begins Marky. Dave looks a little surprised.

'Oh really, first I've heard. What type of work?'

'He's a freelance photographer who also does reviews and interviews with local groups and big acts that come to town.' Dave looks impressed with this colossal lie. He nods his head in admiration.

'So tell me Jimmy, in what rags have you been published?'

'Oh you know, the usual. New Musical Express, Melody Maker, Smash Hits—that sort of thing,' I lie while throwing Marky a pissed off look.

'Great. I know the editor of the Melody Maker—John Hatcher—we went to university together.' Fucking brilliant! I've dropped myself right in the shit! 'Well, I could do with a hand. If you could provide me with a couple of gig reviews each week and the occasional interview every now and then, along with some good quality photo's, I'll see about using them.' Marky grins and I nod nervously.

'Sure thing Dave. What's your deadline for the Saturday edition?' I ask.

'We can go right up to 8 pm on Friday but I prefer to get everything in by mid-week if possible.'

'Okay not a problem,' I reply. Dave suddenly looks concerned and stares at Marky.

'Say, you've cleared this with Bulldog, right?'

'Of course we have. He's organising a press pass for Jimmy tomorrow.' Dave smiles and nods.

'Good, good. Look, I'd love to have a chat but I've got to get this finished,' he indicates at his notes scattered on the table.

'Fully understand, Dave. We'll leave you alone. Catch you tomorrow.'

'Yeah see you Marky, and pleased to meet you, Jimmy. I look forward to working with you.' We stand and walk away into a quiet corner.

'Perfect,' beams Marky. 'This has all gone like clockwork.'

'Apart from the Melody Maker bit. What if he phones his friend for a reference? I'm going to look like a right tool.'

'Yeah, why did you come out with that crap?'

'That was your fault! You were the one who made me out to be some big shot—I had to think of something.' Marky mulls it over for a few seconds.

'Ah don't worry about it. He'll have forgotten by tomorrow. As I say, he's flat out. He's the sub-editor, he doesn't just do the weekly entertainment guide. Right come on, let's get a few more free pints in before the money runs out.'

Marky spends the next hour walking around introducing me to everyone and telling them I'm going to be working for the paper. He's even dropped the freelance part and you'd think I was a full-time photographer on fifteen grand a year with a company car and expense account. Everyone is very welcoming and congratulates me.

Marky looks at his watch. 'Righto, time to go,' he says. I look at the clock on the wall. It's only 10 pm.

'Where are you going? There's another half hour's drinking time left.'

'Ask no questions and I'll tell you no lies,' he cackles.

'Not the "cause" again?' I enquire.

'Shh! Keep your voice down. None of this lot knows about it.'

'They're not the only ones. I'm your best mate and all I know is that at some point in the future, date unspecified, there's going to be an uprising of the masses and the establishment will be overthrown.' He smiles.

'And until that day comes you don't need to know anything else,' he replies with a wink of the eye. I get all serious.

'Marky, you worry me mate. Don't get wrapped up in anything dodgy.' He pats me on the back to reassure me and laughs.

'Jimmy, you know me, I was born under a blue moon. I'm safe.'

'Hey, that's my line! I thought you journalists were supposed to steer clear of plagiarism.'

'Well, it is a good line. Right, I'll see you tomorrow at HQ, 3 pm. Don't be late.'

'Hang on, I'm coming too. I'm not hanging around here, I don't know anybody.' He stares at me with disappointment.

'You should be networking my friend. Integrate and assimilate.'

'Fuck that,' I reply. We walk out of the pub doors and into the fresh night air. Marky zips up his jacket and puts his helmet on, pulling the buckle tight.

'Okay comrade, be good.'

'Hey Marky, thanks for tonight and all you've done. I appreciate it.' He smiles and says,

'That's what friends are for. Love you buddy.' We pump clenched fists together and Marky kick starts his Vespa. I pull my camera out and get a few snaps of him as he speeds off into the night. I begin the long walk to my bus stop.

As I pass a telephone box I notice a flyer stuck to the glass. It's for a band called The Zippers and they're playing at the Granary nightclub tonight. I have a brain wave.

'Why not?' I say to myself. 'After all, you are now officially a freelance photographer.'

3: LOVE

I have a bounce in my step and there's no time like the present. I make my way to the Granary nightclub. It's located only five minutes from Tossers. As I round the corner I notice the imposing figure of Mal standing outside the Granary entrance. Mal is the bouncer. He's a big Geordie fellow who has a gentle manner but is as hard as they come. He's also gay and keeps trying it on with me—in a friendly way—and I assume tonight will be no different. He treats me like royalty and always ushers me to the front of the queue shouting "Stand back, make way, VIP coming through!" It's bloody embarrassing but at least it gets me in from the cold. There's no queue tonight though. I can already hear the racket from the band inside.

'Hey Jimmy! Long time no see, my young friend. What have you been doing with yourself?' I walk up and shake Mal's hand as he slaps me roughly on the back.

'Not much, Mal. You know, signing on, cashing my dole check and taking photos. That's my life in a nutshell really. But all that is about to change. I'm now officially a freelance photographer.' I pull a business card from my pocket and hand it to him with a certain amount of pride. He studies it and reads it out aloud.

'Snap Photography... yeah, I like it, kind of punchy,' he says whilst smiling broadly.

'No, it's more sparky than punchy,' I correct him.

'Punchy, sparky—aren't they the same thing?' he asks.

'Apparently not. What's the band like? They sound fucking woeful from here.' Mal opens the door for me to go inside.

'Not my cup of tea either but they've brought in about two hundred punters, so can't complain.' I walk inside and the noise is deafening. Iris is sitting on her usual perch—behind the counter which, is protected by security glass. Iris is the owner, she's Bulgarian, and she is incongruous in her surroundings. She looks like someone's sweet old granny but she's a smart business operator. She looks over her half-moon spectacles at me. She rarely charges me the entrance fee, unless there's a really big and well known act playing.

'Hello Jimmy,' she says in a weary tone. We always play this game. She knows I won't have any money and will ask to come in for free. She will lecture me about getting a job before begrudgingly shooing me through. But tonight it's going to be different. 'I suppose you want to get in for free again?'

'Well, the thing is Iris, I'm a bit strapped for cash.'

'Jimmy, Jimmy, my boy, you need to work. That is the only way you earn money. Work is good for the soul.' I pull out my business card and hand it to her.

'Well that's the thing, Iris, I am working. I am now a freelance photographer. Tomorrow I will be getting my press card from the Evening Standard and I will be going to as many gigs as possible.' She studies the card nodding her head in a positive manner. She then looks at me suspiciously.

'So how come you've no money if you're now a big shot photographer?'

'I only started today, well tonight, really.' She laughs out loud.

'Oh Jimmy, you're so funny!' I am? 'You always have hope. What I would give to be young again.' I'm not exactly sure what she means by that last statement. 'Go on, go in, shoo, shoo!' I walk to the far end of the room and turn back on myself as I walk up the stairs to the next level. I stop halfway up and pull my camera out of my jacket. I remove the lens cap and begin snapping away at the performers onstage. This is a good vantage point. I get about twenty shots off, then put the lens cap back on and head further up the stairs and through a door.

28

The decibels immediately drop as the door closes behind me. I walk across a narrow glass-lined corridor suspended above the dance floor below, then through another door into the upstairs bar. Nelson is working behind the counter and appears to be the only person here.

'Hi Nelson, how are you going?' He flashes a big Caribbean beam at me, dazzling white teeth almost illuminating the room.

'Not too bad, Jimmy. Although it's so quiet tonight. Not enough customers. I like it when it's busy, although, not too busy. What can I get you? The usual?' I nod and he pulls a bottle of beer from the bar fridge and snaps the top off. I take a good slurp from the bottle and place it on the bar.

'How much?' I ask. He always gives me the first drink for free—but, it's still polite to ask the question. Nelson looks around furtively, to make sure no one's listening. There's no-one here, so there's not much chance of that.

'The first one is on the house,' he whispers, 'but after that, you have to pay, okay?' I nod.

'Cheers Nelson. You're a rough diamond.' He gives me another blinding smile, then looks all serious. He sucks air through his teeth which produces a whistling sound. He whispers again.

'Hey Jimmy, don't tell the dragon in the cage downstairs though, eh, it's our little secret.' I laugh.

'Mum's the word. Nelson, what do you think of this?' I hand over my business card. He studies the words with screwed up eyes.

'Snap Photography, call James. This is you?' he enquires with a startled expression.

'It certainly is, Nelson. I'm now my own business. Keep the card and spread the word.'

'I will tell every single person who comes in here about you. Well done Jimmy. I have a very good feeling about this.' He turns and sticks the card on a notice board behind him. I walk over to the viewing area and watch the band below for a few minutes, their muted sound barely audible now. As I turn around I notice a girl sitting on the floor at the far side of the bar. She's staring straight ahead but I can't tell what she's looking at as she's wearing sunglasses beneath a large, black floppy hat. She's sporting a black dress of lacy chiffon and has Victorian style boots on, all neatly laced up. My interest is suitably piqued. I walk back to the bar.

'Nelson, who's the chick with the hat and glasses?' I ask quietly. Nelson's eyes widen as he shakes his head. He again whispers.

'We call her the "Ice Queen". Comes in here two or three times a week and just sits in that spot. She's a real stuck-up snob,' he sticks his thumb under his nose and pushes it up. 'She's cold, rude and has a sharp tongue in her head. I'd keep away from her Jimmy, she's bad news. Don't you go sniffing around her. There's plenty of pretty young girls out there for you. That one was born under a bad moon.'

'What's she drinking?'

'I'm warning you Jimmy. Listen to your Uncle Nelson. You won't get anywhere with her. I see young men try all the time and none succeed. You'll end up with a bad taste in your mouth. She gives off negative karma, you may get infected by it. She has the very devil inside her.'

'Sounds like a barrel of laughs. Anyway, I like a challenge. So what does she drink?' I ask again, ignoring his honest advice.

'Rum and black.'

'I thought Goths drank absinthe not rum and black.' He pours the drink and places it on the counter. I give him a fiver and he gives me some change. I pick up my bottle, the rum and black and head around the corner. I sit down beside the girl.

'The old Goth look is a bit 1982, isn't it? It's 1984 now if you hadn't noticed.' It's not bad for a first liner—start off with an insult—what could possibly go wrong.

'Ha! That's sweet coming from Mr Mod himself. The Mod revival began and ended in 1979.' Oh wow! Her accent. She could have walked straight out of the Queen's garden party for spoilt aristocratic brats. What on earth is she doing here?

'Touché! But the difference is, Mod is a lifestyle, not a fashion. It's about how you think, feel and act. It's not just about clothes.'

'Really, how incredibly interesting—not,' she replies in an ever-so-bored tone.

'Here, I've got you a drink,' I say as I lift the rum and coke up and try to hand it to her. She looks dead ahead.

'Did I ask for a drink?' she asks curtly.

'No. I thought it might be a nice ice-breaker, that's all.'

'Hmm. There'll be no ice broken here tonight.'

'Suit yourself.' I begin to pull the glass away from her but she stops me. A black lace glove reaches out and touches my hand. Something shoots through my body. I feel like I've been zapped with a thousand volts!

'It would be bad manners not to accept. But don't do it again. I'm not a charity case.' She takes the glass and has a genteel sip before resting it on the floor beside her.

'So what's with the hat and glasses? You got some sort of facial disfigurement that you're trying to hide?' Hard silence. This is going really well. 'What do you think of the band? Really, that's most interesting, I totally agree with you, I think they're fucking average as well.' Nothing, zero, zilch. This is one cold fish. Okay, one last try. 'I've just had a great idea, how about you and me go out on a date next week? I'll let you pay.' As the tumbleweed blows across the floor I contemplate abandoning my efforts, but there's something about her that makes me stay.

'Why would I want to go out on a date with you? You are an annoying and irksome little oik. Besides, we are from different social standings and it would never work. You are obviously working class from the way you speak and the bad language you employ. I doubt you've got any money, and you'll never amount to much. Oh, and by the way, I am not disfigured.'

31

'I can't argue with that. I'll give you a pre-nup before the wedding if that makes you feel any better.' I thought I detected the merest hint of a smile pass her lips—but then again—maybe not. 'So if you're not disfigured let's have a butchers at the old boat race.'

'I've got completely no idea what you just said.'

'You're obviously not an expert in cockney rhyming slang. I said, let me have a look at your face, or are you trying to hide something else? Maybe something mental, not physical.'

'Don't try and psychoanalyse me, you don't have the grey matter for such an onerous task.'

'You said it, not me.' Maybe it is time to give up. A night out with this one would be like chewing on razor blades. But, that touch, that feeling that went through me. Maybe it was static. 'Okay, I give up. You don't know what you're missing out on though. I could have made your heart flip.' As I'm about to stand she turns her head towards me. I stare into her black shades. She lifts her hat from her head and places it on the floor. Her hair is jet black, pulled tightly back into a ponytail. It glistens under the lights. I get a faint whiff of her scent and it enraptures me. She slowly removes her glasses to reveal eyes of sparkling, sapphire blue. My God! I have never witnessed such beauty! My heart rate has spun out of control. I'm breathing erratically and feel dizzy. I've been out with plenty of pretty girls, many gorgeous, but this girl is stunning. She remains completely expressionless and although she's staring into my eyes, it's like she is looking through me.

'Wow!' is all I can say for a moment. 'I'm lost for words…' I mumble like an incoherent fool.

'If only that were true,' she remarks, snippily. 'Right, now you've seen me you can leave,' she adds, with zero emotion. She blinks once, returns the glasses to her face and places the hat back on her head.

'Leave! Why would I leave? I've just seen the future and it belongs to you and me. I'm going to make you mine if it's the last thing I do. We belong together. You are the most beautiful, mesmerising woman I have ever seen. Hey listen, I

32

have an idea. Tomorrow, why don't we get up early and catch the first train to Scarborough. We can head down past the Spa and walk barefoot on the beach. We can paddle in the sea, then build a giant sandcastle together. After that we can waste some money in the amusement arcades on the promenade. We'll snack on sugary doughnuts, washed down with hot sweet tea. Later, we can buy fish and chips then walk up to the castle. We'll find a bench and eat them from the newspaper as we stare out at the sea and the little fishing boats bobbing about in the distance. It will be cold and grey but we won't care, because we'll be together. What do you think? Are you up for it?' I ask excitedly. Silence hangs in the air like a hot air balloon on a becalmed day. Is she thinking it over or just completely ignoring me?

'Well?' I prompt her again after a while.

'No, of course I'm not up for it!' she snaps. 'It sounds perfectly ghastly. Catching trains, trudging across wet sand, going in dirty amusement arcades, eating fish and chips surrounded by unmarried teenage mothers and fat pimply men with appalling body odour. You must have taken leave of your senses. And lastly, I wouldn't go with you if you were the last man on earth. You are clearly deranged and probably quite dangerous. Now if you don't mind, I was busily enjoying my own company a few moments ago until you turned up like a bad penny.' Ouch! I stand up and gaze down on her.

'Okay, you win—for now. One last thing, then I'll go—what's your name?'

'Victoria,' she replies instantly, with a softer tone, almost sad. I'll take that as a small win.

'I'm Jimmy, pleased to meet you.' I hold out my hand in a futile gesture. She lets out a small "harumph" and ignores me. I pull a business card from my pocket and place it gently on her thigh. She flicks it to the ground with contempt without so much as looking at it. I pick it up and put it back in my pocket. I turn and walk back to the bar.

'I told you Jimmy, she's the Ice Queen,' says Nelson shaking his head.

'Maybe,' I concur. 'But I'll be back. I don't give up that easily. I'll let her think about the error of her ways for a while.' Nelson laughs.

'Jimmy, this is what I love about you. You are delusional but always the optimist!' I pull my camera from out of my jacket, remove the lens cap and walk back to where she is sitting. I go down on one knee, aim the camera at her and zoom in on her face.

'Smile, Victoria!' I press the shutter release button and the camera whirs into action. For a split-second, the merest hint of a smile flits across her lips before it is rudely withdrawn, replaced by an impassive stare. Yes! I have her. I know that in that brief moment, she is mine. She may not know it yet but she will, given time. I blow her a kiss and she yawns, which only inflames my ardour.

'I'll catch you later Nelson.' I turn and walk out of the door.

'No worries Jimmy. Take care now!' he shouts after me. I walk back into the wall of sound and decide to get some close ups of the band from the edge of the stage. There's a rather large throng to get through so I lift my camera above my head and shout out above the din,

'Make way, make way, press photographer coming through.' As if by magic the crowd parts. I feel like Moses on the edge of the Red Sea. I barge my way to the front and only get one "Fuck off!" thrown at me.

'Oi! Watch it sunshine or you'll end up on the front page of the Standard.' I stand below the lead singer and get some good shots away. They must be getting to the end of their set as the dry ice machine has gone into overdrive, they also have a good light-show going. I focus on each member and get a handful of snaps. The drummer is the best. He's wild and thrashes his kit. He has long shaggy hair and during the drum rolls he swings his head violently from side to side. Droplets of sweat fly through the air and are illuminated under the dancing lights. I adjust the settings on my camera. I need to catch him on high speed to ensure there's no blur. I rest the camera on the stage and get ready. A minute or so passes and he does his drum roll thing again. I click, wind the film on and click again. My work is done here and I push and jostle my way through the crowd. I'm about to head towards the exit when a girl grabs me by the arm and pulls me into an alcove.

'Hey, who are you working for?' she shouts above the racket.

'The Standard,' I reply. She looks a little disappointed. She was hoping I was from one of the big music nationals. I give her my card which is my last until I see Marky tomorrow.

'Would we be able to get a few copies?' she asks.

'Yeah sure. Listen, why don't you write a review and drop it round to my place tomorrow. I'll develop some photos then drop them off at the Standard. Who knows, it may get in Saturday's paper.' She beams at this. She's very pretty with a short blonde bob and cherubic cheeks. She's wearing a small pink top with matching ra-ra skirt and she's certainly not backward in coming forward on the top half. I retrieve the card from her and scribble my address on the back.

'Say about midday tomorrow?' She slips the card down the front of her skirt, a most peculiar place to keep it.

'Great! How much will it cost?'

'It's on me. You can take me for a drink at my local.'

'Okay, deal.'

It's been a successful day apart from my partial fail with the Ice Queen upstairs. I feel like I'm on a roll.

'Say, what are you doing after the gig?' I ask with the best boyish charm I can muster. She looks disappointed again.

'Sorry,' she replies. 'See the lead singer—he's my boyfriend.'

'Ah well, never mind. Right, see you tomorrow then. Oh sorry, what's your name?'

'Julia.'

'I'm...' she cuts me off.

'You're James.'

'I prefer, Jimmy. Right, see you tomorrow, Julia.'

'I'm looking forward to it,' she says as she trots off. I watch her slink across the dance floor as my male hormones race around my body. My God, I need a girlfriend soon otherwise I'm going to burst.

VICTORIA'S DIARY

I live a boring, privileged life. I was shunted off to boarding school at the tender age of five. I hated it. How can parents do such things to their children at such a young and vulnerable age? It was Daddy's idea of course. He went to boarding school at age five and it never did him any harm, so he says. I beg to differ on that particular point. It makes one cold, passionless, indifferent, repressed—yes, repressed. You need to quickly develop a mask to hide your fear and loneliness. The only time you can show any emotion is in the middle of the night when you can quietly weep into your pillow.

How I missed my mother, my dolls, my treehouse, the great sweeping corridors of the castle. Of course, I came home during the school holidays. I would be ecstatic for the first week. I'd gallop around the grounds on my horse. I would row across the lake, build fires, snoop around daddy's "special place" which was supposed to be out of bounds. By the beginning of the second week, it would start—the feeling of anxiety in the pit of my stomach. I'd begin counting down the days. As each hour passed, the melancholy grew inside.

When my time was up, Mummy would drop me at the train station and wave to me from the platform. It was like I was being sentenced to death. Back to the cold, dreary, crusty old school for ladies. Thirteen years of rules, regulations, of decorum and "what is expected of you". Then, just for good measure one more year at finishing school.

Oh, I didn't waste my time. I read voraciously to keep my mind occupied, to block out the feelings. I took up ballet, I played hockey, I learnt to cook, I sang in the choir. I became proficient in numerous languages. We were taught how to greet and introduce people and what topics were suitable to discuss at the dinner table. It was a factory that churned out young ladies. I'm surprised that on our final day they didn't stamp our foreheads with, "Now suitable for a young gentleman of impeccable breeding".

It's funny, they taught us everything about how to be the perfect adoring wife and mother. Yet, they missed two of the most important parts—they didn't teach us how to love or how to fuck! Such things were never discussed. Loving and fucking were taboo.

Ladies don't fuck, they lay on their backs and think of England. We all must do our bit for the tattered memory of empire.

My mother is a painter, and you'd think being a creative type, she'd be able to express her emotions. But, she's a bit of a cold fish. It's the way she—we—were brought up. I'm sure no-one is born repressed, it is purely down to nurture not nature. The stiff upper lip must be maintained at all times, it's what made Britain great.

I love going home when "he's" not there, which he rarely is. I also love being here in my little flat in the heart of the city. I don't have any friends in the city, well actually, I've only ever had one friend all my life—Penny. Now she is married to some mind-numbing bore and lives in the Cotswolds.

I am six months off my twenty-third birthday and daddy is becoming slightly agitated. He thinks it is time I married and began having children. He views me as a prize sow that needs to start pumping out little piglets. I overhear him speaking with mummy sometimes. She tells him to let me be. All in good time. Let me get it all out of my system first, there's no rush. Daddy is forever playing matchmaker. The names he suggests always make me laugh. High flyers in the City of London. Up and coming young politicians from the Tory party. An Earl here, a Baron there. All obsessed with money or power. I've had enough of that in my short life.

What I want is a real man. Someone who lives life to the full, someone who loves, feels and cares. I want a man who sometimes scares me a little. I don't mean in the way that daddy does, not in a tyrannical or violent way. No, someone who laughs at life and stands up to it, a man with a lust for living. But most of all, I want a man who knows how to fuck.

The men from my background don't know how to fuck. They can fly fighter jets, they can mobilise armies to invade impoverished countries, they can manipulate future markets to make millions—can they bring a girl off? The answer, for me at least, is no!

I've had boyfriends in the past but they never lasted. I've been out with the chinless wonder brigade from Oxbridge, far distant cousins who stammer whilst struggling to put their underpants on. The dreadful bores from the stock exchange—oh dear!

It's funny that I've never had an orgasm with a man. I'm not a lesbian—I'd readily admit it in these pages if I were. There's only one way I can orgasm. I realise it's not normal, but I believe it is all part of the repression. At least it scared some of those simpering sops away.

I spend most of my days reading, practising my writing, updating my dossier on daddy and perfecting new recipes. I go to the gym most mornings and I do a lot of clothes shopping which is rather indulgent of me. I don't feel lonely, but maybe I am.

Then tonight it all changed—or at least it should have—if I had let it. I go to the Granary Nightclub a couple of times a week. It is only a short walk from my flat. I'm not even sure why I do go. I'm not much into modern music. I don't go for the company, as I shun everyone. I think I go because I am alone. Just to hear and see other people living gives me some sort of solace. I have a few drinks and become lost in my thoughts.

There's a West Indian gentleman who serves behind the bar in the upstairs room. I am perfectly dreadful to him. I am not racist, I am dreadful to anyone who tries to speak to me. It's the mask you see. When I put on my floppy hat and sunglasses I become a different person. It's like I am possessed. I am the ultimate spoilt, upper class bitch, sneering and patronising. Anyway, the barman gave up on me a long time ago. We don't even communicate any more. I walk in. His face drops. He pours me a rum and black, I hand over the money. I then take up my usual position, seated on the floor in the far corner of the room.

Tonight was no different. Until I heard the door open and the voice of a young man. He then appears from behind the bar and stares out of the window, gazing down on the stage where some awful local band are playing. He has his back to me and I'm not really paying much attention.

Then he turns around. I do believe my heart actually stopped for a few seconds. I get a tingling sensation all over my body and become quite flushed. He stares directly at me. I devour his body. He is above average height, lithe, very smartly dressed. He is handsome, but still a boy. I stare at his crotch for a few seconds behind the safety of my sunglasses—not the actions of a lady at all. After a few seconds he walks off and disappears behind the bar. I have no idea what to do. The mask forbids me from doing anything. A minute passes and he's back in front of me holding a bottle of beer and a rum and black which, he hands to me.

I am not proud of what ensues. In fact, I am downright ashamed of my behaviour. I turn him away, I spurn him. I insult him and try to humiliate him! Why do I do this? I think I know why. I say that I crave love, but really I am scared to death of it. What if I did fall in love and experience this glorious feeling that poets have tried to put into words for millennia? What if I became besotted, infatuated? What if I loved so hard I could die for it? What if I found love, then lost it?

He made me laugh—I did not show it. He made me giggle—I did not show it. He made me want to drop my mask—and I did—for a few seconds. Then he tells me how beautiful I am, how he is mesmerised by my looks. Any other "normal" girl would have been won over—but not me.

He is working class and ladies don't fraternise with such people, not unless they are fixing something around the home. I give him nothing—worse, I actively discourage him. He suggests that tomorrow we take a trip to the seaside, walk on the beach, eat doughnuts, play the amusement arcades and eat fish and chips at the castle. It sounds wonderful! Oh, to be able to live by the spur of the moment! I have never done anything like that in my life. I give it serious consideration before my anger rises inside me like molten rock in a volcano. I can't go. It would never work. I don't want to fall for this boy. It would only end in a broken heart.

Eventually, even he is beaten and leaves, not before jumping in front of me and taking a photo. I want to laugh, I almost laugh, but I force it back and the most I give away is a split second of a half-smile before my mask slides down again. He places a business card on my dress that I flick away with disdain. He retrieves it. Such a small insignificant moment. Yet, if I had kept the card I would now have a phone number for him. Will I live to regret that moment?

I sit there for another hour, cursing myself. Again, I question my behaviour. Alfred Lord Tennyson once wrote, "'Tis better to have loved and lost than never to have loved at all." I wish I could believe it—but I can't. I could have loved this boy but it would never have worked out. We come from different ends of the spectrum. Our worlds would eventually collide and erupt into a fiery thunderbolt.

Despite all this, I cannot get him out of my mind, this man-boy, yes, that is what I'll call him, *my* man-boy. I fear I have missed out on something truly wonderful, life-changing. I'm not sure what to do. I must find him or he must find me, and when that happens, I will have to remove my mask.

My man-boy's name is—Jimmy.

4: LUST

I wake late and stare at the ceiling whilst mulling over the events of the previous day. I share a semi-detached house with Sofe. It sounds flash but it isn't. I have the upstairs bedroom and Sofe has what used to be the front living room as her bedroom. We share the bathroom and kitchen. I can hear her now taking a leak in the toilet that is adjacent to my room.

'Hey Sofe!' I yell out, 'keep it down will you, I'm trying to sleep.'

'Piss off, Jimmy! You shouldn't be listening.' Shouldn't be listening—it sounds like a bloody Clydesdale in there taking a piss.

'Hey Sofe?'

'What now?'

'Stick the kettle on will you—I'm bursting for a cup of tea.'

'I'm not your slave,' I hear her mumble back.

'Thanks, you're a star.' She flushes the toilet, then I hear her footsteps descend the steps. I dress, then freshen up in the bathroom before going downstairs. I enter the kitchen. Sofe is sitting at the table nibbling on a piece of toast reading one of the high-brow newspapers. There are two steaming cups of tea on the table and the radio is playing quietly in the background. I shovel three teaspoons of sugar into my tea and stir noisily. Sofe looks at me and shakes her head.

'What?' I ask.

'Three sugars is ridiculous. You'll get worms.' I sit down opposite her and sip on my tea.

'So how's Uni going?' Sofe is studying psychology at Leeds University, she's a bit of a brain-box.

'Oh Jimmy, I've got so much work to do. I don't know how I'm going to cope.'

I laugh. 'You've said that every term for the last two years and you always seem to pass with high distinctions.'

'Yeah, but this term is different. I'm really struggling with my thesis.'

'Anything I can do to help?' I offer. She pouts and looks at me with a "really?" look.

'Yes, you can keep out of my hair, for one. So what's new with you?'

'Aha! I do have news for you my beautiful, little flatmate. Things are changing for Jimmy Hooper. My star is on the rise and I can see a bright future ahead.' She smiles at me sweetly.

'Well I hope so because the landlord called around yesterday.'

'And?'

'If we don't get the arrears paid off by Monday—we're out.'

'Bugger! How much do we owe?'

'Fifty.'

'He won't chuck us out because of fifty quid. He's onto a winner with us two mugs renting his shithole.'

'Hmm, I wouldn't be too sure. He was very irate,' she states as she takes another munch on her toast.

'Measly, fucking Scrooge. No, he reminds me of that other Dickens character… the one who used kids to steal things…'

'Fagin?'

'Yeah, that's him. He even looks like the Fagin fucker! He can't just kick us out like that. There are laws… and stuff.'

'Jimmy, I have a few months to go before I sit my final exams. I haven't got the strength or fortitude to move out and find another place to live. I'm almost beat.' She stares at her plate. She does look tired and dejected. My heart weeps for her. I grab her hand.

'Hey Sofe, I promise it's not going to happen. Leave it to me—all right? I'll find a way to raise the money, which brings me back to my good news.'

'Go on then, what is it?' I recount the events of the previous day to her in an excited flurry of words and gesticulations. I tell her of my business cards, the job at the Standard, albeit unpaid, and my ad that will be running in the classifieds.

'So, I have my own business now. I'm a freelancer. My camera, my photography, is not only going to pay the arrears off but also bring in some much needed cash. So don't worry about a thing. You concentrate on your studies and leave the finances to me.'

'Well, well! I'm very pleased for you. I hope it all goes well. But you aren't going to suddenly get work in the next few days. These things take time. Plus, I would never leave the finances to you. You're hopeless with money.' She stands, rinses her plate under the tap and then dries it on a tea towel. 'Oh, hang on,' she says with a concerned expression. 'That means the phone's going to be bloody ringing all day. I'm not going to be your unpaid secretary, Jimmy. I don't have time for it.' I stand up and place my hands on her shoulders.

'Hey, chill girl. I'm not expecting the phone to ring off the hook… not just yet anyway. Once I've got a few paid jobs under my belt I'll buy an answering machine, then you won't have to worry.' She doesn't look convinced. She is a serious girl who doesn't laugh much. She has long frizzy auburn hair that falls down across her shoulders. She never wears make-up, she doesn't need to. Her coffee coloured skin radiates vitality. She is quite stunning, slender, almost delicate.

There's no sexual chemistry between us, which is probably a good thing. I look upon her as I would a sister.

I glance at the clock on the wall. It is already 10:30 am and I remember that Julia is arriving at twelve. I take a big slurp of tea, pick my camera up and notice I have two unused exposures remaining.

'Hey Sofe, I've got two exposures left on my film. How about we do a couple of tasteful nudes?' She stares over the rim of her reading glasses at me with disdain, then suddenly brightens.

'Okay, you get undressed and tell me which buttons to press.'

'Haha! Very good. Sofe cracks a joke. There's a first time for everything I suppose.' She slaps me on the arm as she makes her way back to her room.

'I need to study.'

'Yeah, and I need to get this film developed.'

I'm in my darkroom, which is basically a wooden frame enclosed with four sheets of heavy duty plywood and covered in thick black velvet. It looks like a kinky boudoir. All the equipment used to belong to my Uncle Billy. He was an amateur photographer and I'm not sure why he never took it up full time as there wasn't anything he didn't know about cameras, film, exposure times and developing. He taught me everything.

I first became interested in photography when I was about fourteen and Uncle Billy took me under his wing. I think he was glad he could pass on his extensive knowledge to someone before he passed away. He died from cancer aged fifty-five about a year after my father dropped dead from a heart attack. It was a rough time for me but I always had Marky there by my side to pull me through the shrouds of despair. I loved my Dad and my Uncle Billy—I still do.

I beaver away developing my negatives, putting them through various washes until I have my proofs. It's not fast work, it is slow and painstaking and any slackness along the way can have dire consequences on the quality of the finished print. I am exacting in the process and very rarely lose an image. I chuckle to myself as I hang each print up on the drying line. There's the savage dog from the scrap yard. The photo of Marky zooming away on his Vespa—he looks super cool, I might use that in my burgeoning portfolio. Then come the prints of the band taken from the stairs of the Granary. Now my heart skips a beat and flips upside down. It's the print of the Ice Queen. She's staring straight at me. I can make out the faint outline of her eyes behind her shades. I stare at her sexy boots. There's a sliver of firm milky thigh showing from beneath her lacy dress. Her lips are as full and red as ripe cherries. There's the enigmatic smile. I hang it on the line and study it intently. Victoria, the Goddess, a temptress, a royal pain in the arse. I waste a good ten minutes transfixed by her image.

The doorbell rings and I look at my watch. It's just past twelve. That will be Julia. I hear muffled voices, then the sound of footsteps making their way up the stairs. There's a gentle tap on the door followed by her voice.

'Hi Jimmy, it's me, Julia. Can I come in?'

'I'm in the darkroom. I'll be another ten minutes. Either wait on the bed or go make yourself a cuppa.'

'Okay,' she replies.

I finally hang the last of the prints on the line to dry and turn the safelight off and the normal lights back on. I open the door and poke my head out from behind the curtain. Julia's sitting on my bed reading a music magazine. I smile at her.

'Hi Julia. You can come in now. They're just in the process of drying.' She stands up and walks into the room. Her scent is heavenly. She's wearing a tight and very short denim skirt, above which sits a white boob tube and a denim jacket. She shuffles down the line looking at the prints. She pulls a tatty looking piece of paper from her handbag and passes it to me.

'This is the gig review. I'm afraid it's not very good. Writing is not my area.' I quickly scan the sheet of paper.

'Don't worry. I'll knock it into shape. You've got the song names, band members and the crowd reaction that's all that matters. I can't promise that the Standard will use it though.'

'I know. Just do what you can. These look fantastic, Jimmy,' she says as she walks down the drying line studying the photos intently.

'Okay, pick a couple to go with your review and I'll drop them off this afternoon at the Standard. I love this one of the drummer shaking his head. You see how that spray of sweat is caught in the different coloured lights, each drop crystal clear.' She giggles.

'That's Denny. He's a head-case.'

'Aren't all drummers?'

'Yeah, I suppose.'

'That's probably not a good one to use. You really need a group shot.' She points at two particularly clear and atmospheric shots of the band.

'This one and this one,' she indicates.

'Okay, we just need to give them thirty minutes or so to dry, then they're done.'

'Can I take the other photos with me as well?'

'Of course. Although I'd like to keep a copy of your drummer for my portfolio.'

'Oh he'll love that when I tell him.' She spots the print of the Ice Queen.

'She's beautiful,' she states slowly, in a wistful manner. 'Is she your girlfriend?' I laugh.

'I wish. She's out of my league.' Julia turns and surveys me with a cheeky glint in her eye.

'I don't think so. You're a good match.'

'She's not interested. I tried it on with her last night and she gave me an ice bath.'

'Faint heart never won fair lady,' she grins.

'Oh my hearts not faint but she ain't my fair lady. She can cut you down with just one withering glance.'

'That means she likes you.'

'It does?'

'Of course, it does. Don't you know anything about how girls operate?'

'Apparently not.'

'Try again with her and if you don't succeed keep trying until you do. It took Joey five attempts of wooing before I went out on a date with him.'

'Joey? The lead singer from The Zippers?'

'Yeah. I thought he was a bit of a jerk at first but there was something about him interested me. Anyway, how about we go for that drink while we wait.'

'Sounds good.'

We are sitting in my local pub munching on Cornish Pasties discussing the local music scene.

'So what do you think of The Zippers?' Julia asks. I knew that question would be coming. I place my pasty down on a napkin, have a sip of beer and lean back in my chair.

'You want the truth or do you just want to hear nice platitudes?'

'The truth of course.'

'Okay, well let's start with the positives. They are all competent musicians. They look confident on stage. They have a certain amount of charm about them.'

'And the negatives?' she inquires as she continues attacking her food.

48

'Well, their songs are pretty average, not bad but not great either. They are copying bands that hit the big time two or three years ago. That's never going to work. If you're going to do that you need to be copying bands that are just on the cusp of hitting the big time. That way, when those bands do make it big, the record companies will be running around like headless chickens trying to find a duplicate. They're like that—the record companies, they haven't a fucking clue what's going on. They're always one step behind what's happening on the streets.' I pause for a moment and she notices my reticence.

'Go on,' she probes, looking thoughtful.

'Well… you could take a completely different tack. Go way back. Don't copy what's popular right now, that boat set sail a long time ago. Go back to where it all began.' She finishes the last of her pasty and relaxes back in her chair.

'Rock and roll?' she queries.

'Yeah, you're on the money. Listen to Eddie Cochrane, Duane Eddy, early Elvis, Gene Vincent, Chuck Berry, Bo Diddley, Carl Perkins… even guys like Johnny Cash. Or go even further back, the blues guys; Muddy Waters, Howlin' Wolf, Robert Johnson, John Lee Hooker—that sort of thing.' She arches her eyebrows in surprise.

'Fuck! You really know your stuff! How come you know all these guys? I've never heard of them, apart from Elvis.' I drain the last of my pint and wipe my lips.

'I have three passions in life: music, photography and females.' She smiles, lasciviously.

'In which order?'

'Ha! No, when I say females, I don't mean what you think. I mean I love their company. I love their form.' She looks confused.

'Their form? What does that mean?'

'Their curves, the way they are built. Men are either angular or a fucking mess. Women, well… they're streamlined.'

49

'Even the fat ugly ones?'

'There are no fat ugly ones. Women can be streamlined on the outside, or inside, or both. There's something about women that fascinates me. They're so different, compared to men—more complex, less fucking outwardly aggressive.' She breaks out into laughter. 'Did I say something funny?'

'No, sorry, it's just that I've probably met a lot more females than you and that's not my impression. There's some real bitches out there. Manipulating, nasty, fucked-up pieces of work.'

'Hmm… were they born like that or did they become like that because of the way they were treated growing up?' She clamps her lips together and ponders, then loses interest.

'Not sure. You finished?' she says, eyeing my empty plate and glass.

'Yeah I'm done. Let's go.' As we saunter back to my flat, I offer some further advice. 'And another thing, the keyboard player, that soulless synth sound is fucking horrible! He needs to get rid of it. You've heard of "Green Onions" by Booker T & the M.G.'s?'

'Yeah, who hasn't?'

'They use a Hammond organ. The sound is almost human. That's the sound you should go for.'

'Anything else?'

'Yes, their dress sense is embarrassing. Poncy shirts, leather pants, long flouncy hair, boots up to their knees? That's so old hat, no—worse—it's boring. There are some looks that stand the test of time…'

'What, you mean like your Mod look?' she mocks me gently.

'Yeah! Style never goes out of fashion. But fashion goes out of style. Oh, and one last thing, the name—The Zippers…'

'My, you're really going to town on them aren't you?' she says, with maybe just a hint of annoyance. I stop and stare at her.

'You said you wanted the truth. I'll shut up if you want me to.' She kicks at an invisible pebble, then regains her composure.

'No, go on. Finish the autopsy.'

'There's lots of bands around with naff names like that. Go for something new, original or at least from a different era. Right, I'm finished. I apologise if it annoyed you—but you did ask.'

'Yes I did, and you certainly didn't hold back.' I place my hand on her shoulder and turn her around.

'Hey Julia, I'm not trying to undermine. I'm trying to help. They do have something. They've taken the wrong turn that's all. I can see it even if no-one else can. Have you seen the Hipnotikz?'

'Yeah, Joey's lot once supported them.'

'And what did you think?'

'Fucking amazing! I could bang the lead singer,' she gushes.

'Well, they're my best mates. It won't be long before they hit it massive, and the reason? Because they don't give a fuck about what's popular now. They just take their influences and nuance them into their own material. It's pretty simple really, if you open your eyes.'

'Okay, I hear the message, loud and clear.'

##

I open the front door and let her in.

'Go straight on up,' I say, pointing at the stairs. She climbs the steps as I follow behind. I'm looking at the back of her legs and imagining what's at the top of them. Damn it Jimmy, you need a girl—I know, I know!

I'm standing in the darkroom and touch one of the prints with the back of my finger knuckle to see if the photos are still tacky.

'Yep. They're dry.' I pull the prints down, separate them each with a thin piece of greaseproof paper, then put them into a large envelope and hand them to Julia.

'Thanks ever so much Jimmy. Are you sure I can't pay you? At least for the materials?'

'Nah, don't be silly. Just remind Joey that when his band hit the big time I expect to be getting a phone call from them to do their album covers.' She laughs as she places the envelope down on a bench. She takes a step towards me.

'Maybe I could pay you in kind?' She reaches out and begins to rub her hand up and down my crotch. Despite how desperate I am, I'm not sure I can go through with this.

'Come on Julia, you've got a boyfriend,' I sort of plead.

'Oh don't worry about Joey. I know he's had plenty of girls while dating me.'

'And that doesn't bother you?'

'Well, I'm not over the moon about it, but what can you do. As long as he's discreet and doesn't rub my face in it.' By now she's undone the buckle on my pants, unzipped my fly and her hand is in my underpants working my cock. There's no going back now. She kneels down and takes me in her mouth. I relax back and close my eyes. There's a lot of pent up frustration down there and this isn't going to take long at all. I let out a deep sigh and slowly open my eyes. Staring at me is the Ice Queen, Victoria. I imagine it's her knelt down with me inside her mouth. I look at those red lips and visualise stroking her head, as I tell her how much I love her. Within a few minutes I feel the surge and give Julia a warning.

'Ship ahoy!' I shout like an idiot. Well… it was the first thing that popped into my head. It doesn't distract Julia, in fact, quite the opposite. She now goes into overdrive. I hear her gag slightly but she carries on. I begin to subside and she stands up, removes a tissue from her jacket and daintily dabs at her lips.

'Well that didn't take long.'

'It's been a long time between drinks,' I offer, as a way of apology.

'You need a girlfriend.'

'Tell me about it.' She looks at Victoria again, who has just witnessed my act of betrayal. I know it's ridiculous but I make a promise to myself that I will never cheat on her again.

'She's the one for you. Well thanks again for the photos, your honest assessment and advice. I'm sure we'll bump into each other around the traps. Take care Jimmy.' She gives me a sweet kiss on the side of the cheek. I hear her footsteps descend the stairs followed by the slam of the front door.

5: ACCEPTANCE

I'm standing in the reception area of the Yorkshire Evening Standard as I try to capture the receptionist's attention. The building is made of pebble-dashed concrete and walls of glass. It would have looked quite modern when it was first built in the early seventies, but now it is a bit of a carbuncle. The place is humming and I like it. It emits an energy and excitement that makes me feel alive. It's like a train station or an airport. People coming and going, parcels being delivered while others are picked up and loaded into the back of waiting vans. Phones ring non-stop. There's constant chatter.

'Can I help you?' the receptionist asks.

'Yes. I'm here to see Mr Carmichael to collect my press pass.' She looks down her nose at me, as though how could I possibly have any business with the great Bulldog himself.

'Name?' she barks.

'Jimmy, Jimmy Hooper.' She picks up the phone and lets it ring for about two seconds, then says,

'Sorry, he's busy. Can I try someone else?'

'Yes, try Dave Dee.' I get the same response and she is losing patience. 'Okay, try Marky, sorry, Mark Carlyle.' She presses another button.

'Mark, there's a gentleman here to see you by the name … yes, that's right, Jimmy. Okay, I'll send him right up.' She points at some stairs behind her. 'Second floor, turn left at the top, head through the double doors straight ahead.' I scamper up two flights of stairs and burst through into a cavernous open-plan office. There's a clicking sound of keyboards being hammered by dozens of frazzled looking reporters. Men stand at large drawing boards with scalpels or pens gripped tightly in hands. Marky comes up to me beaming and holds out his clenched fist.

'Comrade, winning the battle?' I tap my fist into his and pat him on the shoulder.

'Baby steps Marky, baby steps.'

Marky spends the next twenty minutes walking me around the room introducing me to everyone, many of whom I'd already met the night before. They all shake my hand warmly and make me feel welcome as Marky not only sings my praises but makes me out to be the next David Hockney. Everyone seems to love Marky and why wouldn't they? He is a life-force, an unbridled fireball of nervous energy that seems to rub off on everyone he talks to.

He then takes me up a floor and we meet and greet all the girls and women from the classified ads department. Same result; all welcoming, all enamoured with Marky. Finally he takes me down three flights of stairs at breakneck speed and into the print room. There is a busy hum in the distance as print rollers spin around and print off thousands of copies of tonight's edition of the Standard. There are more introductions before Marky finally finds his man.

'Hey Jack, this is Jimmy I was telling you about.' He then puts his hand over his mouth and whispers. 'He's the new photographer. How'd you go with the business cards?' I shake Jack's hand and he looks around surreptitiously.

'Nice to meet you Jim. Come on boys, follow me.' He leads us past a whole gaggle of phototypesetters busy at work then into a back room and closes the door. He opens a desk drawer and pulls out four cardboard packages wrapped in brown paper. 'Here you go Jim.' He hands me the parcels and I slip my backpack off and drop them inside. Marky pulls out a fiver from a bunch of notes and hands it to Jack who quickly tucks it into his back pocket.

'Cheers Jack. You're a star. Next time I see you in the Soldiers I'll shout you a few pints,' says Marky.

'Aye, no worries Marky. Just watch out for security. They've been having a bit of a crackdown lately. Apparently, a lot of pilfering has been going on. Some people would rob their own grandmother.' Marky laughs as he pats Jack on the shoulder.

'Right come on Jimmy, back to the control centre.'

'Okay, let's go see Dave Dee and get your press pass,' says Marky, once we are back in the hustle and bustle of the newsroom. We head towards an empty desk that is situated at the far end of the room. On the way, an older guy emerges from a doorway.

'Oh fuck,' says Marky. 'That's John Arnold, resident photographer and the most boring man on the planet. I'll give you fair warning now Jimmy, do not get into conversations with him or show the slightest interest in what he's got to say, otherwise he will bore your tits off for a good hour. Plus, once he thinks you're his mate, he'll follow you around like a lost puppy.' John Arnold makes a beeline for us. 'Here he comes, incoming boredom missile,' whispers Marky.

'Hey Marky, who's the new kid?' says Arnold in a slow, northern drawl.

'John, let me introduce you to Jimmy. Jimmy is a brilliant photographer and is going to be doing a bit of work for us… you know, all the shit you hate doing. The local bands, the acts who come to town on their way up, the bands that come to town on their way down.' Arnold eyes me suspiciously for a moment as he looks me up and down.

'What camera do you use?' he asks.

'Olympus, om10,' I reply with a gracious smile. He sniffs.

'My go-to is the "Nikon FA". Brilliant bit of engineering. I used to use the Olympus but found it a bit too shaky and it's too light. I like to feel something heavy in my hand.'

'That's what I love about it,' I reply. 'It's light, portable. You can have it hanging around your neck all day without even noticing it.'

'Jimmy is great at capturing faces and iconic images. He's a real artist,' gushes Marky. Arnold sniffs again as he jerks his head upwards.

'Hmm, well in this game, what the people want is a clear photo, not some arty interpretation, you'd do well to remember that. Are you full-time, part-time or freelance? No-one's said nowt to me about you starting work here, and I am chief photographer,' he inquires, still looking at me warily. Marky laughs.

'Don't worry John, no-one is taking your spot. Jimmy is just doing a bit of freelance, gratis, for a month just to see how it goes.' Arnold softens his stance and holds out his hand.

'Well, pleased to meet you Jimmy. We must get together at some point and discuss cameras.' His handshake is limp and weak. He has appalling dandruff and is dressed like some bad actor from 1973, with flared trousers, a wide-collared shirt and a Laurel and Hardy tank-top. Cutting street edge, he is not—although, these are strange fashion times we live in. Marky spots Dave Dee returning to his desk just as Arnold starts up again.

'Sorry John, but we really do need to speak with Dave. Catch you later. Oh by the way, didn't see you in the Soldiers last night?' Arnold looks slightly disappointed, then with his somnambulistic brogue he replies,

'No, the old ulcer is playing up again. Doc says I have to keep off the grog indefinitely otherwise I could die.'

'You worry too much, John. It's not the drinking that gives you ulcers, it's stress. If you can't stand the heat get out of the kitchen!' Marky pulls me away and we make our way over to Dave Dee. We stand in front of him like schoolboys in the Headmaster's office. He has his head down and is frantically going over some copy, crossing things out, then adding extras. A half-smoked cigarette lays in an ashtray to the side of him, silently burning away. After about thirty seconds he stops scribbling and pushes his notes aside. He looks up at us.

'Sit, sit!' he commands. We both pull out chairs and take a seat. He pulls open his top drawer, throws a couple of laminated cards across the desk and hands me a small box similar to the one I just collected from Jack in the print room.

'Okay Jimmy, here's your press pass, security pass and a box of business cards. First of all, security pass is required for out-of-hours entry to the building. Before 7 am and after 9 pm. The press pass will get you into most places; University, Polytechnic, Duke Of York, Irish Club, etc, etc.' He now produces an A4 sheet. 'Take this. Here are the contact names and numbers of all the entertainment venues in Leeds and surrounding areas. Mid-morning Monday, ring all the venues and make an appointment to meet the manager or whoever's in charge. Go introduce yourself and give them your business card, that way they know you're legit. Always pays to put a face to a name.' I pick the cards up and study them before slipping them into my back pocket along with the sheet of contacts. I grab the box of business cards and chuck them into my backpack.

'Cheers Dave, ' I say. 'Has this all been okayed by Bulldog?' Dave looks at me sternly.

'It's Mr Carmichael to you and don't forget it. And yes, Bulldog has signed off on it all.' He then pushes another sheet of paper my way. 'These are the acts that are playing in the next month. Thirty of the buggers to entertain this sad and sorry fucking town. I've highlighted the ones I want reviews for in green. As for the others, well I'll leave that up to you. I want good original photos and copy, not the usual shit we get from their PR office. Right, I'll give you a fair crack of the whip for one month and see how you go. If I like the cut of your jib, then we'll take it from there. We'll supply you with film and you'll have access to all our facilities, including the darkroom, at any time. See John Arnold on the way out and he'll give you some rolls of film, make sure you sign for them. Oh, and remember, the film and darkroom are for work related to the Standard. Don't try using it for your own work—understand?'

'Sure,' I reply as he takes a deep toke on his cigarette. He stands up. He is solid, well-built, a naturally powerful man. He turns and opens a grey filing cabinet behind him and pulls out a bottle of whiskey and three small tumblers. He unscrews the cap and fills the glasses with a small shot of the amber liquid then hands them out.

'Here's to the future! If you are half as good as Marky makes out, then you'll do all right.' We all clink glasses.

'Thanks Dave, I appreciate you giving me a go. Chances are hard to come by these days.' He sits back down and is immediately consumed with more important matters. He looks at his watch as I check the clock on the wall behind him. 4:55 pm, I have already been here for two hours.

'Have you got wheels?' he asks as an afterthought. I shake my head in response. He pulls a bulging wallet out of his back pocket, opens it and hands me a twenty. 'This is for bus fares, should keep you going for a while. Keep the ticket stubs, we can claim it back on expenses. If you run short, come and see me. Okay, now fuck off you two. Oh, wait a minute. Marky, are you up for a bit of overtime tomorrow?' Marky grins.

'A Saturday—double time—of course. What's the go?'

'Got a phone call a few minutes ago. Post Office in Armley, armed robbery—bastards! Go around there tomorrow morning and interview the Postmaster and his wife. Get some details of how and what occurred. Go gentle… they're both shaken up… in their sixties. Then get yourself over to Milgarth Police Station and ask to speak with DCI Willis for a statement. He'll be expecting you. They're putting together a photofit. A lot of fucking use that will be. Two blokes with balaclavas over their heads. Anyway, I want a good photo of the couple … you know… shaken and afraid.'

'How about I take Jimmy with me to get the photos? He's brilliant at faces?' Dave stares at him, slightly annoyed.

'No! Take the coffin dodger, he's our official photographer.' Marky turns around and looks at John Arnold who is slicing something up on a guillotine.

'Hey John!' Marky shouts, 'you up for a bit of double-time tomorrow?' Arnold shakes his head.

'Sorry, no can do. Got a wedding. Can't get out of something like that at short notice.' Marky turns back to Dave and smiles. Dave slumps back in his chair.

'Fuck it! Okay, take Jimmy with you. I'm trusting you both. Take a pool car Marky and don't prang it.' Dave rips a piece of paper off a notepad and hands it to Marky. 'Here's the details. I need the copy and a good photo on my desk by noon at the latest.'

'Not a problem Dave, have I ever let you down yet?' grins Marky. We turn and walk away as Dave calls out again.

'Oh, by the way, Marky, you're doing okay—keep it up and you'll soon have my job!'

'I wouldn't want your job for all the tea in China. What time will you knock off tonight?' Marky laughs. Dave stares at his inbox.

'Probably about ten. Then back here tomorrow at eight. It comes with the territory. Okay, now fuck off and let me get on with my work. Have a good night!' We head back over to John Arnold.

'Right Jimmy, you get sorted with John and I'll just tidy my desk up then we'll head off for a couple of pints.'

'You after some rolls of film?' John asks in a slightly bored manner.

'Yeah, Dave said to see you.'

'Okay, follow me.' He opens the door he'd emerged from earlier and takes me into a large storage room. At the far end is a solid looking door, with a red light above it and signage that reads, "Do not enter when red light is on".

'I take it that's the darkroom?' I say, nodding towards it.

'I see you're a bit of a livewire,' he replies sarcastically. 'How many rolls do you want?'

'Give me ten for starters.' He slides a box from a shelf and places it on a table.

'Here, help yourself.' He then pulls a folder out and places it beside the box of film. 'Make sure you sign for it, otherwise there'll be hell to pay. Time, date, name, amount of film, type of film and reason. Never used to be like this. Anyone could walk in here and help themselves to whatever. A perk of the job. This last eighteen months they've been cracking down on everything. You can't wipe your arse without them wanting to know how many sheets you've used.'

'This is all black and white. Do you have any colour?' He stares at me with a puzzled look.

'If you hadn't noticed, the fucking newspaper is black and white.'

'The entertainment guide in Saturday's edition is in colour—if you hadn't noticed,' I reply cockily.

'Smartarse,' he retorts and pulls another box from the shelf. I grab four rolls, lob them into my backpack along with the black and white film then fill out the register. 'Do you want to have a look inside the darkroom?' he offers expectantly.

'I'd love to John, but I need to make tracks. How about Monday afternoon?' He smiles.

'Aye, okay then—that's if I'm around. You never know what can crop up working here.'

I meet back up with Marky in the main office and we head down the stairs then into the daylight and the city noise.

##

We're sitting in Tossers sipping on our pints laughing and joking at the turn of events.

'I can't believe it Marky. Just over twenty-four hours ago I was sitting here with you, unemployed, unemployable and nothing on the horizon but signing on and applying for crappy jobs. Now I have my own press card, a bag full of film, more business cards than you can shake a stick at and a bit of cash in my pocket. Things are looking up and it's all down to you.' Marky laughs and pats me on the arms.

'No comrade, it's down to you. I just gave you the kick up the arse you needed. You've now officially joined the club, you're part of the gang.'

'What gang?'

'The Evening Standard gang. Dave Dee—he likes you. Once you've got your foot in the door then you are in for good. It's like a giant family working there and they look after their own.' I take a gulp of beer then place it down on a beer mat.

'I think it's a bit early to say that Marky. I need to prove myself first.'

'And you will my son, you will. Listen, I've barely eaten a thing all day, why don't we head up to the Taj Mahal for a stinking hot curry then come back here and meet the others later.' Macca, Jonesy and Gerry won't show up for another two hours and I am feeling ravenous. Plus, it will be nice and quiet in the Taj at this time of day and I want to tell Marky about the Ice Queen.

'Okay, sounds like a good idea. Sup up your beer and let's make a move.'

We've just finished onion bhaji starters and are waiting on our main courses.

'What did you get up to last night after you left the Soldiers?' I ask Marky as he's busy poking his teeth with a toothpick.

'Can't say, mate. I'd like to tell you but it's all hush-hush at the moment. You'll find out one day.' I laugh.

'Fucking hell Marky, it's all very clandestine, a bit cloak-and-dagger. Is this to do with the "struggle" and the "glorious revolution"? I thought you were just winding us up, but you're serious aren't you?' He puts the toothpick down and leans forward with a frown on his face.

'Oh yes, I'm serious all right.' He shoots a glance around the restaurant. 'There are forces at play right now. Things are going to change—big time,' he says softly. He worries me. I decide to change the subject.

'Do you want to know what I got up to last night when I left you?'

'Yeah, of course I do.'

'I went to the Granary. There was a band playing and I got some shots of them. Met the lead singer's girlfriend and gave her my card. She came around to my place today and collected some prints.' He's nodding as I speak. 'She gave me a blowjob in my darkroom, payment in kind, if you will.' Marky grins.

'You dirty little fucker. Don't you feel bad fucking someone else's girl?'

'I didn't fuck her. It was just a blowjob—and yes I did feel a little uneasy but before I knew it she had unzipped me and had me in her mouth. There's no turning back at that point.'

'No, I guess not.' The waiter arrives with our curries and plates of chapattis. We waste no time in tucking in.

'Anyway, that's not the only thing that happened.'

'Go on,' he says, his attention now firmly fixed on his beef madras.

'Well, in the Granary, before I met the girl from the band, I also met another girl in the upstairs bar.'

'Fuck! You can't leave it alone can you,' he mumbles as he stuffs a big piece of chapatti into his mouth.

'The thing is Marky, I'm in love.'

'Yeah, sure you are,' he snorts.

'No, I mean it. This girl was... is... the most beautiful girl on the planet. Her looks are breathtaking and I fell for her straight away.' Marky still seems more interested in eating than my tale of unrequited love.

'What's her name?'

'Victoria. I tried all my Jimmy Hooper charm on her and she threw it all back in my face. Couldn't even get her to crack a smile. Plus, she's super posh, I mean like royalty posh.' That got his attention. He places his fork down on the table and dabs at the sides of his mouth with a napkin.

'Forget about her Jimmy. It will never work. You are going to open yourself up to a world of pain. I've told you about their type before. I'm telling you

Jim, those bastards will never let you into their private club. No matter what you do, no matter what you strive for, no matter what you achieve, you will always be a commoner to them—less than zero. They believe they were born to rule and you were born to be their mule. Walk away from it right now.' I stare at him for a few seconds.

'I can't. There's something about her that electrifies me. This isn't lust or wanting something I can't have—it's different—something I've never felt before. Even talking about her now, I'm getting goosebumps. My hands are tingling and I'm getting the biggest boner on.'

'Oh for God's sake man! Show some respect. I'm eating here! Jim, listen to me, this will end in tears. She will chew you up and spit you out when she's ready, once she's had her bit of "rough". She'll break your fucking heart, man! And, you know what you're like, you love too much, you feel too much—you're an emotional sponge.'

'Well, I'm willing to take that risk. In fact, I've taken a vow of celibacy. No more sex with anyone until I've made love to her. Now I think about it, she will be the only woman I have sex with for the rest of my life.' Marky leans back in his chair and takes a large gulp of beer.

'This place does one of the best curries in the city but their beer is shit! So, your vow of celibacy didn't last long, did it?' I'm not sure what he means.

'Come again?'

'Quite. Well, you take this vow of celibacy and less than twelve hours later you're getting gobbled off in your darkroom. There goes that vow.' I pause for thought. He's right, I've failed straight away.

'Well, the vow of celibacy starts right here and now.'

'Do you understand what celibacy means?'

'I'm not stupid. It means abstaining from sex.'

'Yep, any sex. That includes having a wank. Are you telling me that you are never going to knock one out for the rest of your life?' I haven't contemplated this—but now I do—I'm feeling strong.

'Well, not for the rest of my natural. Once I've made love to Victoria, then self-abuse can resume on a normal twice-daily basis.' Marky chuckles then looks thoughtfully at me.

'If she gave you the brush off last night, what makes you think next time will be any different?'

'Not sure. Yes, she did give me the cold shoulder but there was something else, I can't explain it. I got this feeling like we'd been together once before in a previous life. There was this overwhelming feeling of sadness, of melancholy, yet wrapped in deep love.' Marky laughs.

'Fuck me drunk! You've been reading too many of those romantic poets. Well James, my boy, it's your call. But don't say I didn't warn you. And remember, I'm your best mate, so when your heart is laying in tattered pieces on the floor, I'll be here to help you stitch it back together.'

'Don't mention this to the others—right?'

'Okay, if you say so Jim.'

We're back in Tossers and Marky is having another heated discussion with Macca—yep, you guessed it, it's about politics.

'Yeah well, I've heard from a good authority that the miners are going to take strike action—any day now,' states Marky with a certain amount of pride.

'And what good is that going to do?' scowls Macca.

'They are the most powerful union in the land. Once they go out on strike they'll be followed by the steelworkers, the dockers, the railways—the whole country will grind to a halt.'

'Nah mate. The Iron Lady and her crew won't allow that to happen. They're too wily. Times have changed and the people won't support it.'

'Oh yes they will. This has all been carefully orchestrated and planned. There will be a mass uprising and the government will fall. The Labour party will be back in power, then we begin moving the party over to the hard left. A real socialist party. The House of Lords will be the first big institution to go, replaced by an elected senate. Then the public school system will be dismantled, and after that, the royalty.'

'You're fucking barmy! The British love their royalty. What would the tabloids put on their front page every day without them? Sometimes Marky, I wonder about your mental state. You seem to live in a different reality to the rest of us,' laughs Macca. I've heard enough and collect the empty glasses.

'Time for one more pint, then I better get off. Same again boys?' I ask. They all nod. Gerry looks at his watch.

'What's the go with you Jimmy, it's not even ten o'clock yet?' he looks surprised.

'My ad went in the paper tonight; so who knows? My phone may have been ringing off the hook.'

'Not a lot of good if you're not there to answer it,' Gerry replies.

'I have a secretary—her name is Sofe.'

'You take advantage of that girl,' laughs Jonesy. 'Hey, have you and her ever... you know?'

'No, of course not. I love her to bits, but it's not like that. Anyway, a golden rule of mine is, "never hump your flatmate", things could get complicated, plus, I think she might be a lesbian.' Jonesy snorts derisively.

'Why? Because she doesn't fancy you, you assume she's a lesbian?'

'No, not at all. Just a feeling I get.'

I return to the table with the drinks, and thankfully the political arguing has ended.

'Hey boys, Spring is not far away now. It won't be long before we're doing a scooter run up the east coast, stopping off for fish and chips at Whitby, a game of footy on the beach, driving back through the moors and quaffing a few refreshing ales at some glorious English country pub,' laughs Jonesy. Everyone's faces light up at the prospect.

'Yeah, I can't wait,' concurs Gerry. 'It's been a long time since we've been on a run.' All my mates have Vespas and there's nothing better on a fresh Spring day, than riding along on a scooter, or in my case, riding pillion on the back of Marky's. Gerry puts his pint down and taps me on the knee.

'Jimmy, I forgot to mention. You remember, Billy, he used to play keyboards in the band?' I nod.

'What about him?'

'Well, you remember that Vespa Rally he has?'

'Do I ever! 200 cc, beautiful shiny red with white "go-faster" stripes down the side. Who could ever forget that?'

'Guess what? He's selling it and it's a steal. He wants two hundred quid for it.' There are gasps from around the table.

'Two hundred quid!' exclaims Macca. 'It must be worth double that.'

'And the rest,' chirps in Jonesy.

'So what do you think, Jimmy?' continues Gerry.

'What do I think about what?' I reply.

'Why don't you buy it. Then you've got your own set of wheels. You're going to need some transport if this photography lark takes off.' I laugh at him.

'Gerry, I couldn't cobble together fifty quid let alone two hundred.'

'Borrow it from your old lady?'

'Nah, she's on struggle street as it is. It's a nice dream though but a dream nonetheless.'

'Cheer up Jim,' says Marky. 'In a couple of weeks from now, you might be able to afford it.' It's a glimmer of hope, but at that price, someone will snap it up before I have saved up the money.

'Nah,' says Gerry. 'Billy needs the money before the end of next week. He's going to Canada to work the ski season for three months, that's why it's going cheap. He's really short of cash.' Damn! I finish my pint and say farewell to my mates.

'Don't forget I'll pick you up tomorrow at 9 am, Jim,' Marky reminds me.

'Yep, no problem, see you then. Catch you boys later. Love ya.' I depart into the cold, dark night to catch my bus.

6: UPWARDS

There's a soft orange glow emanating through the curtains of Sofe's room. I put the key in the door and turn the latch.

'Hi Sofe!' I call out, 'Only me.' I hear the scrape of a chair, then her door flies open.

'You bastard!' she screams at me.

'What?' I reply, in genuine shock.

'Since three o'clock this afternoon that bloody phone hasn't stopped ringing!'

'Wow! Really? That's great news,' I say, beaming at her.

'No, it's not great news. I've had to break off from my studies so many times that I'm now behind on my thesis. I have to hand it in by Monday morning otherwise I'll get a fail. You need to get an answering machine tomorrow because I won't be playing secretary for you.' I walk over to her and grab her roughly behind the head and plant a great big smacker on her forehead.

'You love me really though, don't you?' I smile at her. She knocks my arms away.

'No, I don't. You are a selfish pig. Right, come on hurry up I need to get back to my work.' She walks over to the telephone stand and picks up a notepad. 'You've had twelve enquiries.'

'You have to be joking?'

'Do I look like I'm joking,' she snaps at me. She shows me the list and runs through each one telling me what they are about.

'This is a woman who wants some family portraits taken. This one, she wants some professional shots of her babies. This is a guy who has a business in the city and he's getting some flyers made. These two are family portraits. Another business, oh, and this one, she said you can ring her back tonight, it's really important. She was quite distraught. It's her wedding next week and she just found out today the photographer she had lined up was involved in a serious car accident and will be out of action for some time. She's tried literally dozens of other photographers but none are available for next Saturday. She kept me on the line for a good twenty minutes. Right, the rest are self explanatory. Oh, this last one, he rung about an hour ago, an older sounding guy, rather posh, wants some photos of him and his wife in the Bauhaus style, whatever that is. Kept going on about the Weimar Republic and the German expressionist movement and asked me if you could duplicate that style. Dotty old bastard. That was a good ten minutes wasted speaking to him. He wants you to ring him back tonight as well.'

'You seen the film Cabaret, with Liza Minnelli in it?'

'Yeah, what about it?'

'I think he's referring to that sort of thing. You know, decadent Berlin of the nineteen twenties. How the fuck can you put that into a family portrait? I suppose I will get the occasional crackpot.' Sofe turns and heads back to her room.

'And don't forget, Jimmy, the rent is due Monday and the arrears. And you'll have to pay more towards the telephone bill.' She looks tired and worn out.

'Yeah, of course. Hey Sofe, thanks.' She looks at me and almost smiles but it turns into a pout.

'You're still a bastard,' she says softly.

'I'll bring you breakfast in bed in the morning to make up for it.'

'Ha, you'll be lucky there's nothing left but a mouldy loaf and a half-can of baked beans.'

'Okay. Night then.'

'Night.' She closes the door behind her and I study the list of potential customers. I suddenly feel extremely tired. It's been a whirlwind twenty four hours. I think about going to bed but decide that as a young entrepreneur I must strike while the iron is hot. I pick up the phone and ring the lady who is having the wedding. The phone rings a couple of times before a woman's voice answers,

'Is that James from Snap Photography?' she asks in an expectant tone.

'Yes it is and you must be Tracy?'

'Yes. Thanks for ringing back so late.' She then launches into a ten minute verbal barrage. She tells me about the wedding, the one hundred and twenty guests that will be arriving. How they have overseas visitors flying in. The catering, the bridal gown, the bridesmaids' dresses and about how her photographer is now laid up in St. James' hospital with a broken back. Her voice rises higher then begins to tremble.

'How can I have a wedding day without a professional photographer there to capture it all? This is a once in a lifetime event and I want photographs I can look back on in fifty years' time.' I've barely had a chance to get a word in edgeways.

'Tracy, Tracy,' I interrupt. She finally stops babbling.

'Yes?'

'Tracy, I will guarantee you that next Saturday I will be at your wedding and you shall have the best wedding photos of anyone in the land.' I can discern her audible relief.

'Oh James, you don't know what this means to me. Thank you so much. I don't care what it costs, you can charge whatever you want, I'm past caring. Have you done many weddings before?' I laugh down the phone.

71

'It's my bread and butter and not one complaint yet.' I check my nose to make sure it hasn't grown tenfold. 'Tracy, I will charge you a fair and reasonable amount and not a penny more. I'm not going to exploit your situation for my financial benefit.' Fuck me! I'm even talking like a young professional businessman.

'What's your husband's name?'

'Gary.'

'Okay, well, how about six-thirty Monday evening I call around to your place and you, me and Gary figure out exactly what you are after, then I can give you an idea of the cost.'

'That sounds wonderful. Tomorrow I'm going to ring the caterers and get them to set an extra place at the table. You can be our guest and have a free nosh-up.'

'Thank you, that's very kind.' I jot down her address, say goodnight and hang up. I feel pretty pleased with myself for a moment and then it hits me. I know absolutely nothing about taking wedding photos or what to charge for them. A shot of adrenalin courses through my veins. I've got quite a bit of homework to do in the forthcoming days. Again, I think of sleep but decide to ring the mad old bastard about his fucking Weimar Republic photos. I'm assuming it will be a crank. He answers the phone in a soft, refined manner.

'Garth Peacock speaking.'

'Hello Garth, James here from Snap Photography, returning your call.'

'Oh good, good. Thank you for ringing back. Yes, I was explaining to your young secretary that I was after some photographs of me and my, ahem, wife. She's very professional isn't she?'

'Who? Your wife?'

'No, no, your secretary. Yes, very charming girl. Before we continue I'd like to ask you a question.'

'Sure. Fire away.'

'Mr Hooper, do you follow politics?' What a strange bloody question.

72

'No. Not at all. I'm apolitical,' I reply.

'Good, excellent. Now, are you aware of the renaissance of the arts in Germany during the Weimar Republic? Berlin in particular?' Of course I'm fucking not, you mad old clunker.

'Yes, yes. I must admit it is one of my favourite art periods. I believe the Bauhaus movement flourished during this time?'

'Yes, yes, oh super! It led to the rise of Dadaism. Of course, Dada himself was as mad as a fruit cake.'

'Ah yes, good old Dada, the world wouldn't be the same without him.'

'Quite, quite. My sentiments entirely. Okay, so how does tomorrow at 3 pm sound?' Sounds bloody great to me.

'Perfect. What's your address?'

'I live out near Ripon and the address is…' I jot it down. Ripon is a good hour and a half's bus journey away, plus a walk on foot to his pad.

'Well Ripon is slightly outside of my area…' I begin, already having reservations about the job.

'Oh Dear. Where are you based? Leeds, I suppose?'

'Yes,' I confirm.

'I would be more than willing to pay you for your travel time.' I'm thinking about turning down my first customer. The overall journey would take the best part of three hours. Another hour on the shoot and what would I charge…thirty, forty quid? 'How about two hundred pounds for the shoot and two hundred once you've hand-delivered the prints, that's if I'm happy with them, of course?' he says.

'3 pm you say? Okay, not a problem. See you tomorrow Garth. Oh, and by the way, will that be cash or cheque?'

'Whatever you prefer.'

'Cash would be good.'

'Cash, it is then.' I hang up and have to pinch myself. Did that really happen?

I burst into Sofe's room, pick her up and swirl her around.

'Fucking hell Sofe! You won't believe it. That barmy old sod has just given me a job worth a possible four-hundred quid and next week I've got a wedding booked. I'm in the money Sofe, no... we're in the money!' I suddenly remember the Scooter. I drop Sofe like a sack of potatoes and she lands with a thump on the floor.

'Ow!' I rush back to the phone and call Gerry. His wife, Sarah answers.

'Hi Sarah, it's Jimmy, is Gerry home yet?'

'Oh hi, Jimmy. No, I assumed he would be still out drinking with you?'

'No, I left early, got a lot on. Can you tell him to call me when he gets in? Doesn't matter what time it is, it's really important, okay?'

'Yes, of course. It's nothing bad is it?'

'No, no, the opposite. Okay, see you soon.' I hang up. Sofe is standing in the hallway rubbing her backside. 'Sorry Sofe. I got a bit giddy. Would you like me to rub it better?'

'No, I bloody wouldn't! You have to be one of the most annoying people on the planet. Now get to bed!'

##

I am laid in bed waiting for the phone to ring thinking about Victoria. I feel a pain in my heart and a strange feeling deep in my gut. I need to go back to the Granary each night and see if she is there. How can I charm her? How can I win her over? Just be yourself, has it ever failed before? Yes, many times. I think of my vow of celibacy and the hardening down below. Fuck it, I'll restart the celibacy vow tomorrow.

I wake with a start. It's Sofe shouting from her room below.

'Jimmy! For God's sake! Answer the bloody phone! I'm sick of it!' I jump from my bed, leap down the stairs and pick up the receiver.

'Hey Jimmy, what's the go? There's a note on the table saying I had to ring you ASAP. Is everything all right, mate?'

'Yeah, it's all cool, Gerry. Listen, I can get the two hundred quid for the Vespa. Can you pick me up about one o'clock tomorrow—I mean today and we'll head over there?'

'Fucking hell, Jimmy. It's half-two in the morning now. I'm not sure I'll be sober by that time.'

'Please Gerry, I know it's a big ask.'

'Aye, all right. Catch you tomorrow at one.'

'Oh, and Gerry, ring Billy first thing and tell him not to sell the scooter to anyone else. I'll have cash for him.'

'Okay, will do. See you later pal, goodnight.'

##

I wake startled. There's a loud rapping on the front door. I roll over and look at my watch. One minute to nine. Damn! I have forgotten all about Marky. He is the most annoyingly punctual person I have ever met. I get out of bed and fly down the stairs. Sofe emerges from her room with a dressing gown on, yawning. I fumble with the latch and pull the door open.

'Morning comrade,' we fist-punch. 'I'll wait in the car, the nine o'clock news is just starting. I can hear the theme tune now. I wanna see if the miners have gone out on strike yet—oh, and Jimmy, shake a leg mate.' He turns and walks back to the Vauxhall Cavalier parked in the driveway. It has the "Yorkshire Evening Standard" logo emblazoned along its length.

'Yeah, I'll be with you in a jiffy,' I reply. I shut the door on the bitter cold and look at Sofe.

'Jimmy, I don't want to stare at that thing first thing in a morning!' she shouts with a look of distaste on her face.

'What?' I reply, puzzled.

'That!' she screeches, pointing at my crotch. I stare down. I am wearing only underpants and I have a bad case of the "Morning Glories".

'Oops! Sorry,' I apologise as I push it down into the fabric of my jocks. It immediately springs back up and points at her like a loaded rifle. I then pull it up so it is laying flat against my midriff but still under its blanket.

'Really Sofe, I don't have a lot of control over it. The fucking thing seems to have a mind of its own. It's like having a second head. You've no idea what I've got to contend with.'

'God give me strength,' she whispers. I turn to walk up the stairs.

'Sofe, don't suppose you can do me a couple of slices of toast and a strong black coffee, could you?'

'Jeez! There's two slices left and they're both mouldy!' She yells back as I enter my bedroom.

'Not a problem! The heat will kill the mould!' I shout back in reply.

##

In a hurry, I scoff down the toast and throw back the instant coffee. Sofe is sitting at the little kitchen table sipping on tea. I pull a tenner from my pocket and place it on the table.

'Sofe, go to the shops and get some bread, bacon, beans and eggs. You need to eat.' She looks at me and smiles in a sad way that I do not understand.

'No, I need to write. Get on your way Jimmy, Marky's waiting for you—we all have things to do. I'll be glad for the peace and quiet.'

7: DEEDS

We get to the post office by nine-thirty and are greeted by an elderly gentleman who is maybe in his early sixties. He takes us through the post office and into a back living room.

'Mary, this is Mark and Jimmy from the Standard. Mark's a reporter and Jimmy is here to get photos.'

'Oh pleased to meet you,' she says shaking our hands. She immediately follows British protocol and insists on making us all a cup of tea before we start. I take a seat and inspect the room. It's neat and tidy, a little threadbare and has a feeling of austerity about it. Marky chit chats idly to Arthur, the postmaster. I've never witnessed Marky in action before and I am suitably impressed. He has a soft gentle tone and points to photographs on the mantelpiece above a three-bar fire that is blazing out radiant heat.

'Are these your daughters?' asks Marky. Arthur picks up a photo frame and looks at it lovingly.

'Yes, this is Gillian, our eldest. She's a doctor in Oxford. Done very well for herself. Always studied hard at school.' Mary returns with a tray stacked with steaming hot mugs of tea and a large plate of assorted biscuits. 'And this is Annie, our youngest. She's no longer with us. She was killed five years ago in a hit and run.'

'Oh, I'm so sorry to hear that, Arthur. It must still be very painful for you.' The old guy looks like he is beginning to choke up, and his wife comes to his aide.

'Yes, it's still very raw. I don't think the pain will ever go. I'm not sure I want it to either,' she says as she passes me a cup of tea.

'She's very beautiful,' comments Marky, in the present tense. He takes the frame from Arthur and studies it intently. 'I lost my father when I was fourteen and it was very traumatic. I couldn't get used to the fact that I'd never see him again, that's what really cut me up. But, after a few weeks, although I couldn't see him, I could feel him. I know that sounds odd, but I knew when he was in the room with me and mam. I could even smell his aftershave. Sometimes on a night I'd lay on my bed and talk to him. I still do actually, and I know that he is there, listening to my boring day or my troubles. I do believe there is an afterlife and one day I'll be with him again.' Arthur smiles and takes the photo from Marky and places it carefully back on the mantelpiece. He laughs.

'That's funny, because me and Mary do the same thing. Some nights we sit here and talk to our little Annie. She's here all right, sitting right there in that chair that Jimmy is sitting in.' A cold shiver slides down my spine.

'I'm not a big believer in God or religion,' starts up Mary, 'but I do believe in the afterlife. After all, what happens to all the love that someone has in their soul when they die? It's got to go somewhere, hasn't it?' Marky smiles at her sweetly as she passes him a cup of tea.

'Yes you're right, Mary. Where does the soul go?'

We sit and chat for another ten minutes or so while sipping tea and munching on biscuits. Marky deftly changes the subject and is relating some of the mishaps that have befallen him as a junior reporter. The old couple chuckle and chortle at his tales. He then takes a dictaphone from his jacket pocket turns it on and places it on the small wooden table.

'Well Arthur, Mary, I know this may be traumatic for you reliving the events of yesterday, but let me explain how the process works. I'm not here to get a sensationalist headline for the paper. I'm here for two reasons. I want to get as many details of the incident as possible. When it's published it may jog someone's memory. It could be something which seems irrelevant to you, such as the way the robber walked or a physical anomaly, but that's the sort of thing we need. Once we've got all the details down, I want you to tell me how you feel, the way this has impacted your life and how you see your future—the human side. People need to read these stories and realise that it's not just another armed robbery on a post office, it's a trauma that has been caused to a couple of loving parents and grandparents—real people.'

As the couple relive their ordeal I study them. He's a stout man with a barrel of a chest. He's trying to put on a brave face but his eyes give it away. He's in a state of shock and he's fearful. Mary wrings her hands and looks like a hunted rabbit. I've seen the headlines many times in the papers but never really thought about the human impact. Here they are, two grafters, running a post office, just getting by. Probably save enough to have a week's holiday in Bournemouth once a year and buy birthday presents for their grandkids. Good people, honest folk, playing by the rules of society. Then a couple of worthless scumbags, carrying shotguns, scare the living daylights out of them and for what? Two and a half thousand stinking quid. Bastards! Action—throw a pebble into a tranquil pond. Consequences—watch the ripples, too many to count, dissipate outwards forever. Two old people will now live in fear, scared of their own shadows. They'll probably throw the towel in and he'll have to start looking for a new job, along with another four million people.

I'm standing on the opposite side of the street with my camera affixed to the tripod. Arthur and Mary are standing outside the post office trying to look brave and stoic. I zoom in and get a few shots of their faces but I'm not happy with the setup. I get some long shots so it captures the couple and the post office signage, but I'm still not happy. I have an idea.

I'm back in their living room and I've now got Arthur with his arm around his wife pulling her towards him in a protective manner. Behind them on the mantelpiece are the photos of their daughters and grandchildren. I take a dozen shots hoping that at least one won't have either or both of them blinking.

We're back in the car and I've told Marky about my upcoming photoshoot and how much I'm getting paid for it. He slaps me on the thigh and smiles.

'These are good days comrade, good days indeed, and they are only going to get better for me and you.' I tell him about the scooter and he fist pumps the air. 'Brilliant, no more riding pillion. Freedom Jimmy, that's what a scooter is, it's sweet, liberating freedom.' He drops me off at the Standard so I can start work on developing the film. He heads off to the cop station to get a statement from the police.

There are not many people in the main newsroom today. A couple of older guys down the far end and the ubiquitous Dave Dee sitting at his desk, slurping on coffee and smoking cigarettes.

'How'd you go Jimmy? Get some good shots?' Dave asks.

'Yeah, I hope so. Bloody hell Dave, that was heartbreaking hearing what that old couple have been through.' He leans back in his chair and takes the cigarette from his mouth.

'I know. I see it every fucking day. Good people left broken and battered. All for what? A few quid. The crime rate is exploding and with the unemployment rate rising, it will only get worse. Cause and effect.' I consider his words carefully.

'You can't really blame it on unemployment, Dave. I've been unemployed but I didn't go out raiding post offices with a sawn-off shotgun.' He laughs at this.

'No, but not everyone's like you. Some people get desperate, some have a drug habit to feed and some people are just plain bad. The takers will always take and give nothing back.'

I begin work in the darkroom, which is state of the art. Once the prints are dry I take them down and study them intensely. The outside shots just don't work for me so I focus on the interior prints. The first two, Arthur has his eyes closed. The next three, Martha has her eyes closed and the following two, they both have their bloody eyes closed—the dreaded blink, every photographers nightmare. There's one print left.

I place the photos in front of Dave Dee, who stops scribbling over some copy. He lights another cigarette and scans the prints. He tosses each one aside after a brief glance.

'Nope, nope, nope,' he throws me a disappointed look. He lets out a huff as he gets to the last one. He freezes momentarily then pulls a magnifying glass from his desk drawer. There's a bang and I turn around to see Marky hurriedly walk through the doors and make his way to his desk in the middle of the room.

'Dave!' he shouts out, 'I'll have your copy in thirty minutes.'

'Make it fifteen Marky. You're not writing war and fucking peace,' Dave shouts back. He takes a puff on his cigarette, inhales, then ejects the smoke from the side of his mouth. He places the photo on his desk in front of him, grabs the others, scrunches them up and drops them into a waste bin. He stares at me for a while.

'Smartarse,' he says without any emotion. 'You're hungry Jimmy.' It's not a question.

'I'm not hungry, Dave, I'm bloody starving,' I reply. He gives me the merest hint of a smile.

'Good, keep it that way. Never lose it. Right, go on, fuck off, I've got work to do.' I walk over to Marky who is already busily typing away as his dictaphone replays the interview.

'How'd you go comrade?' he asks.

'Not sure?' I reply. 'He called me a smartarse.' Marky turns off the dictaphone and grins at me.

'That means he thinks you're a star, my friend. Put another notch on your belt.' I look at the clock on the wall.

'Righto, Marky. I've got to fly. Gerry's picking me up at one o'clock from the flat. Are you going to be at the Soldiers Arms tomorrow lunch to watch The Hipnotikz?'

'Of course. You?'

'Yep, I'll see you then, hopefully with my Vespa Rally parked up outside.'

##

I walk around the shiny red Vespa and marvel at her beauty.

'What's the top speed you've got out of her Billy?' asks Gerry.

'Just over 80 mph,' he replies, with a cocky smile.

'Fuck off!' exclaims Gerry. 'I'm a scooter mechanic and there's no way you can get a Vespa up to that speed!'

'I kid you not Gerry. I've done a bit of work on the engine and souped it up. Remember, it's the Vespa Rally. Fastest Vespa ever built—at the moment. I made a few tweaks here and there and can squeeze a few more knots out of her. I wouldn't advise going at that speed though. Apart from breaking the law, it sucks up the juice something rotten.' I'm still mesmerised as I lovingly stroke the seat. Billy's standing smoking a cigarette and is rightly proud of his machine.

'Any problems with her?' I finally ask.

'Nah. She's run like a dream from day one. I keep on top of her, mind. I regularly service her; oil, filters, spark plugs. She is the smoothest ride you'll ever get and the acceleration is phenomenal. I'll be sad to see her go—but needs must. You're getting it for a song, Jimmy.'

'Okay, can I take it for a test run?'

'Sure.'

'I have a photoshoot in Ripon, how far is that from here?'

'At a nice steady pace, forty minutes.'

'Okay, I should be back in about two and a half hours. You cool with that?' Billy laughs.

'Yeah, just don't leave the country. Say Jim, if you get the cash to me today, I'll throw in a free helmet for you and a couple of side panniers.'

'Sweet. Well, I'm pretty keen I've got to say.' I attach my camera bags and tripod to the back pannier, put my helmet on and jump on the kick-start. She put-puts sweetly into life—ah, that sound, music to my ears. With big grins from all, I rock the Vespa off its stand and trundle down the driveway.

'Hey Gerry, I've got a name for her,' I call out.

'Yeah? What?'

'Shelley.'

'Shelley? Why?'

'After Pete Shelley. She reminds me of the Buzzcocks.' He looks puzzled for a moment, then grins.

'Yeah you're right, she does.'

'Cheers for the lift. I'll catch you tomorrow at the gig.' He gives me the thumbs up.

'Jimmy, don't fucking crash it and don't attract the attention of the police—you're not insured,' Billy calls out after me.

##

I'm cruising down country lanes and through majestic countryside. Marky was right. This is freedom. I have an amazing feeling of well-being. The scooter glides along as though on air. Occasionally, I open the throttle and feel the powerful surge of acceleration. I think I'm probably the happiest man on the planet right now.

##

After a few false turns I eventually arrive at the address. It's a large stone farmhouse situated down a remote lane. The place looks quite palatial and well kept. There are two flash cars parked in a spacious driveway. I remove my helmet, unstrap my gear and knock on the door. A few seconds later an elderly gentleman, with slicked-back grey hair, sticks his head around the door.

'Garth Peacock?' I enquire

'Yes and you must be James,' he smiles politely. 'Come in, come in.' Once inside, I notice his attire. He's wearing a fluffy white dressing gown and a pair of tartan slippers. I find this odd. 'Leave your coat and helmet on the dresser and follow me,' he instructs. We are in the hallway and to the right is a flight of stairs.

'So, where were you thinking of doing this? It's a beautiful fresh day outside with great light. If you've got a favourite spot in the garden we could do some outside shots as well. Maybe get the house in the background,' I suggest. Garth turns and begins climbing the stairs.

'No, no, that wouldn't do at all. Come along, follow me young chap.' He's clearly eccentric and why he wants me to follow him upstairs is a bit of a puzzle. Oh well, he's the customer. I tag along and as we reach the landing he ushers me towards a bedroom. I'm now having some deep suspicions that he might be a sexual predator. I have a vision of myself tied up in a cage wearing a gimp mask.

As I follow him into the bedroom the first thing I notice as is a large bed. The second thing I notice is a woman lying on the bed. She is clothed in a black corset with stockings and suspenders. Her breasts are out, that's plain to see, plus, she's not wearing knickers and she has a completely bald vagina. Not one single hair to be seen! She's reading a book and nibbling on a chocolate. She's probably in her mid to late forties. She has jet black hair with the occasional streak of grey running through it. She's extremely attractive and has certainly kept her figure. Despite the fact that she is pleasing to the eye, I'm in the throes of a slight panic attack. This is not going to be a normal husband and wife portrait shoot.

'Margaret dear, this is James, our photographer.' She stops reading her book, removes her glasses and studies me but says nothing. 'Right James, if you'd like to get set up, then we'll begin.' The entire room is swathed in red and black velvet and the curtains are pulled shut. I cough.

'Ahem, what exactly do you want me to do?' I ask, hesitantly. I firmly hold my gear, ready to make a run for it.

'I want you to capture our lovemaking of course.' Of course—how silly of me. 'I want you encapsulate the very essence of unbridled passion. But most of all I want you to capture the look of ecstasy and pleasure on Margaret's face. You remember our little chat last night about the German expressionist movement? Well, that's what I'm after. Lots of close-ups and the juxtaposition of shadow and light.'

I haven't a fucking clue what "juxtaposition" means, but I'm not going to ask for clarification—one mustn't show ones ignorance, now must one. Garth disrobes to his birthday suit. He's not in as good shape as his wife. His muscle definition has gone. He has saggy skin near his armpits and a slight pot-belly. Jesus! Well, it's hard to miss! He's got a dong like a blind cobbler's thumb! That's some serious jousting pole he's carrying around.

'The problem is Garth, there's not enough light.' I'm hoping he'll call the whole thing off but there's no stopping this randy old bugger.

'Not a problem at all!' He throws back the curtains and bright daylight pours in illuminating the room. Microscopic particles of dust dance in the sunlight. I feel decidedly uncomfortable about the whole situation but I think of that little red beauty parked up in the driveway and how, in a couple of hours' time, it will be mine. I set up the tripod and unpack two cameras.

'Black and white, I take it?' I say, referring to the film type.

'Of course, what else could it be? They didn't have colour film in Berlin in the nineteen twenties, now did they?' Garth replies—mad old fucker. I load the film and attach one of the cameras to the tripod. Garth appears to be a tad impatient.

'Come on, chop, chop, James. Get out of your clothes and let's get started.' Hang on—what did he just say? I stare at him horrified.

'Sorry, I think I misheard you?'

'We can't have two people naked, making love, while another person is fully clothed. It would be incongruous to the situation.' The woman grins at me with wicked intent.

'Oh surely, you're not shy are you?' Well yes actually, I am. I suddenly wonder if they are swingers and expect me to join in. I look at the woman, and she is a beauty, and I do have a thing for older women at the moment —but no, not with Garth in the room. She must have read my thoughts. 'Don't worry, we're not going to ask you to join us, are we Garth?'

'Good Lord, no! He's nothing but a slip of a lad. Probably doesn't know the first thing about proper love-making.' I'm beginning to dislike Garth. Despite their reassurances I still feel reluctant to get my kit off. Garth notices my reticence.

'There's another fifty pounds in it for you.' I pull my shirt off and throw it onto a chair and begin to unbuckle my belt. I am now a whore and money is my pimp. As I take my underpants off I notice that my little friend down below has decided to lay dormant. He's normally in a state of flux between rock hard or healthy, firm plumpness. But not now. Right at the moment when I need him to come out of his corner fighting, my welterweight against Garth's heavyweight, he's decided to take a leave of absence. In his place an impostor acorn has taken up residence. It's fucking embarrassing! Garth and his so-called wife are sitting on the bed looking slightly bored.

'Right, ready,' I proclaim. 'Would you like me to leave the room so you can get started?' I offer graciously.

'No. Let's get on with it. James my boy, remember, capture the ecstasy, the ecstasy I say!' I heard you the first time you bohemian barmpot.

I expect them to be sedate, ageing lovers. I am wrong. They start off in first gear, quickly move to second, third, fourth and are now going at it hammer and tongs in fifth. Garth has all the moves. He must be an avid student of the Kama Sutra and Margaret, a practitioner of extreme yoga. I click away as they get down to it. I set the tripod camera on high-speed shutter release, the one around my neck on auto. The light changes constantly as the clouds drift by outside, sometimes casting shadows, other times shining brilliant luminance into the room.

I go through one, two, three rolls of film as twenty minutes pass. The majority of my shots are of Margaret, capturing her pleasure. Whenever I do focus on Garth he is always sporting a pained expression, like a man who has just had his scrotum stapled to the floorboards.

Garth manoeuvres Margaret into a new position. She is now facing me at the end of the bed and Garth is behind her, doggy-style, and giving it a damn good go! Margaret lurches violently back and forth. With the high-speed camera I capture her look of uninhibited, animalistic pleasure. Her head is about twelve inches away from my partner down south. He has now finished his time in absentia and returned to duty. He stands rigidly to attention like a new recruit on the parade ground, saluting, trying to impress the Sergeant Major. She stares at it studiously as though it is an alien from another planet.

Finally, we get to the climax—thank God! Garth kneels on the bed with his back to me. Margaret is astride him. She begins to moan and quietly call his name.

'Garth, Garth, Garth...' The silver fox glances over his shoulder at me.

'Stand by James, stand by...' he shouts at me, as though he is manoeuvring a tug boat into a harbour and I am ready to leap from the poop deck and secure the boat to a mooring pole.

She throws her head back, closes her eyes and bites her lip. Just at this moment a cloud moves outside and a blinding flash of light radiates across her face, half in shadow, half in light. Thankfully, Garth has got his great big noggin out of the way just in time as he busily sucks on her right tit. She is gone to the world as I click away. A few seconds later Garth lets out a groan like a cow giving birth to an elephant. He twitches, convulses violently, stiffens, then collapses on top of his partner. They both lie motionless. I fear Garth may be dead. I immediately envisage myself in the witness stand at the coroner's inquest.

"Yes Sir, that is correct. As seen by exhibit "A", that particular photograph was taken a split second before the fateful event. I believe Garth Peacock expired at the exact same moment as ejaculation. It was, after all, a rather vigorous fuck fest for a man of such declining years."

"I thank the witness for his time. No further questions—the witness may stand down."

I quickly pull my underpants on shrouding my discombobulated penis - which hasn't the foggiest idea what's just gone down – in darkness. I pull on my jeans, socks, desert boots, top then disassemble the camera apparatus.

'Oh, Viv... I mean Margaret... my aching desire for you will never be quenched. I love you,' Garth mumbles. She pats him on the back as a mother would a little boy and replies,

'Of course you do Garth, of course you do.'

'I'll be downstairs. Take your time Garth, no rush,' I say. As I leave the room I hear her scold him.

'You silly old fool.'

'Whatever's the matter dear?' he replies non-plussed.

'You called me Viv. Discretion is everything,' she whispers angrily.

'Oh don't worry dear, I don't think the boy noticed.'

##

As I wait for Garth I walk around the large kitchen-cum-dining room observing the many paintings that adorn the walls. Some of them capture my imagination. I know a little about the great photographers of the world, but not much about the painters. There's a most colourful and vibrant painting of what can only be described as "a splattering". It is by someone named "Jackson Pollock". Never heard of the geezer! I rewind the film in the camera and replace it with a colour roll. I walk around taking shots of the artworks.

I hear the creak of the wooden stairs and here he is—the silver fox stands before me in a fluffy bathrobe and tartan slippers. He seems almost embarrassed about the past events, whereas I no longer give a fuck. He walks into the kitchen, opens a drawer and pulls out a wallet.

'Ahem, so James, what did we say? Two hundred for the shoot?'

'Yep, that's right and fifty for the clothes thing and another two hundred on delivery of the prints.' He pauses for a second, throws me a quizzical glance, then pulls five fifties from the wallet. I grab them and stick them in my back pocket.

'When can I get to look at the prints?' he asks.

'When do you want them by? I have a rather busy week.'

'Well, I was hoping by tomorrow,' he replies expectantly.

'Wow! Tomorrow. That would mean me working through the night and I've got to say, I'm dead on my feet at the moment.' He looks at me thoughtfully for a few seconds, then opens his wallet again.

'Would another fifty cover it?' I snap up the fifty and stick it with the rest. 'By the way, you will provide me with the negatives, won't you?' he asks, suspiciously.

'Yes of course. Right, I'll be back here at about ten-thirty tomorrow with the prints and the negatives. See you then.'

##

Fuck! I have three hundred quid burning a hole in my back pocket. As I navigate the narrow high-street of Ripon, I spot an electrical shop. It is five-twenty on a Saturday and the shops are about to close. I park up my baby and rush into the store. They have an answering machine on "special" for just twenty pounds. I buy it and head off on my way. I get back to Billy's place by ten-past six and knock on the door. As he opens it I thrust the notes into his hands.

'Deal?' I ask. He smiles as he extends his hand. I shake it.

'Deal,' he grins. 'I'll attach the side panniers, should only take a few minutes. Make sure you look after her,' he warns.

'Don't you worry—I'm going to cherish her.'

##

I'm about five minutes away from the flat and I'm knackered. I realise the only thing I've eaten or drank all day is two slices of mouldy toast, a cup of coffee and tea and biscuits at the post office.

As my little red beauty glides along the high-street I detect an unmistakable aroma in the air. There's no greater smell in the world than freshly fried fish and chips. I spot the chippie two hundred yards away and park up outside. I remove my helmet, go inside and order two serves of fish and chips with scraps, two buttered bread-cakes, two curry sauces and two tubs of mushy peas— plus two cans of shandy!

##

I struggle with all my gear as I turn the key in the door and kick it open with my foot. I drop everything in the hallway and slump back against the wall with a big sigh.

'Hi Sofe! Only me.' Sofe appears from her room in her dressing gown. She's crying.

'Sofe, what's wrong?' I ask, alarmed. She stares at the ground as though ashamed.

'I'm so sorry Jimmy. I finally finished my thesis this afternoon. I was so tired I took to my bed but the bloody phone kept ringing. I took three calls then left the phone off the hook. You may have lost a lot of customers. I'm really, really sorry,' she blubs.' I take her in my arms and comfort her.

'Shh, don't be silly. I'm not bothered. How many businesses answer their phones on a weekend? Not many. They'll ring back. Stop crying now. You're overly tired.' I pull a tissue from my pocket and wipe the tears from her cheeks. 'Anyway, look at this.' I pull the answering machine from its plastic bag and hold it up. She giggles and instantly brightens, which makes me feel better. I look past her into the kitchen and spot the tenner I'd left her this morning, still laid on the table.

'Sofe!' I scold. 'When was the last time you ate?'

'Yesterday, at breakfast. A couple of pieces of toast.'

'You need to eat. You need fuel for this,' I say as I tap her gently on the head.

'I know but I was just so tired. Hey, what's that smell?' She pulls away from me slightly and wiggles her nose.

'Are you up for a fish and chip supper?'

'Am I ever!' she exclaims with glee as she claps her hands together.

'Good. Put the kettle on and make us both a nice cup of tea and I'll unwrap the fish and chips.'

She munches away as though in a reverie whilst rocking gently back and forth. As we enjoy our feast I tell her about my day. The post office, the scooter and lastly, the porno shoot. She laughs hysterically as I go over each gory detail.

I take her outside and show her my Vespa. She looks happy for once. It's nice to see a smile on her face. Back inside we attack the bread cakes stuffed with chips and drizzled in curry sauce. Eventually we are replete and there's nothing left but a couple of golden scraps.

'Oh dear, I think I've eaten too much,' she complains.

'Yeah, me too, and now I feel sleepy. I'm going to head up to bed. I'll need to set my alarm early to get these shots developed. When I get back from Ripon tomorrow we are going to the shops to get stocked up for the next fortnight. Monday we'll pay the bastard landlord his money, that will be one monkey off our backs. You've nothing to worry about anymore Sofe. This is just the start.' She reaches across the table and touches the back of my hand. She looks like she's going to burst into tears.

'Thanks,' she whispers, ever so softly.

'Sofe? Are you alright?' I ask, concerned at her demeanour. Her lips begin to tremble.

'I'm fine,' she sniffs. She stands then hurriedly runs to her bedroom and shuts the door behind her. I stand outside and listen to her muted sobs for a while. It breaks my heart and I don't know what to do. I slowly climb the stairs and collapse exhausted onto my bed.

My alarm rings at five. I stagger downstairs, make myself a strong black coffee, then begin work. By eight o'clock my prints are dry and I go through them one by one. There were over seventy shots and I've selected the best thirty-two to deliver to Garth. Twenty are good, ten very good and two—breathtaking. I place the last two at the bottom of the pile, then slide them carefully into a protective plastic sleeve, then into a large padded envelope. I collect the negatives and place them in a separate envelope. I open the darkroom door to leave, then stop. I can't

91

do it, I can't hand back the negatives. This is art—my art. Some of those photos could win prizes. There's nothing pornographic about them. I realise I can never show them to anyone… but, at least I can add them to my growing collection. I quickly cut up the negatives I didn't use and slip them into the envelope and remove the others. I don't think old Garth will even look at them and even if he does, it would be hard for him to tell if they match the prints.

8: MADNESS

I'm sitting at the table in Garth Peacock's kitchen. He's busy organising coffee for us both. There's a small wood burner in the corner of the room that occasionally, spits and crackles. Orange flames perform a hypnotic dance behind the glass door. There's no sign of the woman from the previous day and I don't ask about her.

Garth places the coffee on the table, then pulls a pipe and a round tin of tobacco from a drawer. He fills his pipe then lays it down carefully at the side of his coffee cup. While he's been doing this, I've been asking him about Jackson Pollock. He seems pleased that I've taken an interest and gives me a brief synopsis on his life, his painting techniques and of his death at the tender age of forty-four. He grabs a large book from a shelf and hands it to me.

'Here, take this. It's a biography about him. It also contains reproductions of his paintings. Return it next time you're in the area.'

'Thanks Garth.' I flick through the pages and gaze at the prints. I spot the one that Garth has hanging on his wall. 'Ah! This is the one you've got,' I say, pointing at the page then at the wall. Garth smiles.

'Yes, "The Uncertainty Of Ritual". Quite a masterpiece.' For some reason I am fascinated by it.

'What does it mean? What does it signify?' I inquire. Garth laughs.

'What does it mean to you?' I stand up and walk over to the painting on the wall and gaze at it intently.

'Initially, it's like an energy. All those vibrant colours. But there's chaos there as well. It's like the inside of my head some days. Millions of thoughts, some real, some abstract, almost dreamlike.' I walk to the other side of the room and stare at it again, squinting. 'Now when I look at it from here, I see something else. Those black, bluey lines, they remind me of death. They're like strands of barbed wire in no-mans land, or maybe dead flower stems or burnt trees. I think of the Battle Of The Somme and the First World War. Yet now, as I move closer, I see chaos again—elegant chaos.'

'I think Pollock would be proud of your interpretation. All art is a contract between artist and the viewer. The artist can try and signify what their intent is, but they have no control over what the viewer sees. You are free to see whatever you like.'

'How much did it cost you, if you don't mind me asking?'

'Six-hundred pounds, including the frame.'

'I don't suppose that's too bad, to say you own a Pollock,' I nod. Garth guffaws.

'Oh my dear boy! That is a lithograph, it's not an original. I may be a fairly wealthy man but not wealthy enough to own an original Pollock—I only wish I were. Right, to the photos. Did you bring the negatives?' I pull the envelope from my jacket and place it on the table. He picks it up, smiles at me, then wanders over to the wood burner. He opens the door and throws it in. The white paper smoulders, turns brown then erupts into flame, revealing its innards. I see the film spiral back on itself, angrily, like a cut snake. A few seconds pass and there's no evidence it ever existed. I'm thankful for my earlier decision. I think I would have broken down in tears if I'd had to witness my artwork being torched like that. He ambles back and takes his seat at the table. I sit down as Garth lights his pipe and takes a few lusty puffs on it. The aromatic smoke fills the air. He picks up the envelope that contain the prints and opens it. His hands are trembling as he slides the plastic cover out and removes the photos. He places them in a neat pile in front of him and studies the first one.

As he pours over them, he gives a running commentary on what he sees. Margaret's beauty, his own wild eyes, how he has the "beast" within him when he makes love to her. He's bewitched by the composition, the shades of light and dark, the pleasure and intensity on Margaret's face. He comes to the last two. The first photo is the one I shot when Margaret was staring intently at my erect penis, mere inches away. He falls silent for an age. He spins the photo every which way to inspect it. He places it back down on the table and scratches his cheek with the end of his pipe.

'How strange...' he trails off.

'What? You don't like it?'

'No, I absolutely love it my boy. But... her expression. At first, I thought it was one of pleasure, but there's something else going on. She's staring at something almost longingly. And here, her lips are slightly parted with the merest hint of a smile. Her look is enigmatic.' I know exactly what she's staring at and I have a bloody good idea what she's thinking as well, but I'm not going to tell Garth that. He picks up the last photo and becomes choked up.

'Oh yes, yes, yes.' The shot is the final climactic scene when the blaze of sunlight hits the top half of Margaret's face, casting a shadow across it. Her head is thrown back, her eyes are half-closed and a couple of pearly-white teeth are gently biting down on the corner of her bottom lip. A bead of sweat is caught on the side of her cheek. She glistens.

'James, you have caught the very essence of Margaret. Not just her likeness, but her love, her passion. She has love in her soul. Do you know what I mean by that, James?' I find his question condescending. How could a nineteen year old boy, working class, from the wrong side of the tracks, until recently a "dole" scrounger, possibly know what he means? Surely people like me only know about football, music, drinking and fornicating—that's what he's implying.

'Actually Garth, I know exactly what you mean. I also have love in my soul. I know you think I'm just a "whip" of a lad—but you'd be wrong. I feel love for people very strongly. My best mate, Marky, always says that I love too much. How is it possible to love too much? He sees love as a weakness, as a vulnerability. I see it as a strength.

Without love what is the point of anything? We may as well be zombies or robots. I love my friends, my mother, my flatmate—I would actually die for them! Sounds dramatic doesn't it? But I mean it. If a gun was pointed against my head and it was either me or them—I'd take the bullet every day of the week. So yes, I do know what you mean by "love in the soul". I live and breathe it every day.' At first he looks bewildered. His eyes flick back and forth across mine as though looking for some mockery or lie. He finds none.

'James, you are a revelation. I suppose you think me an old fuddy-duddy, but I am not. I once had a fire in my belly like you. It is an energy like no other—harness it. Do you have a girl to shower your love upon, like I do Margaret?'

'Yes… well, not yet, but soon.'

'Her name?'

'The Ice Queen.' He frowns and leans forward.

'Oh, I see. Unrequited love, eh?' I nod. 'Deep pain dipped in the thick sugary syrup of longing. It is a bittersweet concoction.' He's nailed it in one, that's exactly what it's like. 'Well James, if you love this girl, then there's only one thing for it—you must chase her! Women love the chase. Woo and court her. Tell her how you feel, tell her you love her, tell her you would walk barefoot over hot coals for eternity to spend just one second in her presence—worship her. Eventually, she will succumb to your charm and boyish looks. If she doesn't, then more fool her.'

He gathers the photos together and slides them back into the plastic cover. 'Some people would look at these and call it pornography. But pornography is crass and indulgent. It demeans the human spirit. But these,' he taps the photos, 'these are erotica capturing the human condition. Two people as one. Well done James. I'll be recommending you to my small circle of friends of a like-minded disposition.' I should be pleased, but I don't want to get a reputation as the camera guy who shoots homemade porn.

'Thanks Garth, but I don't really do this sort of thing. I'm more a family portrait guy, babies, weddings and the like.' He stands up and pulls his wallet out of his back pocket.

'Nonsense, boy. You have a rare talent, don't waste it on the minutiae of life. You have something about you that I can't quite put my finger on. Throw caution to the wind and ride the devil bareback through the gates of hell, whipping him hard on the arse as you do so.' Yep, he's definitely a crackpot, but he's all right.

I'm walking around the supermarket with Sofe doing our weekly shop. Normally our budget is twenty pounds, ten each—but not today. Sofe is brilliant at this. She has her little shopping list for all the essentials and a list of meals for the week. What usually happens is that I put things in the trolley, she removes them, puts them back on the shelf, then chastises me.

"Not that brand, it's too expensive. Look! This is on special—half price. No, we can't afford that, it's a luxury. Don't even think about putting that packet of biscuits in there, it's empty calories. Ooh, look, tinned tomatoes ten pence a tin, we'll stock up." If I were allowed to do the shopping myself I would probably blow twenty quid on a six-pack of beer, a monster pack of potato chips, chocolate bars, expensive coffee and fillet steak. Talking of which, time for a treat.

'Sofe, tonight we are going to eat like kings... erm... and queens. How about a big juicy fillet steak, onion rings and fried chips.' She looks at me, disappointed.

'Jimmy I know you've had a bit of a windfall and you want a treat but you should be saving that money for a rainy day. You're not going to get that sort of cash for every job. You never know when you may need it.'

'You're right Sofe, it may be a long time before I make five big ones in less than twenty-four hours again, but I've got that wedding booked for next week, plus another thirteen enquiries to follow up on. I'm also handing out my business cards next week. I'm now earning. Come on, we've both done it bloody tough for a long time, let me spoil you for once, you deserve it for putting up with me.'

'Hmm, well that's true,' she says with a cheeky smile. 'Okay, a one-off then save your money.'

We wander through the meat section and I spot the fillet steak. I make a bee-line for it but Sofe gets there first.

'Oh no Jimmy! That's ridiculous. Five pounds for two tiny pieces of steak, that's a quarter of our budget.'

'We don't have a budget today, how many times do I have to remind you?'

'It's the principle of the matter.' She walks on and stops at the chickens. 'What about a chicken, Jimmy. It's only four pounds and we can get four meals out of it. I can do a roast for tonight with some carrots and potatoes; tomorrow we can have it cold in sandwiches. We can have the legs and wings as snacks, then I can pick the carcass, boil up the bones, throw a tin of sweet corn in and we have chicken soup another night.' There's no point arguing, she is the queen of thrift.

'Okay. Chicken it is. But I'm going to buy you six bottles of fizzy wine as a treat, seeing as you won't let me buy the steak. Hey Sofe, I've just been thinking. The money I got for a day's work is more than I would get in four and a half months on the dole—crazy isn't it?' She looks at me with sad eyes.

'I know. It's wrong, but what can we do.'

I'm sipping on a pint in the Soldiers Arms talking with Marky. The Hipnotikz are on stage playing their improvised set. This is not their usual performance they play at their proper gigs. It's a mixture of cover versions, slowed down acoustic ballads of their own songs and a general clowning around and telling of jokes. The audience is a mixed bag and everyone loves their off-the-cuff cabaret act. They've been doing this Sunday lunchtime gig for well over a year. They only get thirty quid between the three of them but they get free beer and they have a good laugh.

'It's on Jimmy, in two days time,' says Marky.

'What's on?'

'The miners go on strike on Tuesday morning. This is the start of it. You'll remember this day Jim, for the rest of your life.'

'I doubt it. Your shout.'

'Show some fucking enthusiasm Jimmy. This is a working class struggle and the last time I looked you were working class. You need to be proactive.'

'Why can't everyone just get on with each other,' I sigh. 'All this argy-bargy and hatred of one another just because they've got different backgrounds.' Marky shakes his head.

'Oh James, what am I going to do with you? You're so naïve. You always see the good in people. All the miners want are their jobs, is that too much to ask for, to provide a living for their families? The government doesn't plan to close down just twenty pits—it's got a hit list of over seventy, that's a loss of eighty-thousand jobs—jobs that will never return. Do you understand what will happen to those communities, Jimmy? They will perish and die, they'll become fucking ghost towns.' I'm not in the mood for one of Marky's militant tirades today. It's been a long week and I just want to chill out on a Sunday afternoon, have a few beers and listen to my mates on stage.

'Listen Marky, I do support the miners. I don't want anyone to end up on the unemployment line, fuck me, I should know better than anyone what it's like to be on the dole. It's bloody degrading, depressing, it saps your confidence and makes you fearful. There's always the gnaw of hunger in the pit of your stomach. Sometimes me and Sofe have sat in that cold damp house for five days straight with one loaf of bread and five cans of baked beans to share between us. When that starts to run out, I go back to my mam's to get a decent meal, so that Sofe can eat.'

'Jimmy, your problem is you see no correlation between government policies and the rise in unemployment. This is a concerted effort by the government to undermine the working class. They actually want high unemployment, that way it drives wages down. People will start working for less and less. They don't want to close a few unprofitable pits, they want to close them all, they want a fight with the miners and they want to win. If they beat the biggest union in the land, then there's no union that will ever take them on again. They will be toothless tigers. This is a battle of ideologies.

This country is one of the richest in the world, yet we have mass unemployment, record homelessness, millions living on the bread line and crumbling hospitals. A government is supposed to be there to govern for the people, the majority. Not this lot! They think they were born to fucking rule and they govern for the elite, the one, two per-cent. The rich, the powerful, big business, the stock market, the banks. They're all in it together. If they really cared, they'd start a nationwide building program and demolish the slums and put up thousands of new homes. They'd build new hospitals and roads. It would create millions of jobs. The government would make most of its money back from taxes and people would spend more. Ha! Did you hear what I just said, "make its money back", as though the money belonged to the government in the first place. It doesn't; it belongs to the people and is supposed to be managed by the government.' He finishes up his pint, picks up my glass and heads to the bar. Thankfully, the Hipnotikz have stopped for a break and make their way over to me.

'Okay Jimmy, show us your scooter then. Is it outside?' quizzes Macca. I immediately brighten.

'Yeah, come on she's a beauty.' Macca and Jonesy follow me outside as Gerry heads to the bar.

'Oh wow! She's the bee's knees, Jimmy boy,' smiles Jonesy. 'What's she like to ride?'

'Like riding on glass,' I reply with a grin.

'Give me the keys, I'll take it for a spin,' says Macca.

'No you fucking won't!' I reply horrified at the thought.

'Why not?' he asks, looking offended.

'Because for one thing, I'm not insured and for another, I know how you flog your scooter. This little beauty needs love and tenderness.' Macca backs down as both lads circle the Vespa, gently caressing it.

'Well, you've got the best scooter out of all of us now,' confirms Jonesy. Macca looks at me.

'How's Karl Marx today?' he enquires.

'Don't ask. He's just gone off on a rant about the miners. I'm trying to relax and all I get is the Communist Party manifesto barked at me.'

'Great, best get our pints knocked back quickly and get back on stage. I'm not up for his shit today.' We go back inside and sit down with Gerry. Marky is in the far corner of the pub feeding coins into a slot machine.

'Gerry, how long ago was it that you got married?' I ask. Gerry takes a gulp of lager and thinks for a few seconds.

'Two years ago this April. Why?'

'You sad bastard,' snorts Macca. 'Married at nineteen.' Gerry looks pissed off.

'Fuck you Macca! Me and Sarah have never been happier. Best thing I ever did.'

'Yeah, but why didn't you just live together. I mean, marriage is so… final, isn't it?' replies Macca who seems perplexed.

'Final until the divorce,' laughs Jonesy.

'There's no way me and Sarah will ever divorce. I know marriage isn't right for everyone, but we wanted to show a lifetime commitment to each other.'

'So what are you going to do when we hit the big time and you have groupies falling over themselves to shag your arse off?' Jonesy continues.

'I'll remain faithful of course, as per my wedding vows.'

'Do you remember how much your wedding photos cost?' I ask, trying to get the conversation back on track. Gerry stares down at the table with a puzzled look and rubs his hand over his short hair.

'We got the basic package as money was really tight, but I'm guessing it was about two hundred quid. I'll ask Sarah when I get home, she organised it all and she has a memory like an elephant.'

'How many photos did you get for that?' I continue my interrogation.

'Oh, I don't know, about twenty or thirty, delivered in an album. But the guy made money out of everyone else as well. My mam wanted a full set. My gran wanted a really big photo of everyone standing outside the church. Then, there were other relatives who got some prints. Why? You got a wedding gig coming up?'

'Yeah, next Saturday. I'm going to see the happy couple tomorrow night and I need to get some figures together.'

'Well done Jimmy, I'm really proud of you.'

'Cheers Gerry. I think things are beginning to take off for me.'

'Yeah, well done mate,' says Macca slapping me on the back.

'Jonesy, if I give you a list of prices and packages do you think you could knock up a flyer for me?'

'Yeah, of course Jim.'

'Has anyone got any paper?' Gerry pulls a crumpled up set-list out of his back pocket and hands it to me.

'Here, use this.' I pull a pen from my jacket and begin scribbling away on the blank side. Marky returns to the table and thankfully the conversation turns to football for a few minutes. I quickly finish my improvised flyer and hand it to Jonesy.

'Just tart it up and get my logo and details on the top. If you can get me a handful of copies that would be great.' Jonesy studies it for a few seconds before slipping it into his pocket. 'I'll refine it over the week and when I'm happy I'll get a few hundred printed off.'

'No problem Jim. When do you want it by?'

'I'll pick it up from your joint, about sixish tomorrow night.' He nods.

'Say Jimmy, how'd you go with that photoshoot you did yesterday?' asks Gerry. I beam at them all and take a quick slug of beer.

'Hold on to your seats boys, because you are going to laugh your tits off at this—turns out it was a porno shoot!'

9: SOUL LOVE

It's been a whirlwind two weeks. I haven't had a break and I'm working sixteen-hour days. I am dead on my feet. I did the wedding and made four hundred quid from it and got a free nosh-up. I introduced myself to every promoter and nightclub owner in the city picking up more work. I've done six baby photo sessions and four non-pornographic family portraits. I've been to six gigs and provided reviews with accompanying photos for the Standard. I've stuck my business cards up all over town and already done four shoots with local bands. I have another three weddings booked for next month, more family portraits and a couple of businesses that want photos of their employees and premises for brochures.

Every night before I collapse exhausted into bed, I stare at the photograph of Victoria. I made a larger print and bought a nice frame for it. It hangs on my bedroom wall. I tell her about my day and she listens in silence. I then say how much I love her as I stroke her cheek. I promise her I am coming for her, and not to forget me, and very shortly we will be together. Secretly though, I fear it may already be too late. Who knows where she might be? I've been meaning to visit the Granary every night since I met her but there has not been one second free. I curse myself for not finding the time. There's a growing, sickening feeling in the pit of my stomach. I imagine her in the arms of some other man, someone who is not worthy of her and it nearly makes me vomit. I kiss her slowly on the lips and whisper,

'Hold on Victoria, just hold on a little longer, and I'll be there.'

I have spent all day with Marky, as John Arnold is off sick. I accompanied him on his rounds, snapping photos of the Lord Mayor, a councillor who has been charged with fraud, a comedian who is playing the theatre at the weekend and finally, a woman who found five-hundred quid in a purse and handed it in to the police—the Standard is a regional newspaper after all.

It's Thursday night, exactly a fortnight since I first met Victoria and I am sitting having a well-earned pint in the Soldiers Arms with Marky and the rest of the crew from the Standard.

'You look tired comrade,' states Marky.

'I am Marky. I'm dead on my feet.'

'You need to slow down Jimmy, or you'll burn yourself out.'

'I know, but I can't turn down work. Every time I need to develop photos I have to travel to the other side of the city, back to the flat. I could do with somewhere closer to the centre.'

'Just use the Standard's darkroom.'

'Nah, Dave Dee warned me about that. I don't want to blot my copybook. I tell you what Marky, I could never have done this without the scooter, it has been a Godsend.'

'I told you so. A set of wheels is freedom. Have you got a lot on tomorrow?'

'No, thank Christ. Just some shots to develop for a local band. I'm going to have a sleep in, enjoy a leisurely breakfast, then go for a ride in the countryside, chill out for a while and recharge the batteries.'

'So, you still in love with this mystery girl?' he laughs.

'Of course. I can't stop thinking about her. I've got her photo on my bedroom wall and talk to her every night. Do you think that's weird?'

'Yep, it's fucking creepy. And how is the celibacy going?'

'Only a couple of lapses,' I smile at him.

'Anyone else involved or was it Sister Palmer and her five lovely daughters?'

'Sister Palmer,' I nod. I look at my watch, it's nearly 10 pm. 'Right, I'm going to make tracks after this pint. I'm going to call in at the Granary, see if she's there.'

'Who? Sister Palmer?'

'Very funny. Victoria, you dickhead. If she's not there, then it's home to bed and blissful sleep.' I finish the dregs of my pint and stand up.

'Remember Jim, slow down a bit, pace yourself.'

'I can slow down when I'm dead. I've wasted enough of my life already. Okay Marky, love you mate. Catch you later.'

'Yep, see you soon comrade.'

##

I park my scooter outside the Granary. Mal eyes me suspiciously as I still have my helmet on and he doesn't recognise me. I remove it and he beams.

'Jimmy! You have wheels! Great to see you,' he shouts, as he pats me on the back.

'Likewise Mal. Many in tonight?' I ask, nodding at the entrance.

'Nah, about sixty at the moment. It will start to fill up once the pubs close. So where have you been? I haven't seen you for a couple of weeks.' I spend the next ten minutes chatting with Mal, telling him about my escapades and how much work I'm getting.

'When you go inside, have a word with Iris. She's looking to update the promotional side, she may have some work for you.'

'Cheers Mal. Hey, keep an eye on the scooter, will you? I don't want anyone messing with it.'

'Jimmy, if anyone so much as looks at it, I'll batter them,' he snarls and holds his fist up which is the size of a ham. I walk inside and spot Iris in her kiosk, counting money.

'Hi Iris, can I leave my helmet with you?' She looks at me, annoyed.

' No you can't! Leave it in the cloakroom, that's what it's there for.'

'Aw come on, I'm only going to be a few minutes.' She relents.

'Oh very well. You are a nuisance. Come around to the door, I want to speak with you.' I enter the tiny office and sit down.

'I want some new photos of the Granary.'

'Okay, can you be more specific?'

'I want shots of the bars, the dance floor, the stage, the staff, and the outside—everything. We are going to be doing a bit of advertising over the summer. What is your price for this?'

'For you Iris, fifty quid,' I smile at her.

'Don't be silly. You are no businessman. One hundred,' she scolds.

'Forty,' I reply.

'One hundred and twenty,' she fires back.

'Thirty, but that's my final offer.'

'Okay, one hundred and fifty and it's a deal.' I laugh and we shake hands on it. 'I will give you a call when I'm ready,' she says, with a smile.

I'm bursting for a leak and make my way to the toilets. As I'm standing at the urinals I sense someone come and stand next to me, a little too closely. I look to my left, it's Mal. What a surprise. I catch him having a cheeky peek at my penis.

'So Jimmy, you still playing hide the sausage with the opposition?'

'Yes Mal,' I reply wearily. 'I haven't suddenly turned into a homosexual in the last two weeks. I still fancy girls.'

'How do you know, if you've never tried it?' he persists.

'I think I might know by now, if I prefer pussy or cock, don't you?'

'You don't know what you're missing out on Jimmy.' I zip myself up and turn just as Mal begins to put his dick back in his pants.

'Jesus Christ, Mal! Put that thing away! You could have someone's fucking eye out with that!' He's got a weapon of ridiculous proportions. I move to the basin and rinse my hands as does Mal. He smiles at me through the mirror.

'Well, you know where I am when you finally come to your senses.'

'That's never going to happen, pal. I know what the male body looks like. I stare at my own in bewilderment every morning. Men's bodies are bloody ugly. Compare them to a woman's. They are perfect, a work of art. I'm not sure who God used to design the female form, but he used a different designer for the male body. Right Mal, fuck off and get back outside. You're supposed to be guarding my scooter.' He laughs as we leave the toilet together, squeezing my shoulder.

'One day, Jimmy, one day,' he chuckles in his gruff Geordie accent.

I make my way to the upstairs bar. I greet Nelson and order a beer. He goes through his usual custom of giving me the first one for free. I should just walk around the corner and see if she's here—but I can't. I'm nervous and edgy, partly through tiredness. The thought of her not being here tonight is adding to my stress. I'd prefer to just hear it from the mouth of Nelson.

'Say Nelson, is the Ice Queen in tonight?' I wait for the crushing blow, braced for disappointment. He rolls his eyes to the roof and nods. YES! My heart suddenly jumps out of my chest and begins turning cartwheels across the floor. I have a sudden surge of adrenalin that sweeps away my weariness.

'You're wasting your time, Jimmy,' Nelson advises. I ignore him as I try to recollect what I am going to say. I have practiced my speech a hundred times, but right now, at this critical juncture, I can't remember a single word of it. I stare back at Nelson.

'Wasting my time, eh? Give me a rum and black.'

'I'll bet you five pounds that you will walk out of this room alone tonight,' he smiles at me.

'Okay, I'll take your bet.' I reach into my pocket, pull out a fiver and slap it on the bar. Nelson pulls a fiver from his wallet, picks up mine and places them both carefully on top of the till. I pay for the drink, down my beer in one go and order another.

'You'll need more than Dutch courage to tackle her,' chuckles Nelson.

'We'll see.' I take a couple of deep breaths. It's at times like these I could willingly become a smoker. 'Wish me luck Nelson,' I say. He grins back at me whilst shaking his head.

'Luck? There is not enough luck in the whole world for you to win this bet.'

I collect the drinks and walk around the corner. She's there, sitting in the exact same spot as she was two weeks ago. She's even got exactly the same clothes on. The hat, glasses, black dress and those Victorian-era tie-up boots, which I find inordinately sexy. I stare at her for a few seconds in disbelief. I want to remember this moment for the rest of my life. I can't tell if she's looking back at me or just staring past me. I still cannot remember my rehearsed lines and realise I'm going to have to wing it. I'll speak from the heart, that's all I can do. But first, an irreverent opening sentence—don't want to come over as too desperate—even though I am.

'Fuck me! Don't tell me you've been sitting here for a fortnight. Have you taken root?'

'Oh it's you again. How dreary.' At least she replies this time. Not the response I had envisaged in my dreams, but at least it's a start. I walk over and hand her the drink. She takes it straight away. Progress. I sit down beside her—on her right. 'Please get your drivel out of the way, then leave me alone, there's a good chap,' she spits, pithily. Not the most encouraging of starts, but I'm not cowed.

'I will. I don't intend staying long. I'll say what I have to say then I'll be on my way. For the last two weeks I've been working flat out, I've got to admit, I'm exhausted. Even though I had to be focussed on my work, every spare second my thoughts returned to you. That picture I took, well, it now hangs on my wall. I speak to you every night before I go to sleep. I tell you about my day and the plans I have for us. I know, weird, right? Creepy? You're probably looking for the panic button, right now.

I had a lovely little speech written down. I've spent hours on it honing every word. It's back at my flat underneath my pillow. I can't remember a single word of it now. I guess I'll just have to mumble how I feel.' I take a swig of beer and shoot Nelson a glance. He's polishing a glass and is sporting a smug look. 'I can't explain what I'm about to say, it sounds like bullshit, like I'm delusional. The thing is, I feel like we've been together before, in a different time, a different age. It's like our souls have been wandering around searching for each other, yearning for each other—lost souls. And now they've finally met again. I told you it would sound mad.

I've been warned off by my best mate to not to get involved—it will only end in tears, you will break my heart, he says. I don't care. I'll take that chance. You are all I think of. I wake hot and sweaty every night, my pulse races, every sinew tingles at the thought of you. My heart feels like it could implode. I feel happy, then sad then... bereft. I've missed you.

You said that we come from different backgrounds, well, that's true, we do. But who's to say it can't work? Who makes these fucking rules anyway? Love doesn't care about backgrounds, about class, about colour. It doesn't even care about looks. It doesn't say hello and I suppose it doesn't say goodbye. Sorry, I'm waffling.' I'm starting to choke up. I take another slug of beer and clear my throat. 'Anyway, I have one last thing to say before I leave, then I won't bother you again. Victoria—I love you and I need you. I'll always love you... no matter what happens or doesn't happen. That's it, that's all I have to say.'

There's no response. No put-downs, no snippy sarcasm—nothing. I wait for what seems like an eternity, but all I hear is heavy silence. I've just ripped my pulsating heart out and handed it to her on a silver platter and it has meant nought. I look at Nelson again. He no longer looks smug. He appears sad and shakes his head then lets out a deep sigh.

I suddenly feel exhausted again. A malevolent God has stuck a pin into my balloon. I know what the ensuing weeks, months, years, now hold—regret, misery, aching emptiness. I recall Garth's and Julia's words. Keep wooing, keep chasing. I can't, it's too painful. I shuffle uncomfortably.

'Okay, well that's that then. You have my heart, do with it what you will.' I place my left palm on the floor, ready to push myself to my feet. Her hand darts out and she clamps it firmly on the top of mine. Wow! I get that zap of electricity again. She pulls her legs into her chest and lifts herself upright, without aid. She's tall, nearly my height. Looking up, she towers above me, like a Greek Goddess. Her form is perfect. She exudes grace and power. Oh, and those eyes. I could dive into them, they transfix me.

She peels her hat off, then her sunglasses. She places them on the bar without once taking her eyes away from mine. She shakes her head and her ponytail whips out like a pendulum in perpetual motion. She extends her hand. I grip it and pull myself to my feet. I am mere inches away from her lips.

A tear wells in the corner of her eye. It breaches the dam and trickles slowly down her cheek. I reach out and tenderly smudge it away with the pad of my thumb.

'No, please don't cry,' I whisper softly. She places one hand behind my head and pulls me towards her. Our lips touch. Her eyes now explode into a waterfall. She weeps, silently. We kiss. Her tears congregate as salty pools on the top of our lips. I pull back slightly and open my mouth. They pour in. I taste her for the first time. Her DNA now mixes with mine. I don't care now how it ends. I will remember and cherish this moment until my dying breath. She sniffs and takes a step back. She reapplies her hat and glasses then grips me firmly by the hand and leads me towards the door. She has not uttered one single word in all this time.

Nelson stares at me with mouth agape, his eyes nearly popping out of their sockets. As I pass the bar he hands me the two five pound notes and shakes his head in amazement. She leads me down the steps and across the dance floor. One of my favourite songs is blasting out of the speakers, The Flying Pickets version of "Only You", an a cappella masterpiece. I feel like I'm floating on air, as though I'm ten feet tall. I'm full of pride as people stare at us. She leads me out through the doors and into the cold night, never once relinquishing her powerful grip. Mal looks dumbfounded, and as we step out onto the road he calls out after me.

'Hey Jimmy, what about your scooter?'

'Can you stick it inside once you close? I'll pick it up tomorrow. Cheers Mal!,' I shout back.

'It's not a fucking valet service!'

##

We walk down the cobbled streets in silence for a while.

'Should we order a taxi?' I suggest.

'No. I only live around the corner. Five minutes' walk.' Her voice has changed. She still sounds refined, posh, but gone is the caustic upper class twang.

'Your voice, it's different.'

'Yes. This is how I speak.'

'So what was with the upper class accent back there? Was it all an act?'

'Not an act. Part of the mask.' We turn a corner, head down a tree-lined street and pass a small park along the way.

'Why did you cry? I didn't mean to upset you.' She stops and looks at me.

'Because you said you loved me and needed me.'

'I don't understand?'

'No one's ever needed me before—ever. The last time anyone said they loved me was ten years ago. It was my grandmother. She died not long after. Breast cancer.'

'I'm sorry. Do you still miss her?'

'Of course. Although, she's still with me… sometimes.'

'Surely it can't be ten years since someone said they loved you? What about your mam and dad?'

'Mummy loves me. I know she does but she's not emotional and can be very self-absorbed.'

'Well what about your dad? Dads always love their little girls.'

'Ha! Not my father. He considers himself part of the elite. He's a raging snob and is derelict of any emotion—stiff upper lip and all that nonsense.'

'Okay, well what about brothers, sisters, what about your friends, surely your mates tell you that they love you?'

'Do *you* tell your friends that you love them?' She seems a bit incredulous at this last question.

'Of course I do, all the time,' I reply.

'Hmm, well you're different. I don't have any siblings and I only have one friend, who I'm lucky to see twice a year if that. And no, we don't tell each other that we love one another.' We walk on in silence until she stops outside a large Edwardian townhouse in the financial district, not too far from Tossers. She fumbles for a key, unlocks the door and we go inside. There's an old fashioned gated lift in front of us. To the right, a wide spiralling staircase. On the left there's a number of pigeon holes for mail.

'How many flats are there?'

'Just four. I'm on the top floor.' She slides the grille door of the lift shut and hits a button. The lift clanks into action and we rise steadily into the heart of the building.

'They don't make lifts like this anymore, do they? Just a few bars to keep us in.' She doesn't reply. This is hard work. I'm wondering if she's having second thoughts. We get out of the lift and she leads me to a door. She turns the key and we walk into a small vestibule. She stops, hangs her hat on a coat peg, then opens another door and we walk through. Immediately opposite is a large double bed with two small bedside cabinets nestled either side. At the end of the bed there's a large, floor to ceiling window. I assume it offers a view out over the city. In front

113

of the window a small round table with two chairs. On the far wall is a wooden dresser with a small portable TV positioned on top of it. Alongside this is another set of drawers, then a wardrobe and on the remaining wall is a large bookcase that is packed with hundreds of books all neatly arranged. She begins to remove her earrings.

'This is classy, do you mind if I have a look around?'

'Be my guest,' she replies. A soft sheepskin rug is at the edge of her bed laying above polished floorboards. I walk towards a doorway at the edge of the window. I go down two small steps and into a modern and functional kitchen. Another floor to ceiling window is at one end. At the other is an alcove with a small dining table with four chairs tucked neatly under it. Behind this, is an old leather sofa which looks well worn but comfortable. I go through another door which leads into a bathroom. There's no window, but a wall of frosted glass bricks, instead. There's a large open shower, a toilet, something that looks like a foot bath, a double hand basin and a floor to ceiling glass mirror.

'Swish, very swish,' I whisper to myself. I walk back to the bedroom. 'Is this your place or do you rent?'

'It belongs to my parents but I spend most of my time here.' We stare at each other for a while. The magic and emotion of earlier appears to have dissipated. 'Did you mean what you said earlier, about being in love with me or was it just a ploy to get into my knickers?' I reach out and gently stroke her cheek.

'I know you must think that I bandy the word, "love" around willy-nilly, but I don't. I only say it to those I truly love. Yes, I did mean it. I love you.'

'How can you love someone you don't know?'

'I'm not sure and I don't claim to understand it. I just knew, the first time I laid eyes on you. I thought yeah, this is it.'

'Have you been in love with girls before?'

'No. I've been out with plenty of girls and I've really liked them all and become good friends with some of them, but this feeling I have now, I have never experienced it before.'

'If you've never experienced it before then how do you know it's love?'

'Because my hearts on fire. I am overcome with happiness. My fingers and toes are tingling. I have butterflies in my stomach and now, I can't imagine life without you. What else could it be? It must be love.' She nearly smiles.

'Could you unzip me, please?' She turns to face the bed as I walk up behind her and slowly pull the zipper down on her dress. I see the small of her back and the top of her knickers. She slides the dress off both shoulders and it slips silently to the floor. 'Now my bra.' I carefully undo three clasps and she removes it and throws it onto a chair in the corner. 'Would you undo the laces on my boots please?' I take a step closer and kiss her on the nape of the neck.

'Leave them on,' I reply. I look over her shoulder into the mirror and see a faint smile staring back at me. She puts her thumbs into her black lacy knickers and wriggles out of them. They fall to the ground and she kicks them off. I step back as she slowly turns around.

She is a statue of pure beauty. The jet black hair, the piercing blue eyes. I drop my gaze onto her chest and her full pert bosom with slightly upturned nipples. I trace her body down over her navel and marvel at her completely hairless vagina. This continental craze seems to be sweeping the country.

She has taut powerful thighs and honed calves. I take my camera from around my neck and place it on the sideboard, before kicking my shoes off, peeling my socks away and ripping my top off. I undo the buckle on my belt, unzip and let my jeans fall to the floor. I move towards her. She reaches out and pulls my underpants down. I step out of them. She explores my face before carefully surveying my body. When her eyes reach my penis, she arches one eyebrow, which slightly unnerves me. The flag is already half-way up the flagpole and steadily rising. We kiss, softly, tenderly. A wave of ecstasy floods my body and my chest heaves and falls. She drops to her knees and I caress her soft locks. I think of the darkroom, of her picture staring at me and how I fantasised that it was her, not Julia that day—and now it's a reality. I'm the luckiest man on the planet. She comes back up, plants a hand on my chest and pushes me. I fall back onto the bed and lay there spread-eagled.

We make ardent love for thirty minutes. Each time I feel an imminent release, she stops and kisses me passionately on the lips, on the neck, on the chest, before she begins again. Finally, she changes position and I feel an unstoppable surge. This time she doesn't stop but intensifies her actions. I look up and all I can see are her buttocks rocking back and forth on top of me as though riding a horse. That's all it takes. I let out a groan and push hard into her, grabbing her cheeks as I do. I gasp, twitch, then lay there satiated but exhausted. She climbs off me and removes her boots before disappearing. I hear the sound of water from the bathroom then the flush of the toilet. A few minutes later, she's back, snuggling into my chest. We lay silent for a few minutes before she sits up.

'Right, come on, now it's my turn.' There's no more coldness from her and she offers me a warm, heavy smile. She rolls onto her front, face down into the pillow, spreads her legs and thrusts her hands between her thighs. 'Spank me,' she orders. I'm a bit taken aback, to say the least.

'Kinky, eh?' I say. She looks up at me with a mischievous grin.

'A little,' she replies. I stand up and position myself adjacent to her buttocks. I give her a playful slap on her left cheek.

'I said spank, not slap.' She sounds a tad annoyed. The second time I hit her a lot harder on her right cheek.

'Harder, a lot harder,' she shouts at me. I lift my right hand high and bring it down as hard as I can. She lets out a low groan. Immediately, there is an impression of my hand tattooed across both cheeks and my palm is stinging. After a few minutes, her bottom is flushed red. Every time I bring my palm down onto her she lets out a satisfied moan. With every slap her buttocks begin to change colour, from pink, to red, to angry crimson. I'm distinctly uneasy with it all. The whole thing is too violent. It goes against everything I believe in. I don't want to hurt her—I want to love her. Why does she need to feel pain to experience pleasure?

After a good ten minutes of spanking she thankfully reaches climax and lays quietly panting into her pillow. I feel terrible. Her buttocks look bruised. Tiny lines of broken blood vessels leave crazy streaks against her flesh. I place my hand ever so gently onto her flesh. She flinches slightly. What goes on in her head? Why is this the only way she can get off? I sit on the side of the bed next to her. A cauldron of emotions bubble away inside me. Finally, two of them reach the surface—remorse and shame. I try hard to stop the tears but it's futile. They flow down my cheeks and drip onto the crisp white linen. I sniff. She opens her eyes and looks at me.

'Oh, no! No, no, no!' she exclaims as she bolts upright. She grabs hold of me and pulls me into her soft bosom. 'No, no, I knew this would happen.' She rocks back and forth with me like she's holding a newborn baby.

'I'm sorry, it's selfish of me, but I can't hurt you… I can't cause you pain,' I sob.

'Shush, shush, it's all right. You're not hurting me, you're giving me pleasure.' I feel like a failure.

'How? Why?'

'I don't know why. It's as though… I don't deserve pleasure unless I'm punished for it.' She lets out a long sigh.

We make love another four times during the night, each time, instigated by her. There's no more spanking, only deep sensual love-making. I do not understand her. She is complex and appears bitter with the world for no apparent reason. The only thing I'm sure of, right now, is that I'm in love with her. Eventually, we are exhausted and a deep sleep overcomes us.

10: HAPPINESS

The comforting clink of milk bottles wake me from my slumber. I listen to the tuneful whistle of the milkman as he makes his way down the street. The soft hum of his electric milk cart pulls aways and drives to pastures new. The curtains are partly open but there is no daylight yet. I am on my back and Victoria is snuggled into my side. I adjust my position, gently place her head onto the pillow and slip out of bed. I pull back the curtains and stare down at the twinkling orange lights. They float like aliens in the dark sky, illuminating the lanes and alleyways far below. I glance at the clock on the wall—6:05 am. In the kitchen, I put the kettle on then return to the bedroom. I sit on the side of the bed and stroke her head. There's an aching in my stomach from lack of food. I whisper softly,

'Hey sleepyhead, feeling hungry?' She murmurs and yawns as she rolls onto her back and drowsily opens her eyes. She smiles, a soft, sweet smile and my heart skips a beat.

'What time is it?' she asks.

'Just gone six.'

'I am feeling rather peckish. I have bread and croissants in the kitchen.'

'That's no good. I'm ravenous. Let's go for a proper breakfast.' She lets out a little laugh and stretches.

'There's nothing open at this time of day.'

'That's what you think. I know of a great greasy spoon café near the train station, it opens at five.' She rolls onto her side and supports herself on one elbow.

'Greasy spoon café? Doesn't sound particularly enticing.' Now I laugh.

'Have you ever eaten from a greasy spoon café?' She shakes her head.

'Well, you're in for one of life's little treats then; fried bacon, fried eggs, sausage, fried mushroom, fried tomatoes and fried bread all washed down with hot sweet tea.'

'Is the tea fried as well? It sounds perfectly...' I cut her off.

'Perfectly ghastly!' I say in a posh accent. She flings her arm out and playfully smacks me on the thigh.

'I was going to say it sounds perfectly yummy, actually.'

We make love in the shower and I gently stroke her bruised bottom. I feel bad and tell her so. She tells me not to be silly. We dry each other slowly with warm fluffy towels, exploring each other's bodies as we do so. We laugh and giggle. She brushes her teeth and finds me a fresh toothbrush. She leaves the bathroom to get dressed as I rinse my mouth out with water. I place the toothbrush into a glass next to hers. I stare at them for a moment.

Standing in front of me, she's wearing tight black leggings and a red fluffy jumper. Little ankle boots cover her feet and her hair is pulled back into a tight ponytail. She looks radiant. I kiss her again.

We exit the apartment into the bitterly cold morning air. The streets are deserted as we walk briskly, arm in arm, huddled against the cold, towards the city centre.

The café is already busy with workmen, postmen and a couple of down and outs. I order the full works for both of us and we find a table for two, tucked away in a corner. We attack our food with gusto and Victoria is genuinely amazed at how good it is.

'I'd never have come to a place like this in a million years if it wasn't for you.'

'There's a lot of things you're going to be doing now, that you haven't done before... now you're with me.' She grins.

'I like that.'

'What?'

'Those words; now you're with me. They make me feel safe and warm and... loved.' I shovel more baked beans into my mouth, then pick up a teaspoon and scoop sugar out of the sugar bowl into my mug of tea. I stir then take a couple of satisfying gulps. I feel her eyes boring into me.

'What?' I ask.

'Three sugars! That's ridiculous.'

'Cheap energy,' I reply. She giggles. 'So, first things first. I'm going to have to find a new name for you.' A worried expression crosses her face.

'Why? Don't you like the name, Victoria?'

'I absolutely love Victoria, but, it has too many syllables. Vic-tor-ri-a. That's no good. A name should only have a maximum of two syllables. All I can come up with is Vic or Vicky? What're your thoughts on it?' She bites gingerly into a piece of fried bread dipped in baked bean sauce.

'Hmm... this is scrumptious. Well, Vic makes me sound like a man so you can rule that one out and Vicky...' she curls her nose up, 'that sounds like an unmarried teenage mother from one of those dreadful working class soap operas.' I pause for a moment.

'Okay, how about... Vee? Vee for victory. Short and sweet.' She smiles.

'Yes, I like that. My grandmother used to call me Vee when I was a little girl.' She looks sad.

'Okay, so tell me all about yourself.' She seems a trifled uncomfortable for some reason.

'What do you want to know?'

'Everything. How old are you?'

'Twenty-two. Twenty-three in November. You?'

'Nineteen. Twenty in December. I'm into older women at the moment.'

'Oh dear, I'm a cradle snatcher,' she laughs.

'Does it bother you?'

'No, of course not.'

'What's your last name?' She uses her fork to scoop a helping of beans into her mouth.

'It's Victoria Ha... well,' she coughs and splutters halfway through and points to her throat.

'What's wrong? Did a baked bean go down the wrong hole?' She nods as I pass her a cup of tea. She drinks, swallows and coughs again. 'Nothing worse than a baked bean in the wrong hole. So, Victoria Harrywell, was it?' She nods again and clears her throat.

'Oh, sorry about that yes, Harrywell.'

'And your parents, what do they do?'

'Mummy is quite a famous painter.'

'Oh really! What sort of paintings?'

'Abstract expressionism. When I say famous I mean quite well known over here in the UK art circles. She's not like Jackson Pollock or Andy Warhol.'

'Jackson Pollock, interesting, I'm reading a biography about him.' She raises an eyebrow as though impressed.

'If you like Pollock then you'll probably love mummy's work.'

'And your Dad? What does he do?'

'Oh, he's in politics,' she replies in an offhand manner.

'In what way?'

'He's something in the government.'

'Sounds a little vague. Do you mean a civil servant?'

'Yes, I suppose you could call it that. And what about you? Tell me about your family.'

'Not much to tell really. My dad died a few years ago. My mum's still going but she isn't very well. I have an aunty that I'm close to. No siblings. But I have got my mates.' She looks sad.

'I'm sorry to hear about your father,' she offers. 'Are you close to your mother?'

'Yeah, dead close. She means the world to me. She has funny little sayings that always make me laugh.'

'Such as?'

'One I've heard since I was old enough to walk is, "I was born under a blue moon". She says it to me whenever I'm in trouble.'

'A blue moon? That's two full moons in the same calendar month, right?'

'Yeah.'

'I don't get it, what does she mean by that?'

'She says it means that nothing bad will ever happen to me. That I'm protected.' Vee laughs at this.

'Must be an old wives tale or something. Were you actually born during a blue moon, though?' I shrug.

'Not sure. But, according to my mother, I was. I guess she should know.'

She looks around the room and stares at the assorted characters. She covers her mouth with her hand and leans towards me. 'Do you think those two men sitting near the window are tramps?' she whispers with a worried frown on her face. I glance at the two men.

'Yep, they're derelicts all right. Probably spent the night under the Arches.'

'Poor devils, it must have been below zero last night.'

'Well, they'll have a brazier going all night and probably some blankets… but yes, it wouldn't be very pleasant.'

'Why do they do it?' I don't understand the question and cock my head to one side. 'I mean why don't they find somewhere to live?' I laugh.

'Could be a hundred different reasons. Finding somewhere to live when you haven't a job and look like a tramp is pretty hard to do. Anyway, back to you. How do you earn a crust?' She looks a little sheepish.

'Me, I don't do anything.'

'You must do something, everyone does something.'

'Well, I do a lot of cooking, I read a lot, I go to the gym most days and I help mummy out with her art exhibitions.'

'So where does your money come from? You're certainly not on the dole and that's a pretty swish pad you've got there.'

'I told you last night—that belongs to my parents but I live there most of the time.'

'So, what about money, everyone needs money?'

'I get an allowance from the family trust.' Strewth! How the other half lives.

'How much, if you don't mind me asking?' She leans back in her chair and sips her tea, looking a little uncomfortable again.

'No, I don't mind you asking. I get five hundred pounds.'

'Wow! Per month?'

'Per week.' The warm sweet tea that a few moments ago was gliding effortlessly down my throat, is now unceremoniously ejected back up via my nostrils on to the table. I grab a napkin and dab up the mess. Vee laughs uncontrollably.

'Two grand a month!' I almost shout out before realising where I am. She regains her composure.

123

'Yes. Is that a lot?' Fuck me rigid! The girl has no idea.

'Well, let me put it into perspective. I'm on the dole and I receive fifty-six pounds per fortnight.' She giggles.

'Don't be silly, you do not. No one could possibly live off that.'

'I'm sorry but it *is* true, cross my heart.' She stops smiling and looks concerned. She reaches out and touches the back of my hand.

'How do you manage?'

'I just do. I eke and scrimp and when there's nothing left I go back and stay at my mam's place until the next dole cheque arrives.'

'Hang on, you told me you were a freelance photographer, you even gave me your business card.'

'I am, but I only started two weeks ago. In fact, that was my very first unpaid job the night I met you in the Granary.'

'But you're still on the dole?'

'Yes,' I nod.

'Isn't that illegal?' I nod again 'So what happens if they find out you're working?'

'They stop my dole and my housing benefit.'

'Housing benefit? What's that?'

'They pay eighty-percent of my rent.'

'How much is your rent?'

'One sixty a month.' Her face looks troubled.

'Let me get this correct. You get paid twenty-eight pounds a week on the dole and out of that you pay eight pounds a week in rent leaving you with twenty pounds a week to live on?'

'You're good at maths,' I grin as I finish the last dregs of my tea. 'And you've just paid for breakfast,' she says sadly, looking down at her plate.

'Well, one pound fifty each for a slap up meal that will keep me going all day isn't too bad. Plus, I've picked up quite a bit of photography work over the last couple of weeks, so I'm a bit flush at the moment.' She shakes her head and grabs my hand.

'You live off one meal a day?'

'Yeah, normally. Right come on, let's go for a walk.'

We stroll around the city arm in arm observing the ever increasing traffic and the thousands of people busily making their way to their place of work. We talk non-stop. I tell her about my mates, Marky, Jonesy, Gerry and Macca. I talk about the band, The Hipnotikz and how one day they are going to be huge. My life is laid out in chronological order for her, starting from my earliest school days right up until the present.

We stop off at a cafe and sip on strong black coffee that she insists on paying for. She tells me about her school days and how at the age of five she was packed off to some elite private boarding school, only ever coming home in the holidays. She tells me how much she loves her mother and her late grandmother and how she always argues bitterly with her father.

We emerge from the cafe and saunter down the main street.

'Hey, how would you like to walk around the art gallery?' she suggests.

'Sounds good, anywhere to get in from this bleeding cold.'

'Have you got any work on today?'

'Not really. I need to develop some photos of a band I took the other night. But I can do that later in the day.' She looks a little sad.

'Where do you develop your photos?'

'I've have part of my bedroom in my flat converted into a darkroom. It's tiny but it will do for now.'

'Will you come back after you've done what you need to do and stay the night?' she asks expectantly.

'It might be late, about eight, but if you want me to, I'd love to.' She beams at this.

'Of course I do. The thought of you leaving me makes me feel homesick, the feeling I used to get when I knew I'd be heading back to boarding school—how strange. Hey, what's your favourite meal?'

'Spag bol,' I reply.

'Super, I love spag bol as well and I make a mean one. Do you like olives?'

'Love them.'

'Parmesan?'

'Love it.' She does a funny little jig on the spot which makes me laugh. 'Right, spaghetti bolognaise it is for dinner.'

##

We spend the rest of the day together, talking non-stop, laughing, recounting funny little tales, holding hands and lots of kissing. It gets to 4 pm and I realise I have to go.

'Okay Vee, I'm sorry but I really do need to get going. I promised this band the photos by tonight.' She looks crestfallen.

'You'll definitely come back later? Promise?'

'Yes, I promise.' She beams, flashing her white teeth at me. 'Right, we better head to the Granary and collect my scooter.'

I get a bollocking and a lecture from Iris when I pick my scooter and helmet up. I placate her by arranging a time for tomorrow to come and do her publicity shots. I introduce her to Vee, and she acts a bit aloof with her, but Iris is like that with everyone. I kiss Vee one last time then strap my helmet on.

'Jimmy, be careful on the roads, won't you? There are some terrible drivers around.' I smile and give her the thumbs up. 'Tonight at eight, yes?' she confirms with imploring eyes.

'Eight-ish,' I reply as I sit on the saddle. I kick-start the Vespa, slip it into gear and speed off down the road.

VICTORIA'S DIARY

I am in a state of great excitement but also fear. He came back—my man-boy! I have spent the last two weeks sitting in the Granary each night in the exact same spot as when I first met him. I had nearly given up hope and decided this is probably the last time I will do this.

I fear I have lost him for good. Then, just after 10 pm the door opens and I hear his voice. It's ridiculous, but I get heart palpitations and a bad case of the jitters. I try to compose myself and run through the plan in my head. I will not be rude, caustic or sarcastic. I will keep my dignity and not throw myself at him, but, I will offer him encouragement this time, and overall—I will be nice!

He comes around the corner with a huge welcoming grin and just stares at me for a while. My eyes pore over his body. His hair, his cute smile, his tall lithe frame, his crotch again! He makes a joke about me taking root. I want to laugh and giggle but what do I do instead? I'm rude to him! I cannot help myself.

He hands me a rum and black then sits down next to me. He says he won't stop long, that he's only here to tell me something then he'll leave me alone. My heart sinks. I fear that he's going to give me a telling-off for my appalling behaviour of a fortnight ago. He doesn't, instead out come all these words about how he has been thinking of me in every waking moment. How my ghost visits him in his dreams. He has my photo on his bedroom wall and speaks to me every night before going to sleep. Then—he says the word that I thought I'd never hear

128

again in my lifetime—he says that he's in love with me and always has been! He says he needs me.

There is true emotion in his voice. I feel something inside me burst. It is like a breach in a dam wall. The feeling completely overwhelms me. I am flooded with emotional torment. Sadness, anger, melancholy, homesickness, resentment—and something else, something I don't know the name of. I sense movement as though he is about to up and leave. I place my hand on top of his and he relaxes. I begin to well up and, despite how hard I try to force the tears away, they begin to flow. I'm not sure whether I'm crying because of years of repressed emotion or because of joy—or both.

I stand and hold out my hand for him. I pull him to his feet. I remove my mask and stare into his gorgeous, boyish face. The tears drip from my cheeks and he looks mortified that he's upset me. He uses his thumb to gently push them away. We kiss. A sweet, slow, sensual kiss. My tears streak his lips and I feel embarrassed.

I grab his hand tightly and we head out of the club and down the street. He asks so many questions—too many questions! He tells me about the people in his life, who he loves and who love him. He wears his heart on his sleeve and I envy him for that.

Back in my flat, he asks if he can have a look around. He's back in a few short minutes and stares at me. There is now an awkward moment and I fear he is having second thoughts. I ask how can he really know that he loves me. He says he can't explain it—that he just feels it and knows I am the one for him. I want to release my heart like a songbird from a gilded cage and let it fly and be free, but I cannot. He undresses me, but asks me to leave my boots on. I like that, sex with him will never be boring. He undresses and I marvel at his young, hard, frame. There is not an ounce of fat on him. He is lean and sinewy with a broad chest and strong shoulders. I look down at his manhood which is already on the way up. We kiss, then I go down on him. I push him onto my bed and we begin to make love. Every time I feel he is about to orgasm I ease off and begin kissing him passionately all over his face and body. I change position, ride him hard until I feel him clench my buttocks. He pushes deep into me as I feel him spasm.

I freshen up and lay with him for a few minutes. I think about just laying there until we both fall asleep, but my body is in such a state of arousal that I desperately crave relief. I know the next ten minutes or so could be make or break time. I ask him to spank me. He thinks that it's just a bit of fun and playfully slaps me. I order him to hit me harder. I am in raptures and as I orgasm he keeps hitting me with increasing force. This prolongs my ecstasy and it seems to last forever.

I lay panting and exhausted, my face deep in the pillow. Then I hear that dreadful sound. He sniffs. I look up and his face is emblazoned with tears. I knew this would happen!

I cradle him. He says he cannot hurt me. He wants to know my reasons. I explain that it's to do with feelings of inadequacy. I fear my peculiar fetish has scarred him and that during the night he will slip out of my life forever. I keep making love to him during the night for two reasons; one, because I want to feel him inside me and two, I want to make sure he doesn't leave. Eventually, I fall into a deep sleep, fearful of what the morning will bring.

I hear his voice and my heart soars. He is still here! I can scarcely believe it. He suggests breakfast at some greasy spoon café which sounds perfectly ghastly but I agree. Before we leave we make soft, gentle love in the shower then dry each other, laughing and giggling like little children.

At the café, the food is delicious. I'm sure it's terribly bad for you. I've never eaten in a café like this before. The place is full of what my father would describe as, "common people" and I am fascinated by them. He's now asking more questions and this is where I could lose him.

He asks what my father does. I reply by not quite telling him a lie, but then again, it is not quite the truth either. He decides on a nickname for me—Vee—Vee for victory, he says. I like it. It's what my grandmother used to call me—how peculiar.

Next, he asks me what my last name is. If I tell him the truth it won't take him long to figure out who my father really is, then he'll discard me. Rather fortuitously, some food goes down the wrong way and I cough and splutter just as

I am telling him my surname. He thinks I said, "Harrywell" instead of "Halliwell". I don't correct him, in fact, I confirm it—oh dear, my first full lie to him! It does not sit easily with me.

He tells me how much he has to live on a week. I laugh and think he is joking with me again; he is not. I feel embarrassed and ashamed at my ignorance and at my ridiculous weekly allowance. I get five hundred pounds per week—he—twenty-six! I don't understand how this disparity exists—it does seem most unfair!

We spend a wonderful day together and unlike me, he doesn't hold anything back in describing his life, his friends and his passions. I ask him if he will stay the night and I will cook him dinner. He happily agrees and I try to read him for any artifice but I cannot detect any.

At 4 pm we head back to the Granary where he gets a severe lecture from the owner because he left his scooter there overnight. She is very fierce but underneath I can tell she has a soft spot for Jimmy.

As he departs down the street on his little red scooter, I watch him and become overcome with sadness. I'm now full of self-doubt. Will he come back? Has he had his bit of fun with the "weird" rich bitch, who can only get "off" on pain. He's probably already making his way to the pub to laugh and joke about me to his mates. I finally lose sight of him as he turns a corner and another unwelcome wave of melancholy and sadness engulfs me.

I walk back into the heart of the city and buy the CD of the song we left the Granary to last night, "Only You" by The Flying Pickets. I must confess, it is the only pop song I have ever bought. I play it continuously all evening as I await his return.

He said he'd be back about 8 pm. The clock keeps on ticking and 8 pm comes and goes. The bolognaise sauce is simmering slowly in the oven and the dried spaghetti lays expectantly on the kitchen bench.

As every treacherous minute passes by, a gnawing fear begins to rise inside me and I curse myself for letting my mask down. Now I am going to suffer months, if not years, of bittersweet regret and torment.

9 pm departs like an unwelcome guest at a funeral and I convince myself he has forsaken me. I try reading to take my mind off him but it is futile.

It is now 10 pm and nothing. I am beyond distraught and curse myself for my reckless behaviour. Love is not meant for cold, repressed people like me.

Then, the buzzer for the intercom goes. My heart flips and I have a mini panic attack. It has to be him, surely. No one else would call at this time of night. I nervously press the button and hear his voice. He sounds jaunty and casual,

"Hey Vee, it's me, Jimmy." I press the release button for the apartment entrance and rush to open my door. I go back inside and quickly redo my ponytail in the mirror. I pump the air and shout "Yes! Yes! Yes!" I do a funny little jig on the spot and a Hawaiian dance in the mirror.

I can hear the lift ascending then the clank of the steel grille. As he walks in, wearing a beguiling smile, I act casual and tell him that I had nearly nodded off—another lie. He apologises for being late and I tell him I'll get the spaghetti on. He tells me it can wait. He picks me up, then swirls me around and around. He tells me that he loves me and that even these few hours apart were painful for him. I keep my night of torment to myself. He then dumps me on the bed, rips his clothes off, then mine, and jumps on top of me.

We make passionate, torrid love for twenty minutes. We stop, we eat, then make love all through the night. He is still here in the morning. I am fit to burst with happiness!

11: LEARNING

I'm in front of her bookcase perusing the hundreds of neatly stacked books that are arranged in alphabetical order by author name. I must confess, I'm not much of a reader. Vee comes in with two steaming mugs of hot coffee and two plates of cheese on toast.

'I've made us a bite to eat. We best be quick if we want to catch that film. It starts in half an hour.'

'Yeah,' I reply, distracted by the books. 'This is some book collection you have.'

'Oh, that's nothing. You should see the books we have at home. We have thousands upon thousands of them. Do you read much?'

'Nah, not really. I think the last book I read was at school during one of those dreary English lessons. They always managed to pick boring books for us to read. If I'm going to read, I want something with a bit of action and adventure.' She walks over to me and hands me my coffee whilst taking a bite out of her toast.

'Hmm, okay, let me see.' She scours the bookshelf and pulls a book out and hands it to me. 'What about Treasure Island by Robert Louis Stevenson. That's got action and adventure—and pirates.' I study the front cover.

'Okay,' I say, 'I'll give it a go.' She takes another bite of her food and wipes a crumb away from the side of her mouth.

'I know, how about I pick ten books out for you that I think you'll like. You can be my pet project. I'll educate you on the great literature of the world.' I laugh.

'Okay. I suppose I could do with a bit of educating on the finer things in life. Have you read all these books?' I say pointing at the shelves.

'Yes and the rest.'

'Why do you read so much?'

'I love it. Every book is a new experience, a new adventure. It's like stepping inside the head of someone else. You see the world from a different perspective, through the author's or characters' eyes. It's fascinating.' I take a sip of my coffee as she begins to pull books from their home and stack them on the table.

'Who's your favourite author?'

'Oh, too many to list.'

'All right, what's your favourite book?'

'Way too many to mention.'

'Just name a few?' I ask becoming a tad annoyed.

'Okay, authors: F. Scott Fitzgerald, Dostoevsky, the Brontë Sisters, Jane Austen, to name a few. Books: Pride and Prejudice, To Kill A Mocking Bird, 1984, Wuthering Heights, Catch 22, Lord Of The Flies—the list goes on forever. Okay, here's some you'd like. Dracula, Billy Liar, The Loneliness Of The Long Distance Runner, Live and Let Die...' I cut her off.

'James Bond?'

'Yes.'

'Great film, didn't know it was a book as well.' She throws me a disapproving look and continues studying the bookshelf. I pull another book out and stare at the front cover. The text is completely unintelligible. 'What's this?' I ask as I pass her the book. She glances at it for a split second.

'Oh, that's Homer's Iliad.'

'Of course, it is. It's not in English.'

'No, it's in Greek.'

'You can read Greek?' She stops again and looks at me impatiently.

'Yes, I can speak and read Greek. Is that so unusual?'

'Yes, it bloody well is—unless you're Greek of course. Any other languages you speak?'

'French, German and Spanish. I'm not as fluent as I once was because I don't get to speak them very often. That's why I have foreign language books, to keep my eye in.'

'Jesus, I can barely speak English, and here's you with four languages.'

'Five actually, if you include English. And don't be silly Jimmy, your command of the English language is… commendable, although you do swear too much.' I think she intended that as a compliment, but for some reason, it didn't sound like one. 'Ah! Here we go, Charlie and the Chocolate Factory, you'll love this.' I feel she may be patronising me somewhat.

'Hang on a minute, I'm not stupid, that's a kids book. I can read you know, I just said I didn't read much.' She laughs at me.

'A good book is a good book whether it's written for adults or children. You can still take something away from it.'

'And what am I going to get out of Willy Wonka?'

'Ah, so you are aware of it then?'

'I've seen the film… when I was a kid.' She puts the last book on top of the pile and takes a sip of her coffee.

'Well, although it's wrapped up as a children's story it explores common themes of humanity. There's poverty, disparity, hope, expectations. There's greed, sloth, gluttony, bribery, corruption and finally, redemption.'

'You know your shit, don't you?'

'Well, it's all subjective. What I take from a book may be completely different from what you take from it.' I pull out another book. It's a hardback and looks very old. The cover is a faded green, covered in some sort of cloth. It has streaks of gold dappled across it. There's a picture, well, more like an engraving of a woman's head. She looks fierce and her hair appears to be made of snakes. There's more foreign letters at the foot of the page that read, "Geasa".

'What language is this?' I ask. Vee takes the book from me and places it back in its home.

'That's Irish Gaelic.'

'You speak and read Gaelic, as well?'

'Yes. Irish Gaelic.'

'The chick with the snake hair, I know her, it's Methuselah—right?' I state, proud to show off my knowledge. She laughs.

'No. You're thinking of Medusa. Methuselah is a biblical figure who lived until he was nine-hundred and sixty-nine.'

'Fuck! I bet he was knackered when he finally pegged it.' I pull the book from the shelf and flick through the pages, then refocus on the cover again. 'So, this is Medusa?' She takes the book from me once more and places it back on the shelf.

'It's a very rare and valuable book. And no, it's not Medusa,' She explains as she leads me by the arm to the table.

'So who is it?'

'Morrigan.' I'm none the wiser and drop the subject. I stare back at the tomes for a few seconds as a thought occurs to me.

'Hey I know what, seeing as you are going to educate me in literature how about I repay the favour by educating you about music? I've seen your record collection and every CD you have is classical, not that there's anything wrong with that, but you don't have anything by anybody who is still alive.' She beams at me.

'Okay, deal.'

'I have a huge collection of albums and cassettes. I'll dig out ten classic albums next time I'm at the flat. Now, who do you like?' Her nose twitches as she scratches her head.

'I don't know really. I have never taken any notice of modern music.'

'All right, what about The Who, The Stones, The Kinks, David Bowie, Slade, Bob Dylan?'

'Sorry, never heard of any of them,' she states, almost apologetically.

'Get the fuck out of here!'

'Jimmy don't swear, it's uncouth!' she scolds.

'Sorry. All right then, you must have heard of The Clash, The Jam, Billy Bragg, U2? They're all recent acts,' I explain. She shakes her head. I am dumbfounded. 'Okay, The Beatles, everyone has heard of The Beatles!'

'Hmm, yes I think I may have heard of them, but I couldn't name any of their songs.' I sit down at the table and eat my toast.

'Oh wow! I wish I was you,' I state.

'Why?' she asks with a tilt of the head.

'Because you are going to hear some of the best music from the last twenty-five years. Imagine hearing "Satisfaction" for the first time, or "Let It Be" and "London Calling". Imagine hearing "Imagine". You are going to be blown away.' She smiles as she collects the plates and heads back into the kitchen. I walk back to the bookcase and begin to count the books but give up after fifty. I turn around and Vee is back at the table flicking through Charlie and the Chocolate Factory.

'I can't tell you how many times I read this as a child. It made me laugh so much, and cry. It was a great comfort to me.' I stare at her. I admire her body, her form, the curve of her breasts, her lips and those captivating eyes. She notices me staring and replaces the book on the table.

'What?' she asks.

'Nothing,' I reply, still staring intently at her.

'Jimmy, you have that look in your eye.'

'What look?'

'You know very well, "what look". And the answer is no! We need to get our skates on, otherwise the film will have started.' I walk over to her and reach out to gently grab her. She fends me away but I move in closer. 'Jimmy, I'm warning you! We don't have time.'

'I only want a kiss,' I lie. She relents somewhat and I place my lips on hers and impart the most sensual and passionate kiss I can muster. Her eyes begin to close and the tempo of her breathing increases. I hold the kiss for a good twenty seconds then slowly pull away. Her eyes are still closed and she tilts forward nearly losing her footing. I walk back to the bookcase and turn my back on her.

'Yep, you're right,' I state matter-of-factly. 'We best shake a leg. There's nothing worse than missing the start of a film.' There's a moment of silence.

'You bastard,' she quietly hisses. I turn and look at her. She has smouldering eyes and her cheeks are enflamed.

'Sorry?' I say.

'You bastard,' she repeats as she advances forward.

'What?'

'You know damn well, what!' She grabs me by my shirt front and drags me to the bed where she roughly pushes at me until I fall backwards. She straddles me and begins feverishly kissing at my lips, my neck and my chest as her hands work overtime undoing my belt.

'Vee, what about the film?' I protest.

'Fuck the fucking film!' she shouts.

'Victoria, don't be so uncouth.'

12: BEAUTY

It's 6 am and I'm staring out of the window onto the city streets below.

'Vee wake up!' I say excitedly. She murmurs something unintelligible. 'Vee, wake up!' I repeat, louder this time.

'Huh, what time is it?'

'It's six. Come and look at this.'

'Six, it's too early Jimmy, let me sleep,' she groans, then rolls onto her back and tucks the blankets around her. I pull the sheets back off and she complains bitterly. 'Jimmy! That's mean.'

'Come on Vee, it's perfect,' I encourage. She slowly rises from her bed, rubs her eyes and joins me at the window and peers out.

'What? What am I supposed to be looking at?' she asks, yawning.

'The fog, it's perfect.' She stares at me in disbelief.

'You awoke me from a deep slumber to stare at fog?'

'Yes. Get dressed. Put your black leggings on, those little black boots and that tight black polo neck jumper.'

'Have you gone completely mad?' she demands, incredulous at my instructions.

'No, we're going down to the canal to take photos. The fog will be hovering just above the surface. I'm going to capture you in all your innocent beauty. Come on, chop-chop.'

'Do I have to? Can I get a shower first?'

'No, no time. The fog won't last too long and we'll miss the chance.' She reluctantly staggers her way to the wardrobe and fumbles about inside complaining all the while.

##

'Yep, that's it. Look past the camera and fixate on an object in the distance.' I continually press the shutter release as the camera whirs away.

'Oh perfect. Walk nice and slow towards the bridge and keep turning your head from side to side.' I take more shots. 'Right, this time Vee, look directly into the lens as though you're looking into my eyes. Look sexy,' I command her.

'What does that mean, look sexy? I can't look sexy unless I feel sexy and I'm freezing.' I pause for a second to think.

'Look at me and think the most perverted sexual thought you can imagine. Your secret fantasy, the one that gives you butterflies in your stomach.'

'No! I'm not doing that,' she huffs.

'Come on Vee. Just play the film in your head.' I wait about twenty seconds before I begin to see the change. Her cheeks become flushed. Her eyes narrow and her bosom begins to rise and fall. 'Whoa! That's it. Keep going.' She's now staring at me with the most lascivious, wanton abandon I've ever witnessed. Her eyes flick back and forth across my face. Her lips are slightly apart as she bites gently down on the corner of her lip. For a split-second, a memory flashes across my mind, but before I can discern what it is—it departs. There is movement downstairs but I refuse to be distracted by him. As she expels air it hangs like a ghostly vapour suspended in no-man's land. She begins to tremble a little and I assume she's shivering. All the while I press the shutter.

'Oh my God!' she exclaims, loudly.

'Are you all right Vee?' I ask, concerned.

'I've just had an orgasm,' she gasps.

'Bullshit! You can't have an orgasm without any stimulation.' I know she's playing mind games with me.

'You can if you contract and release slowly and gently build up the intensity whilst thinking perverse thoughts.'

'Yes, nice try Vee. I'm not going to be distracted by your games. Right, let's try a few shots near those iron railings.'

After thirty minutes the fog begins to dissipate.

'How much longer Jimmy?' she pleads. 'I'm cold and hungry. You're so mean.'

'Not long now. We'll go for a nosh-up at the greasy spoon after this. I'm just going to climb up on the bridge and get some shots looking down. I want to catch the viaducts in the background.'

'Oh Jimmy, be careful climbing up there. If you fall you'll end up in the water,' she cries, in a panic.

'Never fear Vee. I'm like a mountain goat.' I take ten good snaps and as I begin to make my way back down I lose my footing and slip. Vee let's out a piercing scream.

'Jimmy!' I manage to grab hold of a railing as I dangle ten feet above the freezing water below. I swing back and forth until I've got enough momentum to launch one leg back up and over the parapet, then pull myself to safety. I look down at Vee with a big grin. She has her hand over her mouth and looks mortified.

'Phew! That was a close call,' I laugh. 'I could have lost all the photos.'

'Jimmy, get down here at once! I'm going to murder you!' she yells, with a fierce expression. I take one more shot and capture her anger.

##

We make our way along quiet streets back to the heart of the city. An old tramp is coming towards us. He's wearing a long Crombie overcoat that is tied across the midriff with a piece of string. The coat is tatty and heavily stained. He has a single rose in the buttonhole. His boots have holes in the toe and the bottom of his pants are covered in mud.

'Don't suppose you could spare fifty pence for a cup of tea, young Sir?' he asks politely. I stop and fumble about in my pocket.

'Here, get yourself a hearty breakfast, it's a cold day,' I say, as I hand him a fiver. He thanks me profusely.

'Thank you Sir, thank you! Much obliged, you're a gent. If there's anything I can do in return, all you need to do is ask.'

'Actually, would you mind if I took a portrait shot of you?' He looks shocked.

'Of me Sir? Why would you want a shot of an old, ugly, wrinkled face like mine?' I smile at him.

'You're not ugly. You have kind eyes. You've lived. I want a shot that captures your experience. I'm putting together a portfolio and I want pictures of real humanity, not sanitised, sterile beauty.' The tramp scratches his head as though confused but agrees.

'Okay, if you want my ugly mug in your portfolio, well, who am I to argue.'

'What's your name?' I ask.

'Jethro.'

'Now there's a name you don't hear very often.'

'Old biblical name, Sir. My parents were very religious. Devout Baptists.'

'Jethro, I'm Jimmy, pleased to meet you.' I hold out my hand and he looks taken aback but shakes it anyway. 'This is my gorgeous girlfriend, Vee—Vee for Victoria.' Vee extends her arm out towards him as he vigorously rubs his hand up and down his pants as though trying to clean them. He delicately takes Vee's hand, stoops slightly and plants a gentle kiss on the back of it.

'Pleased to meet you Victoria, a real pleasure.' He releases her hand, stands erect, stares into her eyes then places a hand over his heart. 'This bud of love by summer's ripening breath, may prove a beauteous flower when next we meet.' He whispers the words softly.

'Have you lifted that from a Rolling Stones song?' I ask. Vee hits me on the arm.

'It's Shakespeare you clot,' she states.

'She's right Sir. Shakespeare—a man who knew all about love. And Victoria has love in her soul, she is beguiled by it. Love dances from her eyes like a billion particles of stardust, entrancing and bewitching all those who witness it. I hope you appreciate her Jimmy because you are the luckiest man in the universe.' I look at Vee, who now has her hand on heart and is choking up. I slowly turn to face Jethro.

'Yeah Jethro, of course I appreciate her—more than anyone will ever know. I realise I'm not worthy of her. I know I'm punching above my weight—a fish out of water, a tugboat against a battleship. But, fuck it... I will prove everyone wrong. I have a fire in my heart that could burn this planet to a smouldering cinder in seconds...because of her—it is an unstoppable force.' Jethro looks shocked, even slightly scared at my outburst. I smile at him and he visibly relaxes.

'Right, come on, let's get this photo done. Jethro, look at the camera then focus on an object in the distance. Don't pull any expression, just wear the one you normally wear.' I get some good shots of his craggy, well-worn face. 'Okay, now just a couple more if you don't mind. Look directly into the camera lens and give me a smile.' This doesn't work. His smile seems forced and false, which it probably is. 'Hey Jethro, have you heard the joke about the priest and the prostitute?'

'I'm not sure Sir?' I tell him the joke and when I get to the punch line he cackles loudly, the laughter lines around his eyes crease up. I click away.

'Jimmy that is the most disgusting joke I've ever heard!' exclaims Vee. 'It's not even funny, it's just offensive.'

'Jethro seemed to enjoy it. Okay, cheers Jethro.' Before he turns to go he removes the rose from his lapel and hands it to Vee who accepts it graciously.

'A rose by any other name would smell as sweet.'

'Oh thank you, Jethro. That's beautiful,' Vee gushes as Jethro heads off down the street.

##

We're in the greasy spoon café and Vee is digging into her food like she's never eaten before. I sit back and stare at her. I love watching her eat. She is so refined. She talks continually and every time she does, she delicately rests her knife longways on the plate and her right hand covers her mouth.

'What have you got on today?' she asks.

'Twelve, I've got a baby photo. Then at two, another bloody baby photo.'

'You don't enjoy it?'

'It depends on the baby. Some are cute and just sit there quietly. Others scream and wriggle around. It can be trying. And they don't listen to a bloody word I say.'

'They're babies Jimmy, of course they don't listen to what you say,' she laughs.

'I was talking about the mothers. Anyway, the money's not bad. Sixty quid a pop.'

'Have you thought about getting your own premises? Then people could come to you instead of you carting your gear all over the city.'

'Early days yet Vee. I don't want to make commitments when I'm not really sure how long it will last.' She looks astounded at me as she bites into a crispy slice of fried bread.

'Jimmy, how long have you been doing this now?'

'Four… five weeks.'

'Yes, five weeks and you've been flat-out nearly every day. This isn't going to evaporate overnight. It's going to get bigger and bigger. You need to have a long and short term goal. Do some planning.'

'Yeah, I suppose,' I shrug.

'You know Jimmy, I'm going to do something with my life, something worthwhile and purposeful. I don't know what yet but talking with Jethro made me think.' She stops and cradles her cup of tea, then takes a gentle sip. I pick up a teaspoon and begin heaping sugar into my mug of tea.

'Jimmy stop. You need to cut down on your sugar.' She grabs my hand just as I'm about to drop the third teaspoon into my tea. 'Two sugars is more than enough.' I pour the sugar back into the bowl. 'Speaking with Jethro just now got me thinking.'

'Yeah, what about?'

'About life. Life should have a purpose. You have your work. Jethro's purpose is to eat and survive. I have no purpose, I'm a kept woman. I need to find something where I can make a difference.'

'Good. I do worry about you sitting in that flat alone all day.'

'Are you going to eat that rasher of bacon?' she asks.

'No, go for it.' She jabs the bacon with her fork and drops it on her plate.

'I don't know what's wrong with me today. I have such an appetite.'

'Listen Vee, did you really have an orgasm back there?' She sips on her tea again and stares at me from above the rim of her cup. A mischievous grin spreads across her face.

'You'll never know the truth—will you? Does it excite you to think that I did?'

'Too bloody right it excites me. In fact, this table is going to start levitating at any moment.' She laughs and places her tea down on the table.

'When we get back to the flat, do you know what I'm going to do?'

'No, what?'

'I'm going to strip you naked and tie you to a chair then tease you. When you're fit to burst, I'm going to do something to you that I was thinking about on the canal bank.'

'Come on, finish up, let's go!' I push my chair back in a mad rush and stand up.

'No! I haven't finished my breakfast yet. You're like a little boy in a sweet shop. You'll just have to wait.' Damn it!

13: ONLY YOU

I have spent the last week flitting between my pad and Vee's flat. If I work late developing photos, then I slump into my bed at night, not before first ringing Vee and telling her how much I love and miss her. She told me to call at any time to say goodnight. Sometimes I feel bad as I don't finish work until well past midnight, but she insists on a call. She says she can't sleep until she's heard from me. I see her every day. I call around at lunchtime and we'll share a sandwich and a cup of tea. Other days she insists on taking me out to a café for lunch.

I'm getting smarter. When I used to go and interview bands, I would turn up about 3 pm as the road crew were setting up. I'd do an interview with one or two band members, then leave. I'd return at about 9 pm as the band were starting the gig, get some photos of them on stage and hang around until the end of the first encore. Not anymore. I now get there at 3 pm and record a quick interview on a dictaphone purloined from the Standard. I take some shots of the band outside, making sure I capture the venue's name. Occasionally I take some portraits, if any of the band have an interesting face. I ask them for a set-list and depart. I rush home, develop a few photos and zoom back to Vee's flat. Once there, I type out the interview on an old typewriter, kindly donated by the Standard. I then concoct a quick gig review and drop various song titles into it from their set-list. I place the photos, interview and review into an envelope, seal it and write, "Dave Dee" on the front, with "Jimmy", scrawled underneath. I'm pretty much done and dusted by 7 pm. Next day I drop the envelope off at the Standard. Dave Dee's happy, I'm happy and the band get a glowing review of the gig I never saw. Vee is horrified at my conduct, but come on, one gig review is pretty much like another. The band comes on, they play some of their hits, then their new stuff, an encore or two and it's goodnight Vienna.

It's late Thursday afternoon and I am going through the routine just described. I finish the review from last night's gig, then pull the paper from the typewriter. I place it in an envelope, along with two good photos. Vee is in the shower, and as I seal the envelope I hear singing and stop what I am doing. At first I assume it's coming from the clock radio in the bathroom. I know the song well, it's "Only You", the song that Vee plays non-stop, morning, noon and night. This particular version I've never heard before. I make my way to the bathroom and stand in the doorway. Vee has her back to me as she is washing her hair. It's Vee that is singing. I've never heard such a melancholy, heart-wrenching voice before. It is pure, innocent, pitch-perfect and full of such sadness. She rinses off and suddenly notices me and stops singing.

'Oh Jimmy, you startled me. How long have you been standing there?'

'Long enough.'

'Pervert. Is that what you get off on, spying on girls in the shower?'

'Of course. I didn't know you could sing?'

'Everyone can sing,' she laughs.

'I can't. I couldn't carry a tune in a bucket. Where did you learn to sing like that?'

'Like what?' she replies, as she begins drying herself with a towel.

'Like that! That is the most beautiful voice I've ever heard. It's so moving, mournful. There aren't many people who can sing like that.' She smiles sweetly at me.

'Oh you're so nice Jimmy,' she says, as though I only offered the compliment because I love her.

'No Vee, I mean it. I listen to a lot of music and I can tell good from mediocre, and your voice is amazing. More importantly, it's original. It's your own voice.'

'Of course it's my own voice, whose voice would it be?'

'Well, a lot of people try and sound like someone. Sing it again.' She looks embarrassed.

'No.'

'Why not?'

'Because.' As I turn to walk away she begins to sing the song. I return my gaze to her, mesmerised. She is combing her hair in the mirror and stares back at me. She finishes the song, then spins around. My God! My heart flutters and I am immediately aroused.

'Why have you made it sound so sad?' I ask.

'Because it is sad.'

'It's not that sad.'

'Do you not understand the lyrics? It's the end of their relationship. He's left her. She's sitting alone in her tiny bed-sit, flicking through a photo album, grieving for him. There are pictures of them on holiday together, giggling and smiling. There's the one that used to make her laugh, of him wearing a silly hat and pulling a face. Of her eating ice cream on a warm sunny day at the beach. The walk in the park, his birthday party. Happy times that will never come back. In the end, all she longs for is for him to touch her one more time. To feel his hand on her. But it's not to be.'

'Fuck Vee, there's nothing about ice creams and holiday snaps in the song.' She giggles.

'Of course there is. You've just got to imagine it.' She moves towards me, places her hand on my groin and rubs it. 'Is that thing always hard?' she smiles provocatively. I gulp.

'It is since I met you. I have no control over the damn thing anymore. I didn't have much control of it before, but now, it's on permanent sentry duty with a will of its own.' She begins to unzip my fly but I grab her hand. 'Not now Vee. I need to drop the photos and review off with Dave. He's waiting on them.'

'Come on Jimmy, just a quick one, here, up against the wall. I'll do that special thing you like.'

'No, sorry Vee. Later, when I get back.' She pushes her bottom lip out and pulls a disappointed look.

'I'll just have to sort myself out then,' she says.

'Vee! Don't say things like that, you know it drives me insane. I won't be able to concentrate while I'm on my scooter. Right, I'm off. I'm going to have a couple of quick ones with the boys in Tossers after I've made my delivery.'

'Okay. Dinner will be ready by seven. Don't be late.'

##

I'm sitting with Macca, Gerry and Jonesy in Tossers finishing off my second pint.

'Hey Jim, how come we haven't met this bird of yours yet?' asks Macca.

'Don't call her a bird! She's my girlfriend,' I reply, with mock offence.

'Ooh touchy,' he replies.

'I don't think she exists,' sniggers Jonesy. 'This great love affair is nothing but a figment of Jimmy's fertile imagination.' They all laugh at me.

'Oh very funny. The thing is she's a bit nervous about meeting you all.'

'Why? We don't bite,' says Gerry.

'I think, that she thinks, you'll all see her as some posh bitch and instantly dislike her.'

'Jesus Jimmy! You should know us all by now. We're not like Marky you know. We don't prejudge people based on their background or upbringing,' says Macca.

'Or colour,' chips in Gerry.

'Or sexuality,' adds Jonesy.

'I know that, you know that, but she doesn't,' I argue. 'I tell you what, I'll try and get her to come to the lunchtime gig this Sunday at the Soldiers.'

'Okay, fair enough. Hey, she better be all you've cracked her up to be. I'm expecting to pass out when I see her,' laughs Macca.

'Oh mate, you are all going to be so jealous.' I finish my pint and am just about to stand up to leave. 'Hey, you will not believe her singing voice, it is the most beautiful sound in the world. I caught her singing in the shower earlier. I got really choked up.'

'Yeah?' Macca replies. 'Maybe we should get her up on stage on Sunday for a solo spot.' I stop and think for a moment.

'You know what, that's a good idea. Once you've done your second set and had a break, tell the audience that you are going to do a duet then call her name out.' The boys laugh.

'What songs does she know?' asks Gerry.

'Just the one, "Only You". But she's fucking nailed it.'

'Okay,' says Macca. 'I'll learn it on my guitar. We'll perform an acoustic ballad. What key and tempo does she sing it in?'

'Fuck knows,' I reply, honestly. Macca looks a bit miffed.

'Well, does she sing it high or low?'

'Neither, just the same range as her normal talking voice, apart from a couple of high bits.'

'And the tempo?'

'Sort of like this…' I begin to sing the song, badly, and tap my hand on the table to beat out the tempo. Macca and Gerry nod.

'Slow, real slow. Okay, well I hope she's a better singer than you are otherwise she's going to get lynched. They're a rough mob that Sunday crowd and don't suffer fools gladly,' laughs Macca.

'Right boys, I'll see you Sunday, love ya.'

'Yeah, you too, Jimmy,' they reply.

##

Vee's nervous. She's already dressed and undressed into four different outfits.

'What about this?' she asks as she parades in front of me. She's wearing tight black leggings and a figure hugging, pink, long-sleeved polo neck shirt. On her feet are a black pair of Chelsea boots. Her hair is pulled into a tight ponytail.

'Perfect,' I reply. I look at the clock on the wall. The Hipnotikz will already be starting their second set at the Soldiers Arms.

'Are you sure? I feel a bit underdressed.'

'Vee, we are going for a couple of pints at a rough pub to watch my pals play a few songs. It's not the Queen Mother's garden party.' She pouts and looks at herself in the mirror.

'Hmm, I know, but I'm feeling really anxious. What will they think of me? I know how much your mates mean to you. What if they don't like me?' I stand up and hug her from behind as we stare at each other in the mirror.

'How could they not like you? What's not to like. You are the most beautiful girl on the planet. You're funny, educated, caring, understanding… oh, and sexy. Anyway, if they don't like you, so what. I'd give them all up for you in the blink of an eye.' She turns and kisses me slowly on the lips.

'Do you really mean that? You'd put me before your friends?'

'Yep. If they don't accept you, then it's just you and me girl. Right, come on let's go. Stop worrying. We'll have a good time, a few drinks, then back to our little love nest.' She smiles and lets out a deep sigh whilst grabbing my hand. She places it on her cheek and closes her eyes.

I'm sitting around a table with Vee and Marky by my side. We are having a ball. I introduced Vee to Marky and the boys earlier. I'm elated at their response. They love her. I was a bit afraid of Marky's reaction and clued him up beforehand not to start banging on about the rich and the working class struggle. So far he's stuck to his word. The Hipnotikz are coming to the end of their second set and there's a large boisterous crowd in the pub. I look across the table at Vee. I've never seen her so happy, it makes my heart soar. Marky stands up.

'Okay, my shout,' he says. 'Same again, Jim?' I nod. 'Vee, lager and black?'

'Ooh, yes please Marky.' I watch as he pushes his way through the crowd to the bar.

'So, what do you think?' I ask. She leans forward and kisses me on the lips.

'I love them all, especially Gerry, he's so kind and thoughtful. They have all been so welcoming to me. I was so nervous.'

'Well, you're in the gang now. You have four new mates who will back you to the hilt and fight your corner for you. Whenever you're in trouble, they'll always be there—don't forget that.' She begins to well up.

'I've only ever had one friend in my life. I can't find the words to describe what I feel, here...' she points at her heart.

The Hipnotikz finish their last song and make their way to our table. We laugh and joke for twenty minutes then Macca gives me a surreptitious wink and heads back to the stage. Shit! I'd forgotten all about the duet. Vee is completely oblivious to what is about to unfold and I regret ever suggesting it. I stand up to try and catch Macca to call the whole thing off but he is already back on stage with microphone in hand.

'Ahem, ladies and gentlemen, and Marky, can I have your attention please.' The busy hubbub of the pub quietens. 'I have a surprise for you all today. I am going to be performing a duet with a great new talent.' A few cheers go up accompanied by a smattering of applause. I am now suffering a mini panic attack. I look at Vee and want to wrap her in a blanket, pick her up and run from the pub with her slung over my shoulder. She looks at me, so excited and happy. 'I'd like you to put your hands together and give a big warm welcome to Victoria Harrywell!' She looks at me, mouth agape as the pub erupts into whoops and cheers. Gerry and Jonesy encourage her.

'Come on Vee, Jimmy here tells us you have the voice of a nightingale. Go for it girl.' She looks absolutely horrified.

'Jimmy! Why did you do that! I can't get up on stage, I just can't. What would I sing?'

'The only song you know.' I have to try and act brave for her. 'Come on Vee, do it for me. Just sing as you did in the shower, you'll knock them dead.' I pull her up and give her a gentle push towards the stage. She's bright red with embarrassment. 'Go on, you can do it.' She throws her head back and marches forward. The girl's got balls—I'll give her that much.

She climbs the three steps to the stage and picks up the microphone as the noise in the pub subsides. I suddenly hate myself and retreat to the far end of the room and lean back against a window. What if it all goes wrong? What if she gets stage fright and is left abandoned up there while the mob boo and jeer? Christ, what have I done?

Macca begins to slowly fingerpick at his acoustic guitar. Vee stands nervously at the edge of the stage looking down at the ground as the intro comes to an end.

'This is for Jimmy,' she whispers, softly. She opens her mouth and begins to sing. Even from the opening note, it starts. I put my hand over my mouth to try and quell the emotion. The quiet constant buzz of the pub begins to ebb as all eyes slowly turn to her. By the end of the first verse, there is not a murmur to be heard. I look around the room. It's as though the entire crowd is frozen in ice. Even the landlord and barmaids are fixated, standing rigid, glued to the spot, like statues. As she begins the second verse she lifts her head and opens her eyes. She's searching for her love but can't find me. I glance across at Marky. He's sniffing and dabbing his eyes. His shoulders heave and rise. Gerry puts an arm around him and pulls him into his side. I see women all around the room wiping tears from the corners of their eyes. Huge, ugly looking blokes stare sadly into their pints, lost in some private sorrow. Even four scary looking skinheads, sitting in the far corner, stare at my girl in mesmerised adoration.

She slowly scans the room, still searching. As she ends the second verse our eyes lock onto each other. She starts the final verse. A couple of tears roll down her cheek. They're highlighted in the spotlight as they slide along her chin, then drip to the floor. That's it, I can't hold back any longer. There's not a dry eye in the room apart from Macca, who is staring fiercely out into the crowd. People occasionally turn around to follow the arc of her gaze, to witness the object of her burning love. I'm not embarrassed or ashamed of my tears—I'm proud of them, I'm proud of her.

I feel her emotion, her pain, her sorrow. She has never known love and now she's addicted to it. The song ends and there is complete silence. No one moves. She stands there, on that lonely stage, vulnerable—a fragile, flawed human, who only ever wanted love.

One of the skinheads stands up and begins to slowly clap. It's like a rising wave, as one by one, people stand and join in. Within a few seconds, the pub is a tsunami of whistles and cheering. She descends the steps and glides toward me. The crowd parts to let her through as if she's royalty. She stands in front of me as the tears flood down her cheeks. She buries her head into my chest and I gently rub her head. Marky comes up and embraces us both. He's still sobbing like a child.

'You know your problem Marky? You're too emotional,' I laugh through my tears.

'I can't help it,' he sobs. 'I started thinking about my dad. I miss him so much.'

'I know you do mate,' I reply, as I pat him on the back. Macca's voice booms out from the speakers.

'Fuck me! How are we supposed to follow that? Sorry folks, but it's all downhill from here on in. In fact, you might as well all fuck off home right now!' Marky eventually releases us both.

'Right, I'll get the drinks in. I need a whisky after that,' he snivels. I grab Vee by the hand and pull her outside into the warm, fresh air. I kiss her softly on the lips.

'Jimmy, will it always be like this?' she sobs.

'Like what?'

'So much pain! So many tears!'

'I don't know Vee, I don't know.' I rub the wetness from her cheeks.

'Oh please, Jimmy, let it last forever.'

'It will last forever, Vee. There will never be anyone else—only you.'

She gazes at me with those big blue saucers, like an alien from another planet.

'Jimmy I will never let you go… *ever*!'

##

We amble slowly back towards our love nest, arm in arm. I'm feeling slightly drunk.

'So, have you enjoyed yourself?'

'Oh yes!' she exclaims. 'It's been wonderful. One of the best days of my life. I've never experienced anything like that before. That pub was full of so many rough looking people. Did you see those four skinheads with tattoos on their necks?'

'Yeah, they're harmless.'

'They don't look harmless. They scare me, and that huge fat one kept staring at me.'

'Marky knows them. Says they're on our side.'

'What does that mean?'

'I assume he meant they're not fascists—they're socialists.'

'The way you forewarned me about Marky, I assumed he'd be ranting on about politics and class warfare all day, but he never mentioned it once... well, not to me anyway.'

'I warned him to be on his best behaviour.'

'He loves you, they all do. Is he gay?'

'Who? Marky! Nah, you got to be joking, why would you ask that?'

'Oh, no reason. Has he a girlfriend?'

'No, he reckons he's too busy for girls. The glorious revolution can't unfold if you're busy fucking all day, can it.' She hits me on the arm.

'Jimmy! Don't be so crude. Is that what we do... fuck?'

'Sometimes we fuck, sometimes we make love.'

'I'm a lady, I make love.'

'You are a lady, but sometimes you're also very naughty. And when we get back to your flat I'm expecting you to be a super naughty lady.' She snorts derisively.

'How many pints have you had?'

'Just the six.'

'Well, I don't think little Tommy Tinker will be able to stand up straight.'

'I'm sure he'll rise to the occasion. He's never let me down yet. Anyway, he won't die wondering.' She giggles. 'So, are you going to take up Macca's offer?'

'No. I'm very flattered that he wants me to sing for thirty minutes each week, but I only know the one song.'

'Just build up gradually. Learn one new song a week until you've got thirty minutes of material. Macca will come around and help you work on the songs. The landlord wants you to do it. I think everyone in that pub today would want you to do it. You were a little star.'

'It was so embarrassing, everyone offering their gushing praise like that. I'm sure they were just being kind. Anyway, I can't do next week as I'm helping mummy out with one of her exhibitions. In fact, I think it's time you ran the gauntlet.'

'What do you mean?'

'It's time you met mummy. She's dying to meet you. You can come and help with the exhibition for the day.'

'What does that involve?'

'Loading paintings into a van. Driving to the exhibition rooms. Unloading the paintings and putting them on easels. Handing out sandwiches, tea and coffee when the invited guests arrive. Making idle chit-chat for a couple of hours, then packing up. The circles that mummy moves in are very eccentric, very bohemian. It's great entertainment. You'll love it.'

'Okay, it's a deal. What about your dad? Will he be there?'

'No, he'll be down in London.'

'You don't talk about your dad much, do you?'

'There's not much to say. He wasn't there for me as a little girl and he's not here for me as a woman. Anyway, I don't need him—I've got you.'

14: ART

It's Sunday morning and I'm standing on the street below Vee's flat giving her instructions.

'So, you can either hold on by gripping the back pannier—here,' I say pointing at the little metal grille that resides at the back of the scooter. 'Or, you can grip the bottom of the seat, or you can hold onto me around the waist.' She looks concerned. 'Shelley will look after you.'

'Shelley?' she asks, looking puzzled.

'Yes, that's her name.'

'Your Vespa is a she?'

'Of course she's a she. Look at her contours—perfection. She is womanhood incarnate.'

'You named your scooter after the romantic poet, Percy Shelley—oh well, I suppose that's sweet... I think.'

'Percy Shelley? Nah, never heard of him. I named it after Pete Shelley from the Buzzcocks.'

'The "what" cocks?' she yelps in astonishment.

'The Buzzcocks. One of the greatest punk rock bands ever. The lead singer is Pete Shelley.' She looks at me as though I'm deranged. 'Right, shake a leg and hop on.'

'Oh I don't know Jimmy. I've never been on a motorbike before, I'm scared.'

'Don't call it a motorbike. It's not a bike, it's a scooter, a Vespa. There's a difference. A scooter is a moving work of art. Look at that styling—it's a design classic that has stood the test of time.'

'Sorry.'

'I forgive you. Now, when we go around a corner you need to lean with the bike…'

'Hang on, you just told me off for calling it a bike.'

'You need to lean with the scooter. When we go around a right handed corner the scooter will lean to the right. You also need to lean to the right. You will probably feel the urge to lean the other way—don't! Otherwise, you'll have us both off.'

'Oh Jimmy, you're scaring me. Won't I fall off if I lean over?'

'You'll only fall off if you don't lean over. Now, make sure you hold on tight any time we set off because the acceleration will cause you to lurch backwards. Here's your helmet.' I pass her the helmet and she goes to put it on her head. 'No, no. You can't wear a helmet with a ponytail. You'll need to let your hair down.'

'But my hair will be a mess.'

'You can redo it at your mam's place.' She has a worried frown on her face as she removes her bob, then shakes her hair loose. I help her on with the helmet and fasten the straps firmly. I kiss her on the tip of her nose. 'You'll be fine. It's actually great fun.'

'If you say so. Promise you won't go fast?'

'I promise.' I jump on the seat and rock the scooter off its stand and kick-start the engine into life. 'Right, jump on!' I shout. She tentatively straddles the seat and places her arms around my midriff in a vice-like grip. It feels nice. 'Ready?'

'I suppose so. Please don't go fast.'

I've taken the scenic route and we are about halfway to Harrogate on a long stretch of open country road. I ease the scooter down through the gears and come to a stop.

'Why are you stopping?' Vee calls out.

'To see how you're faring?' I shout over my shoulder.

'I'm starting to relax a little.'

'Good. Enjoying it?'

'Not really, apart from holding onto you, which I like.'

'Okay, hold on tight because I'm going to burn some rubber.'

'Jimmy, I don't know what that means but I don't like the sound of it.' I rev the engine, drop it into first and rapidly release the clutch. The scooter takes off at lightning speed. Vee lets out a piercing scream as I race through the gears until the scooter reaches its maximum speed. I glance at the speedo—70 mph. We are flying along and I begin to laugh like a man possessed. It is a beautiful warm summer's day, the sky is blue and we're surrounded by a magnificent green vista. There's no better feeling in the world—this is freedom! Vee has gone extremely quiet and I slow the scooter down and turn off the engine. She leaps from the bike and begins beating me on the chest.

'You bastard! You beast, how could you!'

'What's wrong? Didn't you enjoy that?' I laugh.

'No, I bloody well didn't enjoy it. What would have happened had we fallen off?'

'We are on the open road, no traffic, how are we going to fall off? Vee, you need to embrace it, don't be scared by it. You are perfectly safe.' Her cheeks are enflamed and her sparkling blue eyes spit fire.

'I'm not getting back on unless you promise not to go fast,' she pouts, stamping her foot on the road.

'It's a long walk back to Leeds from here,' I tease. I start the Vespa and begin to drive off.

'Jimmy, come back here right now!' she screams. I accelerate away at speed and soon round a bend and lose sight of her. I slow down then stop and sit there for a few seconds. I restart the Vespa, turn around and head back. She's sitting on the side of the road, her helmet is laying on the grass verge. I pull up at the side of her and put on my best cockney accent.

'Awright sweetheart, you looking for a ride? Coz if you are, I can give you a ride of a lifetime, if you catch my drift, darling.' She tries hard not to smile but eventually she cracks and grins, even though it's swathed in annoyance. She puts her helmet back on and gets on the scooter in silence.

'Ooh not the silent treatment, I can't bear it.'

'I will not be speaking to you for the rest of my life. Please proceed to Harrogate at an orderly speed. If you go too fast I will lodge a formal complaint with the police. Now, please drive on James.'

We navigate through the busy streets of Harrogate and as we emerge on the other side I pull over.

'Vee, are you still sulking with me?'

'I don't sulk, I just withdraw my participation from our relationship.'

'Well, do you think you could re-participate in the relationship because you are going to have to give me directions from here?'

'Very well, but don't think I've forgiven you. Keep going straight ahead.' I drive on for another couple of miles and the rolling hills and greenery return. It is the most beautiful countryside and I am enthralled with the views and scents of summer. Vee taps me on the shoulder and points out a junction to take.

'Next left.' The scooter glides along as we navigate down a steep winding hill. We reach the bottom and Vee taps me on the shoulder.

'Stop,' she commands. I pull the scooter over to the side of the road and kill the engine. She points to her right. In the distance is what looks like an old castle. I can see a flagpole and the blue, red and white of a Union Jack fluttering in the breeze.

'What?' I say.

'That's it,' she replies, nonchalantly.

'That's what?' I ask.

'That's home.' I pull the scooter onto its stand, leap to the ground and remove my helmet. I'm looking but I don't see any houses. There's the castle, lots of farm buildings, fields, a lake and wooded hills but definitely no house.

'Where? I can't see it? Is it near that castle? Point it out to me,' I say.

'It *is* the castle,' she replies with an impish grin.

'What! You live in a fucking castle?'

'Yes, and no need to swear,' she smiles. 'Are you impressed?'

'Impressed! I am fucking astounded! Are you winding me up Vee?' She shakes her head. I knew she was from a wealthy background and I'd envisaged a large detached farmhouse or a plush modern home on maybe a couple of acres. But this was something else. People who owned castles weren't just rich—they were seriously fucking astronomically wealthy! I now have butterflies in my stomach and feel a tad intimidated. What am I doing here? I think of what the lads would say if they could see me now. I know what Marky would say, he'd go off on a rant.

'Well, come on. Let's go meet mummy.'

163

I pull up outside an imposing gated entrance and look at the bronze sign that is affixed to a large stone wall. "Ridley Castle Built In 1309". This is crazy. We slowly roll up a ridiculously long gravel driveway and I park up outside the castle. Vee jumps from the scooter and bounds up a series of stone steps to a set of giant double doors.

'Come on slowcoach,' she shouts. She's excited. I remove my helmet and place it on the seat of the scooter. We enter into a hallway which is double the size of the whole house I share with Sofe. I am lost for words. Vee removes her helmet and places it on a large side table.

'Mummy!' she yells out. 'We're here!' I follow behind looking at giant portraits of crusty old generals and men in wigs. Swords, shields and lances adorn the walls. Giant crystal chandeliers dangle from the ceiling high, high above. 'She's probably in the studio out the back,' she says.

'Oh Lady Victoria, I thought I heard your voice.' An older woman of, perhaps, early sixties emerges from nowhere. She is wearing a light blue dress with a white pinafore over it.

'Mrs Beaton, I'd like to introduce you to James, Jimmy.'

'Pleased to meet you, Master James.' She shakes my hand warmly and smiles. Master James! This is not of my world!

'Jimmy, Mrs Beaton is our cook but more than that, she is our friend.' Mrs Beaton blushes. 'How long have you been with us now?' Vee asks. Mrs Beaton wipes her hands on her pinny.

'Well, let me think. I started here when I was fourteen and I turn sixty-two next month, so how long is that?'

'That's forty-eight years,' Vee replies beaming at her. 'We must hold a big celebration when you reach fifty years.'

'Oh, I don't want a fuss made.'

'Nonsense,' replies Vee. 'Is mummy around?'

164

'She's just nipped into town, says she'll be back by eleven. Will you and Master James be staying the night?'

'No, I'm afraid not. We have to head back to Leeds later today.'

'Oh very well Miss. I'll have some sandwiches waiting for you once you're back from the exhibition.'

'Thank you Mrs Beaton, you are a twenty-four-carat diamond.' Mrs Beaton blushes again.

'Be off with you,' she replies. She turns and walks back down a long corridor then disappears through a swing door, into what I can only assume, is the kitchen.

'Right, come on Jimmy, I'll give you a guided tour.'

##

Vee gives me a whirlwind tour of the building. Initially, I try to keep count of the number of rooms and bedrooms but give up. Portraits hang from every wall as suits of armour stand menacingly on guard along corridors that stretch on forever. She has become animated, excited. Her knowledge is astounding. She reels off the names of Kings, Queens, Lords and Barons. She recounts tales of treason, plot and subterfuge. As we pass tables and chairs and stride beneath crystal chandeliers, she shouts out who they were made by and when. The names Chippendale, Thomire and Samuel Bennett are bandied about as though I know who they are. She occasionally points at some severe looking man in a painting, who is invariably dressed in military gear from a bygone era and gives me his resume.

'That's Lord Allenby, he was special counsel to King Henry VIII. He was part of a conspiracy to oust the king.'

'What happened to him?' I ask, intrigued. She laughs at me.

'What do you think happened? He lost his head of course—on the chopping block. King Henry didn't much care for traitors.' There's a library, giant tables, mammoth fireplaces, four-poster beds, exotic looking vases, Turkish rugs, portrait after portrait of grumpy looking men and hundreds of leaded windows. We head back down a sweeping staircase that belongs in a Hollywood movie, then along yet another corridor.

'Come on, I'll show you the grounds,' she suggests. I notice a large sign above two giant oak doors. It reads "The Great Hall."

'Can we have a look in here?' I ask. She stares at me blankly and pauses for a moment.

'Very well, but there's not much to see,' she replies. She opens one door slightly, just enough for me to poke my head through and take a peep inside.

'Jeez! They weren't joking when they called it the Great Hall.' The hall must be one hundred foot long and at least forty feet wide. There's the biggest table I have ever witnessed standing in the middle. The walls are adorned by more paintings and portraits. At the far end is an almighty fireplace. It's framed by massive hunks of sandy stone. The mantelpiece is at least six feet off the ground. Above this hangs the largest portrait of all. A young, handsome man in what looks like an RAF uniform. He's wearing the thinnest of smiles, in fact, I'm not even sure it is a smile. The eyes are the most brilliant cobalt blue and they bore into me. I realise it must be Vee's father. 'Is that your old man?' I ask as I nod towards the far wall. She pulls a puzzled expression.

'My old man?'

'Yeah, your dad?'

'Oh yes. That's father. Come on, let's go outside,' she replies quickly shutting the door behind her. We walk into another room then exit via some French doors into a beautiful courtyard.

'You said your dad was a Civil Servant,' I say.

'No. I said he was something in the government, a bit like a civil servant. Why?'

'Well, this is all very grand for a government worker.' She laughs.

'Oh I see. No, the castle and the estate come from mummy's side of the family. As she was the only child it was all passed to her. Of course, if there had been a male heir it would have all gone to him.'

'Do people still do that shit? Pass everything on to the firstborn male?' She looks at me in a matronly way.

'Oh yes! I know, it's ridiculous in this day and age. It will be different when I'm in charge.' We walk on heading towards a lake.

'When you're in charge?' I ask, not fully understanding.

'Yes, I will inherit all this one day. The castle, the farms, the estates and everything else.' She stands and surveys the family empire. 'Yes, one day all this will be ours,' she says with a certain amount of satisfaction.

'Ours?' I quiz.

'Yes, yours and mine. And we will do it differently. The castle will be passed on to whichever of our brood has shown the most interest in it. It will be based on merit, not gender or pecking order.' Whoa! I feel a tingle down my spine. At first, I think it's excitement but it's not—it's fear. I wasn't born to live in a castle! And what's this about a brood? I'm having a nice sedate walk through life and she's in the Olympic 100m finals racing towards the finishing line. 'Jimmy, Jimmy, what's wrong?'

'Wrong, me, wrong, nothing's wrong.'

'Oh good. For a moment there I thought you were about to have some sort of seizure.' I stare out at the lake that stretches on forever.

'And over there is mummy's studio.' She points at a large glass lined building behind the courtyard.

We walk past fountains then over a small stream that is spanned by a small iron bridge. We come to a giant oak that stands proud not far from the lake. I stare up at its magnificence. In its heart, it cradles a giant house. This was not knocked together by some handyman on a lazy weekend. This is serious stuff—it's on a par with the treehouse from The Swiss Family Robinson. Vee is still gabbling away at a rate of knots. She suddenly stops.

'Jimmy are you sure you're all right? You've barely uttered a word for thirty minutes.'

'I'm just feeling a little... overawed that's all.' She looks worried and rests one hand on my shoulder.

'This doesn't change anything—does it?' I rest my hand on top of hers.

'Well, I don't know...' She now looks extremely perturbed and places her other hand, delicately, on my cheek.

'Oh please no! Don't let it change anything between us. It's all just trappings and history.' I kiss her tenderly on the lips.

'No, it doesn't change anything. The only thing that matters is you and me.' She instantly brightens. 'Hey, let's go up the treehouse,' I suggest. She giggles.

'I cannot tell you how much this treehouse meant to me when I was growing up. I must have spent thousands of hours up there.'

A set of round wooden posts, fixed horizontally to two huge beams, serves as a stairway up to the arboreal abode.

'Ladies first,' I say holding out my arm.

'Well thank you, Master James.' She's wearing a tight red dress that ends high above the knee. On her feet are a pair of red ballet shoes. She begins to climb the wooden steps which are at quite a steep angle. Well, I'm a man and there's only one thing to do in these situations. I stare up her skirt and marvel at her buttocks and the tiny red G-string that is barely concealing anything.

'No finer sight is there anywhere on this planet,' I drawl. She stops climbing and looks down at me.

'Jimmy! Stop it you pervert. That's why you let me go first! You're a dirty old man.'

The treehouse is huge and she tells me how she used to bring all her dolls up here then line them up at one side of the room.

'I would play teacher and they would be my pupils,' she explains. 'If any of them were naughty, I'd put them over my lap and spank their bottoms. If they were naughty again, then I'd pick them up and throw them out of the window.'

'Jesus! What a psycho!'

'I'd be overcome with guilt and would rush down the steps, pick them up and hug them all. One day the whole class got thrown out of the window because they wouldn't stop chatting as I was trying to teach them French.'

'Nice, corporal punishment followed by infanticide. A sweet child were you?'

She is looking radiant and a familiar longing begins to take over. I walk up behind her.

'Hey Vee?' She stops talking and looks at me.

'Yes Jimmy, what is it?' I don't say anything—just stare into her shining eyes. 'What?' she asks again. Finally, she twigs. 'Oh no! Definitely not. I'm telling you Jimmy, that is not going to happen, most definitely, no! Especially here in this treehouse.'

'Why not?'

'Because… because it's sick for one thing. This is where I used to play as a little girl. It would taint my memories.'

'Well, you'd have a new memory, wouldn't you?'

'No! No! No! Plus, mummy could be home at any moment.'

'She's not going to come up here though, is she?' I kiss her and she tries to pull away. My lips drop to her neck and I slip my hand under her dress and part her G-string.

'Oh Jimmy, why do you do this to me. It's not fair.' She suddenly releases her emotion and pushes me hard against the bark of the tree and begins to feverishly tug at the buckle on my belt.

'On all fours,' I whisper in her ear.

##

She's lying in my arms as I stroke the back of her head.

'I could stay here forever. It's so peaceful,' she says. 'Just the sound of the breeze in the trees, the birds and the ducks on the lake.'

'It is tranquil. This is a special place. I can feel it. It's like the ghost of your childhood haunts it.'

'Victoria! I'm back!' A refined voice echoes out from far below.

'Damn! It's mummy!' We both crawl on all fours to the entrance and peek out over a balcony. A woman walks briskly, heading towards the studio in the distance. 'Quick, where's my G-string?'

'I don't know,' I reply, in all honesty.

'You were the one who pulled it off, you must know where you put it?' Vee is now busy scrambling about on the floor looking for her underwear.

'I just threw it over there,' I said pointing towards the far end of the treehouse.

'Did you see where it landed?'

'No. I was too busy staring at a far more interesting sight.' She slaps me on the arm.

'Oh no,' she whispers sadly as she sticks her head over the balcony and looks down. 'It's on the ground at the bottom of the tree. Come on quick! Let's get down!' We both get up off our knees and I quickly dart in front of her to make my exit down the steps first. She follows behind. Halfway down I stop and look up.

'My God!' I exclaim. 'The sight on the way up was pretty good, but the sight on the way down is even better!'

'Jimmy stop it! You don't know how to behave! Go, go, go! Quickly, keep moving.'

We stride across a manicured lawn and enter the studio. Paintings and canvases are strewn about everywhere and there's a comforting smell of oil paint. Her mother is at the far end of the room. She seems to be dusting down a painting with a household paintbrush. The door clangs shut behind us. Her mother doesn't turn around but shouts out, 'Ah! Victoria, we need to get a move on. I'm running late.' We walk up behind her.

'Mummy, I'd like to introduce you to James—and Jimmy, I'd like you to meet mummy,' she says, with a look of utmost pride. Her mother still has her back to us. She puts the paintbrush down on the shelf of the easel and removes a pair of spectacles.

'Ah! Of course, I forgot you were bringing James with you.' I hold out my arm ready to shake her hand.

'Now James, you must call me Vivienne,' she states warmly, as she spins around to face me. Oh no!

15: POWER

A split second of awkwardness hangs in the air as we both stare at each other. I need to think fast. Vee is not stupid and she immediately detects something is not quite right.

'Have you two met before?' she asks with a puzzled look.

'No, no,' I laugh, as I shake Vivienne's hand. 'But I do recognize your mother's face from somewhere.' Vee relaxes and grins at me.

'Oh, mummy's always in and out of the paper. If it's not her paintings then it's her charitable work. You've probably seen her in the Standard.'

'Yes, yes, that's where I think I've seen her.' I regain my composure. 'How very pleasant to meet you Vivienne.' I now realise what I saw on the canal that day. This could be Vee in thirty years' time. The only difference is the colour of their eyes.

'Likewise James. I've heard all about you. Victoria is on the phone nearly every day gushing about you.' Vee blushes.

'Oh mummy, that's not true. You do over-exaggerate,' she retaliates.

'It is true James. The girl is besotted with you.'

'Mummy! Please!'

'She didn't tell me you were so handsome though.' Now I blush. Vivienne pulls a set of keys from a pocket on her smock and hands them to Vee.

'Victoria, be a darling and bring the van around. We need to start loading these paintings.'

'Of course mummy.' Vee takes the keys and walks quickly out of the room. We both stand at the window and watch her as she skips up a grass embankment, crosses the courtyard, passes a giant fountain and disappears through a set of French doors into the castle.

'I don't think I've ever seen her so happy, not since she was a very little girl anyway. I take it she doesn't know?'

'No. Only three people know and that's the way it will stay as far as I'm concerned.' I mentally count up how many people I've told about the porno shoot. Marky, Macca, Jonesy, Gerry, Sofe, Dave Dee, half the newsroom, Jenny, Amy— oh, and the postman.

'Good, good. I must say, I was very impressed with your work. Garth sings your praises to anyone who will listen.'

'Thank you. I had good subjects to work with.' I can't believe we're both standing here, mutually congratulating each other on what was, after all, a fuck-a-thon.

'Victoria tells me that you are putting together a portfolio of portraits and you'd like to exhibit one day.'

'Yes that's right. I love capturing the human face. I have about twenty particularly good portraits at the moment.' She turns and walks back to her easel.

'Well, maybe that's something we could work on together. I have plenty of contacts. Just let me know when you are ready.'

'Thanks Vivienne.'

'Please call me Viv.'

'And you can call me Jimmy.' She laughs.

'Okay Jimmy. Right—to work!' She puts her half-moon spectacles back on and begins barking out orders. 'Those blankets over there,' she says, pointing at a table, 'each painting must be wrapped with one of them and tied loosely with a piece of twine, top and bottom. The paintings need to be carried out and loaded into the back of the van. Aha! Here's Victoria now!' I look out of the window and see Vee emerge from a battered old white transit van. 'Now Jimmy, pay attention. There's a wooden framework set up in the back of the van and each painting fits into a slot. They need to be stacked in the correct order. On arrival at the exhibition rooms, you need to unload them in reverse order, remove their blankets and place them on easels in the rooms. Can you manage that?'

'Yep, piece of cake.'

'Good. Oh, don't tie the twine too tightly. Right, come on my boy, jump to it. One last thing...' She removes her glasses and fixes me with a purposeful stare. 'The photos you took—were they before you met Victoria or after?' I find the question odd and how I answer could affect our relationship, so I lie.

'Before,' I reply. It must have been the answer she was hoping to hear because she smiles and says,

'Good, good.'

The exhibition rooms are a ten mile drive from Ridley Castle situated in a quiet little village. The front of the building is a functioning tea room but around the back is a large modern space that houses the paintings. At least sixty people are milling about and Vee and Viv are busy talking to the guests. They both seem to know everybody. It's an odd crowd, very arty-farty and bohemian but there's a good vibe and I'm enjoying myself. There's one particular painting that I keep returning to. It has me fascinated and I'm standing in front of it trying to figure out what the fuck it means.

'Ah! James my boy, so our paths cross again.' I recognise the voice and turn around and shake hands with Garth Peacock.

'Garth, good to see you. Hope you are keeping well?'

'Never better, my boy. I'm fighting fit. I feel like I have a fire coursing through my veins. How are you getting along with the Jackson Pollock biography?'

'I've nearly finished it. It's been really interesting.'

'Good, good. Well, just drop the book back whenever you're next in Ripon. If I'm home we can have a good old chat about Pollock over a cup of coffee.'

'Great, I'd like that.' He drops his head and pulls a serious expression. He grabs me gently by the elbow and leads me to one side. He moves his head in close.

'Vivienne has explained all. I erm… ahem, take it you have shown discretion? This must never come out,' he whispers. I smile at him.

'Garth, I will take it to my grave—I swear.' His buoyant personality returns and he slaps me on the back.

'Good boy, good boy, that's the ticket. I have passed your details on to a couple of my more exotic friends and you may be receiving a call from them.' I didn't really want to hear this but I act pleased. He thinks he's doing me a favour.

'Thanks Garth.' I turn and look at the painting again. 'Garth, this painting has me puzzled.' Garth puts his spectacles on and stares at the canvas.

'What puzzles you James?'

'None of the paintings have titles so I'm not sure what I'm looking at.'

'Aha! Yes, that's one of Vivienne's little ploys. She believes that titles can influence what the viewer sees. She wants them to look at her artwork with a completely open mind, with no preconceptions. Tell me what you see.' I stand up close to the painting and examine it again.

'These different hues of yellow with flecks of white remind me of life, new life, of a summer's day, like today. It is joyous and uplifting. That swish of green on the left shouts out hope. Yet… those three brown daubs on the right, with an almost translucent cream coloured edge, they bamboozle me. They don't seem to

175

fit in with the rest of the painting. There's something sinister… no not sinister… what am I trying to say?' I tail off.

'Keep going my boy, I'm fascinated by what you see.'

'It's like when life is going perfectly, you can't put a foot wrong and you succeed at everything you turn your hand to. You think to yourself, yes, this is how it's always going to be. Then you wake up one day and it all turns to shit. Life has a way of doing that. It doesn't like you to get too cocky, so it throws a little misery your way to keep you in check.' Garth looks deep in thought.

'Hmm…' he murmurs. I take five good paces back.

'Yet when I look at it from here, I see something completely different. I see a white plate with scrambled eggs on it, a slice of avocado and three rashers of bacon.' Garth guffaws and slaps me on the shoulder

'Oh my boy, you have a wicked sense of humour!' he cackles. I was being serious. He throws a furtive look on his shoulder then moves in closer. 'I know a little secret of Vivienne's. She scribbles the title on the back of the canvas,' he whispers as though it's classified information. He makes his way to the back of the easel and his head disappears for a moment. I then hear him chuckling.

'What? What is it?' I ask. He walks back to me sporting a large grin.

'It simply says, "Eggs". Looks like you were on the money with your second assessment.'

The exhibition is winding down and people are beginning to leave. I've not had a chance to speak with Vee for over two hours and ridiculous as it may sound, I'm missing her. Eventually, I get her attention.

'So, have you enjoyed it?' she asks.

'Yes, it's been great. You were right about the crowd though.'

'Yes, eccentric but interesting.'

'Oh yes, interesting all right. Look at that mad fucker over there,' I say pointing at a man staring intently at a painting. He's wearing a black velvet trilby, a black cape, sports a monocle over his left eye and is holding a silver topped cane.

His goatee beard is fashioned into a long twist that dangles way below his chin. He suddenly exclaims,

'Sublime!' then moves on to the next painting. Vee laughs.

'That's the Hungarian.'

'What's his name?'

'I don't know. Everyone just calls him the Hungarian.'

'I bet he's not from Hungary. He's probably a butcher from Rotherham who likes to dress up on the weekend as a mad beat poet.' I stare at Vee. I want her again. 'You forgot to pick up your G-string up from the bottom of the tree.' She rolls her eyes.

'I know. I hope the gardeners don't come across it.'

'That means you're standing next to me without any knickers on.' She smiles provocatively.

'Hmm, fancy that.'

'I do fancy that.'

'How does that make you feel to think of me with no panties on? Does it excite you?'

'Excite me? It's driving me insane!' She lifts my hand up, grabs one of my fingers, sticks it in her mouth and begins sucking on it. Her tongue gently tickles the end. I genuinely believe she is evil. She pulls my digit from her mouth.

'Aw poor baby, and it will be hours and hours before we're back at the flat.'

'Fuck that for a game of bow and arrows. I can't wait that long.'

'You don't have any choice in the matter,' she replies coyly. 'Now be a good boy and start loading the van up.' I watch as she walks to the far end of the room and engages in conversation with an elderly woman. Tommy's knocking on the door hoping to get out—stupid naive fool that he is.

##

I've just removed the last of the paintings from the van and placed it back on its easel in Viv's studio. Vee and her mother are busy removing the blankets and neatly folding them. I look out of the window and glance at the long curved driveway that leads to the castle. Three cars are slowly snaking through the gated entrance. The first and last are four wheel drives, the middle one looks like something swish, possibly a Jaguar.

'Eh up!' I shout, 'Looks like you have visitors.' Vee immediately stops what she is doing and almost runs towards me and stares out of the window. Her expression is first one of curiosity until she spots the cars. I now witness an expression that I've never seen on her face before—fear!

'Mummy, mummy!' she exclaims, 'It's daddy. You said he was away for the weekend!' Now Viv comes running over, wearing a similar look of horror on her face.

'He was supposed to be spending the weekend on Sir Duncan's country estate. Oh dear. Quick, we better meet him at the front door.' Both women are acting like a pair of cats on a hot tin roof.

'Vee, what's the matter?' She looks at me in a state of horror.

'Nothing, nothing! Come on, quick.' Viv is already bounding up the embankment and making her way across the courtyard to the French doors. Vee grabs me by the arm and almost drags me along behind.

'Do you want me to move the van?' I ask as we pass the battered transit.

'No! Yes, yes, move the van.' I make my way to the van and she runs after me and grabs me by the arm again. 'No, no. Come on, quickly.'

'Make your bloody mind up!' We make our way through the castle, along a corridor and to the entrance hall.

Viv is standing on the stone steps outside. Vee stands slightly behind her and I remain in the hallway, to the side of the open door. I watch as two black Range Rovers with dark tinted windows pull up neatly on the gravel. The Jaguar parks up alongside. Two men jump out of the first Range Rover and another two out of the second. They are all solidly built, with muscular frames and short hair. Each has a walky-talky strapped to their lapel. One man departs along the perimeter of the house to the left, another in the opposite direction, to the right. The other two bound up the steps. When they pass Viv, they slow slightly, nod and say, 'Ma'am.' Viv nods back. They pass Vee and do the same.

'Ma'am.' Vee nods back. They stop, stare at me, then look back at Viv. She tilts her head sharply upwards and the men continue. I watch as they both march briskly down the corridor. One hangs a right and disappears from view, but I hear his footsteps climbing the sweeping staircase.

A chauffeur emerges from the Jaguar. He carefully puts his hat on then opens the passenger door. A tall man emerges from the car followed by a tiny little dog. I instantly recognise him. The chauffeur walks around to the other side of the car and repeats the procedure. A much older gentleman emerges, blinking in the sunlight. He looks like a de-shelled turtle and I again, instantly recognise him. Both men climb the steps.

'I wasn't expecting you dear,' says Viv to her husband. He bends down and kisses her on both cheeks.

'I'm sorry Vivienne, but we had to relocate from Sir Duncan's estate as renovations are happening and we couldn't think straight for the damned noise.' The turtle climbs the steps and bows in front of Viv, then takes her hand and kisses the back of it.

'Vivienne, looking radiant as ever.'

'Sir Duncan, what an unexpected but pleasant surprise,' she smiles politely.

'I'm sorry for the short notice Vivienne, but I forgot about the blasted renovations.'

'Not a problem Sir Duncan. It's always a pleasure to see you. How are Marjory and the boys?'

'Oh Marjory is keeping busy as usual and she's in fine health. Lochlan is in the States heading up one of my companies and doing a fine job. As for Maxwell, I

179

like to keep him closer to home, he needs a little longer in the oven. He's the editor of the Gazette in London.' Viv laughs, a sort of false, hearty laugh. Vee's father notices my scooter.

'Vivienne, can you please tell the gardener not to leave his scooter at the front of the house, it's not a damned supermarket car park!' He moves towards his daughter and kisses her on both cheeks then rests his hands on her shoulders.

'Father,' she replies. She is rigid and looks decidedly uncomfortable.

'Ah Victoria, my darling. How have you been keeping? I hardly see you these days.'

'Fine,' she replies curtly. The turtle now proceeds towards Vee.

'Good Lord, is this little Victoria?'

'Sir Duncan,' she replies.

'My word! It's years since I last set eyes on you. Well, well, how the little bud has blossomed into full womanhood!' he exclaims. I find something slightly disturbing about his sentence.

'Vivienne, she has your stunning beauty, such radiance, such elegance and poise. Yet, she has her father's steely blue eyes.' He bows in front of her and she holds the back of her hand out for him. He takes it and kisses it, lingering a little longer than he should. 'The last time I saw you, you were about fourteen years old. You were having a devil of a row with your father. You wanted a new pony but your father had put his foot down and said, no,' he chuckles. 'Did you end up getting the pony?'

'Yes,' is her one word answer.

'Good for you girl, that's the spirit. If you can beat your father you can beat anyone. Do you still have the horse?' he smiles at her.

'No. I shot him. He broke a leg a few weeks after I got him.' Jeez! Who is this girl? I make a mental note to avoid ever breaking a leg. Sir Duncan looks taken aback and coughs nervously.

'You mean you got the vet to shoot him?'

'No,' she replies. Vee's father now notices me, just inside the entrance.

'Ah! And who do we have here skulking in the shadows?' I'm not skulking—I wouldn't know how to skulk.

'Oh that's James—he's just a boyfriend,' says Vee. Ouch, that hurt! There's a twelve inch dagger right between my shoulder blades!

'Victoria, we didn't spend all that money sending you to finishing school for you to forget your manners. Introductions please.' Vee moves towards me but does not make eye contact.

'Father, this is James, James, this is father.' Her father looks a tad annoyed.

'Full introductions please, if you don't mind Victoria.' She pouts.

'Father, this is James Hooper, James, this is Lord Jeremy Halliwell.' The Lord holds his arm out and we shake hands. I stare deep into his eyes. It's true, his eyes are as dazzlingly blue as Vee's. But, where her eyes are warm and loving, his are like a shark's—dead. He does the power grip thing during the handshake then places his other hand over the top of mine just for good measure. He's trying to let me know who's the boss around here.

'Very pleased to meet you James.'

'Likewise Jeremy.'

'So James what do you do for a living?'

'I'm a freelance photographer.'

'Excellent! Do you work for the newspapers?'

'I do a bit of work for the Standard,' I reply as he finally releases my hand.

'Excellent, excellent! Did you hear that Sir Duncan? Young James here does work for the Standard. Fine newspaper. Is old Bulldog still bullying everyone?'

'Not really. He's a decent sort of bloke. You know where you stand with him.' He laughs at this.

'Yes, a word of warning James, do not get on the wrong side of old Bulldog, otherwise you'll regret it. I've locked horns with him many times over the years, but he is a thoroughly decent chap. So, what other types of work do you do?'

'Oh you know, family portraits, weddings, bar mitzvahs, the odd circumcision here and there.' Okay, maybe not my greatest ever line. He stares at me, unblinking for a few painful seconds. A wry smile slowly spreads across his thin dry lips, at least I think it's a smile. He slaps me on the shoulder.

'Haha! I like a man with a sense of humour.' His shaggy, scraggy, runt of a dog is now growling at me, as though offended by my joke, which to be honest with you, I don't blame her.

'Molly, Molly, stop that, don't be rude!' He picks up the tiny dog and lovingly caresses her in his arms, then kisses the damned mutt on the snout. 'Right, well I'd love to stay and chat James, but I and Sir Duncan have some rather important issues to discuss. Come, come, Sir Duncan. By the way James, I must get you to come and do a family portrait of the Halliwell's. It's been years since the last one.' He heads off down the corridor. The turtle passes me by, eyeing me suspiciously.

'Oh Victoria,' the old turtle calls out, 'you really must come down to London at some point and we'll have dinner together. We could get together with Maxwell. He's still a free agent you know, but he is looking for a wife.' Yeah, thanks pal, don't worry about me—I'm just the boyfriend! I'll carry the fucking bags—shall I? He paddles off behind Lord Halliwell.

'Oh Vivienne,' Lord Halliwell barks back at his wife, 'could you get Mrs Beaton to make us a round of sandwiches and a pot of strong black coffee. We'll be in the Great Hall. Oh and Vivienne, Sir Duncan will be staying the night so we will need something substantial for dinner. No red meat, maybe pheasant.' I hear the sound of their footsteps disappear down the corridor, then the creak of a door and a loud bang. Vivienne walks past me, says nothing, but rolls her eyes heavenward. There's just me and Vee left alone in the entrance hall. She stares down at the floor. Her hands are clasped together as her thumbs continually roll around each other.

'That was fun,' I say. 'Hmm, well... where do I begin? First of all, do you think you could help me?' She lifts her head slightly and gives me an ashamed look.

'With what?' she asks sullenly.

'I can't reach this dagger between my shoulder blades, could you remove it for me? You may need it later for a disembowelment or target practice.'

'You're not funny,' she mumbles, returning her gaze to the floor.

'I know we haven't known each other for long, and I can see how the little things could slip your mind. I mean, Sir Duncan Campbell Menzies, let's start with him. The biggest media mogul in the country, some say the world! Owner of countless newspapers, radio and TV stations. The rabid, right-wing attack dog of the Conservative Party. An old family friend—and yet you've never mentioned him once.'

'Why would I. He means nothing to me,' she replies sulkily, still staring stoically at the floor and twisting her thumbs around and around each other.

'Then we have daddy dearest. Lord Jeremy Halliwell, Home Secretary for the United Kingdom. The second most powerful person in the land, behind our glorious Iron Lady. The pin-up boy of the Tory right. Touted as the next Prime Minister of this sceptered isle. Not sure how that one passed you by.

Harrywell—Halliwell... a slight slip of the tongue while choking on a baked bean. Ooh, that was good, very good. Quite deft in fact. And last, but by no means least—"just a boyfriend". Yes, just a boyfriend like a stray mongrel lurking around your feet, soon to be taken to the vet and put out of its misery, or maybe you could do it yourself. That hurt, that cut me deep. And yet you stand there and say nothing.' She suddenly pulls her arms rigid to her sides, fists clenched tight. She stamps her foot down hard and glares at me. There is a fire in her eyes.

'I didn't tell you who my father was because I thought it would scare you off. I knew I would have to tell you at some point but I wanted to wait until I was certain you really loved me, until our relationships was safe and secure. As for Sir Duncan, he makes my skin crawl and I don't care about him at all or about his stupid fucking sons. As for "just a boyfriend," of course I didn't mean it. You know how deeply I feel about you. I said it to put daddy off the scent. I've told you

183

before that he is a raging snob. If I had told him how I really feel about you, he would try and interfere and break us up.' She's enflamed with passion, her cheeks a deep rouge.

'Why? Why would a father try and break up a relationship where it is quite obvious how much the boy loves the girl? That just doesn't make sense.'

'I've told you, he's a snob, and straight away you opened your mouth he would have...' she trails off.

'Go on, say it, he would have...' There's an awkward silence for a few seconds.

'Because he would have known where you come from. He would have known your background.'

'You mean he would have known I was one of those dreadful working class types. Those uncouth, unwashed, wastrels, who dare to ask for pay rises and sick leave...they should know their station in life, good for nothing layabouts.'

'Yes, that's exactly what he would have thought!'

'Instead, he now thinks I'm a bit of rough that his daughter is toying with. I'll be cast aside once she's had her fun. I'm no threat to his dynasty.'

'Yes!' She softens then melts, rushes towards me and embraces me. 'Oh Jimmy, I'm so sorry. I only did it because I was afraid. I can't let anyone threaten our love, I just can't. I've hurt you and it breaks my heart. I'll never be able to forgive myself and now I'm terrified I'll lose you.' She begins to sniffle into my shoulder.

I can't go on with the pretence any longer. I'm not really bothered about the situation, about the artifice, the withholding of truths or who her father is. I just wanted to torment her a little and now I feel bad. I pull her head up and smile at her.

'Hey Vee, it's you and me against the world girl. Nothing can separate us. I love you so much. Each day I think it can't get any stronger, and yet every day it does. I'd die for you.'

'Oh don't say that Jimmy. I'd never want you to die for me. Come on let's get out of this place and go home. When he's not here this is such a beautiful special place. When he's home it becomes like a prison. He always makes me feel bad. You see what he's like? He's taken the most perfect day and ruined it. He could look at a blossoming bed of carnations and they would instantly wilt. Take me home and make love to me.'

'That's the best idea you've had all day. Come on, to the scooter-mobile, batgirl.'

'I'll just say goodbye to mummy and Mrs Beaton.'

I grab her helmet and wait for her outside on the purring Vespa. I mumble to myself as I wait.

'Pheasant, who eats pheasant? I suppose Lords and Ladies do. They'd probably eat peasants if they could get away with it.' She's back out in less than a minute and jumps on to the scooter.

'Go! Let's go!' she commands as she hugs me tightly around the waist. As we pass through the giant gates at the entrance to the property, I stop the scooter and look at the sign on the wall once more, "Ridley Castle Built In 1309".

'Fuck me!'

'What? What is it Jimmy?'

'A castle, who'd have thought,' we both laugh like drains as we speed off down the road.

16: VIOLENCE

It's heaving in Tossers tonight and there's an unpleasant atmosphere that I can't quite put my finger on. Macca and Marky are in the midst of yet another heated debate about politics and the miners' strike. Me, Jonesy and Gerry roll our eyes heavenwards.

'I'd support the miners if they'd had a secret ballot and the majority had voted for strike action, but they didn't, they just went out on strike,' explains Macca. Marky is staring at the bottom of his beer glass as the amber liquid disappears down his throat. He slams the pint onto the table and wipes his mouth on the back of his hand.

'Of course they had a bloody vote, it was a show of hands. That's the way it has always been done for the last eighty years until the Tories got into power and changed the rules a couple of years back,' retaliates Marky, angrily.

'A show of hands,' snorts Macca. 'That's bullshit! That's bully-boy tactics. If you don't put your hand up then you'd be targeted. It's intimidation,' says Macca as he finishes his pint. Gerry stands up and collects the empty glasses.

'Same again boys?' he asks. Everyone nods.

'I'll give you a hand,' I offer, glad to get away from the duelling duo. Gerry orders fresh drinks and we lean against the bar as we wait for the refills.

'Jesus, don't those two ever stop,' moans Gerry.

'I know, it's bloody painful. Try and change the conversation when we get back. I'm sick of listening to them. They're like an old married couple.' Gerry laughs and hands a tenner over to Jenny. 'It's an odd atmosphere in here tonight,' I say.

'Yeah? Odd in what way?' he asks.

'Not sure…edgy, tense…'

'Yeah, well that's Bill and Ben having a go with each other, that's the problem.'

'Nah, it's not them. It's the crowd that's in. It's not the usual lot.' Gerry collects three pints in his hands and I retrieve the other two. He calls out as we head back to our table.

'Coming through! Watch your backs… excuse me please!' We wend and weave our way through the boisterous crowd slopping beer along the way. There's a group of five blokes standing directly in our path with their backs to us. 'Hey mate, excuse me, can you let us through please?' He receives no response. He tries again. 'Excuse me mate!' He shouts. One guy turns around. He's tall and quite muscular with an ugly haircut, terrible dress sense and I can tell that he's pissed.

'What do you want you black bastard?' he snarls at Gerry.

'Just trying to get back to my table with the drinks and there's no need for that, now is there?' Gerry replies in a calm and measured tone. He's used to racist remarks, after all, he's had it all his life. I sidle up next to him.

'Hey pal, less of the racist shit, right! Now fucking move!' I growl.

'Who are you? The fucking boyfriend? Fancy a bit of black do you?' I barge past him as all his dumb mates let out guffaws. We get safely back to the table and place the drinks down. Macca and Marky are still at it.

'Bloody racist twat!' I say to no-one in particular.

'Don't worry about it Jimmy, it doesn't bother me,' replies Gerry in a resigned manner.

'Well it bloody well should! This is 1984.'

'If it worries me, then they win. If I don't give a toss, then I win.' I sort of understand where he's coming from... well, no I don't actually. How could I possibly ever know what if feels like to be victimised because of the colour of my skin. I can only hazard a guess that it would be bloody painful. Marky breaks off from his argument with Macca.

'Who's a racist?' he asks.

'Oh, that bastard down there,' I say as I nod towards the five blokes. 'The guy who looks like his mother cuts his hair for him.' Marky stands up and sets off.

'We'll see about that.' Shit! Me and my big mouth.

'Oh nice one Jimmy!' berates Gerry. 'Now look what you've done. Marky leave it!' He shouts out after Marky. It's too late. I can see Marky has already launched a verbal assault on the guy. We all look at each other, take a quick gulp of our pints, then replace them on the table. We all stand up.

'Okay boys here we go,' says Jonesy with a resigned air.

'Bloody great! Just how I like to spend my Friday nights, rolling around on the pub floor with some drunken Neanderthal on top of me,' says Macca.

##

I turn the key in the door and walk in. There's a wonderful smell of home baking coming from the kitchen.

'Hi Vee, it's only me,' I call out, as I waggle my tooth for the umpteenth time since we got booted out of the pub by Jenny. Vee appears at the kitchen doorway with a huge smile on her face.

'Oh Jimmy, I wasn't expecting you back for another...' she stops dead. The happy expression on her face changes to one of horror. 'Oh my God! What happened to you!' she screams as she runs to my aid. I've got a thick split lip and I dab at it with a bloodied handkerchief. 'Jimmy, no! Have you been attacked? We must call the police.'

'Not as such. We got into a fight.' She slaps me hard on the top of the arm.

'No! What are you getting in fights for? Who was it with? Who else was there?'

##

I'm sitting on the bed as she gently bathes my lip with cotton wool dipped in warm salted water. I'm explaining the chain of events to her.

'So Marky goes up to this racist runt and that's when it all kicked off. The guy probably looked at Marky and thought that he'd make mincemeat of him. Big mistake. By the time the rest of us joined in Marky had already knocked two of them out. Anyway, it was all over in less than twenty seconds. I got a punch in the mouth for my efforts. I think my tooth is loose. Jenny has banned us for a month, but I reckon she'll let us back in after a week. The other lads are banned for life. She's not very happy with us.'

'No, and I don't blame her. Fighting like common thugs. I'm not happy with any of you either. And how are the others? Are any of them hurt?' she asks as she drips antiseptic onto a scrunch of cotton wool.

'Cuts and bruises, nothing serious. You've got to watch yourself these days though. A lot of people carry knives—cowardly bastards.' She jabs the cotton wool into my cut lip. I flinch.

'Oh Jimmy, stop, I can't bear any more.' She begins to sob. I try to put my arms around her and she pushes me away. 'No, no! I can't speak to you tonight, just keep away from me, I need some time.' She stands and weeps her way back to the kitchen. It has shaken her up and mentioning knives wouldn't have helped.

I channel surf for an hour or so as I listen to the hustle and bustle from the kitchen. The oven door is opened and slammed shut numerous times. Plates crash and bang. Cutlery drawers rattle angrily and glasses are clinked together loudly. Her shock has turned to anger. I ring Gerry and see how he is. He copped one to the eye and as we departed from Tossers it had already swelled to the size of a golf ball. Sarah answers the phone and I get a torrent of abuse thrown down the line at me.

'I'm sick of him coming home covered in black eyes and cuts and bruises! You are not kids anymore! You all need to bloody grow up.'

'Sorry Sarah but we didn't start it,' I plead.

'It sounds like you did to me! Wasn't it Marky who wouldn't let things drop?' She goes on for another minute or so before she softens.

'Right, I'll pass you over to Gerry, oh, and by the way, he's grounded for a month, no more nights out for him.' There's the sound of muted talking and then Gerry's voice.

'Hey Jim,'

'Gerry, how's the eye?'

'Throbbing. I've been laid with a bag of ice on it. The swelling's starting to go down.'

'Can you see all right?'

'Yeah, no damage done. How's the lip?

'Hurts like hell and I've got a loose tooth. Sarah sounds like she's pissed off.'

'She's fucking ropeable man! I'll need to tuck my head in for a few days until she calms down. What did Vee say?'

'She's not talking to me and at present it sounds like she's vandalising the kitchen.' He laughs. We talk for another minute or so then hang up.

I do some more channel surfing, stare at my swollen lip in the mirror and persist in waggling my loose tooth. The noise from the kitchen begins to abate and after two hours of being sent to Coventry, I move into the kitchen doorway. She opens the oven door and pulls out a large tin of scones followed by a rich and aromatic fruit cake. She places them on a cloth on the table, then clicks the kettle on.

'Tea?' she asks.

'Please. Listen Vee, I'm sorry.' She turns and walks towards me. 'It won't happen...' She cuts me off.

'Stop. No talking tonight.' She puts her arms around me and pulls my head into her bosom. I can feel it fall and rise. I smell her comforting and familiar warmth, but I can also sense her sadness and fear.

As I snuggle her in bed, I realise that apart from my three days of self-imposed sexual abstinence, this is the first time I've not made love to her.

I'm warm and still half-asleep under the covers as I hear the sound of cooking and cutlery being placed on the table.

'Jimmy wake up. Scrambled eggs, mushrooms and toast will be ready in five.' I slowly begin to sink back into sleep. Then I hear her voice on the phone.

'Okay, thank you so much for fitting him in. I'll make sure he's there by ten o'clock. And your address is...' I lift my head from the pillow as she hangs up.

'Who was that?' I enquire as I sit on the side of the bed, gently dabbing at my swollen lip.

'Dentist.' She disappears into the kitchen and reappears carrying two plates. 'Come on, eat. You've got half an hour before your appointment.'

'Vee, you shouldn't have done that. I hate dentists, they put the fear of God into me. I can't go.' She stares at me with angry eyes,

'Oh you are going! Even if I have to drag you there myself.'

'It feels better today. It's not as loose,' I lie.

'Let me see,' she commands.' I pull my lip up and she gently prods my right canine. 'You liar! Not only is it loose but there's already a bit of discolouration at the base. You need a dentist to check that out. There'll be no more discussion about it.' I sit at the table and chew carefully and morosely on the food.'

191

The dentist has a right good bloody poke around in my mouth and he's none too gentle. Then I have an X-ray. Now he's got me back in that damn torture chair.

'Well, Mr Hooper. The root is dying and it will only be a matter of time until the whole tooth is dead. You have three options. Option one; I remove the tooth now. Option two; you come back at a later date and I remove it then. Option three; I remove the tooth and at a further date we install a bridge.'

'A false tooth?'

'No. It's a bridge. It's a permanent fixture and you won't be able to tell the difference between it and a real tooth.'

'Will it hurt?' He stares at me.

'Yes, of course it will bloody hurt,' he laughs—sadistic bastard.

'How much will it cost?' I ask.

'To remove the tooth today, twenty pounds. For the bridge, around the six hundred mark.'

'Jesus H Christ! Six hundred quid for a false tooth. No wonder you guys drive around in Porches.' He smiles smugly.

'It's a bridge, not a false tooth. There's a lot of skill and work involved.'

'Aye, and a lot of bloody money. No, just pull the bloody thing out and be done with it. I won't be getting a bridge.'

##

I enter the flat. Vee is sitting at the table reading a book. She looks at me.

'Well? What did the dentist say?' I give her a smile. She throws her hand to her mouth. 'Oh my God! It's gone! He's removed it.'

'No shit,' I reply.

'Have you booked in to get a bridge fitted?' she asks.

'Not on your Nelly! Cheeky bastard wants six hundred quid for a false tooth. I've already paid twenty to get one removed. The butcher's not getting another penny out of me.'

'Jimmy!' she yells at me. 'I am not going out with you looking like that!'

'Looking like what?' I ask, bemused.

'Like a common criminal, like a street thug. It's ruined your boyish looks. You *are* going to get a bridge. I'll pay for it.'

'No you won't.'

'Yes, I will!' She's already dialling a number on the phone.

'Vee, what do you think you're doing?'

'I'm calling the dentist. I'm getting you booked in asap.'

'Vee, put that phone down. I am not getting a bridge put in. It's my mouth and my teeth and I can do whatever I like.' As she finishes dialling she turns to me.

'Well, the choice is clear. You either get a bridge and let me pay for it or there'll be no more sex—ever! And I mean it!' That is dirty! That's not playing by the rules. Although every ounce of my pride tells me to stick to my guns, there is something far more powerful at play. My pride and dignity never stood a chance. I emerge from the trenches waving a white flag.

17: COWARDICE

It's Sunday lunchtime and we're finishing our drinks up sitting in the Soldiers Arms. The Landlord has called time and The Hipnotikz are busy on stage packing their gear away. I'm showing Marky my new tooth the dentist installed a couple of days ago.

'Looks just like the real thing,' says Marky with a cheeky grin.

'Should bloody well hope so. It cost six hundred quid.' Marky's eyes widen.

'That's an outrage! Dental treatment should be free on the National Health. This is what's happened to this country. Healthcare should be free for everyone, but the Tories are slowly privatising it all. How did you manage to pay for that?'

'I didn't. Vee paid for it,' I reply looking over my shoulder towards the ladies toilet.

'She's got a bit of money then?'

'Yeah, you could say that,' I reply, not wanting to divulge too much information. 'I didn't want to accept it but I had no choice. It was either a new tooth or no more sex.' Marky laughs and knocks back the final dregs of his pint. I glance again at the toilet door as Vee makes her way through it. She walks back to us and sits down.

'Well done Vee. You kill 'em every time with that song. Why don't you broaden your repertoire a little?' asks Marky.

'Thanks Marky. I may do in the future. I just love singing that song, it's our song, mine and Jimmy's.'

'Oh you lovebirds, you make me want to vomit. Right, I'm going to help the lads pack their gear into the van.' We watch him as he heads to the stage but he makes a slight detour to the corner of the room where four skinheads are sitting. He seems to be in deep discussion and I'm curious as to what he's saying.

'Those skinheads really frighten me,' says Vee with a worried frown.

'Don't worry. I've told you, Marky says they're all right.'

'Hmm, still. They've got tattoos on their necks. Do they realise that tattoos are for life?'

'I'm sure they do, but they obviously don't care at the moment. When they reach their late twenties they'll realise their mistake. It's all part of the getup. They're just trying to look hard and menacing. They're probably like little kittens underneath their uniform.' We return our gaze to The Hipnotikz who are indulging in some good natured quarrelling.

'They're a great band,' enthuses Vee.

'They're the best,' I agree. 'It won't be long now.'

'Long before what?' she asks as she takes a sip of her lager and black.

'Before they're off, taking on the world.'

'You really think they'll make it?'

'Without a doubt. It's not just the music. There's something about them when they're up on that stage. There's a chemistry that all the truly great bands have.' Vee ponders for a moment and looks a little sad. 'What's wrong?' I quiz her.

'I want them to be successful, of course, but…' she pauses.

'But what?'

'Well, I feel like they belong to us. I know it's selfish but I don't want to share them with the world. I want us to be sitting here in ten, fifteen years time watching them on that stage. Once they make it they won't play here again. I want to stop the world from turning and keep everything as it is right now.' I reach across the table and stroke her cheek.

'Everything changes Vee. These are great times but there'll be even better times to come.' She smiles sweetly at me but doesn't look convinced. Marky makes his way back to our table.

'Oh Jimmy, don't forget I've got that interview tomorrow with the miners. I want you to get some good shots so don't be late. I'm setting off at 8:30 sharp. I'll pick you up from Vee's digs. I'll blow the horn twice. Don't keep me waiting, it's a no-parking zone and last time I nearly got a bloody ticket. Right comrades, I'll see you later.' We fist bump, he then holds his fist out to Vee. She giggles and taps his knuckles with her own.

'Comrade,' she says. Marky smiles.

'That's my girl. We'll soon have you signed up to the Labour Party.' He turns and heads to the stage.

'He actually believes in all this political stuff doesn't he?'

'Oh yes. Marky's been like that since the age of thirteen. I swear he's getting worse though.'

'Worse? In what way?'

'More radical. I worry about him.'

'Have you told him who my father is yet?' I suck in a deep lungful of air.

'No, not yet. I haven't told anyone. Macca, Jonesy and Gerry won't give a toss. But Marky… well… that's a different kettle of Andropov's.' She laughs.

'Who is Andropov?'

'For the daughter of the Home Secretary, you really don't know much about politics do you? Andropov was the Soviet leader up until about February this year when he fell off the perch.'

196

'I hate politics. It ruins lives,' she says sadly as she stares into the bottom of her glass. The four skinheads are making their way to the door and as they pass our table they stop. Three of them are average height and skinny. The fourth is a huge fat bear with a massive potbelly. He wobbles slightly as he stares down at Vee.

'Eh, tell you what love,' he begins, 'you've got a cracking pair of lungs on you,' he gushes. Vee reddens, shoots him a quick glance and stares back at me.

'Oh thank you,' she says politely.

'And your voice ain't bad either.' His three stooges let out sniggers. Vee looks bamboozled.

'Leave it out mate,' I say, coolly to him. The fat bear stares at me for a second.

'Ladies and Gentlemen, time please!' yells the Landlord for about the fifth time. The four skins turn and amble out of the doorway. Vee shivers.

'Ooh, they give me the creeps. Why did you tell him to leave it out? He was only being nice.'

'No he wasn't. He was being smutty. When he said you had a great pair of lungs he was referring to your tits.' She looks horrified.

'Urgh! Disgusting pig.'

'Although technically, he is correct,' I laugh.

'Jimmy, you're incorrigible,' she smiles sexily at me.

'What does that even mean?'

'It means you have a one track mind and you'll never change.' I stand up and shout out to the boys.

'Hey lads! I'll see you in Tossers, Wednesday night!'

'Yeah, catch you, Jimmy,' they all shout back. I grab Vee's hand and we walk out of the pub together into radiant sunshine.

'I love Sunday's like this,' I say.

'Me too. Back to our love nest. I have a casserole in the oven and after that a little afternoon nap.'

'After the sex, you mean.'

'As I said, incorrigible.' We turn the corner and walk past the side of the pub. As we near the pub car park the four skinheads saunter out of a back doorway. We stop dead in our tracks. They slowly tread towards us but spread out in an arc, encircling us.

'Hey love,' says the big fat bear, 'why don't you ditch this little runt and shack up with a real man?' He's wearing a snide smile but behind it is malice and hatred. His three buddies move in closer and I push Vee behind me for protection. She grips me tightly on the top of my arm.

'Okay, leave it out pal. I don't want any trouble,' I state with a confidence I don't possess. The bear laughs and looks at his mates.

'Trouble? Trouble you say... there's no trouble around here is there boys?' His mates snigger.

'No, Tubs. There's no trouble around here,' replies one of them. I feel Vee's fingernails claw into me.

'Jimmy I'm scared,' she whispers.

'So whaddya say, love. How about you and me get it on together? See what a real man is like?' They inch menacingly forward. Their smiles are now gone.

'Right, fuck off!' I shout at them. 'You've had your bit of fun.'

'I wasn't talking to you, you little faggot. I was talking to that pretty little girl of yours.' I half turn my head towards Vee.

'When I shout, "Now", run back to the pub and get the boys,' I instruct under my breath. I realise that I'm going to get a good kicking here. Tubs is a big unit and once I'm on the deck his cowardly little thugs will stick the boot in. I know these types, they're like a pack of dogs. The leader takes down the prey and the rest lunge in snapping and growling. They move ever closer. I figure if I make the first move then I can probably take out at least one of the skinny ones. That will open the path for Vee—at least she'll be safe. I try one last act of bravado. 'Hey Tubs, you're a big lad but you're a fat bastard and you're pissed. You may take me down but I'll make damn sure one of you comes with me.' Tubs flutters his arms in front of me.

'Ooh, look at me, I'm quaking in my boots.' His mates snigger again. He suddenly makes an uncoordinated rush towards me. I hear a shout and look to my right. Marky comes flying around the corner. Tubs turns with the speed of an ocean liner as Marky barges through two of the thugs. At lightning speed he propels himself from the ground and head butts Tubs in the face. Tubs staggers and groans as blood erupts from his nose. Marky follows it up with a vicious kick to the balls. The other three begin to slide away. Tubs falls to the ground clutching his nuts. Marky feigns to run at the others and they turn tail and scarper leaving their glorious leader writhing in agony. Marky flicks at some invisible dust on his collar then turns to me.

'What's going on Jimmy? Why were they having a crack at you?'

'It wasn't me they were after, it was Vee,' I say, breathing a sigh of relief. Marky's face morphs into anger.

'Bastards!' he yells. He turns around and stands over Tubs and unleashes a barrage of powerful blows into his face. I've seen Marky in action many times but his violence always shocks me.

'Enough, enough Marky!' cries Tubs as he tries in vain to curb the torrent of blows. Eventually, Marky stops and stands up straight. He holds his hand out to the prostrate bear who grabs it gingerly. He pulls himself to his feet. Marky retrieves a white handkerchief from his pocket, wipes blood from his knuckles then hands it to Tubs.

'Tubs, you're a big fat dickhead. You know Jimmy and Vee are mates of mine. What do you think you're playing at? Now let this be a warning to you. If you harm one hair on Jimmy's head or frighten Vee again then I'll have no choice but to tell the Russian.' Tubs' eyes bulge from his head in absolute horror.

'No, no please, Marky, don't tell the Russian, please!' he begs.

'Right go on, fuck off out of my sight. You can keep the handkerchief.' Tubs turns and staggers off across the street dabbing at his nose. 'Oi, and Tubs, don't forget, 10 pm, Thursday night, usual spot!' Tubs turns and gives a weak thumbs up.

'Fucking hell Marky, what are you doing hanging around with scum like that?' I snap at him. Marky smiles. Vee relinquishes her grip on my arm, slightly.

'Foot soldiers Jimmy, everyone needs foot soldiers. Right, no harm done. Are you okay Vee? You can come out now.' Vee's head pokes out from behind my back. She offers Marky a weak nod but says nothing.

'Good. Okay, auf wiedersehen. Catch you tomorrow Jim.' With that he turns and heads off back to the pub. I puff out my cheeks and stroke my chin. Vee pushes me hard in the back then storms off down the laneway that leads to her flat. Her arms are clamped tightly across her chest and she's marching at a cracking pace. I run after her.

'Vee, Vee, wait up. What's wrong?' She ignores me. I catch up with her and grab her by the elbow. 'Vee, wait, I know you're upset but…' She stops dead in her tracks, slaps my hand away, then unleashes on me.

'I can't live like this!' she screams.

'Like what?'

'Like this, all this violence. I don't belong in this world. What would have happened if Marky hadn't shown up? You'd be unconscious on the road by now— or worse. And I'd be getting gang-raped in the pub car park!'

'Calm down Vee, you're over exaggerating.' She pummels her fists into my chest.

'Jimmy you've got to stop! It can't go on. It was only a couple of weeks ago since you were in a fight at Tossers, now this! I can't stand it anymore. What if something happens to you? Every time you go out with your mates I live in fear wondering if you'll make it home unscathed. You've got to stop!'

'Stop? Stop what?'

'Stop going to rough pubs and getting yourself in these situations.'

'I'm sorry Vee, you're right, this is my world. It's rough, it can be violent and you've got to be on your toes, but it is what it is. I could walk into the poshest wine bar in Leeds and get glassed in the neck by some psycho who thinks I looked at him the wrong way. You can't hide away, you cannot be cowed by life. Every day is a game of chance. If you end up being scared of your own shadow then life's not worth living. You have to be fearless and take whatever comes your way. Anyway, I was born under a blue moon, remember—so nothing bad can happen to me.' She rounds on me again and slaps me hard across the cheek.

'It's just a stupid saying! Of course you're not protected, no-one's protected. A stupid blue moon won't save you from a stab wound or a kick to the head.' She stops then slowly and tenderly strokes my cheek. 'Oh Jimmy, I'm so sorry, please forgive me?' She falls into my arms and begins to sob. I embrace her and stroke her head.

'Shh…'

'I can't bear the thought of ever losing you,' she sniffles. I laugh.

'I ain't going nowhere Vee, at least, not without you.'

18: TRUST

It's a cold miserable day and blustery. But that's okay. Black and white photos don't tend to catch the weather conditions as much as colour. I'm at the old railway arches doing a photoshoot with "The Sweet Genes", formerly known as "The Zippers".

I've got to say, I'm impressed with the change of image. Gone are the flouncy shirts and bouffant haircuts. Lead singer, Joey, is wearing black denim drainpipes with shiny blue Doc Martin shoes. He sports a crisp white shirt topped with a bright colourful Paisley waistcoat. His band are in similar getup. They are leaning up against the old stone slabs of the arches, smoking and looking cool.

'Okay,' I shout. 'Nearly done, I just need to get some close ups.' Julia is standing next to me and shivers.

'Ooh, it's bloody freezing today.' I look at her skimpy attire.

'Did Joey take much convincing to ditch the name and image?' I ask as I load a new roll of film.

'I didn't convince him. All I did was plant the seed in his head.'

'What did you do?' I enquire.

'I went to the library and got a few photo books of bands from the late fifties; Eddie Cochrane, Gene Vincent, Duane Eddy, Elvis and the like, oh, plus one on James Dean. I then left them around the house. I bought some old rock and roll albums from the second-hand shop and played them continually. One night as we were eating dinner together, I just began thinking out aloud. I said, wasn't it funny that it always seemed to be the "original" bands that made it big and not those that followed in their footsteps. A few days later, Joey took a week off work and wrote a batch of new songs. The rest is history. If I'd have suggested any of this to him, then it would never have happened.' I gaze at her with sadness. The world is fucked in so many ways. Why aren't women treated as equals? Why is the male ego so enormous that they couldn't possibly take advice from a woman? I think of Vee and the way she is. There's so much inside her. She has so much to give—yet, her talents are locked away, hidden. She's scared to pop her head above the parapet in case it gets blown off. I vow, right here and now, that I am going to do everything within my limited power to coax her out of her shell. I won't see her trudge through life cowed and afraid.

'So what's the new music like?' I ask as I wind the new film on.

'It's great. I wasn't sure at first, but after a few listens it really grabs you. It's quite stark, stripped back, not depressing, just edgy.'

'Punchy?'

'Yeah, punchy, is a better word,' she laughs. 'They're heading off down to London after this photoshoot. They've got a few gigs lined up and they're also going to tout their new demo around the record companies.'

'Are you going with them?' She turns and looks at the battered old transit van parked up a few feet away.

'No way! Stuck in a stinky old van with five blokes farting and belching for five hours is not my idea of fun.'

I start to take some close-ups of the band. They're all good looking lads, but Joey is especially photogenic. He's tall and skinny but has an air of arrogance that most good lead singers have. Macca has the same aura.

Once I'm happy with everything, I call it a wrap. The band all jump into the van, thank me for my time and promise that when they hit the big time they will be giving me a call. Joey gives Julia a quick peck on the lips.

'Love you babe,' he coos.

'You too,' she replies as she grips at her ribs, trying to keep the cold out. She waves at the van as it trundles away from the arches, splashing through muddy puddles and swerving around discarded mattresses and old broken bathroom fittings. When the van is out of sight she turns to me.

'Do you fancy coming back to my place for a coffee?' she asks with a mischievous grin. I rewind the film, eject it and put it back in its container.

'Hmm, does that mean coffee or does it mean something else?' I glance at her with a suspicious smile.

'What do you think?' she giggles.

'I'm flattered, but no thanks.' She studies me for a while.

'There's something different about you than when I saw you last.'

'Really?' I say as I scribble "The Sweet Genes" onto the label of the containers.

'Yes, you seem happy, content…wait, it's that girl, isn't it… the Ice Queen. You're going out with her, aren't you?'

'Yep, been a few months now.'

'I told you she was the girl for you.'

'You were right, she certainly is. Right, these photos will be ready in a couple of days. I'll give you a call when they're done and we can arrange a pick-up point.' I put my helmet on and walk over to my Vespa. She follows me.

'Oh Jimmy, I almost forgot.' She pulls a cassette from her handbag and passes it to me. 'This is the latest demo. Have a listen and let me know what you think.' I take the tape and slip it inside my jacket pocket.

'Cheers,' I say. I kick-start the scooter and rev it up. She leans forward and gives me a peck on the lips.

'Thanks, see you later.' She turns and hurriedly walks back to her knackered little Mini parked near the Arches. I watch her as she goes. Joey is a lucky man—I wonder if he knows it.

I'm in the newsroom of the Standard having a chat with Marky. The door opens and Dave Dee walks in.

'Oi Jimmy, can I have a word mate?' he calls out as he makes his way to his desk.

'Yeah, sure Dave.' I follow behind him. He drops a bulging leather bag onto his desk and plonks himself down into his seat. He removes his spectacles and begins to clean them on his jumper. He looks up at me and smiles as he does so.

'So, that band you went to see last night, The Bojo's, how was the gig?' I'd handed the review, interview and photos in to Dave this morning before the photoshoot with The Sweet Genes. I wonder if he doesn't like the photos? I thought they were pretty damn good, especially as the band weren't the prettiest bunch of faces I'd laid eyes on.

'Yeah, it was great. A good Ska band, plenty of nervous energy. Are you happy with the photos?'

'Yeah, photos are fine,' he nods.

'The interview?' He nods again.

'Interview was great.'

'Well then, is there a problem?' I ask.

'Just a small one,' he says as he nonchalantly puts his glasses back on.

'The review? You didn't like the review? Too long or too short?'

'No, no, the review was good, in fact, it was bloody brilliant. One of your best yet.' I smile and let out a sigh of relief. 'Considering...' he adds for dramatic effect.

'Considering what?' I ask, completely at a loss as to what the conversation is about. He slams his palms hard onto the desk and jumps to his feet leaning menacingly towards me.

'Considering they didn't play the fucking gig? The singer had a bad asthma attack and was rushed to the hospital at 8:30 last night. The show was cancelled!' Oops! 'I just found out by chance, ten minutes ago when I bumped into the President of the Students Union. How long has this been going on?'

'It's the first time, honest Dave,' I say.

'You lying little toe rag!' he hisses loudly. 'That review was due to go out in less than twenty-four hours. Can you imagine the furore if it had! The Standard making up its own stories! Do you know what sort of impact that can have on a paper's reputation?'

'Sorry Dave, something came up at the last minute and I couldn't make it to the gig. I promise it won't happen again.'

'Too damn right it won't happen again,' he bellows at me. The door to Bulldog's office opens and out walks the great man himself. He has a stern look on his face.

'I can hear you yelling from my office Dave. What's all this about?' he asks. This is it, I've fucked up big time. My short stint at the Standard is about to come to an end. Not only that, but I'll scamper out of these hallowed doors with my tail between my legs and a stained reputation. Dave sits back down in his chair and looks up at Bulldog.

'Nothing for you to worry about Bulldog,' he says gently. Bulldog looks at me, then back at Dave.

'No, I want to know. What's been going on?' Dave leans back in his chair and points at me.

'It's young Jimmy, here. I told him when he started to keep all his receipts. Well, he's lost a month's worth of receipts and I've already reimbursed him twenty quid out of petty cash. You know what accounts are like, they'll be chewing my fucking ear off about it.' Bulldog studies me carefully.

'How long has Jimmy been here now?'

'Just over five weeks,' Dave replies.

And how long did we say we'd trial him for?'

'A month.'

'Is he on the payroll yet?'

'No.'

'Well, I've seen his photos in the paper. They look pretty good to me. Seems to know what he's doing. What are his interviews and reviews like for the entertainment section?' I am still actually here, not that anyone would notice.

'His interviews are good, really good. As for his reviews, yeah, they're good too—very inventive.' Bulldog pulls a fat wallet out of his back pocket and peels off a twenty pound note and throws it onto Dave's desk.

'Here, stick that in petty cash. There's no need getting yourself all worked up over twenty quid.'

'Sorry Bulldog. It's been a long day, that's all.' Bulldog places his big mitt on Dave's shoulder and squeezes it tenderly.

'I know Dave, I know. Every day is long at the moment.' He turns and begins to head back to his office.

'Oh Dave, get young Jimmy into the system. Casual, we can't take anyone on full time at the moment... not with the way things are.'

'Aye, no worries Bulldog,' Dave replies. As Bulldog's door shuts behind him I let out a mighty sigh of relief.

'Cheers Dave. I owe you one.' Dave stands up and retrieves his bottle of whisky out of the top drawer of his filing cabinet.

'Yes, you bloody well do.' He puts two tumblers on his desk and half fills them, then hands one to me.

'Welcome to the Standard,' he says, holding his glass towards me and smiling warmly. We clink glasses and bolt down the fiery liquid. He sits back down and begins poring over a stack of papers on the edge of his desk. I linger for a few seconds unsure of what to do. After an eternity, he looks up at me.

'You still here? Go on, fuck off and let me get some work done. Oh, and Jimmy, I'll be keeping a close eye on you for a while.'

'Okay, thanks, cheers, Dave, thanks, yep, yep, thanks,' I gush as Dave returns his gaze to his papers and his little red pen. I turn to go as he calls out again.

'Jimmy, the only reason you're still here is because you're a hustler, and hustlers make damn fine reporters and even better photographers.' I nod and quickly walk back over to Marky who is staring at me with a concerned look. I glance at the clock on the wall. It's just turned five.

'What the fuck was all that about?' whispers Marky.

'Come on let's go for a pint at the Soldiers. I'll tell you all about it.'

##

I'm back in Vee's flat and have just finished telling her about my near-miss experience at the Standard. She slaps me on the top of the arm.

'I told you Jimmy! I did warn you. You can't do things like that, making up reviews. You take too many risks.'

'I know, you were right. I'm just so bloody busy most of the time and I don't want to hang around until after eleven o'clock on a night to watch some shitty band. I want to be here with you.' She smiles and rubs the back of my hand.

'I'll always be here, waiting up for you,' she replies sweetly. She suddenly pulls a stern expression. 'Jimmy, I've said it before and I'll say it again; it's time you became legitimate. Sign off the dole, set up a limited company and get your own premises. Once you've done that, take on someone else to lighten the workload. They can do the late night gigs.'

'Yeah, yeah, I know. I am thinking about it. It's just such a big move and it would be bloody expensive. I don't have the sort of dough to do it at the moment.'

'I have plenty of money doing nothing in the bank. I'll help you out.'

'No, no, I couldn't do that. It would be wrong.'

'Why?'

'Because then it's not business is it?' She huffs as though exasperated with me.

'I believe in you. I *want* to help. Think of it as a loan. If and when you can pay me back—then fine. If it doesn't work out, well, then that's also fine.'

'No, if I'm going to do this then I have to do it off my own bat. Not from the helping hand of my girlfriend.'

'Jimmy, whatever am I going to do with you?' she replies in a resigned tone.

'Rip my clothes off and make passionate, debauched love to me?'

19: DESPAIR

I'm dressed only in my underpants, staring into the wardrobe. I'm pretty sure I left a pair of jeans here a few weeks back, but I'll be buggered if I can see them now. I walk to the bathroom. Vee is just emerging out of the shower. She grabs a towel and begins to dry herself. I go to the laundry basket, lift the lid off and start rummaging around inside.

'What have you got on today?' asks Vee.

'Hey? At the moment, only my bloody undies. Where the hell are they?'

'No, silly. I meant work-wise?'

'Erm… this morning I've got another bloody baby photo. Mid-morning I'm going with Marky to Orgreave to get some shots of the miners. Marky's going to do a few interviews.'

'Orgreave, where and what is that? Is it a coal mine?'

'What? No, it's a coking plant owned by British Steel in South Yorkshire, near Rotherham. Hey Vee, have you seen my Levis? I'm sure I left a pair here?'

'Which ones?'

'The 501s, the blue ones.' I place the cover back on the basket and scratch my head.

'Oh, I threw them out,' she replies, nonchalantly.

'You what!' I exclaim, horrified at her revelation.

'They had holes in the knees and had faded to nothing so I put them in the bin.'

'They had another six months wear left in them. Bloody charming! Now I'm going to have to wear the ones I had on yesterday and they have a big coffee stain down them.' She ties the towel around her head and giggles. 'It's not funny. I'm representing the Standard. I need to look the part.'

'Follow me,' she says. She walks out of the bathroom and back to the bedroom, with nothing on, mind you. She opens the wardrobe, swishes some of her clothes out of the way, pulls out a carrier bag and throws it onto the bed. 'Here, I bought you some new ones. Three blue, two black and a white pair. You'll look so sexy in the white ones. Don't wear them to the coalmine though, you might get them dirty.' I pick up the pants and study them.

'Christ Vee! 501s cost about fifty quid a pop. That's two hundred and fifty pounds!'

'So? As you said, you need to look the part. I also got you some new tops. Don't pull a face like that, I know what you like, they're all Fred Perry and Ben Sherman.' She grabs another bag from the wardrobe and hands it to me. I tip it out onto the bed. There are six polo shirts and three long-sleeved shirts of assorted colours.

'Vee, you shouldn't have. Please don't spend your money on me. I can fend for myself now.'

'Don't be silly. I enjoy shopping for men's clothes. It's so much easier than shopping for my own. I think you should get a suit.'

'A suit?'

'Yes. It would make you look more professional. You know, a really sharp suit, the type they used to wear in the sixties. Narrow lapels, slim fit. If you wore a shirt and tie, and maybe a waistcoat, you'd certainly look the part.'

'Hmm, that's not a bad idea. I'll wait until Burtons have a sale on,' I reply as I pull my new 501s on, and struggle doing up the metal buttons. She chuckles. 'What?'

'No, you can't get a good suit off the peg. You need to be measured for one by a tailor. I know just the man. He has a shop at the bottom of Briggate. He makes my father's suits.' She unwraps a shirt from the packaging, extricates all the needles and undoes the buttons. 'Arms out,' she directs. I stand like a scarecrow as she threads the shirt onto me and begins fastening up the buttons. 'Yes, this looks really good on you. Fresh and handsome.' I slip my hand between her legs and she slaps it away. 'No! You haven't time and you had it less than an hour ago. There's something wrong with you.' She fastens the last but one button on the shirt, kisses me on the nose then stands back to admire her handiwork. 'Yes, that's the ticket. Take a look at yourself in the mirror.' I turn and study myself.

'Yeah, nice, I like it.' She stands behind me and rubs her hand over the shirt, ironing out the creases and picking stray strands of cotton from it.

'What's that aftershave you normally wear?'

'Blue Stratos. Sofe bought if for my last birthday. Why? Don't you like it?'

'Of course I like it. Oh, I almost forgot.' She's back to the wardrobe again. This time she hands me a pair of tan desert boots. 'Here you go "Mr Mod". We really must get you some smart shoes at some point. Maybe when we buy the suits. Right, I'll make you a coffee and some toast then you better get going.' I'm still admiring myself in the mirror and murmur, absentmindedly.

'Hmm, yes…' Did she just use the plural when referring to suits?'

##

It's a cold day and the miners have a small fire burning in a brazier. We are standing outside the gates of the British Steel coking plant in Orgreave. The miners have been picketing it for weeks. The plan's a simple one. Blockade the coking plant and prevent coke being delivered to the power stations. This will cause electricity shortages and maybe even a three-day week. The public will be pissed off with the miners but they'll also be pissed off with the government for letting things get out of hand. Slowly, the pressure will build on the government and they'll be forced to back down on the pit closures... or at least compromise. I'm not convinced about the strategy. The government has only recently won a second term in power. The next election is four years away. This government doesn't care about public opinion at the moment. Not only that, but they've been stockpiling coal and coke for years.

Marky is going from miner to miner with his tape recorder in hand getting quotes and interviews. It's funny to watch, funny peculiar, that is. Here's Marky, a short scrawny, cadet reporter mixing with big burly hardened miners and they are treating him like an old friend. They all shake his hand warmly, some pat him on the back and laugh and joke with him. Me? They eye me suspiciously despite Marky singing my praises. After about two hours of hanging around, Marky has got everything he needs. He goes up to a big giant of a man in his mid-forties.

'Barry, we're just about done here. Thanks for your time,' he says shaking the guy's hand. Barry smiles, showing a row of nicotine stained teeth.

'No problem Marky. Make it a good one, eh?'

'Of course Barry. This will be a piece about the human cost of this strike, it will be one of my best. Right, we just need Jimmy here, to get some shots of your ugly mugs, then we'll be out of your hair.' Barry corrals about a dozen miners together around the brazier. I pull the lens cap from my camera and begin clicking away. They all begin messing around pulling stupid faces and taking the piss out of me.

'Aw come on lads,' I cry, 'give me a break. Act normal, if you can.' They make more jokes and push and prod each other. It's no use, I can't get any good shots away. I pull Marky to one side.

'Marky, can you have a word. I need to capture their faces and what lies behind them. I want to see the hardship, the suffering, the fear.' Marky nods thoughtfully, then saunters over to Barry who is standing in the middle of the pack. I can't hear what Marky says, but suddenly the smiles and jokes stop. The men cluster in and listen carefully. Some nod, others throw me doubtful looks. After a couple of minutes, Marky returns.

'Okay Jimmy, they're all yours,' he states confidently.

'Right lads, can you all get in closer and make a semi-circle around the fire.' The men do as I say. Their faces are now sombre. 'Right, think about how this strike is affecting you and your loved ones. Think of the hardship, remember the bitterness. Think about how you are being portrayed in the tabloid media.' Faces harden. I begin snapping away. Some have their arms tightly folded under their chests, others have fists loosely clenched by their sides. One man looks like he's trying to hold back tears. Others look stoic and proud and some just look worn out and beaten. Then I get the money shot. It's Barry who says everything by the look in his eyes. He's looking past me as if in a sad daydream. He wants to believe but deep down he knows the battle is already lost and what that means to these men, to the wives and children back home. Something has died within him—he has lost hope.

We're driving back to Leeds in the pool car and Marky is animated as he steers us home.

'The old Iron Lady may call the miners "the enemy within", but I'm the enemy within their own fucking establishment.'

'What do you mean?'

'The piece I'm going to write is going to change the peoples' views on the strike. And I'll be doing it from within the hallowed grounds of the establishment.' I laugh.

'Fuck me Marky. I think you are having delusions of grandeur. First of all, your article won't change a thing. Secondly, if you go all political it will never get printed. Bulldog and Dave Dee won't allow anything like that in the Standard. That paper has metaphorical splinters in its arse from sitting on the fence so long.'

'You're right, but you're wrong. This won't be a political piece. This will be a human piece. It will be about the guys who have spent thirty years down the pit and are slowly dying of emphysema. I will talk about the mam and dad with four kids and how they live off one sliced loaf of bread a day. It will be about the community, the butcher, the baker…'

'The candlestick maker…' He throws me a disapproving look.

'The newsagent, post office, local supermarket, that are all slowly dying because no-one has any money. People will fucking weep when they read this. You see, if you bludgeon people around the head with facts and figures and who's right and who's wrong, then they switch off.

Create empathy and you change people's minds, that's real power. You're right about Bulldog, he'd never let anything political hit the front page. Dave Dee is another matter. I know he supports the miners even though he can't overtly show it. He'll run my piece if I get it bang on, and a couple of your photos will be sitting alongside it. We can make a difference Jimmy, you've just got to believe and never, ever give up. If you drop your head for a second, the bastards will be all over you. They aim to grind us into the ground and if they do, this country will never be the same again.'

'Marky, it's just another strike. There have been hundreds before it and there'll be hundreds after it. Not everyone sees the world in such black and white strokes as you. Most people just want to get on with living. No one's waiting for the glorious revolution.' Marky shoots me a fierce glance. Then he laughs.

'Haha, you nearly had me there. For one moment I thought you meant it,' he says as he slaps me on the thigh. The trouble is, I do mean it. All I care about is loving, loving and Vee.

'Marky, I've got something I need to get off my chest,' I begin, full of trepidation. Marky slows down as we near an intersection. He shoots me a quick glance.

'Sure, go for it,' he says returning his eyes to the road ahead.

'Well, it's in complete confidence—right? You must never repeat this to a single soul as long as you live. No one, not the boys not your mother, no one at the Standard.' Marky lets out a chuckle.

'Jimmy, you're like a brother to me. Whatever you have to say will stay locked away in the vault forever.' I feel suitably reassured.

'Do you recall that porno shoot I did for that older couple a while back?'

'Recall it, of course, I recall it. It was fucking hilarious! Hang on—no, you didn't? You randy little fucker—you joined in didn't you?' he guffaws.

'No, no, it's not that.' He seems slightly disappointed.

'Go on then, get it out.'

'Well, the woman…'

'Yeah, the older woman—the one that was a bit of all right?'

'Yeah, well… she was beautiful and bloody fit for her age.'

'Yep, yep, go on.'

'Well, she looked a lot like Vee with the addition of thirty years and different coloured eyes.'

'You've never mentioned this before. But anyway, what about it?'

'Well, the reason she looked like Vee is because it was Vee's mother.' Marky hits the brakes hard, flicks on the indicators and pulls over at the side of the road.

'Get the fuck out of here!' he roars.

'It's true.'

'Oh my giddy aunt! What happened when you met her?'

'There was a moment of awkwardness that Vee picked up on straight away. She's as sharp as a tack.'

'Then what?'

'I said that I recognised her mother and Vee said that it was probably because I'd seen her in the Standard at some point. She's quite a well known painter.'

'And?'

'It hasn't been sitting easy with me. You know how much I love and adore Vee. The thing is, I don't want to keep any secrets from her.' Marky slaps himself on the forehead and stares intently into my eyes.

'Are you fucking crazy? Please God, tell me you haven't told her?'

'No, no. That's why I wanted your advice first.' He shakes his head in disbelief. He reaches out and rests his hand on my shoulder.

'Jimmy, you must never, ever, tell Vee about this. It would break her. You'd lose her. It's a secret you need to take to the grave.'

'You think?'

'Yes, I do think. Where are the negatives?'

'They're hidden in my darkroom.'

'Right, the next time you're back at the flat you need to get those negatives and burn them. Are there any more prints lying around?'

'No. I only made one batch of the best shots and they were given to the bloke.'

'So, I take it this bloke is not Vee's father?'

'No. He's the lover.' Marky strokes his chin thoughtfully.

'Okay, just cover your tracks and get rid of the damn negatives and never mention this matter to anyone else for as long as you live—do you understand?' I pause for a moment.

'Yeah, you're right. I feel better already now that I've told you. I don't know what I was thinking.'

'Sometimes secrets are necessary Jimmy, to protect those we love.'

##

It's Thursday afternoon and the early edition of the paper has just hit the streets. Marky's miners' piece along with my photos are plastered across the front page underneath a headline banner of "Hope Within". I've got to say, Marky has absolutely nailed it. I nearly found myself crying after reading the piece. Then, there's the photo of Harry looking into the distance. A man without hope. I reckon if Lord Halliwell himself read this piece he'd be up on the barricades with the miners tomorrow. Dave Dee was elated with it, although he's not a man to wear his heart on his sleeve. Apparently, his comment of "Two fucking smart-arse twats for the price of one" was high praise indeed. Dave is looking decidedly tired these days. Bulldog has been recuperating from a bunion operation, so Dave has been in charge in his absence.

I'm sitting with Marky at his desk. We're both swigging on sweet milky coffee. There's a busy good natured humour that permeates the office. Marky's feeling particularly pleased with himself as people pass him by and say, "Nice piece Marky", or "Great work." There's a loud bang to our left as the double doors are thrown so violently open that I fear they may fall off their hinges. It's Bulldog. He's got a swathe of white bandages around his left foot and he hobbles along with the aid of a robust walking stick. He doesn't look too pleased. His face is bloated, ruddy and he appears to be suffering from tremors. Silence engulfs the room. He marches right up to Dave Dee's desk and bellows at him.

'In my office, right now!' Dave Dee calmly rests his cigarette in the ashtray and relaxes back in his chair.

'Something wrong, Bulldog?' Bulldog turns and scans the room before his eyes fall on Marky. 'Marky, you little fist fucker, in my office now!' his voice booms out. Marky looks at me sheepishly and says,

'Wish me luck. This should be fun.' Bulldog totters off through his office door as Marky makes his way over to Dave Dee. Dave opens his top drawer, pulls out a bottle of whisky and two small tumblers. He slowly and carefully pours a small measure into each glass and hands one to Marky. They both put it to their lips and knock it back in unison before quietly entering Bulldog's office, closing the door behind them.

If you like free entertainment then you couldn't go past this. For forty minutes the bellicose Bulldog lets fly. He was not happy with the front page spread and he's already ditched the story for the later editions. He's had phone calls from people very high up. He kept stating, then restating the Standard was apolitical. It did not take sides. It reported the news fairly and objectively without fear or favour. At first, only Bulldog's raucous voice could be heard. As time went on, Dave Dee's voice began to answer back in ever angrier tones. Not a peep from Marky though. The entire newsroom is enthralled. Some look worried, other's sport impish grins. The argument rises to a crescendo until finally, I hear Dave Dee cry out,

'Right! That's it! I'm out of here. You can run this fucking newspaper yourself!' Marky emerges from Bulldog's office first, looking red in the face. He's immediately followed by Dave Dee, who slams Bulldog's glass door so hard behind him, that the glass shatters and falls to the floor. Dave pulls his jacket off the back of his chair, collects his fags and marches out of the newsroom. As he does so, filing cabinets are slammed shut, drawers are closed and locked. There is a mass exodus out of the newsroom as nearly everyone follows Dave Dee, the pied piper, out of the building. The only people left are me and John Arnold. I look over to him as he slowly cuts up paper with the guillotine. He raises his eyebrows heavenwards then skulks off into the darkroom for safety. There is now an eerie silence. The room, which is always full of life, is now like an empty cathedral. I collect my backpack and begin to walk towards the exit. I stop as I hear the sound of crunching glass. I turn to see the imposing frame of Bulldog standing a few meters away. I smile weakly at him. He looks tired and bedraggled. He pulls a bottle of pills from his pockets and heads over to Dave Dee's desk. He grabs Dave's bottle of whiskey, unscrews the cap and takes four mighty glugs of the amber liquid to wash down the pills. As he replaces the cap on the bottle he stares at me and his face softens.

'There's no blame on you for any of this,' he states in a conciliatory fashion. 'It's those two buggers, subversive bastards,' he mutters.

'So, what happens now? You can't run a newspaper without a newsroom.' He laughs and sits down on Dave's chair which lets out a loud expulsion of air in annoyance.

'Do you know how long I've been in this game, lad?' I shake my head. 'Fifty years, that's how long. Another year and I'm hanging my pencil up and not a moment too soon. Everything is changing Jimmy, and not for the better. What Dave and Marky don't see is the bigger picture. This paper is not run in isolation. We have shareholders and vested interests that we have to appease. It's a balancing act between putting out newsworthy stories, keeping circulation up, bringing in the advertising dollars and not upsetting anyone. There are people that could close this paper down with a click of their fingers… then, where would we all be.' He takes another mouthful of whisky. 'He'll be back, they'll all be back. He'll saunter in tomorrow as though nothing has happened. We have these sort of bust-ups two, three times a year. You'll get used to it lad.' He stands wearily and in obvious pain. 'Right Jimmy, you may as well bugger off too. They'll all be over at the Soldiers getting pissed. You may as well join them.' He begins to head off towards his office, but stops and turns to me. 'Oh Jim, by the way, nice photos.' I watch him as he limps off muttering under his breath, 'Where am I going to find a fucking glazier at this time of day?'

20: ABSTINENCE

We've spent a perfect, lazy Sunday together. We woke late and made love. We had brunch at a small café, feasting on croissants, raisin toast and cups of strong black coffee. Back at the flat, we both read for a little and then make love again. In the afternoon we went to the cinema to watch a film followed by a gentle stroll along the canal for an hour. Back at the flat, we make love once more. I then doze off like a doddery old man and when I awake I can hear Vee busy in the kitchen.

'What are you cooking?' I shout to her as I pick up, "To Kill A Mockingbird", a book, that for some reason, I am struggling with. Vee appears in the doorway.

'Chicken Kiev with creamy mash and sugar peas,' she says.

'Yum, sounds great.'

'How are you getting on with the book?'

'It's not doing it for me at the moment. I'll give it a few more chapters. If it doesn't grab me by then, I'll give "Treasure Island" a go.' I focus on the words on the page. Vee remains standing in the doorway. I glance at her, then back at the book. She's doesn't move. I put the book down and study her. She has a twinkle in her eye that I know well.

'Chicken will be ready in twenty,' she says. 'Up for it?' she asks, referring to sex.

'Thing is Vee, I'm a bit sore down there?'

'Oh diddums, poor baby,' she mocks. I ignore her.

'I've got a slight cut and it hurts like hell. I think we may have to lay off it for a while, you know, two or three days.'

'Wimp.'

'Pardon?'

'You heard. Wimp. A real man would satisfy his lady in her time of need. But, if you can't manage it…' I put my book down and walk up to her.

'Wimp eh? I'll show you who's a wimp.' I pick her up like a caveman and throw her over my shoulder, march to the bed and drop her. She yelps.

'You bastard!' She's already breathing hard and her face is enflamed. I begin to unbutton my shirt. 'Wimp,' she says again as her foot massages my groin.

'Oh you've asked for it girl, you'll rue the day you called me a wimp.'

'Oh yeah, we'll see about that.' She quickly kneels up on the bed and begins madly unfastening my belt and pulling at my jeans.

##

'So, where's this little sore located?' she asks scrutinizing my penis.

'Half-way down, on the left,' I say as my breathing begins to slow.

'What, this little thing here?' she asks, jabbing her fingernail into it.

'Ow! Holy crap Vee, that bloody hurt!'

'Oops, sorry. It's only a tiny little scratch.'

'Tiny it may be, but it's as sore as hell. Can you put the thing down and leave it alone.' She relinquishes her grip and lays next to me.

'So, how long are we going to go without sex?'

'I don't know, two to three days and it should come good.' She snorts derisively.

'Ha! Seventy-two hours without sex—you wouldn't last more than four hours,' she taunts. I bristle at this and sit up.

'You really know nothing about me, do you?'

'I know you can't go three days in sexual absentia.'

'My willpower is made from iron girders. When Jimmy Hooper decides to do something then wild horses cannot drag him off course.'

'Okay. How about little Jimmy Hooper and Victoria Halliwell have a little wager on it. Say, ten pounds, that you cannot last three days without *any* sexual activity? And that includes the serve-yourself-cafeteria.'

'Right, you're on—in fact, let's make it twenty quid to keep it interesting.'

'Okay, Iron Girder man, shake on it,' she replies, as she spits into her hand. I shake and squeeze it tightly.

'Ow! You pig!' she protests.

'That's for jagging your fingernail into my todger, earlier.' She looks at the clock.

'It's exactly 8 pm on a Sunday evening. No sex of any sort until after 8 pm Wednesday…agreed?'

'Agreed. My self-discipline is a force of nature, you'll see.' She jumps from the bed and heads back into the kitchen, laughing derisively.

'What a poor, hopeless fool you are. You know what they say about a fool and his money, Jimmy?' she yells back. I'll show her, she doesn't know what she's up against.

##

The first day is a breeze—well, not a breeze exactly, but I was so busy I barely had time to think of anything else but work. I get in late after a Hipnotikz

223

gig. I have some great shots of them and I have a short interview that I'm hoping Dave Dee will run in the Saturday entertainment section. Vee is already tucked up in bed with the light off. Only a thin shaft of light emanates from the kitchen.

'I've saved you some dinner. It's in the oven keeping warm,' she mumbles sleepily.

'Thanks Vee, I'm famished.' I wolf my dinner down, hop in the shower, brush my teeth, then snuggle into bed.

'Cuddle me,' she demands. I pull her nice and tight into me and breathe in her heady perfume. She wriggles her naked buttocks back and forth against me for a few seconds. Hmm, this is no good, the man from down under thinks it's playtime. I release her and lie on my side. A few seconds later, she sits up in bed.

'Phew, is it me or is it really hot tonight?' she asks as I feel her pull her top off.

'It's you, I'm freezing.'

'I'll cuddle you then. Take some of my heat.' She lies down and grips me tightly. I feel her nipples rub against my back. I know her game, she doesn't fool me. Ha! Does she really think I'm that weak?

After what feels like hours, I hear her heavy breathing. She's asleep. I gently disengage from her and roll onto on my back as my mind slowly sinks into nothingness.

Day two, and I am a fucking mess! I cannot focus on anything. People have conversations with me but I can't even decipher what they are saying. I accidentally run a red light and nearly get knocked off my scooter. I retreat back to my flat and my darkroom for my own safety. I completely stuff up thirty prints by putting them in the wrong solution. I go downstairs and into the kitchen to make a strong coffee as Sofe walks in.

'Hey Jimmy, how's it going? Haven't seen you for a while?'

'Oh hi, Steve. Have you seen the cat lately?' I walk past her with my brew and head for the stairs. She looks puzzled.

'We don't have a cat! We've never had a cat and did you just call me Steve? Are you feeling all right Jimmy?' she calls after me.

'Yeah fine, fine, never better. Gotta keep going, I have a lot of Pollock Jacksons to decipher.'

'What? You mean develop?' she asks staring at me from the side of the stairs.

'Not now Marky, I'm too busy. But, if you see the dog, don't forget to feed him.' I enter the bedroom and stare at the framed photo of Vee on the wall. I am mesmerised. I think of her hair, her soft cheeks, those brilliant blue bewitching eyes. The fullness of her breasts, her nipples, the soft down on her neck, the curve of her back, her buttocks, her thighs… stop it you fool! I put my coffee down, unzip and carefully inspect my penis. The sore has nearly gone. Maybe we could call it a draw, I've nearly gone a day and a half. No, no, I have an iron will. I will not be beaten!

I stay late and when I get back to Vee's flat she is brushing her hair in front of the mirror, preparing for bed. She asks me about my day and I make some bullshit up, because to be with honest with you, I haven't got a fucking clue what I've been up to. She makes me a bowl of soup and I sit at the table as she tells me about her day. I try hard to avoid eye contact. She seems oblivious to my mental anguish—which is good. I'm going to win this bet. I tell her that I am feeling unwell and may be coming down with a cold so I'll sleep on the sofa tonight. She comforts me and gets me a couple of paracetamol and a glass of hot milk and honey. She asks what I am doing tomorrow. I have nothing on, the first break in over two weeks. She smiles and says that's wonderful, we can spend the whole day together. God, I pray to thee—give me strength.

It's 4 pm, only four hours to go and victory is mine. Today has been absolute torture. Every move she makes, every word she says, every sway of her ponytail, enflames my arousal. I need to extricate myself from her presence for a

225

while and chew up a couple of hours. I'm with her in the kitchen. She's making spaghetti bolognaise, my favourite.

'Hey Vee, I've just got to nip out for a while,' I lie.

'Okay, what for?' she enquires.

'Erm, I have to speak with Dave Dee.'

'What about?' What is this, the fucking Spanish Inquisition!

'Oh, just about a couple of photos he wants.'

'Why don't you just ring him? Save yourself a journey.' God damn you woman!

'Nah, you don't know Dave. He spends most of the day with his phone off the hook, he gets that many interruptions. I've tried that before.'

'Okay, well don't be too long. Dinner should be ready about six. I just want to give this sauce a good long simmer.' I'm already making my way out of the door.

'Yep, I won't be late,' I shout back at her.

##

I walk into the newsroom and it is unusually quiet. I can't see Marky anywhere. Dave Dee is sitting at his desk, scribbling away as usual.

'Hi Dave, how's things?' Dave barely looks up.

'All's good Jimmy. You?'

'Yeah, yeah, never better. On top of the world.'

'Oh good,' he drawls slowly as his red pen works overtime.

'So Dave, how's things?' He puts his pen down and stares at me suspiciously.

'You just asked me that,' he replies.

'I did, haha! Who'd have thought?' He leans back in his chair.

'Are you feeling all right Jimmy? You seem a bit flustered and disorientated.'

'Never better Dave, never better. Chipper, always chipper. Is Marky around?' Dave picks up his pen and resumes his work.

'No, he's at the courts. Not due back until five.'

'What about John Arnold?' Yes, I am that fucking desperate!

'No, he's out and about somewhere. Is there something I can help you with?'

'No, no, all's fine.'

'Good. Well fuck off and let me get some work done.'

'Yep, yep. No problem Dave, I'll fuck off right now. If Marky comes back early tell him I'll be in Tossers until about six.' He doesn't reply and I leave the building.

##

I walk to the bar in Tossers. I'm the only customer.

'Hello Jimmy, you're starting a bit early aren't you?'

'Hi Janice,'

'It's Jenny…'

'Oh, hi Jenny. No, I'm only having a quick one then I'll be on my way.'

'What are you having?' she asks.

'Erm, a pint of pork scratchings please and a packet of lager.' She screws her face up.

'A pint of what?'

'Erm, a pint of lager, I mean.' She starts chatting to me as she pulls the pint and I smile and nod at her as I think of Vee back at the flat stirring the bolognaise sauce. She's wearing white, skin-tight leggings that show every voluptuous curve. On top, she has a baggy blue vest. She is braless and barefoot. I can see her shiny red toenails. Jenny puts the pint down in front of me and I hand her a tenner. I retreat to the far end of the pub. I sit down and sip on my pint.

'Jimmy, your change,' Jenny calls out. I stand and walk back to the bar. She drops the change into my outstretched palm. 'Is everything all right love?' she asks with a concerned look.

'Yep, never better. All's fair in love and war—as they say.' She now looks puzzled.

'Everything okay with you and Vee?' I laugh like a drain.

'Me and Vee, me and Vee. Sweet as, just perfect.' I resume my seat. I think of football and the forthcoming fixtures—for about ten seconds then my thoughts return to Vee. I can see her sitting, propped up on the bed, intently reading a book. She always has a serious expression when she reads. It's beautiful, I could sit and watch her for hours. Stop it! I look at the clock on the wall—5:15 pm. I'll dawdle here for another half hour, then take an extremely long walk home. I'll get back at about six—that will leave two hours to go and victory and gloating rights will be mine. I look back at the bar. Jenny and Amy are in discussion. Jenny nods in my direction and says something to her daughter. Amy shrugs. They are both beautiful, sexy and attractive women but they don't come within a million miles of my Vee— no woman does. I finish my pint as the clock ticks past 5:40 pm. I place it on the bar and say goodbye.

I wander the busy streets and buy a copy of the Standard. I walk at a snail's pace and return to the flat at exactly 5:55 pm.

She's still in the kitchen busily stirring the sauce.

'Hi Jim, did you get it sorted?'

'Get what sorted?'

'The photo thingy with Dave.'

'Oh yeah, all sorted. Not a problem.'

'Good. Here, taste this sauce it's the best I've made.' She dips a wooden spoon into the pan and scoops out a bit of sauce. She holds it side on and as I lower my head to taste it she draws the spoon away from me towards her own lips. I follow the arc of her movement until my lips touch the spoon at the exact same moment as her own do. Our lips are but a hair's breadth away from each other. She's staring directly into my eyes with those big blue marbles. My heart skips a beat and there is an immediate reaction from my rapid response unit down below. We both taste the sauce at the same time. She swallows, then sticks the tip of her tongue out and slowly rolls it around her full red lips in a provocative and completely uncalled for manner.

'Hmm, that is gorgeous,' she says as she turns away from me. 'Do you think it needs just an extra splash of red wine?' she asks.

'Maybe.' She accidentally knocks a teaspoon off the counter and it clatters to the floor. She bends over, slowly, with her back to me and picks up the spoon. I stand in awe of her backside. It's amazing how many times today she has dropped things, then very slowly bent over to pick them up. I fear she may be suffering from the rapid onset of motor-neuron disease. She lifts the bottle of wine and pours a drop into the pan. As she retracts the bottle a splash lands on her leggings. Here we go!

'Oh no! These are my best leggings. I'll need to get them in the wash straight away.' Of course she will. She walks a few feet to where the washing machine is, puts her thumbs into the elastic of her pants and wriggles out of them. She then bends over, again, and takes an age to open the washing machine door and deposit them inside. Her buttocks are staring me in the face. She is wearing a "G" string, for what it's worth. It is more akin to a piece of tooth floss and the important part has disappeared into a familiar crevice. I look at the clock. It has just turned six. Two hours to go—the iron girders are beginning to bend under such a withering onslaught and I fear it may be just the beginning.

We sit and eat tea together. I try and listen to the news on the TV, hoping it will distract me for a few precious minutes. She is sitting opposite and stares continually into my eyes. Occasionally, instead of rolling her spaghetti around her spoon and eating it that way, she sucks a strand up. I watch as she does it again. The spaghetti slowly slides upwards and disappears through her pouting mouth. Then out comes that tongue again to roll around her lips, all the while her eyes never leave mine. I rush my food down as quickly as possible.

'You stay here love and put your feet up. I'll do the washing up.' I pick my plate up and make a grab for hers.

'Hey! I haven't finished yet,' she exclaims.

'Oh sorry, of course. Bring your plate in when you're done.'

I wash the pans three times and dry them three times, as I do with my plate and cutlery. I swear to God, the clock on the wall has stopped. 6:30 pm—one and a half hours until we have lift off. I suddenly feel her presence behind me. I have my hands in the washing up bowl as she pushes me slightly sideways. She reaches across in front of me to place her plate and utensils into the soapy water. I feel her breasts and nipples rub against my chest. As she moves back her head stops directly in front of mine, our lips once again, only millimetres away from each other. Damn those eyes! I can feel her warm sweet breath on the top of my lip. The back of her arm brushes against my crotch. My penis is rock hard pressing against its fabric prison. I can hear it screaming, "Hey come on, let me out of here, what's going on? Was it something I said?"

She grabs a tea towel and begins drying up as she gently sings a song. I finish my duties at the sink and decide now would be a good time to rearrange all the food in the pantry.

'Whatever are you doing?' she asks.

'Pantry, the pantry… it needs sorting. Been meaning to do it for ages. It's all mixed up. No organisation. No time like the present, eh?' I fuck around in the pantry for a good twenty minutes. By the time I've finished, it's completely up the shit. I'm not sure what I did, but there's a mismatch of food types all over the shop. I look at the clock—nearly 7 pm. One hour to go Jimmy, my son. You can do it, hang in there. She can't trap me with her arousal tactics. This boy's not for turning.

'Right, well that's the pantry done. That's a lot better.' I shut the door quickly before she can look inside and see what a gargantuan fuck-up I've made of it all. 'There's a documentary starting in a minute about the miners' strike. You don't mind if I watch it do you?'

'No, not at all. I'm going to get a shower, redo my nails, then read before bed.' I slink off into the bedroom, change channels on the TV and sit at the little table as the intro to the documentary begins. Vee comes in and opens a drawer of her dressing table. She has now blocked my line of vision.

'Oh sorry, Jimmy. I won't be a minute, just need to get some things.' Oops, here we go, she's dropped something else, yep, and there she goes bending over, this time facing me so I can see her breasts dangling freely inside her loose top. She leaves the room—for about a second, and is now back again.

'Oh sorry, Jim. I forgot something.' Oh dear, now she's dropped a hair tie. 'How's the documentary?'

'I'm asking myself the same fucking question!'

'Sorry, I'll be out of your hair in a mo.' Finally she leaves the room but is immediately back again minus her possessions.

'Hey Jim, can I ask you a question?'

'Sure, I'm not doing anything else.' She peels her top off and stands naked in front of me.

'Do you think I've gained weight?' She slowly spins around. I am captivated by her perfect body. She is well toned and firm in every department. She is a marble Goddess. 'Well?'

'Maybe,' I reply. Yes! Take that! I've got one back for the team. She narrows her eyes, pouts and looks at me spitefully. Then, she raises one eyebrow and gives me an enigmatic half smile, as though to say, "Oh, so that's your little game is it? We'll see about that." Maybe I'm reading too much into the situation. At last she's gone and I hear the shower start, followed quickly by her beautiful voice singing away. I try to focus on the talking heads on the screen but it's all in vain. I imagine her in the shower soaping herself down. Her hands rubbing suds into her breasts and buttocks. Her hands between her legs. Stop! Stop! Stop! What am I doing? This is self-sabotage.

I try to refocus. There's some fat bloated politician on the screen telling us that the "age of entitlement" is over. Yeah pal, over for the rest of the country but not for you though. You'll still get your expense allowance, your electorate office allowance and your pension for life once you pull the pin or get booted out.

My mind is in a fever. I hear the shower stop, then a few moments later she's back in the room. It's 7:30 pm—thirty minutes of torment left. She has one towel wrapped around her head and another wrapped around her body, tucked under her arms. She goes back to that damned drawer.

'Sorry, just looking for my pink teddy?' What the hell is she talking about?

'I've never seen you with a pink teddy?' I enquire. She laughs.

'You think I mean a teddy bear, don't you?' I nod. She pulls an item of clothing from the drawer and holds it up below her neck.

'This is my pink teddy.' It's her long-sleeved top that ends at the hips.

'Oh,' I say. 'I thought that was your pyjama top.' She takes the towel from her head and shakes her hair loose. She then throws the body towel onto a chair and pulls the teddy over her head. She's still standing in front of the TV, absolutely no underwear on and I know this is going to be a bitter war of attrition for the next twenty-five minutes. Off she goes again. And now she's back. She sits down on the floor in front of me with legs akimbo and begins repainting her fucking toenails! The part of my brain that controls my eye movement seems to be impaired. No matter how much I try to fixate on the TV, my eyes slowly swivel back to her. They're like one of those ack-ack guns from the second world war, where you crank a pair of handles and the gun slowly rotates.

Every time she looks up at me I quickly avert my gaze back to the screen. She's now got the hairdryer out, drying her toenails, contorting into all sorts of unnecessary positions as she does so. I genuinely believe she is evil. The documentary finishes. 7:40 pm—twenty minutes to go.

'How was the documentary? Was it balanced?' she asks. I have no fucking idea whatsoever.

'Yes, it was fair and balanced. Told both sides of the story.'

'Oh good. Was daddy on it?' she enquires. I'm not sure, he could have been. They could have had Coco the Clown reading the Gettysburg Address and I don't think I'd have noticed.

'No he wasn't. Right, time for a shower.' I get up and make my way to the bathroom and breathe a sigh of relief. I stand under the shower and wash myself from head to toe. Then I do it again. Then once more for good luck. I look at the clock radio that sits on the vanity sink top and see it's red digital lights staring back at me—7:48—twelve minutes to go. My penis is rock hard and all a quiver. At any moment it could self-detonate and explode through the frosted glass blocks, then speed high over the cold night sky of Leeds. On through the stratosphere it could go, within minutes, circling an outlying galactic planet.

"Houston, we have a problem. An unidentified flying penis is orbiting Neptune at the speed of light… over."

I put a ridiculous amount of shampoo into my hands and begin lathering my hair. I suddenly feel a hand on my shoulder that makes me start. Then, her voice.

'Thought I'd come and scrub your back for you. Here let me do that,' she says as she pulls my hands from my head and replaces them with her own. Her long slender fingers begin to slowly and sensually massage my scalp. These are dirty tactics. She knows that massaging my head sends me into an absolute sensual frenzy. Her thumbs knead the back of my neck and around my ears. Her nails scrape along my scalp. I open one eye and look at the clock—7:54—six minutes left. I can see the finishing line dead ahead. I am in the lead but I can feel her filly breathing down my neck—quite literally.

'Ow! Shit!'

'What's wrong Jim?' she asks in a concerned tone.

'I've got soap in my eye,' I complain.

233

'Here, turn around and tilt your head back.' She runs her hands back through my hair, away from my forehead and I hear the gloopy splat of soap suds hit the shower floor. She delicately uses her thumbs to wipe soap away from my eyes.

'Keep you lids closed and let the water run over them.' Another minute passes and I am completely rinsed. She grabs a loofah and soaps me up all over. She then uses her hands to rinse me off. She spends an inordinate amount of time on my buttocks and I feel her finger slip between my cheeks and slowly slide down to my balls. I look at that damned clock—the fucking thing must be on the blink—7:56—four minutes left! I am finally free of suds and she turns the shower off.

'Stay here, I'll get you a warm fluffy towel.' She's back in seconds rubbing me vigorously all over, continually brushing against my purple love balloon. She drops the towel to the floor.

'There, all done.' She gives me a motherly peck on the cheek and I think she's going to go—but she doesn't. She stares at my aching erection and giggles.

'So, how's little Tommy Tinker getting on?'

'He's fine! Don't touch him!' I snap at her.

'He doesn't look fine to me. He looks like he could pop his top at any moment. He's all red and angry and keeps twitching. I think he might be having a heart attack.' I ignore her taunts. 'How's the sore?'

'It's gone.'

'Are you sure?'

'Yep, perfectly.'

'Here, let me have a look.' She grabs the tip of my penis between forefinger and thumb and traces a line down the side of my shaft with the pad of a finger. 'About here, wasn't it?'

'Yep.' She circles the spot around and around. 'Yes, it's all cleared up.' Then, in an act of sadistic and malevolent intent, that would get her twenty-five years in maximum security by any male jury, she slowly drags her fingernails up my

234

shaft from the very base to the very tip. She lets go of me and gives the whole thing a playful slap. I swear to God, if she lays one more finger on Tommy, he will erupt!

I look at the clock—7:58—surely I can't fuck it up from here? My girders are at breaking point and my iron will has turned into a tattered, ragged flag, flapping limply in her breeze.

'Oh well, that's good news then. Another two to three days and little Tommy Tinker will be back in action.'

'What!' I exclaim.

'Oh sorry Jim, but my period is due at any moment and I prefer not to have sex when I'm on,' she replies, nonchalantly. Nooooooo! What trickery is this? What witchcraft is at play here? Sorcery in the ascendancy! This cannot be happening! No man in a relationship can be expected to go six days without sex— that transgresses the immutable laws of nature—surely! My world has just spun out of control and crash-landed into the Sun.

'But...' is the only word I can manage. It's as though my brain has been deleted.

'Oh you look so disappointed. Tell you what,' she says with a breezy smile, 'I'll go put the kettle on and make us a nice cup of tea—that will cheer you up.' A cup of tea—to cheer me up! She has got to be fucking joking! The only thing that could cheer me up right now is a swift jab to the jugular with a syringe full of cyanide! She turns to leave. I reach out and grab her by the shoulder.

'Wait! Not so fast—nice try. You had your period last week.' She pulls a puzzled expression, pouts and taps one finger back and forth against her lips.

'Oh yes, silly me, how could I forget.'

'You bloody minx,' I whisper. I lean forward and put my hands on the back of her thighs and lift her up. Her arms encircle my neck as her legs girdle my hips. I turn and push her up against the shower wall. I gently lower her down and slide effortlessly inside her, thrusting hard upwards.

'Ooh, someone's got a lot of pent up frustration, haven't they?' She bends forwards and begins to kiss my neck and bite on my ear lobe. There's a repetitive beeping sound that echoes around the bathroom.

'What the fucks that?' I ask.

'The clock radio alarm,' she whispers softly in my ear. 'I set it for 8 pm exactly, just so there could be no disputes. I said you had no willpower Jimmy Hooper, and I was right—I win. You were so easy. I could have snapped you like a twig—any time I wanted.'

21: LECTURE

I turn the key in the lock, push the door open and walk inside. Vee follows me in.

'Hey Sofe, it's me! There's someone I'd like you to meet,' I call out. There's the sound of a scraping chair before Sofe emerges from her room and stands in the corridor. She looks a bit taken aback.

'Sofe this is Vee, Vee this is Sofe.' Both girls walk towards each other. They shake hands politely.

'Pleased to meet you, Vee. I feel like I already know you. Jimmy never shuts up about the great love affair.'

Vee laughs. 'Pleased to meet you too, Sofe. I've also heard a lot about you. I sometimes think he's having the love affair with you,' she laughs. Sofe looks a tad embarrassed. I go up to Sofe and plant a big smacker on her forehead and give her a big hug.

'Jimmy, stop it!' she says and tries to push me away.

'Ah Sofe, I love you. How have you been? Still studying hard? I've barely seen you this last week.' She wriggles free and slaps me on the chest.

'Yes, I have been studying hard. I've got to admit it's been peaceful without you here. I've been able to catch up on all my work. That bloody phone hasn't stopped ringing though. When was the last time you checked your messages?'

'Yesterday. I check them nearly every day, it just so happens you haven't been home when I call around. Hey Sofe, be a pal and put the kettle on will you, I'm gagging for a cuppa. Come on Vee, I'll take you to my lair.'

'That's all I am to you, isn't it? A char-lady,' replies Sofe with mock annoyance. I walk up the stairs into my bedroom. 'So, here you are, this is the nerve centre of Snap Photography. What do you think?' Vee stares around the room and looks less than impressed.

'It's so small, how can you work in here?'

'Easy, I just do.' She sticks her head into the darkroom and turns the light on.

'Oh my God! This is disgusting!'

'What?' I reply, following her in. I look around the room. Okay, it's maybe a few weeks since I had a cleanup, but it's been worse.

'That bin is overflowing with empty pot noodles, there are old coffee cups everywhere. Ugh! This one has mould in it. And what's this?' She grabs a scrunched up ball of newspaper and opens it. 'It beggars belief! Old fish and chips, and over there, a half-eaten curry, and here, what even is that?' I stare at the object for a few seconds and try to recollect what, in fact, it is.

'Erm, I think it's a battered sausage—or maybe a battered Mars Bar.' I can't recall the last time I bought a battered sausage or Mars Bar, but it must be well over six months ago. She curls her nose up.

'Battered sausage? Battered Mars Bar—I didn't realise there were such things. And what's this under the table?' She bends over and picks up a slew of magazines.

'Pornographic magazines! Jimmy, how could you?'

'Well, it can get lonely in here on long nights. I only read the articles about cars. I don't look at the pictures—honest.' She drops the magazines to the floor.

'And what's that smell?'

'That's the different solutions for developing the photos.'

'It stinks. Is it toxic?'

'Nah, just saline and a bit of acid that's all.'

'Oh my God! Let me out of here.' She barges past me back into the bedroom. I turn the light off and shut the door. I walk over to my sock drawer and pull it open. I fumble about in my trouser pockets and pull out large handfuls of scrunched up notes and wads of rolled up tenners with elastic bands wrapped around them. I throw them all into the sock drawer.

'What is that?' she exclaims, pointing at the drawer.

'It's my sock drawer, what do you think it is?'

'The money, I'm talking about the money! No Jimmy, you can't do that. You need to get it into the bank… how much is there?' I scratch my chin and have a wild stab in the dark.

'Not sure, about seven, eight hundred, maybe.'

'I'm horrified. You can't run a business like this. It's like the other week when you were ill and I asked you where your diary was and you said you didn't have one. All your appointments were written on tiny scraps of scrunched up paper stuffed into your pockets.'

'The system's not perfect, I'll grant you that, but it does work. Apart from the day I turned up at the wrong wedding.' She stares at me in disbelief.

'Jimmy, you need a proper system. A business has two sides to it; the front end where you do the photographs, liaise with clients and develop your photos; and the back end where you keep track of your income and expenses and plan for the future.' I grab hold of her buttocks and pull her towards me.

'I prefer the back end,' I smile as I lean in to kiss her. She whacks me on the shoulder and pushes me away.

'Jimmy, I'm being serious! You can't go on like this. You need to get that money into a bank and sort yourself out.'

'That's where the porno mags come in,' I laugh. She hits me again.

'Stop it! I'm worried about you!' she scolds. She means it.

'Look Vee, I can't put the money in the bank because I'm still signing on. And yes, the darkroom does need a bit of a tidy. I'll get onto it at the weekend.'

'Jim, you need to go legit. You don't need the dole anymore.'

'I'm just being cautious. You know, the work may dry up then I'll be stuffed.'

'We've been through this before. It's not going to dry up. This is a going concern and you've got room to develop it and expand, but not the way you're going.'

'How come you know so much about business?'

'I studied Business Economics at school.'

'Strewth! That sounds like fun.'

'It may not have been fun, but it was practical. You're just winging it. I'm surprised you are making so much money with the set up you have. Right, when we get back to the flat I'm going to help you draw up a business plan. You are going to have a system, it doesn't have to be complex.' I am suitably chastised. I peer into her eyes. She looks bloody annoyed with me.

'Say Vee, do you fancy stepping into the darkroom for a few minutes?'

'Yes, I bloody do mind! I won't be going back in there until it's been fumigated, disinfected and de-cluttered. It's a health hazard.' She suddenly spots her photo on the wall and walks over to it. She strokes the glass frame. 'Wow! Who was that girl, I barely recognise her now,' she says wistfully. 'That's only a few months ago and now, she doesn't exist.' I put my arms around her.

'Jimmy, Vee, your brew is ready!' Sofe calls up the stairs. Vee turns to me.

'You never told me she was so pretty?'

'Who, Sofe? Yeah, she's a looker all right,' I reply nonchalantly.

'Do you always greet her with a kiss and a hug and tell her that you love her?'

'Not always, but sometimes. Why?'

'I just find it a little odd. You've lived with an attractive girl in the same house all this time and nothing's happened between you?'

'Oh I see, the little green eyed monster raises its head. I love her like a sister, like I love the lads like brothers. It's a different kind of love. My love for them is like driving down a flat straight road, nice and sedate. My love for you is like being on a rollercoaster as it hurtles down the tracks, your stomach jumps into your chest and you think you're going to pee yourself. Except, the rollercoaster never reaches the bottom, it just picks up speed each day. I love them. I love you, but I'm also in love with you.' Her eyes soften and she apologises.

'Sorry Jimmy. I do get a little jealous. I know what you're like.'

'Come on, let's go get that cup of tea, and afterwards, we can relax on my bed,' I wink at her. She stares at my bedsheets and shakes her head.

'When was the last time you washed your sheets?' she asks very slowly, as she gingerly lifts a corner of the sheet up to inspect it. It's a damn good question, and to be honest, I cannot recall ever washing the sheets, but I'm assuming that response would not go down too well. What would be a reasonable amount of time between washes?

'Oh, about three months ago,' I reply, reckoning that makes me slightly obsessed with cleanliness.

'What! That is absolutely disgusting Jimmy. I will not be going anywhere near that bed, let me assure you!' As she turns to leave she goes back to the sock drawer and begins to count up the money, carefully straightening crumpled notes and removing rubber bands.

'How much did you think you had? Seven or eight hundred pounds?' I nod 'There's one thousand seven hundred and fifty-eight pounds here!' I scratch my head.

'Hmm… only one thousand and a bit out,' I reply. 'Oh hang on, there's also the tin… nearly forgot.' I pull an old biscuit barrel out from under the bed, pull the lid off and empty the contents onto the sheets. She gasps, then repeats the process of counting up.

'One thousand two hundred and twenty pounds. Together, that's just shy of three thousand.' She shakes her head at me as though I'm a naughty schoolboy. She slips all the money into her handbag.

'What are you doing?' I ask.

'I have a safe back at the flat. You can keep it there.'

'I've never noticed a safe,' I say, puzzled.

'Isn't that the point of a safe? To be hidden?'

'Where is it?'

'Behind mummy's painting, above the bed. It's built into the wall.'

'Well there you go! Hey, give me three hundred back.'

'What for?'

'I like to leave some behind for Sofe, she is a student you know. I can't bear the thought of her going short.' She peels off three hundred and I put it back in my sock drawer and push it shut.

##

We're all sitting around the kitchen table sipping on tea and munching on the sawdust biscuits that Sofe insists on buying because they are cheap. It's an enthralling conversation as both women bitch about me as though I'm invisible.

'Have you seen how much money he keeps in his sock drawer?' begins Vee.

'I know, it's ridiculous. I don't know how many times I've told him to either put it in the bank or at least find a decent hiding place. We only have a Yale lock on the front door, if someone broke in they'd have a field day.'

'Have you seen his darkroom?' Vee continues.

'Oh my God! I know, I refuse to go in there now. I'm scared I'll catch something. If I make him a cup of tea I leave it outside the door.'

'And he hasn't washed his bedsheets for over three months,' says Vee, relishing my public humiliation. Sofe arches one eyebrow and fixes me with a cold, suspicious stare.

'Three months, eh? I cannot recall seeing Jimmy's bed sheets hung out on the line—not once, and we've been here nearly two years now.' I cannot let my good name and character be besmirched like this. Time to make a stand.

'Ha! Well, that's where you're wrong, Miss Starchy Knickers, because I washed them three months ago, it was the weekend you went back to visit your folks.' That'll show them, that's one back for the boys.

'How convenient,' Sofe drawls. 'Hang on, the last time I visited my parents was well over six months ago!' They both turn and stare at me with upturned noses as disgust drips from their open mouths.

'Right, who's up for another brew? I'll stick the kettle on.'

We have another cup of tea and more sawdust as they rip me apart. Apparently, I'm annoying, untidy, talk in my sleep, don't know how to cook, loud, clumsy, have the ability to say the most inappropriate things at the wrong time, oh yes and I'm stubborn and sulk if I don't get my own way.

The slaughter-fest eventually ends and as the blood slowly seeps away into the trough, they both look at me with soft, sad smiles.

'Okay, Burke and Hare, you've listed my bad points, now what about my good points?' They both turn and look at each other with blank expressions. There's at least fifteen seconds of silence.

'Oh I know,' says Vee, excitedly, as though she's just found the formula for alchemy. 'He's clean, I mean bodily clean, he always smells sweet.'

'Yes he is clean, very clean. And he's always smartly dressed,' states Sofe.

'Oh yes, very smart. The uber Mod.' They both fall silent again as they rap their fingers on the table. At least a minute passes by, accompanied by numerous tumbleweeds.

'Well, is that it? I'm clean and dress smart?' They both stare at me, thinking hard.

'He's very loving,' says Vee, softly.

'Yes he is,' concurs, Sofe. 'A redeeming quality.'

'You can forgive a man anything, as long as there's love and respect.'

'Yes, I suppose you can.'

I stand up. 'Well, you know what they say, a bird in the hand is worth two in Kate's bush! Come on Vee, we best make tracks.' They both look at each other and shake their heads in despair.

##

There's something a little odd about Vee. Not all, but most work days, I head back to her flat for lunch. Because of my schedule I'm never really sure what time I'll arrive. It could be anytime between 11:30 and 2 pm. Yet, without fail, whenever I walk through the door, there's a plate of food and a cup of tea waiting for me on the table. I asked her about it one day.

'Vee, how come every time I arrive for lunch you have it waiting for me? You can't possibly know what time I'm going to arrive?'

'Oh, I just sense it.'

'You sense what?'

'When you will arrive. It's like your thoughts travel to me.'

'What?'

'Yes, it's true. I'll be busy cooking or reading and then it will hit me. Aha! Jimmy is heading back for lunch,' she says in a disconcerting matter-of-fact way. I didn't press the matter any further.

Then there was the time when I entered the vestibule and was hanging my coat up. I heard voices, or at least I heard Vee's voice. I walked into the bedroom and I could hear her chatting with someone in the kitchen. I assumed we had a visitor. When I walked into the kitchen she was busy kneading bread on the table. I looked around the room and there was no one else there.

'Oh hi, Jimmy,' she says, as she purses her lips and leans towards me. I give her a quick peck on the lips.

'Have we visitors?' I ask, assuming whoever it is, has gone to the bathroom.

'No, why would you ask that?'

'You were talking to someone.'

'I was chatting with grandmother,' she states, without a care in the world.

'You were talking with your dead grandmother?' I ask hesitantly.

'Yes,' she smiles back at me. 'She's not really dead. Only her body has left.' I'm intrigued but also a little freaked out.

'Right, okay. And what were you talking about?'

'Oh nothing in particular. Just telling her about my day. She asked after you.'

'And what did you say?'

'I said you were fine, that your business is really taking off. She's pleased for you.' As fucking weird as all this is, another thought comes in to play.

'She isn't here, when we, you know…'

'Know what?'

'You know, when we… fuck?'

'Jimmy!' she scolds. 'Don't be so crude! And no, of course she isn't. She has manners and respects our privacy. Put the kettle on will you, I could murder a cup of tea.'

You see what I mean? Odd.

22: IDYLL

We walk down to the lake hand in hand and lie on the bank for a while soaking up the sunshine.

'This has to be one of the most peaceful places in the world,' I say.

'It is beautiful,' she replies. 'There's an even more peaceful place than this. A secret place, daddy's secret place. Or at least that's what he thinks.' I roll over and stare at her.

'Intriguing. You can't end there, come on where is it?' She giggles.

'Across the lake, then a short walk through the woods. When I was a little girl I used to watch him from my window. Every Sunday morning he'd walk down to the lake with a bunch of Sunday newspapers tucked under his arm and a flask of tea under the other. He'd jump into the rowing boat, row across to the far side of the lake, then disappear into the woods for a couple of hours. He doesn't know I know.'

'Show me,' I command. She sits up.

'Come on then! Can you row a boat?'

'Can I row a boat? Ha! Of course I can row a boat. It's not rocket science. What a question! Can I row a boat indeed…'

I clamber into the little wooden boat and hold Vee's arm as she climbs aboard. I take a seat, facing the pointy end and grab the oars. Vee stares at me.

'What?' I ask as I shuffle to make myself comfortable.

'You're facing the wrong way,' she states with lips pursed. 'You row with your back facing the bow, not the stern.'

'The bow? The pointy end?'

'Yes,' she nods.

'Well that's bloody daft. How are you supposed to see where you're going?'

'I take it you've mastered the ability to turn your head?' she replies, caustically. I spin around and take up my new position. Vee sits opposite me.

'Head in a nor'westerly direction,' she advises as I dip the oars in the water and pull back on them.

'Just point,' I say.

We make painful progress across the lake as the oars keep slipping from their oarlocks, which sends me flying back in the boat. Every time it happens Vee laughs hysterically.

'There's something wrong with these oars,' I moan.

'You're hopeless. Your rhythm's all wrong. Here, let me show you. You man the rudder. Can you manage that?' she snipes. We exchange seats. She leans forward and pulls back hard on the oars. We are soon skimming across the lake.

Every now and then a few drops of water are splashed onto me. I'm certain she is doing it on purpose. I marvel at her taut skin, the well defined muscle in her arms. As she leans forward her breasts launch towards me only to be reined in by her blouse.

'What?' she asks as I stare at her intently.

'Nothing,' I reply. 'Just admiring poetry in motion.'

'Oh stop, you charmer.'

'You stop. No, really, I mean stop rowing—right now.'

'Whatever for? We're over half-way there now.' I grab one oar and bring it to a halt. She looks annoyed.

'Jimmy, you've upset my flow. I'll have to start over again and that's the hardest part.' There is silence between us as our eyes engage. She suddenly comprehends the moment.

'No! Absolutely not! Not in the boat, we could be seen from the castle. I mean it Jimmy, it's not going to happen!'

We lie snuggled on cushions as the boat rocks slightly from side to side. The gentle slap of water against the hull relaxes me.

'You're a beast,' she says softly as she strokes my head.

'You weren't saying that five minutes ago. I hope no one heard your screams of pleasure back at the castle. They'd have thought I was murdering you.' She slaps me on the chest.

'I did not scream, you liar.'

'You bloody did. I'm deaf in my left ear.' We rest in blissful silence for another fifteen minutes until she pulls herself upright.

'Come on, let's get going.'

We disembark at another small jetty and tie the boat up. She grabs my hand excitedly. We walk towards a thick dense copse by following a slight path through bushes and tall trees. As we start to climb a steep hill she talks to me.

'I sometimes used to come here with my dolls when I was little.'

'How did you get across the lake?'

'Oh I didn't row, I wasn't strong enough back then. I'd walk here.'

'Didn't your parents notice you missing? That must have taken quite some time?'

'You've met my parents, you should know the answer. Daddy was hardly ever here, apart from weekends and well, you know how mummy is with her artwork. She can disappear for days in her studio.' I feel desperately sorry for her.

'So who looked after you?'

'Mostly, myself. Mrs Beaton would always look out for me and make sure I got fed and watered. But, I was pretty much free to come and go as I pleased.' I stop and pull her towards me and kiss her gently on the lips.

'I'm so sorry,' She looks puzzled.

'For what?'

'Your childhood. It sounds so lonely. It's not right for a young child to be cast adrift like that.' She laughs and kisses me.

'Don't be silly, I had a great time. Plus, I wasn't alone. I had some friends from boarding school who would come and stay for a week or so, and I have a million cousins who were also dropping in. Anyway, I liked being alone, just me and my dolls living in my make-believe world. It was exciting.

Right, we're nearly here, just got to find the opening. It's been a while since I was last here.' She stops and scours the bush and thickets in front of us.

'Ah yes, here we go. Watch yourself on the damn gorse, it can scratch you to hell.' She half bends, pushes a thick bush aside then drags me through as we sidestep a gnarly gorse bush and a clump of benign looking stinging nettles. After a few more steps we emerge into a slight clearing. The first thing I notice is a mighty oak tree directly in front of us. The girth of its trunk is huge. The canopy hangs over like a protective umbrella. The clearing is encircled by numerous stones, almost like gravestones. Some are pointed at their apex, others have been snapped off halfway up, like an old man's teeth.

'What the fuck is this?'

'Jimmy! Don't swear—not here!' she scolds. 'It's an old Druid site.'

'Fuck!'

'Jimmy!'

I notice a huge circular stone buried in the centre of the stones. I walk over and study it for a moment. Inscribed words stare back at me. Their font is of an angular nature and it is hard for me to comprehend the letters, which are well worn.

'Ban... du... ri?' I slowly spell the letters out. 'What's that mean?' I enquire.

'Not sure. Maybe Celtic,' she answers in a vague fashion. My attention now turns to my right-hand-side. There's a simple wooden bench, sitting lonesome at the edge of what can only be described as a shallow cliff. We are quite high up. I walk over to it. One side faces into the stones and oak tree, the other, out onto a most magnificent panoramic vista.

'Wow!' is all I can say. In front of me are verdant fields, dappled with yellow hues. Behind them, undulating dales and escarpments. They stretch as far as my eyes can see. On the horizon I spot the ruins of some sort of church and the sparkling twinkle of what must be the North Sea. After a moment's reflection, I ask the question,

'What's that old church in the distance?'

'That's Whitby Abbey.'

'Get out of here! That must be over seventy miles away!' I exclaim.

'Hmm, by road. Probably only forty or fifty as the crow flies.' I sit down on the wooden bench, captivated by the view. Vee comes up behind me and begins to slowly massage my shoulders.

'Do you like it?' she asks.

'What? The view or the massage?'

'The view, silly. I know you like the massage.'

'I'm lost for words.'

'Well that's a first.'

'Damn?'

'What's wrong?'

'I should have brought my camera. I could get some brilliant shots up here.'

'Don't worry, we'll visit again—many times.' This is what I love about Vee, she always says "we", never "you".

'Have I ever told you how much I love you?' I ask as I rub the back of her hand.

'Not for about ten minutes,' she replies softly. I sit in silence for a while, then rise and circumnavigate the huge oak, all the while rubbing my hand across its gnarled brown bark. Halfway around I notice something cut into the bark of the tree, two initials. I shake my head and give a wry smile.

'This must be hundreds of years old,' I state as I get back to my starting position. Vee is leaning back against the trunk of the oak.

'There's a similar one in another part of the estate and daddy once paid for an arborist to come and estimate its age. That one, which isn't quite as big as this, was estimated to be over five-hundred years old. So this one could be six, possibly seven hundred years old.'

'No! How long do they live?'

'Up to one thousand years. Of course, once they hit seven hundred, they are well into old age and begin slowing down.'

'Like humans to the power of ten. You'd want to be slowing down and taking it easy after seven hundred years hard graft.' She giggles.

'You're funny.'

'Imagine the things this tree would have witnessed. The English civil war, Cavaliers versus Roundheads charging through fields. Henry VIII firing cannonballs at monasteries. Shakespeare, Queen Elizabeth, the Jacobite uprising, the first railways. It makes me feel so small, so insignificant. What are we handed, three score years and ten—if we're lucky. I'd love to live to be a thousand years old.'

'Really?' she seems surprised.

'Yes, really. A thousand years on this planet with you.' I move towards her. 'Seventy-years is not enough, it's not fair.' I kiss her on the lips, gently at first, then passionately. She places her hand on my chest to hold me back and breaks away from the kiss.

'Jimmy, you cannot be serious! It's only half an hour since we made love in the boat, you can't possibly want it again!' I smile at her.

'Wanna bet?' I move in to kiss her on the lips but she turns her cheek away.

'No Jimmy, not here, this is a sacred site. It's would be wrong.' I drop my lips onto her neck and find her sweet spot that drives her wild. I feel her soft breath begin to increase in intensity. I kiss the top of her breasts and make my way back to her lips. 'No, no. It's wrong,' she states again, with less conviction.

'That's what makes it more exciting—things that are taboo.' As our lips touch, she explodes with passion and responds vigorously. I feel her hand slip into my pants. She unzips my fly and pulls me out. I spin her around. She places her hands on the tree and arches her back. I lift her skirt up and pull her knickers down.

##

I tuck myself away and zip up my fly. Vee is still in the same position, bent over with her hands on the bark of the oak. She's breathing hard and her legs are trembling.

'Sorry. I was a bit rough. I got carried away. Did I hurt you?' I ask. She pushes herself away from the tree and stands upright.

'No, not at all. It was good, better than good. I've never had an orgasm like that before. I'm shaking all over. God, my legs are like jelly.'

'It's hard work making love standing up.' She retrieves her knickers and slips them on as I pull a penknife from my pocket.

'What's that?' she asks.

'It's a Swiss Army Knife my mother bought me for my sixteenth birthday. Not sure why, as I have no intention of ever joining the Swiss Army.' I walk back around the oak tree as she follows me.

'Have you seen this?' I ask

'What?'

'Your dad's carved his initials into the tree. Must have been a while back as it's nearly grown over.'

'Yes I know, I spotted it when I was a little girl.' I begin to chisel at the tree.

'Jimmy, what are you doing? Stop, daddy will know we've been here.' I ignore her and continue on, scratching away.

'Don't you find that odd? A man comes here and carves his initials into a tree but doesn't carve his sweetheart or lovers initials underneath it.'

'Yes, it is odd. There's only one person in daddy's life—and that's himself. Jimmy, please stop,' she begs.

'No, fuck him! He doesn't own this tree or this place.'

'Ahem, well yes, actually he does.'

'Well, granted, he may own it on paper, but he doesn't *really* own it. How can anyone own a seven-hundred-year-old tree? This mighty oak will outlive all of us; our children, our grandchildren, even our great, great-grandchildren. But at least they will be able to come here and see the initials of their ancestors. JH 4 VH FOREVER IN LOVE IN LIFE IN DEATH, surrounded by a heart with an arrow through it.' I scrape away for a few more seconds, then stop what I'm doing and look at Vee. She's quietly weeping. She puts her fist to her mouth and bites down on it.

'Vee what's the matter?' I whisper gently. I put the penknife back in my pocket and smother her fist with my hand. 'What is it? I've stopped now. All I've done is redo the JH so far, no damage done.' She shakes her head.

'It's not that,' she sobs, as I dry her tears with my thumb.

'Well, what then?'

'It's what you just said. That's the most beautiful thing I've ever heard, and yet it's also the saddest. It's making my heart break just thinking about it. Our children and grandchildren and how one day we won't be here anymore.' I take her in my arms and hug her tightly.

'Hush, hush, now. We've got a lot of living to get through before that happens. I promise I'll live to be a hundred if you promise to live to be a hundred and three.' She half laughs, half cries.

'Why?' she sniffs.

'I'll have to be the first to go. I couldn't bear it here without you.' I think my words will cheer her up and make her giggle but they don't, in fact, quite the opposite. She now begins bawling and throws her head into my neck. I feel a rush of tears trickle down my shoulder.

'Oh Vee, I'm sorry, I'm only joking! You know me, I don't know when to stop.' I hold her for a good ten minutes until the heaving diminishes and her taps are finally turned off. She stands back and rubs her face with the palm of her hand.

'Do it,' she commands. She suddenly looks fierce and determined.

'Do what?'

'Carve our initials into that tree. Every year, on this date, we'll come back and refresh them so they don't fade away. We'll bring our children here and show them. After that, our grandchildren then our great-grandchildren.

When we're old and tired we'll come here one last time with all of them and tell them it is their duty to keep these initials fresh and alive—forever.

Those initials will be here for as long as this mighty oak stands. We'll explain to them how important it is to *love* and be *loved* and to *show* it. Even when we are gone, our souls will still be here, looking out for them, joined for eternity.'

I pull the penknife from my pocket and attack the tree with renewed vigour. It's hard work but I want it to be perfect. I put little flourishes on the letters and take extreme care making sure the love heart is perfect. After twenty minutes, I am done. Vee is beaming at me. She walks to the tree and delicately traces the letters with her finger. I stand back to admire my handiwork.

'JH 4 VH FOREVER IN LOVE IN LIFE IN DEATH,' I read the words out aloud, with a certain amount of pride.

'Jimmy Hooper for Victoria Halliwell. Now, doesn't that just make your heart soar?' I ask. Vee begins to giggle, then laugh, then laugh hysterically. She's holding her ribs as tears flood down her face.

'Vee, what? What is it?' I probe, slightly bemused. It takes an age for her to control her laughter and reply.

'It's… it's… the initials,' she sputters.

'What about them?' I quiz, non-plussed, becoming slightly annoyed.

'JH 4 VH! That could be read as, Jeremy Halliwell for Vivienne Halliwell,' she bursts out laughing again.

'Oh fuck! I never thought of that. I can just imagine your father's face the next time he comes up here and sees it. He will assume your mother has done it. He will be enflamed with passion, sprint back to the boat then row across the lake like a man demented. He'll dash up the bank, into your mother's studio, throw her to the ground, rip her clothes off and give her the biggest seeing to of her life. All the while, she'll be wondering what the fuck is going on.' We both collapse to the ground in hysterics and roll around like we've got the devil inside us.

##

I watch on as Vee slowly rows us back across the lake. She can't stop smiling at me and I lap it up.

'This has been the best day of my life so far,' she says.

'Me too. It's funny, it just gets better and better. Every time we do something together, it always becomes the best day of our lives… until the next time. It's like we keep lifting the bar. I wonder if it will always be like this?' She looks annoyed with my words.

'Of course it will, why wouldn't it be?'

'Yes, of course it will.' I placate her and her smile returns.

As we near the jetty she pulls the oars in and the boat drifts along, unpropelled.

'Jimmy, did you mean what you said earlier?' I grab hold of the mooring pole, leap from the boat onto the jetty and secure it with the rope.

'What did I say?' I ask as I lean over and offer her my hand, pulling her up on to the jetty.

'About children and grandchildren?'

'Of course I did. It's the natural order of things. I don't mean like now, or any time soon. We've got too much living to do. But maybe in five to ten years from now, I'd like to start a family.'

'Oh God, I can't believe this is happening to me. I almost expect to wake up at any moment and find out it's all been a dream. I never, ever, thought I'd find someone to love or to love me. Yet now I have—how strange.'

23: DEPARTING

'I see, so you're all abandoning me. A fine bunch of pals you lot turned out to be,' I say as I place my pint down on a beer mat. Macca laughs as he stuffs a handful of peanuts into his mouth.

'Jim the offer's still there. There's room for one more in the van if you want to join us.' The Hipnotikz have been offered two weeks' worth of gigs playing on the Reeperbahn in Hamburg. Normally I would have jumped at the chance to go with them. After all, I am a massive Beatles fan and the Reeperbahn was where the Fab Four cut their teeth before they hit the big time. I push my bottom lip out in fake disappointment.

'Nah, can't do it. I have a full diary for the next two weeks. I can't let my customers down, I'd get a bad reputation,' I explain. Gerry laughs.

'You've turned into a right businessman, haven't you?' he teases.

'It beats being on the dole.'

'Hang on a minute,' interjects Gerry, 'you are on the dole!'

'You know what I mean. It's better to be busy all day working in a job I love, than hanging around with no money in my pocket. Vee keeps telling me to go legitimate but I'm a bit reluctant to bite the bullet.' Jonesy returns to the table carrying four fresh pints.

'What's holding you back?' asks Jonesy.

'The unknown, I guess. What if it falls flat on its arse. Then I've got to go through all the rigmarole of being interviewed and assessed by the dole office to see if I can get my benefits reinstated. That can take months, not to mention the humiliation of it all.'

'Stop being a pussy,' says Macca who is scoffing down the peanuts like he hasn't eaten for a week. 'Listen, when I started out in the transport game, I was the same; full of doubt and fear. Before I knew it, business was booming. After a year, I looked back and wondered what it was I was scared of.'

'Jimmy, you want to watch out for the dole snoopers, they're really cracking down on people now. If they catch you working and signing on they'll hit you hard. If you ever do need to go back on the dole, they'll make your life hell,' advises Gerry.

'Yeah, I suppose you're right,' I concede.

'Anyway Jim,' begins Jonesy, 'Vee's not short of a bob or two. She wouldn't see you starve.'

'No she wouldn't. But that's not right is it, sponging off your girlfriend. I'd lose authority. I'd be a kept man.' They all burst out laughing.

'Ha! Authority, I think you lost your authority a long time ago in that relationship. There's only one person in charge there!' guffaws Macca. I am a little offended by his comment.

'And what do you mean by that?' I bristle. Macca takes a large slurp on his pint then smacks his lips together.

'Come on Jim, face facts. She has you wrapped around her little finger. If she says jump, you ask how high.'

'That's not true,' I contend. 'We are equals, as one, with maybe me being a little more equal than her.'

'No, Macca's right Jimmy. You, my friend, are well and truly under the thumb. And to be honest with you, I think you enjoy it. In fact, I'm sure I can speak for everyone here when I say, we'd all like to be under Vee's thumb. She's a Goddess and a bloody nice lass. You've done well there, don't ever lose her.' I'm annoyed at their assessment.

'I am not under the thumb!' I yell, just as Marky makes his way down the stone steps and joins us at the table.

'Hey Marky, is Jimmy under the thumb?' goads Jonesy. Marky looks at me and points at my forehead.

'See that mark there? That's Vee's thumbprint. It's like a fucking tattoo.'

'All right, all right you pack of bastards, let's move on,' I say as Jonesy stands up.

'Marky, it's my shout. What are you drinking? A pint of bitter?' Marky shakes his head.

'Nah, thanks Jonesy. I'm not stopping,' he replies with a cheeky grin.

'What!' exclaims Macca. 'It's Friday night, where are you going?'

'I'm heading home to pack,' he states triumphantly.

'Pack? Pack for what?' I ask. He places his hand on my shoulder and squeezes it.

'Jimmy, I am catching a flight from Manchester Airport tomorrow to Cuba.'

'Bullshit!' laughs Gerry.

'I shit you not.'

'No fucker goes to Cuba for their holidays,' says Jonesy.

'I do. I was coming back from court today and passed a Travel Agents window. I popped in, asked about Cuba and booked my tickets. Two weeks in the sunny Caribbean.'

'Of course, where else would you go? Who are you staying with, Fidel Castro?' chortles Macca.

'You can laugh all you want Macca. But while you lot are sweating your peanut sized testicles off in some grubby underground cavern on the Reeperbahn, I'll be getting oiled all over by a delicious Cuban lady as I lay on the beach.'

'Who are you going with?' I enquire, bemused by Marky's impromptu decision.

'No one. I'm going on my Jack Jones.'

'Thanks a lot,' I reply. 'Didn't you think of asking your best mate?'

'Jimmy, you wouldn't go anywhere without Vee. You're like fucking Siamese twins. You're joined at the hip.' Everyone laughs again.

'There's only one thing worse than a smartarse and that's four of the twats!'

'Okay, well, I'll have to love you and leave you comrades,' he says as we all do the obligatory fist bump. I watch as he disappears up the steps. Gerry chuckles to himself.

'What's funny?' I ask.

'I wonder if Marky's aware the wet season begins in August, usually accompanied by hurricanes.'

I bid farewell to my mates and wish them the best on their Hamburg stint and head back to Vee. As I walk through the door she is sitting upright on the bed reading a book.

'Oh, hi Jim. You're home early.'

'Yeah, the lads are having a quiet one as they have to drive down to Dover tomorrow to catch the ferry. They've got a two week gig in Hamburg.'

'Wow! That's great. Couldn't you have gone with them? You said you didn't have much work on for the next fortnight.'

'Nah, no room in the van. Not only that, but Marky's flying out to Cuba for two weeks holiday tomorrow as well. Even Sofe's heading back to her parents for a fortnight.' She puts her book down on the bed.

'What's wrong Jimmy, you seem a bit annoyed with everyone.' I flop down on the bed next to her.

'I don't know. It just feels like the gang is splitting up. Everyone going their own way.' She rolls on top of me and kisses me on the forehead.

'Don't be silly. It's the height of summer. Marky's just grabbing a break. The boys can't miss an opportunity like the Hamburg gigs and Sofe is entitled to visit her parents occasionally. Anyway, that means I have you all to myself.'

'Hmm, I guess,' I reply sulkily. 'Vee, how do you see our relationship?' She sits back up and retrieves her book.

'In what way do you mean?' she asks, almost absent-mindedly as she flits back to her page.

'I mean, do you see us as equals, together as one, sort of give and take on both sides.' She lifts her eyes momentarily from the page.

'Of course I do. That's exactly what we are—equals. Why do you ask?'

'Oh no reason.'

'Jimmy, be a sweetheart and make me a cup of tea will you.'

'Yeah sure,' I reply as I jump from the bed and head to the kitchen.

'Oh and would you bring the chocolate biscuits back in with you as well. Oh and Jimmy, there are some damp towels in the washing machine, can you get them out and place them on the clothes horse to dry and put my knickers in the washing machine. They need to be on hot. Thanks Jim.' As I pass through the kitchen doorway I stop and think.

'Hmm, how high…' I mutter under my breath.

##

We're eating breakfast together in the flat.

'Are you okay Jimmy,' Vee asks. 'You've been awfully quiet since you got up.'

'I'm fine,' I reply honestly.

'You seem a bit down. Are you feeling under the weather?'

'No, honestly I'm fine, never better.' Her eyes narrow and she looks at me suspiciously.

'Hmm…' She goes back to her cereal as I spread butter and marmalade on my toast.

'Hey Vee?'

'Yes?'

'Do you know how many times a day I say that I love you?' She giggles.

'I don't know, twenty, maybe thirty. And don't ever stop. Whenever I hear those words my tummy flips.'

'And yet,' I continue, 'in all the time we've been together you've never once said, "I love you" to me.' She leans back in her chair and smiles at me.

'Don't be silly Jimmy. I tell you all the time. You mustn't be listening, that's all.'

'No, it's true. I've been waiting for it all this time. I would definitely have heard it if you had ever said it.' The smile falls from her face and she looks a bit annoyed.

'Jimmy, I'm always talking about our love and feelings for each other and how I'd never leave you.'

'Yes, you do. But you still haven't said those three little words to me.' She drops her spoon into her dish.

'Jimmy, I'm not talking about this. I have said those words, you just haven't heard them, that's all,' she states, impatiently.

'Go on then, say them, say, Jimmy, I love you.'

'Why are you teasing me like this, it's not like you?' She looks hurt.

'You can't say them, can you?' She grips her hands together and rolls her thumbs around each other. I feel mean and annoyed with myself. Why would I toy with her like this and make her unhappy? I put on my biggest, widest beam. 'Hey Vee, I'm only messing with you, I don't mean it. Say, why don't we get on the scooter and go visit your mother?' She brightens immediately.

'I'd love to, but I still haven't met *your* mother yet. Are you embarrassed by me?'

'Don't be silly. Mam's been a bit off-colour lately and if she knew you were coming for a visit she'd wear herself out cleaning the house. Tell you what, we'll visit your mother this weekend and next Sunday I'll take you to meet my mother. How does that sound?' She beams broadly.

'It sounds wonderful!'

'Oh hang on, is your dad going to be around?'

'No, daddy's not home this weekend, I was speaking with mummy yesterday.'

'Okay then. We could stay the night and maybe tomorrow we can head on up to Whitby and eat fish and chips on the pier.' She reaches out her hand and grasps mine tightly.

'And maybe we can find a quiet spot in the country and make love on a picnic blanket,' she says licking her lips.

'We could do it at the end of Whitby pier. Put on a show for the trawlermen.'

'Jimmy, why do you always take things too far?'

##

I'm staring out of the window at the street below waiting for Vee who is getting ready in the bathroom. Vee begins to sing and her dulcet tones dance and pirouette out of the bathroom, through the kitchen to where I'm standing. She's learnt another song—another sad song. I slowly walk to the doorway and rest up against the frame and gaze at her in admiration. She's singing the Beatles' classic, "Yesterday". She's fully dressed and is bent over combing her long shiny black locks with a brush. She sees me but is not embarrassed and eventually comes to the end of the song. She stands up straight, throws her head back and quickly arranges her hair into a ponytail.

'Do you think she ever came back?' she asks. I'm puzzled.

'Who?'

'The girl in the song?'

'Well, if I wrote a song as beautiful as that about you, would you come back to me?' She laughs.

'Don't be silly Jimmy. I'd never leave you—no matter what you said or did. I like to think that she did come back. After all, it was only something he said that upset her. They're only words, not deeds.'

'You really psychoanalyse lyrics don't you?' She turns, walks over to me and drapes her arms around my shoulders.

'Words tell the story—the music moves the soul. I wonder why she didn't tell him the reason she was leaving?' She's back on to the lyrics again. I kiss her on the lips, grab her hand and lead her through the flat.

'Maybe she found someone else and she didn't want to upset him.' She stops abruptly and looks annoyed.

'Jimmy, that's a terrible thing to say. You've spoilt the song for me now.'

'Well, maybe it serves himself right for treating love as a game. It's not a game, it's deadly serious—it's what makes life worth living. Come on, let's head to the castle.'

VICTORIA'S DIARY

He sleeps as I write this. He's noticed, I knew he would; it was just a matter of time. I feel ashamed, embarrassed and as bad as those emotions are, I feel something much worse—I feel disloyal—a fake. I have read back through these pages and not once have I said those three words. I can't even put them down on paper in my secret book.

I've been aware of this since the very first day I met him. I've thought long and hard about it and have been at a loss as to why I just cannot utter those words. I now think I have the answer.

Since Jimmy entered my life I have become a new person. I am now blissfully happy, content in myself and grow more confident each day. I think his ebullience and unbridled enthusiasm for life is rubbing off on me. It is infectious. He wakes with a smile. When he walks in through the door after a long day he is wearing a smile. He goes to bed with a smile and he sleeps with a contented, happy countenance on his face.

I look at him now and I could eat him up. I want to wake him and talk to him about anything and everything. I want to make love to him. I want to delve around in his mind and open secret doors. But, he is exhausted. He works too much. He is like one of those performers who spin plates on top of long slender poles. Forever running back and forth ensuring the plates keep spinning.

I'm trying to think back now, and I cannot recall one single time when he has ever bad-mouthed anyone or anything. He seems to be constantly on a high. It's true what they say; people can make or break your day. What a contrast to when I lived at home, eating breakfast in the Great Hall with my parents. Father would be poring over the Financial Times or raging about some politician or political commentator. Mummy would sit in stoic silence, her misery smouldering away like a fire of damp garden leaves.

My Jimmy is a force of nature and he is projecting that energy onto me. If I could have one-half of his enthusiasm for living, I could achieve anything.

When he's not here I think about him every second. I worry when he goes out for a drink with his friends. I fret and try and occupy my mind by reading, cooking, cleaning, anything to block out the nagging fear that something dreadful is going to happen to him.

Even when he's at work, I cannot help but think of him whizzing around on his scooter. He drives way too fast! What if he gets knocked off or some idiot runs into him?

He has given himself to me one hundred percent, unconditionally, unilaterally. Yet I hold a little back—the three words. Why? What is my illogical reasoning for this? The truth is I am scared. I am scared that if I say those words then it may be the beginning of the end. After all, once I have said them, then there is nothing greater I can ever say to him. He will have conquered the mountain and then what? Will he become bored with me, will his eye begin to wander for the next conquest? I do love him, I am in love with him, I adore him, I worship the ground he walks on and I would gladly lay down my life for his. I believe he knows this, but he wants more, he wants the ultimate.

At some point, I *will* say those words he so desperately wants to hear and pray that my fears don't come home to roost. I will have a practice run right now.

Jimmy, I love you—more than you could ever imagine! You make my heart soar and my veins tingle. Just a smile from you is like a hurricane against my senses. A touch from you is like setting torch to a dungeon full of gunpowder. And, when you say those three little words, so simple, so short, I feel soul love.

During my musical education, he has introduced me to a man called David Bowie and his album Ziggy Stardust, (apparently, an alter-ego). I don't know much about this musician, but Jimmy raves about him. He says this man has been touched by the hand of God. One of the songs he sings is called "Soul Love". I've listened to this song over and over to try and decipher what the lyricist is trying to say. It took me weeks and weeks to understand it. Then one day, I finally got it. It is a hymn to love in all its many forms. All love comes from the soul. It describes Jimmy's love for me and my love for Jimmy. We should never have met. We should never have been together. But, we are, and I will never give him up and I pray that Jimmy will never give me up. Some higher force brought us together.

Okay, one more time, because as they used to say at finishing school, ad-infinitum, "Practice makes perfect—girls";

Jimmy, I love you, I will always love you—only you!

24: SACRIFICE

It has been a pleasant day—no, much more than that—it has been a perfect day. We stop off in Harrogate and saunter happily around an outdoor market eating doughnuts and drinking strong black coffee.

I spot a beautiful, pure white, silk scarf hanging in a market stall and insist on buying it for Vee. She protests that it costs too much and she will buy it instead—for me. We very nearly have an argument, in public, about it. She takes it and wraps it around my neck. I take it off and wrap it around her neck. I say it is a testament to our love—pure and simple—unblemished. She backs down and says she will treasure it for the rest of her life and she'll never go anywhere without it.

I park the Vespa outside Ridley Castle and we alight. Vivienne is already waiting on the steps for us. She looks less than happy and I detect that something is amiss.

'Hello mummy,' says Vee, with a buoyant smile on her face as she takes her helmet off. I know Vee, and I suspect she is putting on a brave face.

'Hello dear. Hello Jimmy,' she replies as she clasps her hands together in front of her like a protective shield. I nod at her.

'Hi Vivienne,' I reply slowly, as I remove my helmet and stick it under my arm. Vee walks up the steps and scans her mother's face.

'He's home, isn't he?' she says, her face now full of worry. Her mother simply nods. I hear his voice boom out from the confines of the castle.

'Vivienne!' We all walk into the grand entrance hall. Vee deposits her helmet and scarf on a side table. Before I can do the same, he is standing in front of us.

'Ah! Victoria, Vivienne, I want you both in the Great Hall now! I have something to discuss with you,' he yells. I wouldn't speak to a dog like that, never mind my wife and daughter. He fixes his attention on me and glares. Our eyes lock for what feels like an eternity but is maybe only a few seconds. There's something in his eyes—anger—no, more than anger—contempt and disdain. How can he hate me so much for simply loving his daughter? I sense that he is going to march up to me and strike out. I take the helmet from under my arm and clench it tightly in my fist. I'll let him throw the first blow if he so wants, but if he does he will be getting a crash helmet to the head. I momentarily think of how proud Marky would be of me. Breaking the jaw of the Home Secretary, with a crash helmet, what sweet justice. Marky would be able to dine out, with his revolutionary home guard, for years on that one.

I glance at poor old Viv. She looks like she's going to wet her knickers at any moment. She slinks off down the corridor already cowed and defeated by her dictatorial husband. Not Victoria though—oh no! She pauses for a few seconds just to rile him.

'May I ask what this is about?' she says, with an almost regal quality.

'In private...' he snaps back. She pauses for another few seconds, then begins to walk with such poise and elegance it is a sight to behold. Her father turns and follows. I am so proud of her. She has more grace in one single step than he has in his entire body. There's an almighty bang, as the door to the Great Hall is slammed shut. I slowly begin to follow. I hear a woman's voice.

'It's not right, what he puts those women through. He should be ashamed.' It's Mrs Beaton, heading down the corridor towards me, carrying a large earthenware bowl. She has her head down and doesn't immediately spot me.

'Hello Mrs Beaton,' I say, without any joy. She jolts and looks surprised.

'Oh, Master James, you gave me a start.'

'Is this a regular occurrence?' I enquire, nodding towards the door. She shakes her head in a worried fashion.

'It's not my place to say, Master James.' She continues on her way. It's the first time she hasn't asked if I intend to stay the night. It only confirms the fact that Lord Halliwell's impromptu meeting is about me.

I can hear murmuring but cannot discern the words. It's Vee and her father talking. As the seconds pass, the volume increases and now I hear everything and it's not good.

It appears Lord Halliwell has done his homework on me and my friends. Vee is in a rage with him and accuses him of snooping and spying. He says some quite nasty things about me, but I don't care. I think about barging in and confronting him—but decide against it. This is one battle Vee must fight on her own. She wouldn't want it any other way. I can hear her voice crack, the sobs, the sniffles. But, from somewhere she digs deep and grows strong. For every missile he launches, she fires two back at him. Back and forth it goes for a good five minutes. Still no sound from her mother.

Then, he issues the ultimatum.

My legs become jelly. I stagger slightly. I feel fuzzy headed. My heart races. I gaze down the corridor. A medieval suit of armour, clutching a broadsword, stares back at me—malevolently.

"What are you doing here?" it asks.

I lift my head and see a miserable looking 18th century naval officer cast his eye over me, from a painting.

"What are you doing here?" he asks. Next to him, a judge. He sports a red gown and wears a wig adorned with a black cap—the hanging judge. He has an accusatory look in his eye.

"What are you doing here?" he accuses. "Take him to the gallows!"

Indeed, what am I doing here? I don't belong. This is not my world. I realise I have been foolish. All this belongs to Vee, eventually. I can't, I won't hinder that. There's only one thing to do—the right thing.

I must save her! Save her from herself, save her—from me! She loves this place more than anything. She was born to it. I don't mean just because of her genes, her parentage, no, she has always been here—her soul resides here.

I love her, I adore her—but I have to save her. The only way I can do that—is to give her up. It ends tonight.

I quietly close the door behind me as I make my way to the scooter. I cast my mind back to the very first time I met her in the Granary. She said it then—she knew!

"We are from different social standings and it would never work."

Her words sting me a second time. I was never meant to be part of her world, and she was never meant to be part of mine.

I straddle my scooter, rock forward, and push it off its stand. I use my feet to propel the bike forward until it has enough momentum to begin freewheeling down the long driveway. Tears stream down my face as Marky's words stab at me.

"I'm telling you Jimmy, those bastards will never let you have access to their private club. No matter what you do, no matter what you strive for, no matter what you achieve, you will always be a commoner to them—less than zero. They believe they were born to rule and you were born to be their mule."

I stop at the cattle grid, grip my head in my hands, and weep uncontrollably. My heart is ruptured. I hear her scream. She calls my name over and over. I turn and see her fly down the driveway. Her beautiful ponytail swishes madly from side to side. The white silk scarf, flutters from her wrist. She runs like a lioness after its prey.

I must go. If she reaches me, I know I will succumb. I have to save my Vee, so she can go on to lead the life that was always destined for her.

I throw my helmet onto the grass, turn the key, then kick-start Shelley. I shoot off across the cattle-grid and onto the road. I slow for a second and gaze back at her. She calls out.

'Jimmy, Jimmy!' she shrieks at the top of her lungs. 'Come back! Jimmy, Jimmy, *I love you!*

No! no! no! That's not fair, that's uncalled for, why did she have to say that now!

'I love you too Vee. Always have, always will, only you,' I whisper through the cascade of tears.

I will not back down, I will not be beaten. The only thing that matters—is Vee.

I struggle to breathe. I rev the scooter, then take off at an alarming speed. For the last time I witness her. She collapses to the ground and beats her fists into the cold heartless earth.

I smash through the gears until I have reached top speed. The tiny beating heart of the Vespa screams in agony as does my own. I whizz down winding country lanes hoping that some idiot will be overtaking on a blind bend or on the brow of a hill. If the narrow country lanes don't get me then the city streets will, as I don't intend stopping at any red lights.

I hurtle along, a puny fragile human, made of skin and bone with a pumping heart as big as a balloon. A heart that loves too much, a heart that was never built for this world, a heart cleaved in two. There is nothing for me now. I pray for oblivion. Please God, for once in my life, let me get what I want.

25: CONFRONTATION

I know there is something wrong as I see mummy come out of the castle entrance and await our arrival on the steps. Jimmy parks the scooter up and we dismount. Her face says it all. *He* is home. I put on a brave face and hope and pray it is something else that influences her mood.

'Hello mummy,'

'Hello dear. Hello Jimmy.'

'Hi Vivienne,' Jimmy replies, in subdued fashion. He has obviously summed up the situation.

'He's home, isn't' he?' Mummy gives a gentle nod. Then, his voice reverberates out. I feel my insides flip over. We make our way into the hallway. I place my helmet and precious scarf on the table. As if out of nowhere, he appears, the architect of my misery.

'Ah! Victoria, Vivienne, I want to see you both in the Great Hall now! I have something to discuss with you,' he bellows and points the way to the Great Hall, as though we don't know where it is. He stares at Jimmy with such contempt, such loathing, that I could slap him. How dare he!

'May I ask what this is about?' I enquire politely, with calm and decorum.

'In private!' he barks at me. I deliberately pause for a few seconds to show him that I am not intimidated by his bellicose behaviour. I walk towards the Great Hall, with poise, with dignity, just as we were taught at finishing school. *He* follows behind. I throw a glance over my shoulder and take one last look at Jimmy. There he stands, tall, looking rugged, handsome. It gives me fortitude. As I enter the hall, father, in a petulant fit of rage, slams the door so hard behind him that the whole castle seems to groan its annoyance. Mother is sitting in her usual spot as father takes up his position at the head of the table. I stand half-way between him and the door.

'Could you please explain what all this is about?' I ask quietly. Father puts on his spectacles and pulls a sheet of papers from his briefcase.

'Yes, I'm about to get to that,' he says in a calmer tone. 'Please be seated.'

'No. I'd rather stand.' He looks over his glasses at me, annoyed.

'Very well.' Now he begins in earnest. You'd think he was addressing the House of Commons, he yells that loudly. He obviously wants Jimmy to hear everything. Well, two can play at that game. I'm just hoping that I have changed.

These types of confrontations always follow a familiar path. He yells—I yell back. He continues yelling and I begin to feel a well of emotion rise up inside. He yells some more and I begin to cry and become incoherent. He yells again, and again, then I run from the room, beaten, distraught—he wins. Well, I'm not the girl I used to be—not since I met my Jimmy.

'I have some information about Mr Hooper and his associates that I'd like you to hear,' he begins. I cannot believe it! I immediately go on the offensive.

'What! How dare you! You've been snooping and spying on Jimmy!' I scream at him.

'It is not spying. A man in my position cannot be compromised or tainted by association. It is standard government protocol to run a background check on anyone who enters the radar of a Minister of high office. Now, where was I? Ah, yes: James Hooper, aged nineteen and a half, left school at sixteen with two O' levels; English and metalwork. Since that time he has been on welfare benefits despite the fact that he is now working as a freelance photographer and earning money. You and he are both well aware that this is benefit fraud.

Mark Carlyle, aged twenty, left school at 16 with three O' levels; English, economics and history. He has been employed as a junior reporter for the Yorkshire Evening Standard since that time. He is a member of numerous far-left Marxist groups, some of which may be in the pay of the Soviets—which is tantamount to treason.

Colin McKenzie, aged twenty-three, self-employed delivery driver. Had his licence suspended for six months for drink driving.

Gerald Merton, aged twenty-two, employed as a scooter mechanic for Turbo Scooters in Leeds.

Steven Jones, aged twenty-two, studying graphic design at Leeds University.

All three play in a local rock and roll band of dubious quality and integrity.

Mr Hooper's flatmate, Sofia Tucker, aged twenty-one, studying psychology at Leeds University. Her father is an illegal Jamaican immigrant who works as a porter in Sheffield General Hospital.

Well, I suppose the last two do have one redeeming quality—at least they're trying to do something with their lives. As for the rest, it's a rogues gallery. Hardly the most salubrious lot.'

'So what!' I yell.

'So what? I'll tell you so what! I cannot allow my daughter to fraternise with this bunch of misfits, fraudsters, lawbreakers and subversives. I have a political reputation to maintain.'

'They're not misfits! They're good, honest people!' I scream at him. He ignores me.

'A daughter of mine needs to be engaged to a man of breeding, pedigree and standing in the community, someone like Charles Whittington or Gareth Winston-Browne or even Sir Duncan's boy, Maxwell.' I sneer at him and guffaw.

'Ha! For your information, Charles is a raging gay. Gareth is an inbred simpering sop and Maxwell is as thick as two short planks. Maybe you should have done a background check on them! If it wasn't for Sir Duncan's wealth and influence then the only position that Maxwell would qualify for is the local village idiot!'

'Victoria! Stop!' he yells. I will not stop.

'Not only that, but he looks like his father—like a turtle. Do you really want a hatchling as your heir? Anyway, you don't have to find anyone for me. I have already found him, he is the love of my life and I will never give him up—his name is Jimmy!' He removes his glasses and rubs at his eyes.

'Victoria, I've cut you a bit of slack and I really hoped this relationship would have fizzled out by now...' I interrupt him with a vengeance.

'It will never fizzle out! It grows stronger each day,' I reply. The barbs fly between us for a few more minutes as his head turns purple and spittle begins to fly from his grotesque lips. He says some terrible things about Jimmy, I pray he cannot hear it. I begin to feel tears sting my eyes at the injustice of it all. He is now incandescent with rage, as he reaches a crescendo.

'I will never accept an heir that has been spawned by HIS seed, that... that... commoner!' The tears begin to roll down my cheeks, as I begin to wilt under his withering onslaught. I take a deep breath, then fight back.

'You want an heir? I'll give you an heir! I'll give you ten fucking heirs and every one of them will be from Jimmy's seed because he knows how to fuck me like a real man!' I scream at him. I think his head could explode at any moment. I throw a glance at mummy who grips her silence like a waif clutching a loaf of bread.

'Do not use that kind of language towards me!' he slams his palm down hard on the table.

'I'll use whatever language I damn well fucking choose!' I retaliate, slamming my hand even harder into the table.

'You will end your relationship with that boy this evening, forthwith—I COMMAND IT! I cannot have my career, all I have worked for, jeopardised by your association with undesirables!'

'I will not end it! And who are you to command me? I'm not one of your Junior Ministers. I am not a little lapdog, like fucking Molly.'

'I am your FATHER!' he rages.

'Yes—that's a cross we both must bear,' I whisper.

There is a break in hostilities before he begins again.

'Very well Victoria, I didn't want it to come to this but you have left me with no further choice. First thing, Monday morning, I shall meet with my lawyer. I will instruct him to remove you from the family trust. Your allowance will be stopped immediately. You shall vacate the flat in Leeds within one week, otherwise I'll have you forcibly ejected. You shall return the car and you will not set one foot on Ridley Castle Estate again until you have come to your senses. Furthermore, I will remove you from my will. You shall not inherit this hallowed house and all its history while ever you are with that boy! You will be disowned, disinherited and abandoned. We'll see how long your precious "Jimmy" hangs around when he realises the golden goose has stopped laying. It won't be long before you're wandering the streets like a common whore!' Silence breaks out for a moment and I take the opportunity to compose myself. I breathe deeply, rhythmically.

'I don't want your money, your flat, your car, or to be in your will. You can go to hell,' I reply calmly. He suddenly looks tired and old, as though the wind has been knocked out of his sails. I hope he is having a heart attack. If he does, I shall stand over his body and piss on him. 'I will never leave Jimmy. I love him. He is the only man I will ever love.'

'Ha! You talk of love—what do you know of love?'

'More than you ever will,' I reply, as I turn and walk towards the door.

'You will not leave this room until I have finished, you cheap little slut!' he roars at the top of his voice. Mother leaps from her chair and slams both hands down on the table with a bang.

'Jeremy! Enough!' she screeches. My father looks shocked. The mouse has finally roared. I stand at the doorway and pause. I am overcome with a burning resolve. I feel quite invincible. Something inside has died, something else has been born. I turn to face him one last time.

'You are dead to me now,' I state without emotion. 'Cross swords with me again and you shall pay dearly.' Our eyes lock in a battle of the wills. Finally, he blinks. I shut the door behind me on my way out. I let out a sigh of relief as my mother and father now lock horns and begin fighting fiercely.

I walk to the entrance expecting to see my Jimmy. He's not there.

'Jimmy, Jimmy?' I call out. I get a sinking feeling in my stomach. I turn and race down the corridor, barge through the kitchen door and nearly scare old Mrs Beaton half to death.

'Mrs Beaton, have you seen Jimmy?' I gasp at her. Her hand is planted firmly on the top of her chest.

'Oh! Lady Victoria, you gave me a fright! I saw him about five, ten minutes ago, standing outside the Great Hall—but not since,' she explains as she breathes in a deep lungful of air. I turn and race back down the corridor. As I pass the doors to the Great Hall, I hear mummy and father still arguing and that stupid mutt barking.

'Vivienne! Lower your voice, you are upsetting Molly!'

'To hell and damnation with the dog! I will wring it's bloody neck unless you leave right now!' she screams at him, a little too late. I fly up the staircase and head towards my bedroom. Oh please be here, Jimmy, please be here. I fling open the door hoping he is laid on the bed with that mesmerising smile on his face. It's now dark. I flick the light on. Oh no! He's not here! I turn and sprint back the way I have come, all the while yelling his name.

'Jimmy! Jimmy! Where are you?' As I descend the stairs in a panic, a sandal falls off, causing me to almost trip and hurtle headfirst into the unforgiving marble stairs. I stop myself from falling and kick off my other sandal. Back past the Great Hall, I race.

'Get out!' I hear mother yell. I'm at the entrance hall and pause to catch my breath and think. Maybe he's gone to the courtyard or the lake—one of his favourite spots—he loves the lake. I half turn then something catches my eye. It's my helmet and scarf sitting on the little table just inside the door. If he were still here, then his helmet would sit alongside mine as it always does.

'Oh, no, no, no,' I murmur as panic begins to seep into every fibre of my being. I grab the scarf, tie it to my wrist and fling open the door. I look out, down the driveway. A full moon is in the ascendancy as I spot the tiny silhouette of a scooter at the very end of the driveway.

I leap the steps and begin to run.

'Jimmy! Jimmy!' I scream. I race like the wind, as fast as I have ever run before. Sharp, jagged gravel, attacks my bare feet, as pain courses through my body. On I go, faster, nearer.

'Jimmy! Jimmy!' I scream. I'm getting closer and he is still sitting there, head in hands—he's waiting—waiting for me!

'Jimmy, wait, take me away from here!' I scream. My legs burn, my heart pumps, my feet bleed. I'm now less than fifty feet from him. He throws his helmet on the ground. What is he doing? He stands up, then thrusts back down and his scooter roars into life. Oh, no, no, please, no! I hear the unmistakable rumble as he shoots off across the cattle grid. I can barely breathe. I want to vomit. I want to piss. He cannot be abandoning me—no—not, Jimmy? He stops, momentarily, on the far side of the road. He looks in my direction. Yes, he's going to turn and come back!

'Jimmy, Jimmy, come back, *I love you*!' I screech with every ounce of air left inside of me. I hear the roar of the scooter and he accelerates away. I see the little red taillight begin to diminish. I throw myself to the earth and begin to beat it with my fists.

'No, no, no,' I weep uncontrollably. I pummel the gravel for a lifetime until my fists are bruised and bloody. Through my avalanche of tears, I fixate on the scarf. It is stained with dirt and blood—no longer unblemished. The sound of reluctant footsteps on gravel interrupts my misery. Mother kneels beside me. She strokes my hair and kisses me on the nape of my neck—a rare sign of emotion.

'Shush, shush, now,' she comforts. 'Come Victoria let's go back inside.' She helps me to my feet as I continue to sob. I can barely speak as my stomach continually spasms and involuntary hiccups thwart my words.

'He's...l...le...lef...left me. He's...go...gone...'

'Shush, shush,' her only reply as she drapes her arm around my shoulder. We walk back to the castle. I gaze at the creamy moon. It hangs like a giant orb on the horizon. It weeps with me for my loss. I am spent, exhausted, there is nothing left inside. All I crave is sleep—oblivion.

I spot my father's Range Rover slowly moving towards us, its headlights low. It stops outside the entrance. The door to the castle is flung open and father descends the steps in a hurry. He has an overnight bag slung across one shoulder and Molly tucked under his right arm. He opens the passenger door and places Molly on the car seat just as we reach him. The damned dog continually barks and yelps.

'There, there, Molly dear. Yes, it's been a fraught night for us all,' he says, in that pathetic "baby-coo-coo" voice. He turns and rests his arm on top of the car door.

'Victoria, I understand your pain, I really do. But in time, maybe a few weeks or months, you will see that I was right. This relationship could never have lasted. At some point, in the future, you will thank me for my actions tonight. James never belonged in our world, and you never belonged in his.' I move closer to him as he speaks. There is one last surge of anger and energy that springs from the well. I launch myself at him. I jag my nails deep into his neck and claw downwards. Instantly, a thin streak of blood appears. He screams. I attack him with my puny fists and unleash a barrage of uncoordinated blows at his head. I scratch, hiss, fist and kick at him. He tries to fend my blows off by cowering and raising his arms above his head. I attempt to get into a position to scratch his eyes out—I will kill the fucker here—tonight. Mother tries to restrain me but she is such a limp biscuit, her efforts are futile. I feel two vices grab me by the wrists and

I become powerless. The chauffeur is obviously a bodyguard as well. He holds my arms aloft. I am immobilised as father slinks into the passenger seat.

'Ma'am, ma'am! Please calm down,' he pleads. I have nothing against the man. He is merely doing his job. My tension releases. He notes the change in my demeanour as weariness crashes on my shore once again. The driver jumps back into the car as father dabs at the blood on his neck with a white, pristine handkerchief.

'Damn and blast it Vivienne! The girl is out of control! She has the very devil inside her! I warned you this would happen!' he bellows at her.

'For God's sake Jeremy, it's not the devil that's inside her—have you no memory? Just go—leave,' she replies with an exhausted sigh. Father slams his door shut and the headlights of the car flick on as it pulls slowly away. I bend and grab a handful of gravel from the driveway and hurl it at the car.

'Go! Fuck off and don't come back!' I screech at the vehicle. I chase after it and bang and slap, violently at my father's window.

'You bastard, I fucking hate you! I hope you fucking die!' He turns to me. His face is ashen. For the first time in my life, I witness something in his eyes I have never seen before—fear! He nods to the driver and the car speeds up and accelerates away.

As I lay in bed, mother rubs a wet cloth against my outstretched hand. She wipes and dabs at the blood and grime. When my hands are clean she begins on my feet. The only thing to break the silence is the sound of water as she wrings the cloth out into a metallic bowl. The coarse perfume of antiseptic assaults my senses. I am in a stupor. I still heave and sniff, occasionally. I am now officially dead but still breathing. Please let the breathing stop, then I can get out of this place.

Mother wrings the cloth out for the last time.

'I won't bandage them. We'll let them breathe.'

282

'There'll be blood on the sheets.'

'Your hands and feet need air. They'll heal quicker. Sheets can be washed, my dear.' She pushes my hair back and kisses me on the forehead. 'You need to rest. Things will seem different in the morning.' If she thinks she can get away with fucking platitudes she can think again. Rubbing blood and dirt from me does not account for twenty years of her indifference.

'Where were you when I needed you?' I scream at her. 'Why do you never defend me? You know what a tyrant he is. All my life I've been at loggerheads with him. How do you expect an eight, ten, fourteen-year-old girl to stand up that monster? Go! Get out! You're as bad as him! Go, fuck off!' She looks shocked, hurt. She stands and makes her way quickly to the door. I leap from the bed, pick up the bowl of water and launch it at her in a fury. It slams into the back of her leg. The cordial of water and antiseptic splatters her. She visibly jumps, then calms. She turns, picks up the bowl and leaves the room. I hear her footsteps trudge along the corridor, accompanied by quiet sobs.

'Oh no... mother, I didn't mean it,' I cry quietly, as my torment intensifies. The devil has stolen my heart and replaced it with a burnt, charred claw.

VICTORIA'S DIARY

It has truly been the worst week of my life, and that says it all really. No, that does not do it justice. Let me start anew.

Misery, heartbreak, abandonment, horror, torment, guilt, purgatory—even these words are toothless in trying to express how I feel. Grief is a better word. Yes, that is the overriding feeling. I grieve for Jimmy. I grieve for myself. I grieve for our love.

##

I have spent the last seven days in a stupor. I cannot remember sleeping, only crying. My mother or Mrs Beaton brings me food. Soup, sandwiches, cold chicken, salad, pasta—I eat nothing.

I ring the flat constantly and leave messages until the answering machine tape is full, but I know he will not be there. I realise now that I know so little about him. At first, it was Jimmy who divulged all the information—about his friends, his family and it was I, who kept secrets. But, after a while, I introduced him to mother, my home, my life.

The tears and distress are constants. The only way to take my mind away from my distress for a short while is to think of my father's demise. I wish him dead!

My flights of fancy start off small.

I hear the phone ring and my mother's distraught voice. The hurried footsteps up the stairs. The door bursting open and my mother standing there in shock and disbelief,

"It's your father, he's been decapitated in a car crash!" Or, "Your father has been blown up by the IRA!" Or better still, "It's your father, his car was surrounded by an angry mob of commoners and he was beaten to a bloody pulp!"

These sweet thoughts are interludes to my grief and they are too short. Over the hours and days, I rewrite the play.

Daddy has a stroke. He cannot speak and he is wheelchair bound. I become the loving, doting daughter. I will nurse him better. After all, mummy is far too busy with her paintings, exhibitions and charity work to do that.

I put ground glass in his soup. I piss into his morning cup of tea. Late at night, just before his bedtime, I put laxatives in his brandy nightcap before lovingly tucking him up in bed.

He will soil himself during the night and lay in that stinking putrid mess until the next day, whereupon, after having a sleep in and a leisurely breakfast, I will open his bedroom door then scream out aloud, making sure everyone in the household comes running. We will all hold our noses and stare at the disgusting beast in disbelief.

I will pinch him hard when no one else is around. I will strip the shirt from his back and slice him ever so gently with a razor blade. I will puncture him with a blunt screwdriver. I will tie his arms down and slap him hard across his face, over and over, until he is a ruddy blue colour. When people ask what happened, I will say he fell from his wheelchair.

I will take him for long walks around the gardens and lake, all the while divulging every last detail of mine and Jimmy's lovemaking. He will hear of the time we went for a walk around his secret place and how Jimmy took me from behind and fucked me hard up against the sacred oak tree. How he carved our undying love into the precious oak. I will list every place we made love; the treehouse, the rowing boat, mummy's studio, the tower and even on the table in the great hall as mummy entertained the vicar in the next room.

One day, after three or four months of this sweet torture, I will push his wheelchair down towards the lake. I will ask him why he's never once told me that he loves me?

I'll park his chair on the steep incline near the boat ramp and carefully explain that today he is to die.

"Yes father, that's right—you are going to die. In a moment I will release the handbrake on your wheelchair and off you'll trundle down the grassy slope. When you hit the bank you will be jettisoned into the water.

You will writhe and flap around for a while, all in vain. Slowly, the water will begin to fill your lungs and you will gasp for air. The panic will have already set in—which only makes it worse—and I will stand here, on the bank, laughing, uncontrollably. Your last vision will be of me, your beautiful, loving daughter, howling like a Banshee at your pathetic demise.

I do hope it's true what they say about drowning; that your life flashes before your eyes—how utterly dreary it will be for you—a man who has never loved! But, before I release the brake, there's one last thing I need to tell you.

Jimmy and I never split up. Your vitriolic tirade, on that fateful evening, only brought us closer together.

I see Jimmy every night when you're tucked up in bed full of brandy and laxatives. We fuck in your old study surrounded by your RAF medals and congratulation letters from the Prime Minister. I'm surprised you haven't heard the unbridled screams of pleasure reverberating down the corridors.

Oh, and by the way, I almost forgot, we are now man and wife—yes, that's right we are married. Even better news, I am pregnant!

Oh come on daddy, at least give me a smile. Yes, nestling safely in my womb is a baby boy—your heir—the heir you always wanted.

One day, all this will be his. The land, the castle, all your wealth and the title. I will call him James—he will be Lord James Halliwell... hmm... on second thoughts, maybe we will change the name to Lord James Hooper... yes, that has a better ring to it.

He will take a seat in the House Of Lords—I'm sure he will make a very good lord—for someone who was spawned from common seed.

And when the police have departed and the ambulance has taken your lifeless body away, I will call Jimmy. We will take down every photo and painting of you in the house and we will light a funeral pyre in your honour. As it burns, we will fuck like wild beasts in the grass next to it.

Goodbye daddy dearest. I'm sure I will see you in hell one day—where I will become your carer again."

I release the handbrake and watch with glee and satisfaction as he rolls down the hill and into his watery grave.

##

These reveries give me solace and some form of retribution. But, as I replay the film in my head, two, three times a day, they begin to lose their potency. After three days they are but hollow men and all I am left with is an aching and bloodied heart.

I spend a lot of my days staring out from my bedroom window at the long driveway and the country roads beyond. I pray that I will see him tootling along on his red scooter as he makes his way back to the castle. He never arrives.

26: HOPE

There's a tap on my door and mother enters carrying a tray containing a bowl of soup, bread and a dish of semolina pudding. She places the tray down on a table and makes her way to my bed.

'Come Victoria, sit up,' she commands.

'I'm not hungry,' I mutter. She grabs hold of my arms and pulls me upright, then plumps up the pillows and places them behind me.

'You've barely eaten in a week. Today you are going to eat. Mrs Beaton has made your favourite mushroom soup with freshly baked bread followed by your favourite pudding.' She places the tray on the bed in front of me. I stare down at the food. The aromas ignite my hunger and I begin to spoon the soup into my mouth while ripping hunks out of the bread. I am suddenly ravenous. Mother sits and watches me in silence until I have finished. She removes the tray and sits back down, closer to me. She runs her fingers through my hair.

'Feeling better?' she enquires softly.

'A little. No, not really.' She lets out a deep sigh.

'Right my girl, you are going to listen to me...'

'Oh no, mother! I don't want to hear it. You had your chance to speak up during father's tirade,' I interrupt her.

'You're damn well going to listen to me, my girl! Tomorrow, after a hearty breakfast you are going to leave this house of misery and return to your flat in Leeds. You are going to find Jimmy, and you are going to tell him how much you love him and to hell with your father. Do I make myself clear?' I slump back into my pillows.

'Don't you get it mother? He left me. I don't blame him for that. He couldn't stomach the thought of forever being insulted and looked down upon by my father. What person would put up with that for the next thirty years? He's probably feeling relieved that he's escaped the clutches of this family. I hope he finds a nice girl whose family is accepting, loving, caring. He deserves it, he deserves love.' Mummy raises her eyebrows in surprise.

'Oh my… you silly girl!' she exclaims.

'What?' I reply, confused by her reaction.

'You really don't understand a thing, do you? Jimmy didn't leave you because of your father—he doesn't give two hoots about him.'

'I don't know what you mean. Why did he leave then?' Mother laughs, then instantly cups her hand to her mouth.

'Sorry, dear, I shouldn't laugh. Jimmy left to save you.'

'To save me?'

'Yes! To save you, you dull-witted girl! He loves you so much that he couldn't bear the thought of you losing everything, your allowance, your flat, your inheritance. Don't you see? He paid the ultimate sacrifice for you.' My head is in a spin. Could it be true? A shard of light shines through the flock of ravens that have been circling my body all week.

'But I don't care about the money or the inheritance. All I care about is Jimmy.'

'I know that, you know that—but silly, young, misguided Jimmy doesn't. You must find him—you will find him,' she states resolutely as she stands up. 'As for your father, well, next time he resurfaces, he's going to be told some home truths. For a start, any changes to the family trust requires two signatures, mine and

289

his. So, your allowance, flat, car and inheritance won't be changing. Another thing your father forgets is that this castle is my ancestral home—not his—it belongs to the Kilpatrick family not the damned Halliwell family.' I begin to believe again. Energy floods my body. I glance out of the window and as if by a miracle, the sun wanders sleepily out from behind a dark ominous cloud and bathes me in sunlight.

'Oh my God! I've wasted so much time. Why didn't you tell me this earlier about Jimmy?'

'I assumed you realised.' She sits back down on my bed and holds my hand. She stares into my eyes, her demeanour is one of concern.

'Victoria, it's time for you to grow up. You've spent these last few years like a spoilt child. You need to leave the girl behind and become a woman, make a life for yourself. Your father will keep a low profile for a while as he licks his wounds and ruins someone else's life. But, once the dust has settled, he'll try again. He expects to become PM one day—his ambition knows no bounds. Before that day arrives, he will make sure that all his little tin soldiers are lined up in a row. Anything that could jeopardise his tilt for power, however slight or inconsequential it may seem, will be dealt with—and that could include Jimmy. What I'm saying is, if you want to be with Jimmy, then you are going to have to be on your mettle. You will always need to be one step ahead and never, ever, let your guard down. Jimmy is powerless against your father—but you're not.' She stands up and kisses me on the forehead. 'Do I make myself clear?' I smile at her and nod.

'Yes, crystal.'

'At last! We have a smile.'

'Couldn't you just throw one of your spells at him? I grin. She picks up the tray and makes her way to the door.

'I'm afraid my waning powers would be useless against your father. His spirit is too strong. But, when I saw you stand up to him last week, I realised what love has done to you. You have a fire and a fury in you that could bring down the walls of Jericho—use it wisely. Will I see you in the Great Hall for dinner tonight?'

'Yes… yes, you will,' I reply, already lost in thought.

'Good. Oh, and Victoria, please get a shower, you smell ghastly and you look like something the cat has dragged in.' I smile at her and laugh.

'I'll take one right now.' As she makes her way out of the door she turns to me.

'Remember Victoria, your father plays a long game.'

I am now inflamed with an indefatigable resolve. I won't be beaten by my bastard of a father. I will find Jimmy, even if I have to walk to the edge of the world and back—I *will* find him! And when I do, I will let him know how I feel. I will tell him how much I love him, and will always love him. No-one can hold me back now—no-one.

I don't yet fully comprehend what has gone before. I certainly don't profess to know what is going to unfold in the days, weeks, maybe even months ahead. However, I do know one thing, with a resolute certainty that is now unshakeable; my future is with Jimmy. I pull my diary out from under my bed, pick up a pen and begin to write.

"Dear Life, unleash your slings and arrows of outrageous misfortune. Herald the trumpeters to blow a sound so deafening it wakes the dead. Corral your battalions of walking cadavers and signpost them my way. Send me your pestilence, your swarms of locusts. Call forth the tempest and cajole disease into action. Command your ogres, monsters and fiends to throw their fury at me. Please, I beseech you, send them all my way—for you shall be beaten!"

Twenty minutes ago, lying in this bed, was a sobbing child—a girl. Now, here sits a woman with a beating heart, so strong, so powerful and so loving—unwilling to be beaten. Yes life, throw your worst at me—there will only be one winner. And why will I be victorious? Because of love—it shall conquer all!

THE END

Download a free copy of the prequel. Details below…

THE SOUL LOVE SERIES

I hope you enjoyed book 1 in the Soul Love series. There is far more to come, we have but taken a little step in the journey. If you would like to enjoy a free copy of the prequel – "Soul Love" then all you have to do is sign up to my monthly newsletter.

Download your free copy of Soul Love here.

Not only do your get the prequel for free but once a month you will receive my entertaining, humourous take on life. Plus, I always have lots of goodies for my subscribers throughout the year. You will not be bombarded with emails or given the "hard sell".

Soul Love: Prequel – OUT NOW

Love Is The Goal: Book 1 – OUT NOW

Love On The Roll: Book 2 – January 2020

Love Of The Coal: Book 3 – 2020

Love In The Soul: Book 4 – 2020

All books will be available in paperback and ebook.

REVIEWS

All reviews are greatly appreciated.

Follow on Facebook or BookBub

https://www.facebook.com/snorthousebooks/

https://partners.bookbub.com/authors/5007629

Visit my website: www.snorthouse.com

THE SHOOTING STAR SERIES

Arc Of A Shooting Star

Catch A Shooting Star

Fall Of A Shooting Star

The Resurrection Tour Diaries

About the Author

Simon Northouse writes books that entertain. His stories include hefty doses of self-deprecating satire, ironic farce and droll bathos delivered in a deadpan Yorkshire voice. However, as many of his fans have pointed out, there is much, *much* more to his books than laughter.

He touches on social issues that have plagued humans since the first man pointed at a woman on the back of a woolly mammoth and shouted, "Oi, love, come down from there. That's a man's job!" Racism, misogyny, sexism, elitism, classism, anxiety, self-doubt and entitlement are just a sprinkling of issues that intersperse his works.

He's also big on love, mateship, truth and loyalty and their darker flip sides. Yes, there is humour, bonding, ridiculous situations and tender touching moments of true feeling that live alongside each other on the page. His philosophy is simple, *entertain!*

Oh, and lastly, Simon Northouse is not a New York Times or USA Today bestselling author. He has yet to be nominated for the Booker Prize or Miles Franklin Award and he is still waiting on a call from the Nobel Foundation—the clock is ticking people.

He is the author of the Soul Love, The Shooting Star and School Days series. He also puts out a cracking monthly newsletter which you can find by just typing, "Discombobulated Newsletter" into your web search engine—I kid you not!

www.ingramcontent.com/pod-product-compliance
Lightning Source LLC
Chambersburg PA
CBHW050141120726
47903CB00002B/451